Copyright 2021 for Red Cape Publishing

Cover design by MJ Dixon

Edited by P.J. Blakey-Novis, Red Cape Publishing

First Edition Published 2021 by Red Cape Publishing

CASTLE HEIGHTS

18 STOREYS, 18 STORIES

A HORROR ANTHOLOGY

Foreword

The journey to Castle Heights started around September 2020 with the inkling of an idea; a tower block full of individual horror stories all set on one fateful night. I bounced the idea off my friend, filmmaker MJ Dixon, and between us it quickly grew into an eventful night with set events that could lap over into each tale.

Of course, the year 2020 brought devastation to the world. It has been a real-life horror for all of us and too many have lost loved ones, I lost my father who I loved dearly. I'll never stop missing him.

But, in times of struggle we are stronger when pulling together. Strength in unity. United we stand. An anthology seems quite apt; a collaboration of some very talented and rather nice people coming together with one purpose - to entertain you. Well, scare you.

I'd like to give huge and sincere thanks to everyone involved in bringing this book to life; MJ, for his ideas and efforts in shaping it and pulling together the writers, Red Cape Publishing who have been patient and incredibly supportive, the talented writers for bringing such a variety of styles and tones to their individual floors, and you, the ever-valued reader.

Thank you!

Until next time, look after each other, stay safe and...

Enjoy the frights of Castle Heights!!

Tony Sands

CONTENTS

A Hole in One

David Chaudoir

"We are all just passing through, we are all just on one long conveyor belt to death." So said Detective Chetwyn's bleak internal voice that had chimed in as he was staring blankly at a tub of hummus whilst slowly walking around the supermarket. What on earth had he contributed, what had he done to leave a lasting mark on this world? *Nothing,* he thought, and it bothered him.

Detective Chetwyn was a semi-retired C.I.D. detective who had worked for the Metropolitan Police in London for thirty years before his colitis had unceremoniously reared its ugly head and forced him to take early semi-retirement. Working in a records "facility" in a god forsaken industrial estate in Croydon was the equivalent of a punch-drunk boxer given the broom so he could sweep the gym and make way for the new generation of young pugilists, or in his case, detectives eager to climb the greasy pole.

He would while away his lonely days surrounded by dusty files and cabinets, mulling or "stewing", as his wife called it. Since the children had left home she had become even more intolerant of him around the house. "Stop hovering!" she would snark at him, whilst he was "rootling like a pig" for snacks as Megan was cooking. His waistline had increased alongside his dissatisfaction with his marriage. What had happened to the lovely girl he had married? He actually could see malice in her eyes when he crossed her, which didn't take much these days. Truth was, he was bored, lonely and isolated as much at work as he was at home.

He spent long hours indexing old case files stored at the south London facility, reading, in the vain hope, that he might find something to stimulate his atrophying intellect. So far, he hadn't.

The Castle Heights case fell into his lap or, expanding on the metaphor, bounced off his paunch and then fell into his lap.

After doing his shopping at the supermarket, during an extended lunch hour, something he never used to do when he cared, he went back to the industrial unit where the records were housed. An old policeman had given him words to live by; "Be nice to people on the way up because you are sure to meet them on the way down." There stood a detective he had met on his way up the greasy pole, Detective Kitty Valletta was just such a person he had been pleasant to on his way up within the firm and was now reciprocating during his slow descent into career obscurity.

She was ten years his junior and he had a bit of a soft spot for her, she still occasionally appeared in his fantasies as he would envision her in her WPC outfit and her black stockings, the uniform she was wearing when they first met at a crime scene many moons ago.

"Saw these and thought of you," she said, as she dumped an evidence bag on Chetwyn's small desk that contained a series of black notebooks.

"Thank you for coming down to my dusty lair," quipped Chetwyn.

"They were probably going to pulp these, but I wondered if you had a home for them?" She cast her eye across the acres of metal shelving.

Chetwyn had removed one of the notebooks and was peering at the elegant ink handwriting on the pages when he felt she was looking at him. He caught a look of pity on her face, a look he had seen before. The force was changing so fast that Chetwyn felt like a fossil, whereas Valletta was the future. There didn't seem to be room for old white men in the Met anymore, despite their experience.

Detective Valletta had brought food too, a few Tupperware boxes were relieved of their lids to bring forth olives, mozzarella cheese salad and Italian bread. This food was slightly outside Chetwyn's limited palate, so he politely made an excuse and watched the detective perch on his desk and munch through it as they spoke.

"You'll be needing a nice chianti with your Italian food, Valletta."

"And some fava beans!" she joked back, knowing Chetwyn's love of the macabre.

"There's some proper spooky goings on in them books," she continued.

"Oh yeah?"

"I got this from the clean-up squad at a residential tower block. This chap they found dead, perfectly mummified with his arm up pointing at the window. They reckon he might have been dead for almost a year. Proper eerie it was, right up your

7

alley."

Chetwyn was hardly listening as he looked at her face which he had the sudden desire to grab and kiss. A rush of passion had welled up and consumed him. The lack of human warmth at home had propelled him toward his idiotic yearning.

Only when Kitty Valletta had left did he calm down and return to a semblance of sanity.

As the daylight faded from the semi-opaque sky, Chetwyn reached into his tweed jacket and removed his Turkish cigarettes, lit his one a day constitutional smoke, and set about reading the books now in his possession. Turning on the tiny desk lamp beside him instead of the antiseptic strip lights, he inhaled the heavily scented smoke, adjusted his glasses, and settled into the chair with a slight growl of contentment.

I am Raymond Garrick, psychologist and Lecturer of Criminal Psychology at King's College, University of London. I am currently on a sabbatical whilst I write a book. The dean suggested I take this as a sabbatical since my research is not for a peer reviewed paper but a manuscript I am hoping will be picked up by a publisher of lighter factual material. I suspect the dean is doing this to quash any arguments about salaries as well as prevent any grumbling which the fellows and other professors might have on the nature of my proposed book; Ghosts, a clinical psychologist investigates. The dean actually choked on his wine when I told him the proposed title. I imagine he saw my one-time appearance on a morning television show and didn't want any more embarrassing incidents. He could keep me at arm's length from the University and cut me off, if my book became successful, without bringing further shame on the department. It was fine to have an Iranian lecturer who actively worshipped and advertised her belief in a supernatural deity, but heaven forbid a middle-aged nutter who claimed he saw a ghost as a child and was planning to write a book about it.

Why that bit? Chetwyn puffed on his cigarette and drew down a plume of heavy white smoke, he reached for his thermos flask and topped up his coffee cup. A tingle of boyhood excitement travelled through him, akin to the feeling he used to have on Christmas Eve as a child or hearing a good ghost story. Chetwyn attributed his desire to join the police force and his love of all things supernatural to watching the black and white film *The Hound of the Baskervilles* with Basil Rathbone and Nigel Bruce. In fact, he could directly credit his first experiments with smoking due to that film, that and his aforementioned love of ghostly stories.

Opening the first notebook to the first page he read;

I, Raymond Garrick, am a Professor of Psychology at King's College, University of London, and I believe in ghosts. This rather unfashionable belief stems from the time I met my dead grandfather.

I was eight years old and I was walking home from school in the village of Levisham, Yorkshire when I saw my grandfather sitting on the stile out of the big sheep field near The Horseshoe pub. My grandfather had once been the local smithy's boy and usually wore a sixpence piece that he had punctured a hole in, on a leather lace around his neck. It was strange to see him in his black suit, smoking his pipe. "Hello Ray, did you enjoy your learnin' today?" he said with his gold tooth glinting and his thick white hair standing up like Stan Laurel. I told Grandpa that I had and he reached out his hand, pulling the lace and sixpence out of his pocket, the memento he had made as a boy, which he put it in my hand. "Keep on working, Ray, you's as bright as a button lad, you'll go far." He got down from the stile, patted me on the head and walked down the path beside the sheep field. As I walked away, he called out, "Look after thy mother."

When I arrived back at our cottage I was greeted by my mother in the kitchen. She was sat at the old oak kitchen table. She had been weeping and there was pink around her eyes and fresh tears on her cheeks. She quickly wiped her face. She sat me down and explained that she had just taken the bus back from the hospital and grandpa had passed away.

"But I've just seen Grandpa, and he gave me this," I said, reaching into my grey flannel shorts pocket and pulling out nothing. There was no sixpence on a lace. It had gone.

Mother exploded in grief and anguish. She thought I was "telling one a y' jokes."

Two weeks later, at the funeral, Grandma gave me an envelope with "Ray" written in a rough pencil hand by my grandfather. Inside was a note saying "Look after your mother. Grandpa," and the sixpence on the lace. I've kept it ever since.

No physical evidence remains but I was not, at the tender age of eight, suffering a psychotic episode and the experience is so clear and deeply ingrained as to be indelible.

This experience has led me on a lifelong quest to seek out other convincing and baffling stories that may or may not have a supernatural bent.

The next day Chetwyn felt full of energy, despite the crick in his neck from sleeping on the sofa, the one he'd been banished to by Megan, his vengeful spouse. He felt fleet of foot, his spirits lifted. This had a lot to do with seeing detective Valletta as well as doing a bit of his own detective work around the Raymond Garrick case, if in fact there was some to be done.

As Chetwyn entered one of the incident rooms, Valletta was bending over a desk, looking at some case files alongside an Indian detective. Very erotic images of Detective Valletta flooded his mind and it was difficult to prevent himself from putting his hands on her hips in a lover's welcome. If he acted out his fantasies he would be off the force and out on the pavement before you could say Harvey Weinstein. Not only that, he was a gentleman and had never partaken in boorish behaviour.

Chetwyn waited patiently until Kitty Valletta was done. When she spun around she had a furrowed brow that relaxed into a warm smile.

"It's got its hook into you, hasn't it?" She looked at him at the angle that accentuated the way her right eye pointed in slightly. A defect that Chetwyn found endearing.

"Let's just say it's got me intrigued."

"An eminent university professor obsessed by things that go bump in the night, found mummified in a rather down-at-heel residential tower block in mysterious circumstances. Let me get you the case file."

Kitty Valletta bent again slightly as she reached into an archive box under her desk. Her sturdy legs in tights, her charcoal grey suit skirt revealing a little panty line. *Jesus, man, get a hold of yourself,* that phrase bounced around Chetwyn's cranium. She booked him a car and he soon found he was on his way to Castle Heights with his pulse racing and damp patches under his arms, luckily concealed under his sports jacket. As the constable drove him, he looked through the file Kitty had slipped him. His brain snacked on the information but was constantly diverted back to Valletta's bottom.

The WPC who drove Chetwyn to the tower block said almost nothing apart from the obvious.

"We've arrived Sir, I'll wait for you here."

Chetwyn nodded and walked through the double doors into the foyer of the tower block, a musty stench of damp from the stairwell hitting his nasal passages. He was relieved he didn't need to climb them as the lifts looked unreliable and the flat was number one, on the ground floor. He pulled the one remaining strand of police incident tape off the door as he entered.

The interior of the flat required, what an estate agent might euphemistically describe as, some updating. Chetwyn surmised that the flat must have been owned by a little old lady. Lladro porcelain dogs cluttered the shelves and the mantelpiece above the three-bar gas fire. A gaudy painting of a clown holding balloons stood above the same gas fire in the living room. Dated furniture, dated brown Formica kitchen, very dated avocado coloured bathroom.

If he had concentrated on the way over, Chetwyn would have learnt that the flat was owned by Irene Smith, a spinster of eighty years who owned the flat that Raymond Garrick was discovered sat bolt upright in. He was found in a kitchen chair with his arm outstretched and pointing at the sliding doors that lead out to a fenced-off patch of grass with ornamental pots and a patio.

Chetwyn turned the key and slid open the door. He walked out into the garden and had he not been concentrating would have fallen into a round deep hole in the grass. He stood peering at it. He found the sensation brought a profound sense of discomfort because he couldn't see the bottom. He went back into the house and grabbed a porcelain dog. Tossing the dog into the hole, he heard it clatter downward then nothing. Chetwyn stepped backward into the flat. A more youthful man might have exclaimed WTF, but Chetwyn: "What on God's green earth?"

Once home and ensconced in his shed, he properly went through the accumulated paperwork as well as an entry by Raymond Garrick in his collection of notebooks. Flicking through the last notebook he picked up, Chetwyn surmised it to be the psychologist's final one.

Often explanations of hauntings are attributed to aberrant mental behaviour or even illness. The final case I wish to share is that of Irene Smith who is going blind and apparently suffers from Bonnet syndrome.

This case was referred to me by the Consultant Ophthalmologist at University College Hospital.

Irene Smith is a cheerful woman in her seventies, a former seamstress of a West End theatre. She puts her failing eyesight down to re-attaching sequins onto the chorus line's costumes during the ten-year run of a hit show. Despite the ophthalmologist explaining this is not the case and her oncoming blindness is in fact due to an inoperable degenerative disorder, Irene prefers her explanation.

Bonnet syndrome is a phenomenon named after Charles Bonnet, a Swiss psychiatrist who wrote about it in the late eighteen hundreds. When sighted people begin losing their vision, they oftentimes start experiencing complex hallucinations. In Miss Smith's case, she started to observe people appearing on the land outside the Tower Block that had been designated as gardens for the ground floor residents.

Again, Miss Smith defied the wisdom of the

consultant in favour of her own explanation that in fact these were the ghosts of the "ancient people".

At first I didn't understand what was going on but soon enough I knew these were people from beyond the veil.

Over the telephone she described in detail that the people must be the ancient Britons because the costumes they were wearing were like a play that she'd once worked on.

"The costumier did a lot of research, she did. Won an award for it, she did, despite the play being a flop. Anyhow, these ghosts are wearing the same clothes," Miss Smith explained.

When pressed about what she saw these "ghosts" doing in her garden, she quite matter-of-factly explained that this was an ancient burial ground and that she could see the trees in a circle where the garages now stood.

Whilst this might appear laughable and indeed the hallucinations of a woman suffering from Charles Bonnet's syndrome, I had to investigate her very detailed description of a series of wooden poles in a large circle and this is where things got stranger. It turned out that Castle Heights had been built on the edges of one of the few discovered wooden henges in Britain. The cultural and historical significance was lost on the developers of the hideous erection of Castle Heights.

I decided I had to investigate.

This is hotting up nicely, thought Chetwyn as he absentmindedly reached into his tweed jacket, drew out the Turkish cigarettes and lit the second of the day. Turning a page of the notebook, he saw a strange diagram. It looked like the same design as the Swastika Stone of Woodhouse Crag, an image Chetwyn had seen before.

I must try to describe accurately what I saw when I spent the evening at Irene Smith's flat last night. I arrived at eight thirty pm whilst there was still some residual daylight and had a cup of tea. At nine, Miss Smith fumbled her way across the living room and turned off the lights. She made a giggled remark about what the neighbours would think about a young man being seen in her living room at that hour with the lights off (despite the fact she was a partially blind woman in a darkened room sitting with a middle-aged professor in sight of nobody.) We sat sipping tea with Miss Smith explaining, "They'll be here soon." Infuriatingly, she made this remark several times over.

This last sentence was struck through with a line. *The old bird was pissing him off,* thought Chetwyn.

Peering into the gloom of her back garden, only illuminated softly by streetlamps, I began to enter the strange nether world of Irene Smith and her "hallucinations". In the shadows I started to see the drifting black wisps of something, perhaps smoke?

"Here they come," whispered my companion.

The loose smoke coalesced into straight columns like tree trunks placed at regular intervals and described the edge of a circle. Now other plumes of smoke rose from the ground and began to move. Human motion was easily detected, even when fleshed out by this strange spectral smoke or mist, whatever it was. In the gloom, one blinks to try and gain definition and bring what one is seeing into focus, but there is no clarity.

Then a confusion of mist gave way to a flailing of limbs and a woman in rags was being dragged by four men. The silhouettes became fuller, the mixture of light from centuries ago and the yellow sodium streetlights fused into three-dimensional forms that crossed into the here and now.

I saw a huge circular stone with a strange carving upon it. The woman was dragged onto it before one of the men lifted a huge rock and smashed it downward on the struggling wretch's head. The body twitched. Another man in a cape and pointed hat moved to the centre of the rock and slashed at the woman's neck. The men lifted the woman's body upside down and, like a slaughtered pig, the blood drained on the rock.

"Fancy a brew?" came Irene Smith's voice from behind me.

I remained transfixed on the scene still playing out before me. The woman's body was tossed into a huge dark hole very close to the patio door in Irene's garden. A hole that I had not seen earlier. The woman's body landed like a rag doll on the lip and bounced on the edge of the chasm before falling in.

Oh my God, the hole, thought Chetwyn, *is that what it's for?*

The next morning, he himself had commandeered a car and driver from the pool and was driven from his house to Castle Heights. Sod the paperwork, he'd deal with it later.

It was the same monosyllabic WPC who dropped him at the tower block before.

He still had the keys with him from the previous day and was soon in the vacant but still furnished flat. As he'd crossed the lobby, Chetwyn had seen who he assumed was the concierge, leaning on a broomstick, eyeing him suspiciously. What had happened to Irene Smith? He jotted a note in his pocketbook to locate her before he strode into the living room. He unlocked the patio doors to the garden and gingerly walked towards the grass. No hole? He went back into the living room and looked about him as if he had let himself into the wrong flat. He felt truly discombobulated. Out in the garden he felt the ground to check the earth was solid; it was. He got on his knees and slowly examined the grass.

Back inside the flat, he spun around on the spot in confusion, trying to reassure himself that he was in the right place. An uneasy excitement grew within him.

That Saturday evening Chetwyn sat in his shed, "stewing" on the case. He pulled out from behind a book on his shelf a small hip flask of very expensive malt whiskey and totted his coffee with it. He lit his fourth cigarette of the day, gulped at the warming brew, inhaled the deep rich smoke and read Garrick's notebook once more.

I returned several nights in a row. Thankfully Miss Irene Smith has been taken into Denville Hall, a retirement home for theatrical professionals, so I wasn't disturbed by her inane wittering (omit / remove). Activity seems to be gaining momentum. In the gloom I spy garlands of flowers and lit torches around the stone with strange symbols. According to Professor Dunitch's Esoteria of Pagan Practices, a festival of Mabon, "a gathering in, or precursor to a harvest festival." Tonight I believe something momentous is about to happen.

A bolt of realisation hit Chetwyn. *The date of the festival in the book. That's tonight. Sod it,* thought Chetwyn as he got into his battered old Volvo and sped to Castle Heights.

He was smoking almost nonstop now, his blood pressure through the roof with excitement. For the first time in months, he felt alive again.

Chetwyn skipped across the lobby to the flat and called a cheery "Good evening" to the gormless concierge, who nosily had stuck his head out of a doorway to gawp at him.

Once inside the flat he switched on the lights, availed himself of Miss Smith's toilet and drew up a kitchen chair close to the patio doors. He then readjusted the lighting in the living room to prevent reflections by turning off the central lighting, favouring a little lamp resting on the shelf with the gaudy porcelain dogs.

He cupped his hands on the glass so as to see by the yellow light of the sodium streetlamp what was going on.

Nothing happened, not until eleven fifteen. Then, in the nether world, the strange plumes of smoke belched from the earth, just as Garrick described, and soon murky, shadowy people were moving about in front of him. Then he noticed it. The huge gaping hole in the ground, then the flat stone with a design carved in. He had heard about this but not seen it himself. The excitement gave way to unease, but not fear, as what was happening outside the glass appeared almost as if it were a faded film playing out. Chetwyn turned the key in the patio door and slid it open a little way so as to get a better look. There appeared to be six caped men, twenty-five feet away.

Chetwyn pulled his flask from his pocket, twisted off the cap and swigged. The flask slipped from his fingers, causing him to look down.

He felt a sudden cataclysmic crushing pain in his chest as the whiskey was flowing down his neck. He looked up again as he fell to his knees, seeing the six men standing in front of the opening in the patio door. It was like a bizarre game of grandma's footsteps. Suddenly they were right in front of him. They were still dark shadows but now they also appeared solid too. They were all pointing at him. He realised they had come for him. The flat's lights flickered as the six men grabbed him and pulled him into their world. Chetwyn tried to open his mouth and scream as he saw the men, blood on their hands, illuminated by the flickering torches, the sodium street lamps and light from the flat. The men wrestled with him as they dragged him onto the large flat stone. He could hardly breathe, the pain and dread constricting his whole being. In the torchlight he noticed one of the hooded figures had a tattoo on his chest of the same strange four-pointed design. They pinned him down onto the cold stone surface. He looked back at the flat. The lights flickered once more and he saw three women standing over his body in the flat. It was Kitty, Megan and the monosyllabic driver. They all had smiles on their faces as Chetwyn saw himself writhing on the carpet, clutching his chest.

Chetwyn was somehow in the flat and outside at the same time. He decided he was dead already.

The rock was raised above his head by one of the pagan priests and brought down swiftly. A neurological bolt of lightning locked his right arm and leg as pain exploded in a canopy of stars across his vision. They then dragged him to the hole. His broken soul moaned like a wounded animal as he was tossed into the pit.

***

In the darkness of the flat, Kitty Valletta lit a cigarette, illuminating Chetwyn's wife Megan and the police driver. The driver switched on the torch of her phone, illuminating Kitty and Megan as well as the immobile crumpled heap of Chetwyn close to the sliding patio doors. All three women were wearing gold pendant necklaces with the same strange symbol.

Kitty exhaled and gripped Megan's hand tighter.

"Now you've joined the order, I told you would always answer our sisters' prayers."

Apartment 10

Anna Dixon

Scarlet sat at the kitchen table in her new apartment staring at her open laptop. On the screen was the social media page of Charlie, the love of her life, the person she had trusted more than any other, the man who she now knew had lied, cheated and deceived her for years. She read through his last few posts:

15:00 FREEDOM! Sun's out, guns out. Where you at?

17:30 I'm going out, out. If you want me, you know where to find me!

He was moving on and so should she. She was a mature, responsible adult and she didn't need the safety net of a sham relationship. She grabbed the open bottle of vodka from the table and drained the last of it, discarding it in a pile of similar bottles by her feet. She got unsteadily to her feet and crossed the room to the kitchen, dodging the various boxes she had not yet unpacked and noticed the clock on the wall. 21:00. *God knows what or who he's doing now! And who even cares!?* She carried on towards the kitchen, opened the freezer and retrieved another bottle. As she closed the freezer door, she saw her phone on the work surface. There were unread messages. She opened the first, from Charlie. Her heart jumped into her throat:

Yo! Got the house to myself, got a bottle of vino and ain't got nothing goin' on...

That heart in her throat turned to bile as she resisted the urge to text back exactly what he could do with that bottle of 'vino'. She opened the next message, also from Charlie:

Scar, that wasn't meant for you. It was honestly for Sean. Please come home. Or just call so I know you're ok.

Her resistance is futile. She started to text back: *Well, tell 'Sean' he's probably best to drop by the clinic on his way home tomorrow...* She was cut off by her phone ringing. It's Justin, her oldest friend, and she sagged a little with relief. She owed him so much lately, he'd got her out of her place with Charlie and set her up with this, admittedly dated, but well out of her price range apartment on the first floor of Castle Heights.

She'd found out about Charlie when she and Justin had gone for a full-on nostalgia fuelled night out, of bands, booze and bad dancing. She'd been riding a wave of euphoria at the time, although she couldn't explain why, she was just deliriously happy to be out and free and... then they bumped into Charlie. With his arm around a girl. A girl young enough to be his daughter. He had looked up at her and the guilt was written all over his face. She didn't need to see or hear any more, and she had turned from him there and then and had never looked back.

Justin had known exactly what to do and here she was, just a week later with her own place and not dependent on anyone. She answered the phone:

'Hey, man.'

'Hey Scar Face. Just checking in. You settling in okay?'

Scarlet tried to keep the slight shake from her voice and picked up the chilled bottle of vodka as she headed back to her computer. She forced herself to smile.

'Yeah, absolutely fine. This place is amazing. You're a good man to know.'

'You sure? You not heard from, well, He Who Shall Not Be Named?'

She faltered for a moment and decided honesty isn't always the best policy. Justin hated her getting messages from Charlie and she could totally understand why. He always seemed to be able to charm her back with a smile and a sweet word in the past. All those times she'd had emails with photos of him out with the other girl, screen grabs of his messages, receipts from restaurants he swore he'd never been to.

'He wouldn't dare. He knows what a mouthful he'd get'.

The line went quiet and Scarlet again started to look through Charlie's page on the computer, seeing if he had updated anything since she'd last checked. Nothing.

'You sure? I wouldn't be surprised if he was trying to pull on those heart strings of yours – why do you never go for nice guys?'

The response was silence. He continued.

'Do you need me to come over? That old building can be weird at night when you're not used to it.'

Scarlet rolled her eyes. Justin was amazing, but he had a bit of a saviour complex. He treated her like some ludicrous damsel in distress.

'I'm okay, thanks dad.'

Her voice was kind and teasing, but she knew it had been the wrong thing to say.

'Fine. You're one of these 'strong, independent women' I keep hearing about. If you need me, though, you call. Promise?'

She owed him and his heart was in the right place. 'Promise. Thanks, Ju. I do appreciate it.'

They said their goodnights and she hung up the phone. She *was* a strong, independent woman who didn't need to rely on anyone or any*thing*. She flicked the cap of the new bottle of vodka and took a healthy swig, looking thoughtfully at the contents. This didn't count as 'anything', right?

Her laptop screen had gone dark from inactivity and she caught a look at her reflection in its surface. Yesterday's makeup and unbrushed hair was not an empowering look, she decided. She got up and headed to the bathroom, dodging the debris of takeaway cartons and discarded bottles littered around the room.

She turned on the tap to the bath and let the water run, sitting on the side of the bath she looked at her phone to check the time, wondering where Charlie would be now and then hating herself for wondering. 10pm. *He's probably half-way into a bottle of Jack...or half-way down a girl's throat*, she thought bitterly. As she was lost in thought, a loud knock from the apartment's front door startled her.

Her brief fear turned to annoyance. She would put money on this being Trevor, the all-too-helpful concierge, once again making sure she felt 'safe' in the creepiest way possible.

She gave herself a once over in the mirror, tried to straighten her hair and makeup and then gave up, exasperated, and left the room to head towards the door. The loud hammering continued as she stormed towards it and, throwing the door open with some force, yelled, 'Do you have any idea what time...' to thin air. She stopped in her tracks, baffled. She looked up and down the corridor at the other silent apartments on her floor. There was no-one. She frowned and shut the door carefully. She stood for a moment, confused, and then exclaimed, 'the bath!' and rushed back to the bathroom.

She bustled in, a little wrong-footed, and turned off the tap, slightly scalding herself in the process. She tried to brush off the weird feeling rising from the pit of her stomach. She spotted her old friend Russian Standard sitting innocently on the cabinet. She smiled, swiping up the bottle and putting it to her lips. She was about to take another huge swig when the loud banging from the door made her lose her grip. The bottle smashed on the floor around her bare feet and she stifled a scream. She sighed, carefully picking her way around the broken glass and out of the bathroom. Keeping her eyes focussed on the door, she edged slowly towards it as the frantic banging continued. She slowly reached out her hand to the door handle, but the knocking stopped abruptly, as quickly as it had started. She hesitated for a moment. Thoughts raced through her mind as to what she should do next, when she caught a glimpse of a reflection of a figure, distorted but definitely human, standing behind her in the mirror next to the door. She tried hard not to react as the panic started to rise within her chest. She tried to subtly look around for something, anything to defend herself with and settled on her old, battered umbrella leaning against the wall. She could see the dark figure in the reflection, silently edging closer to her and she forced her tense and terrified body to relax. 'Is that glass?' she said aloud, in what she hoped was a calm and disinterested tone, as she bent down to grab the umbrella before spinning around, her back against the door.

The empty corridor loomed in front of her. Scarlet's eyes darted around, but there was nothing there. She took a second to take stock of the situation and closed her eyes, trying to bring herself under control. She felt the breath on her cheek almost before she heard the word, lilting, almost like it was being sung to her. 'Scaaarlet.' She lashed out with the umbrella and, hearing a satisfying grunt from her left-hand side, ran back towards the bathroom. She stumbled in, frantically locking the door as she fell to the floor and shuffled backwards against the bath. She breathed heavily, staring at the bottom of the door as a shadow drifted in front of the gap, blocking out the light from the hallway.

As she stared at the dark space under the door, her phone buzzed loudly from the side of the bath where she'd discarded it earlier, snapping her attention away from the door for a moment. When she looked back, the shadow was gone. Keeping her eyes on the door now, she fumbled for her phone and, with some effort, looked down at it. There was a new message from Justin. Not even reading the words, she hit the call button, shooting her eyes back to the door and keeping them fixed on the sliver of light underneath. Justin answered immediately and cheerfully he said, 'Scar! I was just thinking...'

Scarlet cut him off, a mixture of relief and renewed panic rising in her chest. 'There's someone in the flat. I don't know how they got in...I...' She trailed off. How did they get in? She struggled with the thought for a moment.

Justin cut in, breaking her concentration, 'What!? What do you mean? Who's there? Where are you now? Are you hurt?' Scarlet looked down at herself. She had forgotten the broken glass on the floor and hadn't realised that she had crawled through it in her effort to escape. 'I'm okay. I think I'm okay.'

Justin didn't sound convinced. 'Wait there.'

She let the phone fall from her hand onto the glass and blood-soaked bathmat. Her attention was drawn back to the light under the door. She could hear her blood pulsing through her veins, her heart racing, and she tried to calm herself down. She started to try to get up and to remove the glass from her skin. She unlocked the door and went to open it as the familiar shadow fell under the door, blocking the light. She gasped and recoiled as the bathroom door handle slowly started to turn and

her breath caught in her throat. As the door began to open, she kicked it shut again and heard a muffled, 'Fuck!' from the other side.

'Scar, it's me!'

'Ju?'

Scarlet's tone was questioning and, still suspicious, she cautiously opened the bathroom door, umbrella in hand. Justin was standing in the hallway outside, his face a mask of concern, his police uniform in slight disarray. Gratefully, she grabbed him and hugged him closely to her. He looked down at her, at first smiling, then noticing the blood and umbrella and wrinkling his nose at the overwhelming smell of vodka.

'What the hell happened to you?'

She looked down at herself, realising how inexplicable this all looked. She suddenly felt foolish and more than a little crazy. She dropped the umbrella and put her face in her hands.

'I don't know where to start...'

Justin smiled kindly at her and put a hand on her chin, lifting her face back up to look at his. 'You get changed, I'll put the kettle on.'

Justin put the two mugs down on the coffee table in the living room as Scarlet, now cleaner and feeling slightly more together, slumped down on the sofa, throwing her head back with a sigh. As Justin took the seat next to her, she recounted the events of the evening as best she could. It seemed ridiculous now she put it into words and Justin's face screwed up into a slightly confused expression.

She watched him take in the mess in the living room, with the various bottles strewn across the table and floor. She followed his gaze, seeing the conclusion forming in his head and she sat forward, slamming her cup down indignantly.

'I can see what you're thinking!' she exclaimed in frustration, 'and I know what I saw!'

His eyes darted back to hers, a guilty expression clouding his face. He held up his hands in a gesture of submission.

'No, I'm not thinking anything! I'm just worried about you. Maybe you need a bit more looking after than you let on is all? I can clock off for the evening and stay.' He moved in closer to her and put his arm round her shoulder.

She looked at him incredulously. 'I don't need any looking after! I'm not a bloody goldfish!'

She shrugged his arm off her and stood, heading over to the mantelpiece and grabbing another half full bottle of a slightly cloudy liquid. She ripped the top off the bottle, sniffed the contents experimentally, shrugged and downed the contents, glaring at Justin.

Justin sighed and stood, holding his hands up in surrender.

'I didn't mean to hurt your feelings, really. But you called me from your bathroom, covered in blood and booze and talking about vanishing intruders...'.

He trailed off, looking away. Scarlet could tell he was trying not to offend her and the more she thought about it, the crazier it sounded. She shook her head and looked up at Justin, adopting a more conciliatory tone.

'I'm sorry, you're right. I'm probably just going more nuts than usual...but I'm okay, really I am.'

His face lit up as he took a few steps towards her.

'Great to hear, shall I get us takeaway? You feeling spicy or Italian this even...'

She cut him off, shaking her head. 'No. You go, get back to work – catch some real bad guys, not my imaginary ones.'

She smiled, kind but firm. Justin took a step back, his face falling into a mask of concern. 'Are you sure about this? I feel wrong leaving you alone...'

Scarlet forced a nonchalant smile and nodded. She put her arm around him in a friendly hug and led him from the living room and towards the front door, ushering him out into the dark hallway.

'C'mon, what time is it?'

She checked her phone and noticed a new message from Charlie. She tries to hide her expression and failed. Miserably.

'Gone half eleven! Man, I should be in bed.'

She began to close the door, now distracted by the message. Justin checked his own watch, nodded and smiled, a little defeated.

'You'll call if you need me?'

She nodded, not really listening.

'Yeah, you too.'

She slammed the door and leaned back against it,

her breath catching in her throat. She looked back at her phone and opened the message:

You're not safe there, baby. We need to meet. Now.

She looked at the message, baffled. He didn't know where she was. This was not the late-night text she had been expecting but, really, what did she expect? Another apology she wouldn't believe? Another suggestive message sent to the wrong person? But this was just...weird.

As she stood in the hallway trying to make sense of this, the TV blared to life in the living room, making her jump and causing her to drop her phone.

'...AND THE 'SLEDGE' IS REALLY HAMMERING HOME HIS INEXPERIENCE HERE, TROY...'

Scarlet walked cautiously towards the living room as the commentators screamed deafeningly from the set.

'...I'M NOT SURE HE'S GETTING BACK UP FROM THIS...'

She looked around the door into the living room. No one was there. She noticed the TV remote on the arm of the sofa and went towards it, picking it up.

'...OKAY, HE'S GOING FOR THE COUNT...'

As she stood, she thought she noticed the same reflection in the window, a distorted figure standing behind her. A man, she thought, presumably dressed in black from head to toe as she couldn't make out any features. She tried to keep calm. The TV announcers continued...

'...OKAY, HERE WE GO! 1...2...3...'

Suddenly the flat was pitched into blackness as the electricity cut out, enveloping the room in darkness and silence. Scarlet stifled a scream and spun around to look where the figure had been a moment ago. She could see nothing by the limited light afforded to her by the streetlamps outside.

She crept back towards the hallway and, seeing the faint glow of her phone by the door, she edged towards it, trying not to disturb the deep silence. As she bent down to grab the device, something gripped her throat from behind, pulling her backwards. She struggled to free herself and fought for each breath as she was wrenched back and slammed into the wall of the hallway. She slumped to the floor, slightly dazed, and felt around her throat. There was nothing there. Her head buzzed as she tried to collect her thoughts. She saw her bedroom door, invitingly ajar. There was a lock on the inside, she remembered. She got to her feet, trying to appear more disorientated than she was and then ran. She flew through the door, slamming it behind her and bolting the lock. She held her ear to the door, listening intently to every sound. There was nothing.

She leaned her forehead against the door and checked her pockets for her phone. *Damn!* she thought. It was still in the hallway. As she stood at the door, thinking out her next move, a whisper in her ear made her blood run cold and she froze with fear.

'Scar by name, scarred by nature.'

She felt a sharp pain in her neck and tried to turn

around to face her demon. As her vision blurred, and before the world went completely black, she grabbed at the outstretched hand in front of her, scratching and grabbing as she fell, clinging to something to help her stay upright. The something broke away and she fell, unconscious, to the floor.

Scarlet started to come round on the floor of her bedroom, her arm twisted painfully underneath her and her head throbbing from the pain. She couldn't tell how long she had been there. The flat was still in pitch darkness and her ears were ringing. As she regained control of her senses, she could make out that the ringing was coming from the hallway. It was her phone, still on the floor by the door. As she listened, the ringing stopped. She staggered to her feet and looked down at her fist, still clenched in a grip from her struggle. She opened her hand and saw half a strap from a watch sitting in her palm. Her fingernails were stained with blood. She dropped the strap on the floor and staggered out of her bedroom and into the dark hallway. She could see the glow of her phone on the floor and half ran, half crawled towards it, grabbing it and backing up against the front door as she looked around her.

She tore her eyes away from the shadows surrounding her that seemed to shift and distort, and looked down at her phone. She had missed calls from Charlie and Justin, and she paused for a moment, looking at the two names. She took a deep breath and hit the call button for Charlie. As she listened to the call tone, she heard a phone ringing in the flat. She moved towards the noise which led her back into the living room and she saw another phone in the middle of the floor, ringing quietly and moving with the slight vibration. She let her phone drop from her ear and stared as the phone became silent and, eventually, went dark. She shook her head in disbelief, bringing the phone back up to her face and dialling again. This time, Justin answered.

'Hey man, what happened to that early night?'

'He's been here. He might still be here. Can you come?'

The line was quiet for a minute.

'I'll be there in ten. Get somewhere safe.'

The phone rang off and she stood motionless, staring at the offending phone on the floor and trying to take in the room around her.

Scarlet wasn't aware of the time passing, of the banging on the door and of Justin calling her name. He let himself into the flat and she felt his arms around her shoulders, gently spinning her around. She let herself fall into his chest and let him lead her back to her bedroom and onto her bed. She sank gratefully down onto the covers, as he pulled a blanket over her.

'You're safe now. I'll stay with you.'

A sudden hammering on the door made Scarlet sit bolt upright and caught Justin off guard. 'I'll check it out,' he said, soothingly.

He helped her lay back down and stroked her hair affectionally. She watched him leave the room and listened as he answered the door. She looked around the room and reached for her bedside light, flicking the switch. Still nothing.

'It's out in the whole block,' Justin cut in from the doorway. 'Seems like a serious threat, they've got the army out door knocking'.

Scarlet sat up again in bed, looking confused. 'The army? God, what time is it?'

Justin came to sit next to her and went to check his watch. Scarlet noticed it wasn't there and saw the deep scratches on his wrist. Her heart stopped in her throat and her head began to swim. She darted her eyes upward, trying to keep her expression neutral.

'Do you know, I'm not sure,' Justin said. 'Maybe half three-ish?' Scarlet started to get back out of bed.

'Well, I need a nice hot shower and decent cup of coffee,' she said, slightly too cheerfully, trying not to meet his gaze.

Justin smiled as she headed from the room. She crept towards the door, turning the handle as quietly as she could. She slowly opened the door an inch as a hand slammed it shut again. She looked in the mirror by the door and into the distorted face of her old friend.

'Why do you never go for the nice guys?'

Too late she saw the syringe jab into her hand, felt the pain in her neck, his next words echoing through her head.

'You're mine now.'

And her world went black.

The Demon of Apartment 13

Jason White

"Danny, I'm starting work now. I have to keep my door shut as there are lots of Zoom meetings and my clients don't like to be interrupted. If it's an emergency text me on my mobile and I'll read it. There's money for a pizza or whatever you and Georgia want on the side. £30 should do it, yeah?"

Mum gave Danny a smile and proceeded to take a cup of tea and pack of chocolate digestives with her into her bedroom. Shutting her door, Danny heard the key turning on the other side until it locked. It was obvious that Mum wasn't working a normal 9 to 5 job. Since Dad had died Mum had done anything to make ends meet, but no matter how many jobs she had done, the pittance they paid didn't bring enough money into the house. Mum had started the customer service job three months ago and life had started to get a lot better, although they hardly saw her at all some days.

Danny knocked on his Mum's door, placing his head against it to see if he could hear what was being said behind it. Absolutely nothing.

"Mum, what did you want to eat? Is pizza okay for you too or did you fancy something different? I could cook for you if you didn't want takeaway. I don't mind."

Mum spoke from behind the door, not even attempting to unlock it and speak to him directly.

"Pizza's fine darling. Could you get some garlic

bread with cheese and some mozzarella sticks too please? I'll eat it once I've finished work. Love you, beautiful!"

Danny nodded his head in agreement. Not that she could see him do it behind the door.

"Okay Mum. Don't forget Mask of Thorn is on at 9pm. You said you wanted to watch that! I thought Saturday night was supposed to be a weekend?" Danny said, walking away from her bedroom. He would be very surprised if she came out at 9pm to watch the film. She seemed to spend most of her time in her bedroom. *At least when we had less money, I saw more of her*, he thought to himself. He looked at the clock. 4.15pm. Georgia would be home in a minute. As long as she didn't get distracted by Johnnie next door at apartment 15.

He took a can of drink out of the fridge and snapped back the ring pull. He listened as the bubbles frothed their way to the top. Taking a sip, he placed it on the table next to the armchair in the living room. Sitting down, he closed his eyes and drifted off to sleep.

***

"Hi Trevor! How's it hanging? To the left, to the left I bet! Cheer up mate. It's not that bad, is it?"

Georgia always spoke to Trevor as she made her way to the lifts in the lobby of Castle Heights. He had worked there for eternity as far as she knew. Some people said if they cut Trevor open you would find he was made of the same concrete that held the block together. He never answered her back, but her Mum had always taught her to be courteous to anyone she saw on a regular basis. *You never know when you might need their help,* she heard her mum say in her head. Chuckling to herself, she clicked the button to open the lift door. As she got inside, she clicked to go to floor three, which is where her apartment, number 13, was. She gagged as the lift started its journey upwards. The lift had its own fragrance of sick, piss and excrement which lingered in the air even after copious amounts of Zoflora and thick bleach. Next time she would remember to take the stairs.

The lift doors opened and she stepped out into the passageway of the third floor. *Home sweet home,* she thought to herself. Reaching into her school bag, she searched for her door key, rummaging about for what felt like minutes.

"For fuck's sake! Why do I remember everything except my blood door key? I have my makeup, mobile, hand sanitiser and even the kitchen sink, but door key? Hello! No sign of it anywhere! Prepare to get moaned at by dickhead Danny, Georgia," she said to herself, still rummaging about and in the vain hope of finding it and not having to endure the irritating whiny whinging voice of Danny's *I told you so* voice.

"Hi beautiful! How was your day? I missed you. I can't wait for you to finish school for good, so we can spend more time together."

Georgia's heart melted as she heard Johnnie's voice ringing in her ears. She turned round and gasped as his lips met hers, his tongue prodding her mouth, forcing it open. Their tongues met and she felt a shiver flowing from her shoulders down to where she wanted him to end up later that night. Just as she was lifting her head back in anticipation, he pulled away, curling his lips into a seductive smile.

He opened the door to apartment 15 and gave her a look which spoke the words *Are you coming in then?* He pushed his dirty blond hair back away from his face and she gazed at his chiselled boy band looks. He took her hand and placed it under the black t-shirt he was wearing. She smiled as she felt her way up his chest, stroking his abs as she felt the urge to yank the t-shirt clean off, out in the hallway, and to push him to the ground. The thought of this made her laugh out loud. He looked at her puzzled as she removed her hands from under his top and let it fall back down.

"I have to go in. Danny will be waiting for me. He is stricter than Dad was when he was alive. I can't even go to the corner shop without him either questioning where I'm going or wanting to come with me. Mum's too busy to notice I'm not in the house, bless her."

Johnnie took Georgia by the hand, trying to persuade her to walk into the apartment with him. Georgia seemed to be swayed towards his way of thinking but was interrupted by Danny opening the door of apartment 13.

"Georgia! What do you think you're doing? You know not to hang around with him. He's a junkie lowlife with no future ahead of him. Get indoors now!" Danny screamed so loud that his voice echoed down the corridor. Georgia scurried into the apartment, giving Danny a dirty look as she barged past him. Johnnie looked unimpressed, walking over to Danny, looking ready to punch him.

"Am I not good enough for your sister? I was good enough when you wanted to come in and smoke weed with me and play on the Xbox, wasn't I? I really like Georgia. I wouldn't do anything to hurt her or let anyone else hurt her. You know that."

Johnnie stepped back. The last thing he wanted was to look too threatening, even though he wanted to punch Danny so hard. Sometimes his emotions got the better of him and the only way to release them was to punch someone out or hit a wall. Normally he would hit a wall, which was usually a big mistake as it killed. *Not today,* he thought to himself.

"Johnnie, I don't do drugs anymore. That version of me has long disappeared. Doing drugs helped me lose my job and my girlfriend too. I have to look out for Georgia's best interests. She's fifteen. You're twenty. She should be going out with boys her own age, mate. I'll see you later."

Danny walked in and closed the door. Johnnie was right. They had both been tight not too long ago. He blamed Johnnie for introducing him to drugs, but at the end of the day, he had taken them. He had made the decision. Johnnie hadn't forced him to do it. *Perhaps I should speak to him tomorrow and patch things up,* he thought to himself.

"I hate you!" Georgia screamed at him as he walked back into apartment 13. She gave him a dismissive look, walked to her bedroom and slammed the door shut as she went in. Danny went to the kitchen and took the pizza menu out of the top drawer where Mum always kept it. Walking back to Georgia's bedroom door, he knocked on it lightly.

"Hey! What did you want from Papa Joe's? I was thinking Pepperoni, stuffed crust, extra-large, garlic bread with cheese and mozzarella sticks too. Mum wants the bread and the sticks. I'm sure we can stretch to a large tub of ice cream too. There's a horror film on at nine. I think you'll love it! Come out mate. I'm sorry. I'm just being the responsible dickhead brother!"

Danny walked away from Georgia's door. He had to be the responsible adult. Mum was too busy with her work and neither of them really had a role model in their lives. When Dad was alive, he always tried his best to steer them on the right path. He had been the one who had shown Danny how pointless smoking weed was and had even managed to find a place who would take him on as an apprentice. He missed his dad.

Georgia opened her door, still looking a little worked up, but she managed half a smile.

"At least you admit you can be a dick at times. Can we get chocolate chip cookie flavour please? If we can, I'm in! When can we order? I'm starving," she laughed and jumped over the sofa to sit on it.

Danny ordered the takeaway, and when it arrived they sat down together and laughed and joked like they hadn't done in years. Things were looking like they were going to get better.

***

Danny cleared up the ice cream bowls and put the remainder of the chocolate chip cookie ice cream in the freezer for Mum to eat when she decided to stop working for the night. Georgia had screamed throughout Mask of Thorn, but he could tell by how much she had chattered about it when it finished that she had actually really enjoyed it. He put the slices of pizza, garlic bread with cheese and mozzarella sticks that were left on a plate for his Mum and placed it in the microwave. It was now 11.25pm and she had still not come out of her room once since she had started work. *That was seven hours ago. Was she not entitled to breaks?* he thought to himself.

"I'm bored Danny. Is there nothing else we can do? Have you still got the board? You know what I mean?" Georgia tugged at his T-shirt, giving him a doe-eyed look.

"I'll get it, but if Mum finds out she will kill me! She is very sensitive you know. You know it's going to be midnight soon, don't you?" Danny said, hinting that he would actually prefer to go to sleep instead.

"Come on Danny. Just a couple of goes and then I'll go to sleep. I promise." Georgia gave him the doe-eyed look again.

Knowing she wasn't going to give up, he went into his bedroom. Bending down, he reached under his bed to pull out the Ouija board and planchette. He really didn't think it was a good idea. *Mum's bound to come out whilst we're using it,* he thought to himself. Knowing resistance was useless and still feeling a little guilty about earlier, he took them from his room, clearing the coffee table to make room.

"Place your hands on the planchette. I'll ask the questions. Who did you want to contact?" he said, knowing the answer would be Dad.

"Dad!" Georgia said.

"How original!" Danny said, winking at her.

"Is there anybody there?" Danny said, as they both held the planchette. It moved over slowly to the word **Yes**.

"Nice one Danny," Georgia laughed.

"I didn't move it. Honestly, Sis," Danny said. "I thought it was you."

"No, it's you. Stop mucking about. It's only a game. For God's sake, don't pretend it's real. I'm not a child you muppet," Georgia said, laughing. Her head tilted back as she chuckled. The planchette started to move on its own.

B – I – L – L – Y

"Billy," Georgia said.

"Well done, spelling bee champion," Danny said sarcastically.

N – I – G – H – T

"Billy Night! How the fuck do you know about

44

him Georgia? You aren't funny. That sick bastard is just a myth. The kids in the block have been told about him for years, so they don't play up and run out of their parents' sight. Did Johnnie tell you about him?" Danny said, starting to get angry and slightly losing his composure.

"Who's Billy Night? Never heard of him. You're winding me up. Stop playing about. I'm not thick. I stayed at school. You didn't," Georgia said, keeping her fingers on the planchette.

"Okay, if you want to play games, so be it," Danny said, pressing more firmly on the planchette, to ensure she didn't move it again without a struggle.

"Billy Night, what do you want? You're a dirty old man who preys on the suffering of children. I've heard about you. I bet you haven't got the balls to move this planchette have you? You tosser!" Danny spoke like he was serious. There was no Billy Night. Never had been.

The planchette sprung out of Danny and Georgia's fingers and started to move by itself, spelling out two words which sent shivers and chills down both of their spines.

Y – O – U – R - S – O – U – L

"This is not fucking funny anymore! I don't want to play this stupid game ever again. Take the magnet out from under the coffee table Danny and let's pack the game up. Well done, nice wind up!" Georgia said, leaning down to take the planchette and Ouija board away.

As she leant down, she recoiled as black smoke

began to ooze from the board. The planchette glowed a fiery green colour and started to spin around erratically. Incessant laughter resounded around them and they felt themselves being held down on the sofa seats. Danny forced his head up to look at the clock on the wall.

11:40pm

"Mum!" they both screamed in unison. Hearing the commotion, Mum took her headset off and ended the live chat with Fred from apartment 49. He looked at her with frustration as she ended the live session. *Fred must have been ready to shoot his load,* she thought to herself. She put her hand on the key in the bedroom door to unlock it, but it wouldn't budge. The key wouldn't turn.

"Hold on kids! Just one sec. I'll be there in a minute!" she said, finally managing to turn the lock. As the door opened, the power in the apartment failed. All she could see in front of her was darkness. She hated the dark. Always had done since she was a little girl. In case Billy Night appeared and snatched her away.

"Kids! Are you okay? Where's my mobile? It has a light on it. I can use that. Let's go and find it. It must be on the table in my bedroom." Mum said this with a tinge of fear in her voice. She always felt as though the darkness would wrap itself around her like a cloak and squeeze her, draining the air from her lungs until she collapsed in a heap on the floor and died.

"Where the fuck is it?" she said, hands clambering about for it on the table. It was probably right in front of her, but the dark was a cruel individual who could hide what they wanted to when you least expected it. She put her fingers out, and finally found the mobile. She swiped the screen and the phone lit up. Turning on the light app she walked out of her bedroom and froze in her tracks. As the light shone, she could make out a figure standing in the front room, which was definitely not Danny or Georgia.

"Hi Monica. Do you want to play or are you still afraid of the dark? You always were a little frightened mouse who would piss themselves at the slightest fright. How's David? Oh, I forget, he's dead. Poor you. It must be so hard being a single parent slut, always willing to turn a trick to make ends meet. How do you get promoted when you're a Cam Girl again? It's not like they can buy you stars, is it?"

As the person moved into the beam of light from the phone, she let out an anguished cry. *It was him! But he wasn't real...*

She had dreamt of him as a child, but as she got older the dreams had faded away and evaporated into dust particles which travelled through her mind until they disappeared.

"If you're some sicko dressing up and pretending to be Billy Night you can do one and fuck off out of here. You're not him! Who are you, you dick?" Monica screamed with determination, despite her inward fear telling her that she should make a run for it and come back for the children later. She couldn't do that and she would have to stand her ground, despite her reservations in doing so.

"I don't have to go anywhere. The kids invited me in. They used a spirit board to conjure me, and unfortunately they're too stupid to figure out how to banish me. What a pickle you're in, my poor child. Bet you wish you didn't work from home now, you cocksucker!"

Billy smiled, widening his black lips to show razor sharp teeth. Maggots fell from his mouth and he pretended to heave. She screamed as the stench of vomit, blood and rotting flesh wafted from his mouth. He stuck his fingers down his throat and proceeded to force his arm within his mouth. She gagged as he pulled his arm out. Attached to it were his entrails. Throwing them in her direction, they landed at her feet. She screamed as they started to squirm towards her on the floor. This intensified as they began to make their way up her legs. She tried to brush them away but flinched as pus oozed from their pulsing veins. They pulsed faster and faster as they slowly crawled up her legs. She bent down and put part of the entrails in her mouth, clamping down her teeth on them. Pus exploded in her mouth and the entrails screeched, releasing their grip and falling to the floor. She stomped on them erratically, until they exploded all over the carpet.

The sight of this made her stomach retch and she vomited herself, chunks of sick falling to the floor, making squelching sounds as they hit it.

"Where are my fucking kids? Don't mess with them! You'll have to get through me first. I'm not scared of you! Give it your best shot!" she said, racing past to the kitchen. Opening the kitchen drawer, she pulled out a bread knife, making sure she didn't drop the mobile phone, as she would lose her only source of light otherwise. She ran at him, plunging the knife into his chest. He slapped her across the face with such force that she hurtled towards the sofa, falling over it and hitting her head on the floor. As she drifted into unconsciousness, she felt a pair of arms cradling her.

"Mum, are you okay?" Georgia said, her voice trembling with fear. Monica went to speak but couldn't form any words and then passed out.

"Georgia, leave her on the floor. We'll have to sort this monster out. I should have let Mum know we were hiding here. What we need to do is trap him in something. I have an idea that might work. Do you think you'll be able to distract him whilst I grab the Ouija board? I'll lead him into my bedroom. There's a way I might be able to trick him into agreeing to trap himself for good!" Danny spoke with a determination in his voice that Georgia had never heard before. She nodded her head, standing up off the floor and running towards the kitchen. Opening a cupboard door, she took the first thing that came to hand, which was the largest frying pan they had.

"Hey Billy! How do you like your eggs in the morning?" she said.

He looked puzzled.

"I like mine with a kiss. Well kiss this, you arsehole!" she screamed, running at him. He hissed at her and she recoiled as venomous spit landed on her top, causing it to smoulder. She whacked him with the frying pan and laughed as blood started to gush from his nose.

"You little bitch! I'm not putting up with that! Still scared of spiders, are you?" Billy said. He started to retch again, several times, and she could make out something long and spindly starting to appear from his mouth. It looked like a tarantula. Screaming in intense fear, she hit Billy several times again with the frying pan. He took a lot of blows, clawing away in the hope of reaching her and causing her harm. With one final blow she used such force that she knocked him out cold.

"Danny! Pick Mum up and get her to your room now! Make sure you've got the Ouija board too. This has to end tonight. Hurry up! I love you!"

Danny lifted Mum in a fireman's lift. He ran to his bedroom, all the while ensuring the Ouija board and planchette were tucked safely under his arm. He placed Mum on his bed, squinting to see a little clearer in the darkness. He fumbled about for the torch he kept in his bedside cabinet. He had left his mobile phone in the living room in the rush to get Mum and the Ouija board and planchette out of Billy Night's reach. Finding the torch, he shone it in his mum's eyes, which caused her to wake up with a startled look on her face.

"Fucking hell! Get that torch out of my eyes Danny! Where's your sister? Where are we?" Mum said, blinking to make out her surroundings.

"Mum, we're in my bedroom. I had to carry you in here. All the electric has gone out in the apartment. There's this man in the apartment calling himself Billy Night. He appeared after me and Georgia messed about with this!" Danny said, holding up the Ouija board in the torchlight.

"I'll ask you again. Where is your sister? Please tell me you haven't left her in there with that thing. We don't know who he is. He says he's Billy Night, but Billy isn't real. We need to get back out there, get Georgia and leave the apartment. I swear if that fucking weirdo has touched a hair on my baby's head, he is done for. Have you still got that baseball bat under your bed? It will be next to those dirty magazines you hide under there. Get me it quick. We can go out there and bash him on the head and run out. We don't need to use the lifts. The stairs will be fine. I need a workout anyway."

Danny looked at her with confusion. Knowing there was no time to waste, Mum reached under the bed, scrambling about for the baseball bat. Finally finding it, she clenched it in both hands, making her way to the bedroom door.

"Danny, come on! Shine the torch around so we can nail this fucker! Georgia, honey! Please tell me he hasn't hurt you beautiful!"

Danny ran out into the living room with torch blazing. His heart raced as he swung the torch around until he found what he could only describe as his worst nightmare. Billy Night had his hands around Georgia's throat and was strangling her. What made Danny gag was the sight of Billy Night rubbing himself against Georgia's body, clearly trying to get off on the fear visible in her face.

Danny could see she was frightened and was not moving as she had been paralysed by his perverse actions.

"Leave my sister alone you dirty cunt! I ain't having you touch her up like some paedo rapist! Mum, hit him with the bat. Come on! Hurry up!"

Danny screamed the order at his mum as though he was a sergeant in the army. Mum raced at Billy Night with the baseball bat, striking him several times in the stomach. The force of her blows was enough to make him loosen his grip around Georgia's throat. Gasping for air, Georgia slumped to the floor. Now it was time for Mum to bark her orders.

"Danny, get your sister in your room! Quickly, there's no time to waste. Let me know once you're in there, okay?"

Danny ran to Georgia and tried to drag her away from Billy Night. Clearly enjoying the taste of fear, Billy grabbed Danny by the arm, intending to keep him as well.

"Come join the fun, Danny! I will love the taste of your fear too! Boys' fear is always the sweetest to taste. Umm!" Billy Night licked his lips and was about to lick Danny's face when he received an almighty smack across the head from the baseball bat. His grip upon Danny loosened. Danny grabbed Georgia and raced with his mum to his bedroom. She locked the door tight and grabbed Danny's bookcase. Books flew all over the floor.

"Danny, put Georgia on the bed. We need to barricade ourselves in. Come on, look sharp son! He will be in here otherwise, and we really don't want that!"

Danny placed Georgia lightly on the bed. He helped his Mum move the bookcase and they put it at a slight tilt against the door, budging it under the door handle, which would prevent any movement outside or in.

"Give me the Ouija board Danny! Quick. I'm going to make sure this fucker is gone for good. He is one evil mother of Christ. Give me your lighter too!"

Mum waited for the Ouija board to be passed to her and Danny opened his bedside cabinet again to locate his lighter. Mum lit the lighter and placed the flame against the corner of the Ouija board. It started to catch alight. Flames and smoke started to billow and soon it was starting to blaze.

"Danny, open your window please. I call upon the angel Gabriel to cast the spirit of Billy Night back to the fires of Hell. Hear me, oh holy God! This demon does not belong here on Earth and needs to be sent back to whence he came. I cast this board out into the sky. With the board let the demon fly!"

Monica ran to Danny's window, flinging the board as far as she could into the air. As the board fell to the ground it started to spark, and for a moment it looked as though someone had lit fireworks and set them off. The board struck the concrete floor of the car park and exploded, causing a display that reminded Danny and his mum of the local firework display they attended every year. It wasn't the same without Dad, but they still went, eating jacket potatoes, lighting sparklers and getting merry on pints of lager and cider. Danny snapped out of his reminiscing as Georgia awoke screaming, lashing her arms out.

"Keep away from me! Don't hurt me please!" she cried. Shining the torch on her seemed to calm her down. Mum smiled at Danny and they both smiled at Georgia, who looked confused.

"You had us worried there for a minute beautiful. I thought Billy Night had got the better of you and you were a goner. He's been dealt with now. You have nothing to worry about. I love you darling."

Mum bent in to give Georgia a kiss on the cheek. As she did, they heard an almighty thud against the bedroom door. *Bang.* Then silence. *Bang.* More silence. *Bang.* They screamed as the top of the door started to splinter causing a hole to gradually form. As the banging continued, the hole grew bigger and bigger until a hideously deformed, burnt and scaly hand poked through and darted left and right, looking for whatever was blocking the door from being opened.

"Fuck off! You have got to be kidding me!" Danny said, shock etched on his face.

"Mum, he's going to kill us. He's going to kill us! Mum!" Georgia screamed.

"He won't do any such thing. I know what he wants to do now. He wants to play a game. Winner takes all. Well, Billy Night, if I open the door and let you in, do you promise not to do anything until the game is won fair and square? I'll move the bookcase out of the way if you do."

Danny and Georgia looked at Mum as though she were mad. She smiled and gave them both a wink.

"Danny, help me move the bookcase! Don't take all day!" she said starting to move the bookcase herself. Danny reluctantly helped her. Once it was moved, Billy Night bashed at the door, forcing it off its hinges. His left eye was completely burnt away and he smelt like charred flesh. The spell had worked a little bit, but not enough to completely destroy him. He stared at Monica and then curled his lips up to form a wry smile.

"Monica, are you ready to play the game?" he bellowed with a stench of rotting flesh, sick and excrement.

"Yes. I am. Ladies first though, yes?" she asked with a questioning smile.

"If you must. Go ahead then!" he bellowed.

"We're going to play the *I bet you can't do that game*. You know how to do that, don't you? I say I bet you can't do something, and you have to prove me wrong. Is that okay?" she said smiling innocently.

Billy Night nodded his head. He would amuse the mortal for a while. Once he got bored, he would devour her and her children's souls.

"Okay. First challenge. I bet you can't disappear inside Danny's bedside cabinet mirror! Bit difficult that one. Are you up for it or are you afraid of the challenge? I don't think your powers can stretch that far!"

Mum had a cunning plan. Billy Night nodded his head in agreement.

"Easy as 1-2-3!" he laughed manically, making himself evaporate into smoke. As he did this the smoke started to enter the mirror. The torch caught the last of the smoke and Monica grabbed the opportunity by the horns. With the torch in hand, she pounded on the glass until it shattered into a myriad of pieces.

"Quick, pick them all up before he has a chance to form again. Quick," she screamed.

They shone the torch on the floor and frantically picked up the pieces, scanning again to ensure nothing was left.

"Throw your pieces out of the window in opposite directions. Make sure they are thrown really far apart. The slightest chance they can meet back together could allow him to form back into himself!" she said.

"How do you know all this, Mum?" Georgia asked, puzzled.

"No time to explain now. Just do as I say!" her mum said with a determined stare.

Danny and Georgia threw the pieces with all their might, making sure none of them were anywhere near each other. Finally, Mum threw her pieces with such ferocity that when they hit the ground they shattered into a multitude of tinier pieces.

"Let's go! We can't stay here any longer. I'd rather be outside in the freezing cold than stay in here tonight. There's a horrible stench lurking.

Keep your windows open Danny!" Mum said.

As they stepped out onto the landing of the second floor, they were greeted by the fact that the whole block was in complete darkness. Making their way to the fire exit, they intended to open it and make their way down the stairs into the cold chill of the night air, but it felt like it was jammed tight.

"Mind out of the way guys! Let me open this fucker!" Danny said.

He barged against the door several times. With each shove he could feel the door starting to ease open. He decided to kick the door with his left foot and it crashed open, making an echo which resounded through the landing.

They heard the door to apartment 15 being opened and Johnnie stepped out in just his boxer shorts, clearly wondering what the racket was he had just heard. Georgia for a moment felt she should answer him and go to see how he was, but her mum and brother pulled her into the fire exit and rushed downstairs.

"What's all this noise?" Johnnie said, failing to notice that black smoke had started to billow behind him from his apartment. A black deformed hand reached out of the smoke, grabbing him by the hair and pulling him back inside. The door slammed shut with immense force.

"Now it's time to play my game," Billy Night chuckled maniacally from inside the apartment.

"Winner takes all!" he declared as Johnnie screamed in response. Billy Night stuck a finger in each of Johnnie's eyes, pulling both eyeballs out and chewing on them. The game would be over for Johnnie tonight for sure.

Bloody Nightmare in Room 19

Bob Pipe

It was dark. Martin was running. Running again. Running through the bowels of the old apartment block, clutching onto a heavy ancient device. Why did it always have to end this way? Just as he was getting to grips with this body. Martin hadn't always wanted to be a God, but he hadn't been given much choice in the matter and now he was just making the most of it. Shame everyone seemed to want to kill him.

He was about to reach the red door he had reached a couple of dozen times before, but something was different this time. He always did something to try to sway the outcome. This time he had been more of an asshole to everyone he met. He wasn't naturally an asshole, but it got him to where he is now in a much faster time than any other previous attempts. But then he heard the sound.

It was a low growl. Demonic.

Martin cursed to himself under his breath. His heart rate started to increase. He'd hoped he'd changed the outcome enough not to have to encounter the Demon Dog again. Martin's time was running out. It was getting closer. It started barking. If he was going to live, he'd have to make it through the red door.

The snarling beast was practically at his heels now.

Martin grabbed the handle, turned it and began to

enter… but he was too late. The evil dog latched itself to his ankle. Martin screamed and practically threw the package he was handling with care up until that point. Still holding the door handle, he smashed the door against the beast's head a few times till it let go and ran away yelping in distress.

Martin slammed the door shut and lay on the floor breathing heavily, staring up at the cobwebbed wooden beams above him. He'd never made it this far before. Is this the end?

"Thank you for returning the device to me, Martin," said a voice from across the room.

Martin sat up to see who was in the room with him. Whoever it was, was old.

"A valiant attempt but alas you failed again… you're getting better though," said the old man slightly patronizingly.

"That beast out there…? Does it belong to you?"

"Ha! It took a lot of attempts to get that working. A nice touch, huh?"

Martin knew that voice… "You bastard. It's you!"

"Time to go back Martin. I can't thank you enough for bringing this back to me, I have a lot do."

Martin jumped to his feet to strangle the old man to death when two robed figures lurched out of the darkness and pulled Martin back. "Let go of me!"

The old bastard was now in front of him and a third robed figure moved behind him and stuffed a wet rag in his mouth. "Stay calm Martin or you'll give yourself a heart attack."

Martin's strength was leaving him and his knees went lax. The robed figures were pulling his eyelids apart and now the device was in front of him, it whirled and buzzed and made noises unheard by human ears before.

"I'm not going through that door again," Martin slurred.

"We'll see," he heard as white light enveloped his world.

***

Martin suddenly awoke, fully clothed on the hotel bed. He propped himself up and looked at his watch. "Damn!" He pushed his legs off the bed and projected himself into his wheelchair. He was back in the hotel room. He was so close. Fuck that old man and those robed twats! He looked at his watch again. "Damn."

Martin wheeled himself into the bathroom, turned the cold tap on and threw some water on his face in the sink. Panic was starting to set in. "I'm sorry Eric," Martin said to himself in the mirror.

BANG, BANG, BANG.

Martin's heart nearly jumped out of his mouth. He should be used to it by now but what he had to do never came easy. He slowly wheeled himself to the door and opened it. Eric gave a nervous smile.

"Sorry I'm late."

"Get in here!" Martin grabbed Eric by the jacket and pulled him into the hotel room.

"You wouldn't believe the…" Eric was

beginning to explain.

"Come on, hand it over!" Martin interrupted as he slammed the door behind Eric.

"That concierge is a strange fella…"

"Yeah, yeah, yeah, just give me the box."

Eric began to hand the box he was carrying to Martin. "Hey! No need to snatch."

Martin gave Eric the death stare. "I'm warning you."

"What happened to you? You never used to be like this."

Martin pretended not to hear Eric and placed the box on the bed. He then took a knife out of his pocket and sliced the box open.

"Are you going to tell me what this is all about?"

Martin said nothing, just continued staring inside the box for what seemed like an eternity to Eric.

"Anything? I'd love to know why I put my life at risk," he persisted. "It wasn't easy breaking into that apartment. That place is messed up. Like, evil. With a capital E. EVIL. Biblically evil. And it stinks like evil too."

Eric waited for a response. Nothing.

"You know, if evil had a smell, that'd be it."

Still nothing.

"Okay, I'll go then. We're even now?"

Martin slowly took his gaze off the contents of the box and turned to Eric.

"Sit down Eric."

Eric let out a sigh. "Can I take a look first?"

"In time. Sit down."

Eric went and sat at the dresser as Martin spun

his wheelchair around to face him.

"I stole it from the army."

"You did what?"

"I stole it from the army."

"Stole what?! What's in that damned box?"

"It's a device… of sorts. An ancient mechanical device. The experts think it could be the first computer…"

"Okaaaaayyyy."

"I was part of a team who were assigned to protect it and bring it back from the Middle East during the war. The army has been studying it for years. They finally got it to work. It opened a portal to another dimension, a parallel universe… only they unleashed…"

"Shut up Martin. What the hell is it?"

"Fine. Don't believe me. It's easier that way."

"Okay, why did you steal it?"

"To put things right."

"Put things right? What are you blathering on about?"

"Some really bad things have been happening since it was turned on and I mean to do the right thing. Thought it would be nice to get my friends involved."

"Sorry, what? Have you gone mad? Okay, okay, so how did this… device get to Castle Heights?"

"Another… friend took it there. I'm just part of a chain. We all have a part to play. We only know our small part. Only I couldn't do my part of the plan - that's why I needed your help."

"Glad I could be of service. So seriously, what

does it do?"

"If I told you, I'd have to kill you."

Eric laughed but Martin just stared back.

"You'll have to catch me first," Eric chuckled to himself.

"Come take a look then."

Eric stood up, walked over to the bed, bent down and opened the flaps of the box. It was old, for sure. And made of gold. Or possibly brass on closer inspection. It looked like a large version of the insides of an old clock or maybe a nautical device. Old yet new. Martin was right, it was beautiful. Martin pushed himself over to Eric and got as close as he could to his face. A bit too close.

"Look into the box," he said gently in Eric's ear.

The hairs on the back of Eric's neck stood up.

"I'm looking…" Eric could feel Martin's breath on his ear. He wanted to turn to face him but he couldn't take his eyes off the contents of the box. Suddenly the cogs started turning and wheels started moving. It made a gentle ticking sound and started to glow.

"What the…" was all Eric could get out.

"I trust you, Eric. You're my friend and I think with your help we can put things right."

Eric suddenly felt Martin's hand round his neck.

"Hey, what you doing?!" Eric screamed but Martin just pushed his face deeper into the device.

"I don't know how or why this happens but I'm going to need your body now."

"Get the fuck off me, you lunatic!"

"Shush Eric. Stop struggling." Martin was much

stronger than Eric realized as he tried to fight him off.

"Now go to sleep…" was the last thing Eric heard as his head became swampy and his eyelids suddenly weighed a ton, he felt as though he was melting.

"That bastard Martin," he thought to himself as he was about to hit the hotel room floor.

Only he didn't. He just kept going. He watched the ceiling of the hotel room getting further and further away. Down he went until the ceiling was no more than a dot and one of many dots. Stars twinkling in the night sky.

He was suddenly hit by a blast of cosmic sound, it vibrated through him and increased into a crescendo. The most beautiful angelic music he had ever heard. It moved through him and off into the distance in the form of cloud. He no longer felt like he was falling but rushing upwards, as if he had been turned inside out, his body obliterated into atoms.

He saw the universe in front of him. The horizon stretched out before him but in a blink of the eye he was the horizon. He felt simultaneously massive and tiny at the same time. Many luminous spikes rose up as his eyes tried to focus on what was in front of him.

He took a huge gasp of air as he woke up on the hotel floor carpet, his face buried in the rug. He had clearly been drooling. He spat some fluff out of his mouth and took a look around the room. It was empty. Martin and the box were gone. Eric tried to get to his feet but his legs weren't working.

"Martin? What's going on?" He thought he must have fell awkwardly and his legs had gone to sleep.

He dragged himself to the dresser, pulled himself onto the chair and looked in the mirror. "What the hell?!"

That wasn't his reflection.

"What the…"

He leaned into the mirror. Martin was looking back at him. "What have you done to me?" he said to himself… to Martin.

RINGGGGG RINGGGGG

Eric jumped across the room to the hotel phone but missed and fell on the floor. "Owwwww."

RINGGGGG RINGGGGG

He lifted his arm and fumbled around for the phone, which fell on his head.

CLANG

"JESUS!" The receiver lay next to him. He put it to his ear. "Yes?!"

"Eric Tavener?" the deep voice on the other end of the receiver enquired.

"Yes! Is that you Martin?"

"No, this is not Martin…"

"Where is he?" Eric/Martin interrupted.

"…but he asked me to contact you," the voice continued.

"That bastard! What the hell has he done to me?!"

"I want you to relax Eric."

"RELAX? THAT BASTARD STOLE MY BODY!"

"Please calm down Eric. Erratic behaviour will not get you out of this situation."

"Situation?!"

"I need you to calm down Eric."

"This is ridiculous," Eric mumbled to himself.

The voice recounted how Martin had contacted Eric earlier that day and asked him to pick up a box from an apartment complex called Castle Heights and bring it to the hotel. He then explained he would have to do the same.

"You've got to be fucking kidding me?"

"Now I won't tell you who to choose but it will need to be a someone you trust. An old college friend, a cousin or drinking buddy maybe? Someone you can rely on, someone who owes you a favour. But not close family."

"That bastard Martin!"

"You are really trying my patience, Mr. Tavener."

"Sorry."

"Do you remember the address Martin gave you?" the voice asked.

"Of course. He made me repeat over and over. I wasn't allowed to write it down."

"Very good. A box has been left there. You'll need your chosen person to go and collect it and bring it back to you. We will call you back in five hours, by which time you will hopefully have retrieved it."

"But what if I can't get anyone to do it?"

"Tell them you will give them a thousand pounds for doing so."

"And what about the words?"

"Say them whilst staring into his or her eyes… the rest will be simple. Someone will be in contact in five hours with further instructions."

"Please tell me why this is happening."

There was a long silence. Eric held his breath.

"All will be explained when you have retrieved the box. Now call that person and get this done. Goodbye for now, Eric."

"What about my face?!" Eric shouted to no-one.

***

For half an hour Eric stared at the reflection of his friend Martin Dunbar in the mirror. "Why? Why did you do this to me?" He knew Martin was into some dodgy things when they were growing up, but he never asked details. Then, in his mid-twenties, he sorted himself out and joined the army. It was totally unexpected and out of character.

They lost touch after that. But then a few weeks ago he got back in contact. An email out of the blue.

They met for drinks and caught up. Martin had had quite an adventure in the army. He barely recognized the Martin from his youth. He'd also lost the use of his legs. He wanted to ask how it happened, but Martin quickly changed the subject whenever they mentioned the wheelchair.

They met a few more times after that. Martin seemed to have a lot on his mind and was full of energy, the conversation was non-stop, his mind zipping from one subject to another. Eric could barely get a word in.

But he could tell something was wrong. Then, last night, he called to ask him to pick up the box. He was edgy and nervous, he said it was really important - that it could really change his life. He said he couldn't leave the hotel and that people were after him.

"What have you done Martin?" Eric said to himself... to Martin in the mirror.

His mind raced through their friendship. To twenty-five years ago and meeting on the bus going to college. Bonding over horror movies. The music they listened to and the clothes they wore. All the drinking, the drugs, the dancing and, of course, the fun they had.

Innocent times before experience and life changed them into the men they were now.

And then a memory tumbled into his head. An incident he hadn't thought about for a long, long time.

It was after they had both left college, the mid-nineties, the summer before Eric went to university. Eric and Martin were in their late teens and playing in a band together. Him, Martin... oh, what was his name? Whispers! And Lucy of course. For a few years back in the nineties they were the best of friends. Inseparable. He cringed at the memory.

Martin was in love with Lucy... but one night after band practice they'd got drunk together. Martin was passed out on the sofa... one thing led to another...

"Oh god," Eric said to himself... to Martin in the

mirror. "I'm sorry." He remembered what he had said to Martin. "I did you a favour! I told you she was a slag." He cringed again. "Oh god, I'm so, so sorry. I was young… I didn't know what I was saying… what I was doing. No-one does at that age."

Nothing was said about Lucy when they had met up in the pub.

"Shit… is this revenge for Lucy?"

Then Eric started to remember what Martin had said in the pub that night, five pints and three tequilas in; "I know how to make things better for us. I know how to change the past."

Eric had laughed but stopped when he noticed Martin was not laughing with him. "Sorry, please continue," Eric had said but Martin just glared at him.

"I've said too much. I'll tell you more some other time," Martin had replied, his eyes darting over the other people in the pub.

Eric had forgotten about the conversation; they were very drunk at this point in the night but now he wondered if all this was related…

"Lucy!" Eric shouted to Martin's reflection. "I should call her." He took out his mobile phone and searched for her name in his address book. It had been a few years since he'd seen Lucy, but he had her number. "I wonder…"

He pressed CALL and waited.

***

A few hours had passed and now Lucy was lying on the hotel room carpet. He couldn't believe it had worked. "Oh Martin, you didn't have to go through all this just to see me," she had said to him just before he said the words.

He had practiced the words over and over in his head as he waited for her to arrive. When it came time to say them it was as if someone, or something, took over him. In fact, it was as if he was in a trance. The last few hours had all been like some weird dream. Living in someone else's body.

Lucy had taken some convincing on the phone. "Is this a trick?" she asked about five times. "Or some kind of prank? I'm not going to be on TV, am I?"

He reassured she wasn't, he explained he was in a wheelchair now and that he really needed her help. "I wouldn't ask if it wasn't important."

"Okay, what's the address?"

Lucy was a good person, a care worker, he knew she would do it. He didn't even need to use the money angle to convince her. And then he remembered the box which was still in his lap.

He went to open it when the hotel phone started to ring.

"Hello?" he said when he had wheeled himself over to the hotel phone by the bed.

"You have the box?" The voice was familiar, but it wasn't the same voice he had spoken to previously.

"I do."

"Very good. Put the body in the bath."

Eric didn't argue. He dragged Lucy to the bathroom, doing as he was told. He wasn't sure why and was past trying to make sense of it. It wasn't easy without the use of his legs, but he got it done and then went back to the phone.

"Okay, it's done."

"Now put your head inside the box, close to the device."

Again, he did as he was told.

Before he knew what was happening the device had attached itself to his face. He tried to scream but his jaw was now part of whatever was in the box. The pain was unbearable and, as he was falling to the ground, he thought he was dying.

But he didn't land on the floor.

He once again found himself tumbling through space, then becoming the space and at the moment of realisation, he felt himself tumbling towards the earth and suddenly he woke with a gasp in the hotel bathroom. "Fuuuuuck!"

He clutched the sides of bath and pulled himself out. The world was a blur and swirling. He ran the tap and splashed water on his face. His vision was returning as he stared in the mirror. "Lucy? Ahhh, not again."

Eric's mind was racing. He thought back to those times with Martin, Lucy and Whispers. Those crazy nights that turned into days. He remembered how he had hurt her. And Martin. And…. Whispers? Had he ever hurt Whispers? He was the one that was elected to fire him from the band… but that was long ago…

The sound of the phone ringing pulled him out of his reverie. He belted out of the bathroom, like a newborn elk, unused to this frame and nearly tripping over Martin's unconscious body before making it to the hotel phone in a crash. "What have you done to me?" Eric squawked, not used to these vocal cords.

"Oh... Sorry, Miss... your car is here," the voice on the other end of the receiver said.

"Who is this?"

"Reception. The car you ordered is waiting outside."

"I... I'll be right down." He tried to compose himself. "Thank you."

"Thank you, Miss."

The driver was waiting by the car as Lucy approached. "You must be my driver."

"Lucy Richards?"

"Yes... that's me."

"Very good. Would you like to put that in the boot?"

Lucy hesitated, wondering what he was referring to but then it dawned on her - the box! She had forgotten she was holding onto it. "Oh, no, it's okay. I'd rather hold onto it."

"As you wish." The driver opened the door and in moments they were winding through the back streets of London.

"Castle Heights?"

"Sorry?"

"The address; Castle Heights Apartment Complex?"

"What about it?"

"That's where you're going?" he asked whilst looking in the rearview mirror. He was waiting for a response, but she gave none. "Strange is all. Heard a lot of odd stuff about that place."

Lucy turned and looked out of the window.

"Can I ask you something, Miss?" the driver asked, looking in the rearview mirror again.

"Yeah... sure."

"What's in that box? I mean, it must be something very special if you don't want to let go of it."

"Oh," Lucy thought for a moment. "It's an antique."

"Must be pretty expensive."

"It is."

He stared at her for an uncomfortably long time then put his eyes back on the road. They continued the journey in silence until they came to what looked like an industrial area.

"This doesn't look right," Lucy said, leaning forward but the driver didn't answer.

"Hey! This isn't right!" she said, banging on the glass divide, but still he didn't answer. She started to feel panic rising through her body. The driver parked up in front of a garage. Lucy attempted to open the door but it was locked. "Hey!" she shouted at him as he got out and opened the garage.

"Let me out!"

"My boss would like a quick word," the driver said through the window.

"This is nuts!" she shouted.

He opened the door, as if expecting her to launch an attack. She didn't, there was no point, he was far too big and from the look of his face he was used to getting into fights. "He'll be here soon," the brutish driver said.

"Who will?" she sighed.

"My boss."

"Yeah, but who is your boss?" She was at the end of her tether now.

"You'll see."

A small man of slim build strode confidently into sight. He was clad in a long, white leathery coat embellished with cream fur trim. The collar bunched up high around his ears. His black shirt was unbuttoned at the top, revealing a hairless chest, and was tightly tucked into black jeans. Brown suede boots completed his look.

I know that prick, thought Lucy.

"Whispers?"

"Lucy! No, wait… it's Eric, isn't it? I always get a bit muddled at this point… what with all the body swapping."

"Is that you Whispers?"

"No… you're not going to believe this but I'm you… sorry, Lucy. Whispers doesn't mind - he's currently being you but let's cut to the chase," he smiled. "I want that box now. I've been waiting a long time. It's my turn."

"What are you talking about?"

"It's complicated… but I'll tell you as it may come in handy in the future. There are alternate versions of me, you, Martin and Whispers roaming through time and destroying things."

"Sorry, what?"

"Every decision, every action changes us and sets us on a course for how we turn out. Well, to cut a long story short, the future versions of us are complete bastards. Closest thing to evil I've ever seen. It's the box - turns everyone who comes in contact with it into Gollum. My precious," Whispers cackled.

Lucy just stared at him blankly.

"You've seen the film, right? Oh never mind. Just hand it over and this will be less painful."

Before she could answer, three robed figures came out of the shadows and grabbed hold of her.

"Funny how things turned out, Eric?" Whispers was now in front of her, an evil look in his eyes.

But behind Whispers eyes she could see herself... how did she ever become like this?

"First comes the pain..." Whispers began to say as the wall behind him exploded.

Three sprightly robed figures entered through the smoke and falling rubble.

"What the fuck?" was the last thing Whispers said, a laser blast having left a hole in his head.

The robed figures who were holding onto Lucy screamed and let go of her. They tried to run but they too were hit with laser blasts and their bodies hit the ground with smoke rising from the newly acquired holes they had sustained.

The darkly robed figures raced toward her, futuristic sniper rifles in hand, their hoods concealing their faces. "Come with us..." one said, as a third robed figure drove a rusty blue van though the hole in the wall and up beside them, "if you want to live."

The van took them to Castle Heights, a tall, ominous building. Evil seeping out of every crack.

Lucy got out of the van and followed the robed figures into reception with the box still clutched close to her. The concierge, an elderly looking gentlemen, raised his head, let out a long, deep sigh, then looked back down at the crossword he was in the middle of. He had seen it all in this place. Lucy followed the robed trio to the stairs.

"Er… shall we take the lift?" she said.

"No time. It's only three floors," replied one of the figures.

"Come on!" said another.

"Stairs it is," said Lucy.

***

They took her to room 19 and knocked three times. The door opened and an elderly woman who looked familiar led them into the living room. Lucy looked around the room. The elderly woman joined three elderly men sitting in a circle. Faces she recognized but couldn't place. It took her a moment but then it came to her.

"We're time travelers, Eric," Whispers announced. "The device gets turned on at 23:40 Eastern Standard Time from this room tonight and unleashes all kinds of mayhem. We've spent the last twenty-five years trying to put it right."

"And have fun of course," Old Whispers interjected.

She looked at the three elderly men and women... It was Martin, Lucy, Whispers and... himself. She turned to the robed trio, they pulled their hoods down to reveal Martin, Lucy and Whispers, but young. Like they were when they were in college together.

"Holy shit," was all she could muster.

"I'm sorry I got you involved in this Eric, but I didn't know who else to turn to," said the elderly Martin. He stood up and walked towards him. "It was selfish of me... but you always said you owed me for persuading me to join the army."

"I was joking!"

"It doesn't matter, what's done is done. I'm just glad I have my friends with me - I couldn't do it without you." He looked around the room nodding and smiling and they in turn nodded and smiled back.

"There are a lot a crazy people out there trying to get hold of this and I needed people I trust."

"And besides," said the elderly Eric, "the next twenty-five are going to be a lot of fun. You'll see."

"Let's get you back in your own body before the army arrives," said the elderly Lucy. "I think you've had enough use out of mine."

They all gathered around the box and began to chant... a majestic light blasted out and filled the room. An unearthly musical note resonated in Eric's head. He went from feeling spiritual to wanting to scream in agony in milliseconds. Suddenly, it was as if the gates of hell had opened up beneath him and his insides were burning up. He felt his flesh tearing off. He looked around the room and sure enough the skin of each of them was tearing off.

Out of the corner of her eye, Lucy noticed Eric grab the box and run...

***

He wound down the stairs into the basement... why was this basement so big?! It clearly had been an underground bunker of sorts. He kept on running, the demon dog didn't surprise him this time and he ran past the red door... he kept on running, running and running, the evil dog at his heels. He tripped and he knew it was over... perhaps he'd try being less of an asshole on the next go.

Martin suddenly awoke, fully clothed on the hotel bed. He propped himself up and looked at his watch.

"Damn!"

A Guilty Feeding on the Fourth Floor

Teige Reid

- 11:36 p.m.-

Every terrible decision I have ever made has been made sober. Case in point, I was stone cold sober when I decided to get this blind drunk. It's been twelve years since I so much as nosed a glass of wine, and now I don't think I could tie my shoelaces. If I had my choice, I would have preferred to down a bottle or five of pinot, but there is no wine here. Fortunately, scotch has few peers when it comes to inducing a state of moribund semi-consciousness. It is no small thing to flush twelve years of sobriety, but fear is one hell of a bad influence.

I am not one who frightens easily, unless you count spiders; those things are the terrors that keep nightmares awake and should be hunted to extinction. I am more the frightening type, though I don't look it. When people meet me, they might be jealous, or shy, even amused, but never frightened—not until it is too late. No, a pretty face and great tits may be things to be stared at or invited home, but they are not things to fear. That has always been my advantage—even the most cautious let their guard down when they see me, which is why it was so easy for me to get close to one Mr. Tom Beattie.

I don't fit the typical image of a hired killer,

which allows me to kill with an intimacy that few of my male counterparts can hope to risk. You might think that the secret to being a successful killer is to be the kind of person people don't look at twice, but the truth is that standing out is a much easier way to become invisible.

While I was still at school, long before I junked becoming a doctor and joined the army (crushing my parent's hopes and dreams and discovering my aptitude for killing) I had a place where I liked to study. It was nothing fancy, just a window table in a tiny café near my flat. Every Saturday, I would drag myself there as close to 8:00 a.m. as the residual effect of the night before would allow. I would often stay all day. I was friendly with the girls who worked there, and I always ate, so they never minded my loitering—they made great sandwiches.

Across the road from the café was a formidable looking office building. If ever a building could have a high opinion of itself, it would be that one. It seemed so out of place, a tall glass obscenity in an otherwise quaint town. It was overdone in every way and the design was an odd mix of a bold futuristic vision and a desperate need to seem important—I would bet everything I ever had that the architect was male, a Trekkie, and a virgin. The office was set back from the road and had a curving drive that swept across the front of the main doors. An unnecessarily tall and inexcusably phallic sign, emblazoned with the company name and logo, sat on the oval of grass created by the drive.

One Saturday morning, a truck pulled up and

parked in front of the doors. Two men got out and stood arguing. After a few minutes one of them came over to the café to grab some food. The other one stayed across the road holding a clipboard, looking annoyed, and studying the two spotlights that sat, like a pair of giant testicles, amid the bushes and flowers at the base of the sign. These lights illuminated the sign and each of them was roughly the size of a piano.

Over the course of the day, the two men dismantled and loaded the lights onto their truck. Every now and again I would look over to see how they were getting along. I remember that they smoked a lot of cigarettes, took a lot of breaks, and that they argued a lot. They were gone by 4:00. That was all I was able to tell the police when they came into the café to ask about the theft.

I'll never forget that lesson: when the police come asking about my work, the best they can hope for is a mention of the colour of my dress or shirt to go along with "she had a pretty face and a great set of tits." I even use my real name. The people who hire me assume it's a fake, a simple trick which makes it the perfect alias.

Transitioning from being a person who wanted to be a doctor, to save lives, to someone willing to kill for King and Country, to someone who freelances in dealing out death, is not as hard as you might imagine. It's a slippery slope generously greased with lots and lots of money. I don't care why someone needs to be taken out. It doesn't matter to me what they've done or not done to earn themselves a visit, I simply don't care, so long as I get paid.

What I do can take a toll, I won't deny that. Everything has its price and money isn't the only currency; you might say that the emotional exchange rate for being a killer can be murder. Guilt is a nasty, horny old bastard and it will fuck you dead if you let it. I've seen what happens to the people in this gig who can't keep a lid on their feelings, so I keep mine locked down tight. I'm not saying that my conscience hasn't taken a beating— it's bruised and battered, for sure, but you don't last too long in this line of work if you can't compartmentalize and keep guilt out of the equation.

To my mind, the people who hire me are not looking to kill nuns and schoolchildren. Like the bride said: *people get what they deserve.* Every person I have ever killed has brought it on themselves; they must have, or I wouldn't have been necessary. Which is why I am good with the money. When the job does start to get to me, I break the guilt all down into small, easy to swallow and manageable bites. Bottom line, these jobs need doing, and someone will always step up to do the work, so why shouldn't the someone lining their pockets be me? I'm not even thirty-five and I am looking to retire. How many people pillorying their souls 9-5 can say that?

People get what they deserve.

I am a professional, a survivor, in my line of work those two things are virtually indistinguishable. I've been in plenty of tough spots and had my fair share of close calls. A clean and easy job just about never happens. I am careful and methodical but there's always the unexpected, always some risk of collateral damage, but I am good at what I do, adaptable, flexible, and decisive. I have never come up against a situation that I couldn't handle … not until tonight. I take a big drink. Tonight, has been off the charts crazy.

My phone buzzes, startling me. The screen says *Caller Unknown,* but I know who it is. Bennie Monaco is exactly the type of guy you'd expect to find living behind that name. He is not the kind of guy you lie to and he's not the type to take no for an answer, not twice anyway. I've never let him down, but I've 'worked' with a few luckless bastards who have. Bennie has a zero-tolerance policy when it comes to failure. Not taking this call would be almost as big a mistake as answering.

I hit the green button.

"Is it done?" he asks, his voice pleasant and friendly. But I know better. Bennie's reputation imparts a brass knuckle clarity to everything he says, no matter his tone. I look over at Tom's body, bleeding out onto the kitchen floor.

"Not yet, Bennie," I slur, the full weight of more than half a bottle of scotch sitting heavily on my tongue.

"Are you drunk?"

"Very."

"I thought you didn't dri …?"

I hang up and my screen goes blank. Bennie

Monaco is not the kind of someone that you hang up on, but right now his injured pride is easily the least of my problems. Tom, the dead guy in the kitchen, is picking himself back up...again.

***

I have never been religious; I have always put more stock in the tangible fiction of Star Trek than the inconsistent fairy tales of the church. As far as I am concerned, organized religion is nothing more than QAnon+Time. I have never given any credence to the afterlife, or ghosts, any of it. It was all bullshit to me. My unshakable belief in the absolute finality of death was always a great comfort to me; it was one of my strongest anti-guilt firewalls. I believed that there was no point worrying about the morality of killing for money if it wasn't going to matter once I was dead myself. Now, sitting here swigging whisky and watching a dead man get back up onto his feet for the umpteenth time tonight, I'm scared that I may have been wrong. As paradigm shifts go this one is tectonic.

I finish off my glass and refill it with a liberal and clumsy pour that empties the bottle, and splashes whisky over the table and onto the floor. I raise the glass to my mouth and take a generous gulp. Once I'm sure that I'm not going to throw it back up, I take another swallow.

People get what they deserve.

Tom's corpse is standing now, unsteady, and uncertain like a drunk at closing, or a toddler new to walking. After a few stumbles he gains his balance and looks around. His eyes move across me, but don't show any sign of noticing me. He has the confused and pained look of a heavily hungover tourist trying to read a bus schedule in the rain— I've seen more than my fair share of holidaying Canadians to recognize the symptoms.

There's blood matted in his hair and his shirt is dark and wet with the stuff, but the wound has sealed again. He looks at his bloodied hands as though trying to remember what they are for and starts muttering to himself. I've had too much to drink to make any sense of what little I can make out. It's garbled nonsense, garbage his mouth is spitting as his brain resets.

I feel as though I am watching a memory brought to life—almost as though this is a play. There are subtle variations between each performance but each moment, each movement follows a precise pattern, like the product of well-rehearsed blocking. The repetition is exhausting.

He turns away from me and notices the blood and brains, his blood, his brains, splattered on the wall and counter. Subtle changes in the angle and position of his head betray the path of his eyes as they track the gore. Without taking his eyes from the wall, he reaches out with his right hand and opens the fridge. Bracing the door with his shoulder, he reaches in and grabs a can of beer and moves to place it on the counter, freezing when he notices that there is a can of beer already there. The fridge door swings to shut but he blocks it with his right leg.

He picks the can up from the counter with his left hand and studies it closely, contemplatively smearing the blood on the label with his thumb. Then he returns the can in his right hand to the fridge and closes the door. Almost as an afterthought he sets the can in his left back down on the counter. He looks around, as though he has lost something. This bit is always a little different, but he always finds the gun, eventually—it never falls far. Stooping to pick it up, he takes a step, slipping on the blood that has pooled on the floor, almost but not quite losing his balance. Then he looks at me, becoming aware of my presence as if for the first time. I suppose even though he has done this so many times, for him, each time could be like the first. My mouth and throat are dry. I take a drink, but it doesn't help. You can't drink away a fear thirst. He tilts his head and frowns as though he is listening to a voice that only he can hear.

"Make yourself comfortable," he says, and I mouth the words along with him. I have heard them over and over tonight; they are burned into me. He is handsome, just under six feet, early 30s, with the kind of body that I would very much have enjoyed exploring. Yesterday he was a name, a photo, an address, and a sizeable advance payment, now I don't know what he is.

"He'll be here soon," we say together. "Have a drink, Emily,"

"Been there, done that, Tom," I say, solemnly, raising my glass.

Then he puts the gun in his mouth and blows the back of his head off. This has happened so many times that the blood and the brains on the wall look more like a poorly applied first coat of paint than the splatter pattern from a suicide.

People get what they deserve.

If you can believe it, the first time he shot himself, I was pleased. It was a surprise for sure, but I wasn't complaining. Whether I do it or they go the self-checkout route, I still get paid. I was a little upset about the gunshot, I had been planning on a quiet, intimate kill with a knife, something of a specialty of mine, but the gun was as noisy as it was messy, so I got out of the apartment as fast as I could. Though this wasn't how I had planned it, he had done me a little bit of a favour. If I was spotted leaving, or if I happened to run into police investigating a suspected gunshot, it was a suicide—open and shut. All I would need to do was play the scared and traumatized date.

"I didn't know him, officer, I met him tonight at the pub, I'd never seen him before, but we were chatting, and he asked me to come home with him."

[Cue the waterworks—I can cry on command, a useful skill with a multitude of applications.]

"He seemed nice. I thought we were having a good time [sob], but when we got here, he started acting strange and then he … [sob] then he shot himself. I didn't know what to do, so I ran. I'm not in trouble, am I?"

Writing that script in my head, and only seconds after his body had hit the floor, I had turned on my heel and walked out the door and back to the lift. That's when I began to realize just how much trouble I am in.

When I left the apartment, I headed straight to the lift, listening for anyone brave enough to open their door and risk a peek to investigate what that shocking loud bang was. There wasn't a peep from any of the apartments, but I had no doubts that there were a lot of scared and curious eyes and ears pressed up against each door, and probably in the apartments upstairs and downstairs as well. The walls of this place looked so thin I doubt you could keep a fart private, never mind a gunshot.

The lift door opened, and I stepped on and pressed GROUND. I only had to bluff my way past the concierge and then I was smoke. He had been on the phone when Tom and I had come in, less than fifteen minutes ago, and he hadn't looked up. I had faith in the proven power of a quick smile and a wave (not to mention a pretty face and great tits) to get me out the door, and I had my teary-eyed, frightened damsel persona at the ready, just in case. The lift opened, and I froze: I wasn't on the ground floor; I was staring at the peeling green paint of the wall opposite the 4th floor lift.

BANG!

The gunshot startled me, and I stumbled back into the lift. Wishing I had brought a gun of my own, I pressed GROUND again and hit DOOR

CLOSE for good measure. I started to weigh the odds of there being two hits scheduled for the same floor of the same building on the same night. It didn't add up, and it was no coincidence.

The doors of the lift opened; I was back on the 4th floor again.

BANG!

I pressed GROUND and this time I watched the numbers over the door, counting each one off in sequence: 3-2-1-G.

The door opened.

BANG!

I pride myself on being able to stay calm, cool, and collected but I was starting to sweat, just a little.

I pressed 10.

BANG!

12.

BANG!

15.

BANG!

18.

BANG!

Ground

BANG!

I looked out into the 4th floor corridor. There was no one. I pulled the knife from my purse and pried the cover off the panel, exposing an orderly array of circuits and wires. I didn't know what I was looking for, or what I expected to be able to do but my mind was in survival mode, looking for answers. This was a trap. Tom must have known that I had been sent to kill him, and he had brought me home anyway. Maybe he was supposed to kill me but had decided to kill himself instead. Why? My mind played the scene over again, stopping at the part when Tom said: *he'll be here soon*. Who? Monaco? No, that made no sense. Bennie could get me any time he wanted. This had to be someone else, someone looking to pay me back for someone I had killed. They'd have had a contingency plan in case I got Tom before he got me, which meant that whoever had set me up had either mocked up every floor to look like the 4th or they had tampered with the lift. The golden rule when you want to kill someone is to keep things as simple as possible, so tampering had to be it. I wasn't important enough to warrant the time, effort, and expense of what was basically an 18-story practical joke. I couldn't tell what they had done to the lift, but I hacked and slashed at the guts of the thing out of spite until I'd shredded the components. If someone wanted the lift to stay on the 4th floor, it could stay here till doomsday for all I cared.

BANG!

Another shot. But not at me? There was still no one in the corridor. I checked my watch, nearly 10:45 p.m. I looked at the second lift. No good, at best I'd run into the concierge riding it up to find out why the other one was stuck on 4, at worst it would be filled with guys with guns. For a moment I considered running back to the apartment to get Tom's gun, but that last shot sounded like it might have come from there. This easy job had gone completely sideways. The lift was a literal kill box, and the stairs would be watched, and either way they were sure to be in the lobby, but I had no choice, I had to get off this floor. Knife in hand, I ran to the stairs.

The stairwell smelled of piss and sour vomit, but it was empty. I moved down cautiously, listening. When I got to the 1st floor, I stopped. My plan was simple: break into the apartment next to the stairs, run like hell and jump off the balcony. Hopefully, I could be long gone before whoever was waiting for me in the lobby realized I was a no show. I pushed the door open and stepped out into the corridor.

BANG!

I froze. I was back on the 4th floor, but this time I wasn't alone. There was someone standing between me and the lift, and it wasn't a puzzled concierge or a gun toting thug.

The woman turned to look at me, surprised by my sudden appearance. If I wanted to be generous, I would say that she was in her late-80s, but honestly, she looked as though she'd been dead that long. Her skin seemed as brittle as a dried leaf. She was wearing an ill-fitting wedding dress that had faded yellow with time, and her face was a tragedy of poorly applied makeup. Her withered face and toothless mouth were unpleasant, but it was the blood stains on her dress and the decapitated head of another woman that she was holding in her right hand that had my attention.

Behind her, at the lift, a man in his 20s, wearing a black suit, was desperately pressing the button for the lift.

"Please, please, please! Oh, god, oh god, please," he sobbed.

The old lady shook her head, tut tutting.

"Would you excuse me for a moment, my dear," she said nodding politely to me, her voice a rasping whisper with the faintest glimmer of an Irish accent. "I must see to Michael. Me and him have been having words. I don't know where he thinks he is going, but he really should know better, shouldn't you, my love?" she said, shaking her head like an annoyed schoolteacher. She started off down the hall, with the unhurried and carefree shuffle of a pensioner on her way to the shops. Almost unconsciously, I found myself following her. The head swung gently, banging off her leg as she walked.

"We have talked about this, Michael," she said with a rattling gasp. "… to have and to hold from this day forward, for better, for worse, for richer, for poorer, in sickness and in health, to love and to cherish, till death do us part …" with each phrase, her tone became more and more angry.

"Do you remember those words, Michael? You should. You said those words, you made those promises to me, and seeing how neither of us is dead … the words hold."

"I'm sorry, I'm so sorry, please, stop doing this, let us go, please," the man sobbed, collapsing back against the wall, blubbering and incoherent. The distance between them closed, with a remorseless tidal certitude that chilled me—she wasn't moving through the space between them, she was devouring it, like a snake swallowing a water buffalo. I wanted him to stand and run or fight. He was strong and healthy, in his prime, he should have been able to knock this woman over with a stern look. The severed head spun to face me, the mouth moving in a silent scream, the eyes rolling and blinking in wordless agony. Michael rose to his knees and raised his hands as if to ward off a blow.

"Please," he sobbed. "No more."

"Ah, poor Michael, my love, I would if I could, you know that. But you know what he says, *people get what they deserve.*" I don't make the rules, my love, I just live by them," she said kindly. "As you should have!" she added in a hate filled screech as she swung the severed head across her body, striking Michael in the face as though playing a backhand shot in tennis. He spun to his left, and she brought the head down again and again, swinging it by the hair like a flail. Michael's body jerked and shook as seizures wracked him. On the last swing, Michael's skull made a sickening crunch and his body fell still. The impact crushed the head the old lady was holding and tore the scalp from the skull. The head fell to the floor, a shapeless mess of blood and brains. She tossed the dripping scalp aside and grasped Michael by his shoulders. With no more effort than if she were lifting a pillow, she raised his limp body till his crushed face was close to her own and then she kissed his broken mouth. She turned her head and looked at me over her shoulder.

"I loved him, and he said that he loved me," her voice came in a scratching death-rattle-wheeze that quivered with age and emotion. "I believed him," she said as tears streaked her face, upsetting her already messy makeup. "Stupid child that I was," she said, as she kissed him again.

"He fucked her," she snapped, spitting at the head on the floor. "On our wedding day. I caught them, in the cloakroom, while our families and friends were dancing and celebrating. We had been married less than three hours and he fucked *her*. I had no choice, I had to kill them, husband, and sister both. It felt good. I hit him with my shoe," she laughed, raising her dress to reveal white high heels. "It was all I had. The heel stuck in his head, right in his head, can you believe that? Then, she started screaming so I choked her dead, just to shut her up. He stole my life, my youth, my happiness, but people get what they deserve," she added in a sad, reflective tone and sank her teeth into Michael's neck. I leant against the wall for support, reeling and unable to process what was happening.

I watched as she drank his blood and as I watched the years fell from her and her youth returned. Her back straightened and she grew tall, filling out the wedding dress and revealing the beauty she had once been. With a satisfied sigh, she let the desiccated body fall to the floor. Michael now looked as ancient and spent as she had. She turned to look at me. Her face was a grisly confused mess of blood, makeup, and tears, but her eyes burned with a defiant light.

"It is a terrible thing, to love," she said, her voice now clear, strong, youthful, and compelling. "I would advise against ever loving, it can make a person do … terrible things …" she said with a smile that revealed a mouthful of blood-stained teeth. I didn't know what to say or do, so I nodded. The wretched body on the floor groaned and began to move. His left arm reached out and touched her foot.

"I'm so sorry," he wheezed, blood burbling from his broken mouth. She knelt beside him and lifted his head, stroking it tenderly.

"I know you are, I know, I know, I know, I know," she said quietly, like a mother soothing a sick child.

"Forgive me."

"Forgiveness is a myth, Michael; people get what they deserve."

She twisted her hands, and there was a sound like boots turning on gravel and his body slumped again.

"I was a beautiful bride, was I not?" she said sadly, as she stood. She began to sway and dance, humming a light air as she twirled and spun down the hall. She moved with a true dancer's grace, her every step accentuated by her dress which flowed, rippled, and snapped in perfect time with the tune. As she danced, a headless horror in a maid of honour's dress appeared from the open door of apartment 30 and groped its way along the wall like someone looking for a light switch in the dark. The bride reached out and took the thing by the hands and began to drag it through the hall in a grotesque mockery of a waltz.

"Grab the bitch's head, would you Michael," she called out over the shoulders of her sister's body. I looked back and saw Michael's body struggling back to its feet. "I do prefer her without it, but I suppose we can't just leave it out here in the hall. What would the neighbours think?"

Michael gathered up the pulverized skull of his erstwhile lover, cradled it in his arms like a baby, and followed the pair as they danced into the apartment. At the door he turned to look at me. His injuries were healed, and his youth nearly completely returned. Likewise, the head in his hands had become whole again, the eyes and mouth open wide, screaming in mute terror and agony.

BANG!

I flinched at the sound of the gun, Michael didn't so much as blink.

"He will be here soon, you should go back to the apartment and wait for him," Michael said. "If you don't, the building will make you. There's no escaping this place. People get what they deserve."

As the door closed behind him, I caught a glimpse of the bride, now frail and aged again but still dancing with her headless sister. I tore away from the door and sprinted to the staircase at the far end of the hall. I threw myself down the stairs, jumping entire flights in a reckless race to the ground floor. I exploded through the door at the bottom of the staircase.

BANG!

I was back on the 4th floor. Screaming with a feral panic, I kicked the stairwell door, hard enough to dent the metal. The wall beside the stairs began to move toward me, I stepped back and realized that the entire floor was contracting, both ends of the hall rushing together as the floor collapsed in on itself. When it stopped, I was standing in front of the door to Tom's apartment, the ends of the corridor closed so tight to me that I could reach out and touch them both. I had no choice. I pushed the door open and stepped inside.

"Make yourself comfortable, Emily. He'll be here soon. Have a drink."

BANG!

- 11:39 p.m. –

"Make yourself comfortable, Emily. He'll be here soon. Have a drink."

BANG!

My nerves are shot. I'm a mess. I can't remember when I caved and poured the first drink, but it feels like it was years ago. Every reasonable fibre in my body is rejecting the evidence of my own eyes and ears but there's nothing reasonable about any of this.

"Make yourself comfortable, Emily. He'll be here soon. Have a drink."

BANG!

I had hoped that he would run out of bullets and bring an end to this, no such luck. It's all part of the floor show—his head heals, he stands, the gun reloads. If this goes on much longer, I'm going to grab that gun and use it on myself. I shake my head;

that's the whisky plotting, that's not me. I'm a survivor, I'll find a way out of this. I just need to think. There must be a way.

The lights go out, and I shriek with fright. Embarrassing, and to make matters worse I dropped my glass. It's a miracle it didn't shatter. That's all I need, broken glass on the floor. The relative unimportance of that thought almost makes me laugh. Almost. It looks like the lights outside are off too. This looks like a big power outage; I wonder how much of the city is out.

Using the flashlight on my phone, I find my glass and refill it, this time with Irish. I take a large swallow and sit back and stare into the blackness. There's not much else I can do. I hear Tom still going through his routine, his gruesome enthusiasm for the role unimpeded by the lack of light. The darkness that follows the flash of his gun is bad, but the silence is worse.

True silence is oppressive, it is not something we often encounter. We live our lives surrounded by constant noise, even those times we think of as quiet really are not. Whether it's the hum of electricity, the rumble of traffic, or the cadence of a distant radio or television—there's always something to fill the quiet that we so innocently mislabel as silence. True silence is frightening, isolating, and, for lack of a better term, deafening. I can feel my mind reaching out, searching for noise, any noise, like a junkie, desperate for a fix, rummaging through rubbish looking for something to sell. I rub my eyes and realize that I have been crying. I don't know when I started, it might have been in the elevator or the stairs, it might have been while I watched the bride dance. I can't remember, and for some reason that makes me cry even more.

"Make yourself comfortable, Emily. He'll be here soon. Have a drink."

Within the taut silence that exists between the pulling of the trigger and the violence of the gun firing it is possible to hear the universe sigh. It is a sound that humans were never meant to hear. I have come to know it well.

BANG!

"Stop it. Stop this, please," I pray, begging the darkness and the silence for pity. I slip from the chair down to my knees, rocking, drunk, and weeping. I am done. I am broken.

A light grows behind me. Not a pleasant, or warm light, but a sad and sombre light that suggests the dismal radiance of decay. Once, and only once, I opened the curtains in my grandmother's apartment to let some light in. She smoked like a chimney and I remember feeling sick at the hopelessness of the sunlight that struggled through her nicotine-stained windows. I realized then why she kept her curtains closed. No one wants to see light get strangled like that, but I would gladly take the dead light of that apartment over the grim twilight spreading across this room and introducing a winter-graveyard texture to the air.

"I do enjoy the quiet and the darkness, don't you? They are such rare things in this modern world."

The voice is poised and has a strange inflection—an accent I can't quite place—and evokes a darker underpinning of menace than Monaco could ever engender. "When they built this block of flats, the night was still filled with stars and the day knew endless birdsong. Now what passes for both is a sad mockery of what was. Such is progress, I suppose."

Still on my knees, I turn to look for him. He is leaning against the glass balcony doors, looking out at the darkness. The cold, sickly glow is radiating from him.

"Are you Death?"

He laughs. The sound is soulless, joyless, and cruel.

"I am much, much worse than She."

"There's nothing worse than Death."

"Death brings peace, I do not," his voice has all the warmth of a naked razor.

"Who are you?"

"It would be better for you to ask who I was."

He tilts his head slightly, narrowing his eyes as he stares at me. I have been on the other side of this type of a conversation enough times to know the drill. He's here for me, I'm his target and it's already too late. I never gloated like this. I was all about the money, this guy is enjoying himself. I am drunk, confused, and scared, but I am still me. A thought fights its way up through the muddiness that clogs my mind: Tom drugged me, at the bar. That's the only thing that makes sense. This is all hallucination. A multitude of scenarios and possibilities flood my mind, dragging hope along with them. But as I look at him, in my heart, in my soul I know that I am lying to myself. The idea that this is a drug induced nightmare is nothing but panicked desperation; I might as well be drowning and clawing at clouds for purchase.

"Make yourself comfortable, Emily. He'll be here soon. Have a drink."

BANG!

"Why are you doing this to me?"

A smile tugs at the corners of his mouth.

"I am not doing anything to you. This is all your own doing."

His accent makes "own doing" sound like "undoing", and the cruel smile spreading across his face tells me that it wasn't a coincidence. He really is enjoying this.

"Surely you must feel it?" he says nonchalantly.

"Feel what?"

"Your guilt."

"I don't feel guilty … I … have … I don't have anything to feel guilty for."

He raises his right eyebrow in mock surprise. My mouth, dry already, becomes even drier, painfully so.

My stomach clenches, and my gut spasms. I wrap my arms around my sides, trying to hold my insides in. I'm going to be sick.

"Guilt is a treacherous and wormy thing, Emily," he says, drifting over to me. "It might lie dormant, and you may think that you have it under control, but guilt cannot be bargained with, it will not be ignored. And even if you swallow it, as you have done, you can't digest it. All your guilty feelings have been hiding in plain sight, waiting for their chance to strike, not unlike a certain hired killer I know. And here in this place, they are free to fester within you, twisting, and multiplying like maggots boiling on a corpse."

A second stabbing pain rends my insides and I retch and convulse, gagging on my own bile. He kneels beside me, brushing my hair back from my eyes with his left hand. The gesture is almost tender. I groan, as my body shudders through another paroxysm of pain, and I puke; a sour, molten, whisky-scented puddle of vomit spreads out across the floor in front of me. Vomiting brings no relief; I feel as though I am being torn apart from the inside.

"What do you know of farming, Emily?"

I scream.

"Nothing useful, I imagine," he continues, completely ignoring my pain. "I was a farmer, the *first* farmer—not counting dear old Dad, I suppose. To be fair, he technically gets pride of place there, but then he was more of a gardener than a farmer. But there is no question that I was the first to murder, the first to take another human life, the first to suffer the torments of that distinct species of guilt."

I writhe and twist on the floor, howling in agony and rolling in the warm wetness of my own spew.

"Guilt literally shattered my soul when I killed my brother."

Still screaming, I puke again.

"Like most of the stories in the Bible," he continues casually, "the one about me is mostly wrong. I didn't die an ironic death beneath a collapsing stone house. Truth be told, I didn't die. And now neither will you."

I curl, foetal, gripping my knees tight, as though trying to hold my body together.

"I was distraught, Emily, miserable, the guilt was tearing me apart, consuming me," Cain drones on. "I turned to God, begged, and prayed for him to ease my suffering but … as if cancer in babies wasn't a big enough clue … God is a rat bastard. I don't expect you to take my word for it, my reputation being what it is, but God is the alpha and the omega of assholes. I wandered for decades, lost, and tormented, trying to put my fractured soul back together, but I couldn't. Sigmund Freud wasn't so much as an itch in the loins of history at that time so there was no 'help' to be found for my … affliction."

"Make yourself comfortable, Emily. He'll be here soon. Have a drink."

BANG!

"I couldn't go on suffering endlessly, so, I buried the pieces of my soul in remote and quiet places across the globe. All those numberless thousands of years ago the world was basically all quiet and remote, so I could pick anywhere. As time went on, I began to suspect that my process had not been as arbitrary as I believed. I had been drawn to these sites by forces more ancient than even I can imagine.

I roll on the ground, gasping and gagging.

"Pay attention, Emily, this is where the farming comes in. I should have realized that I wasn't simply burying my soul, I was planting it. I never realized that it would take root, burrowing deep into the earth, reaching into realms best left ... undisturbed.

"Over time, around the world, cities grew, and buildings were built, and people came and lived and died everywhere that I had planted my soul. Buildings such as this one, which was itself built upon the foundations of others, and they upon others, stretching back through time. The depth of malevolence in my soul's guilt made for fertile plots where guilt, and other even worse things might flourish. This site, this building, produces particularly ripe harvests of all kinds. The Ground Floor, for example, is intimately acquainted with human sacrifice, a horrific practice you must agree and one that bears no small association with your own vocation.

"When something special comes along, something like you, this place calls to me, drawing me back to bear witness to the torments I have cultivated. The manifestations of guilt are always unique to the individual, which is very entertaining. Given what I am seeing here, yours will be magnificent."

"Make yourself comfortable, Emily. He'll be here soon. Have a drink."

BANG!

"That poor bastard is the undying embodiment of "'wrong place, wrong time'". He's no saint, but the portion of my soul that is buried here had no interest in him, until you showed up. He got caught in the maelstrom your presence created. Though you should be glad, he did know who you were, and why you were so eager to chat with him in the pub. That gun of his, he was going to kill you with it, but my soul couldn't let that happen, so it intervened. He makes a fine appetizer, but you, my dear, are the main course."

Thrashing violently, I scrabble at my neck as something massive forces its way up my throat. I am being suffocated from the inside. My screams are choked off as a grown man emerges from my mouth, erupting from within me like a snake sloughing its skin. I give a final spasm and expel him onto the floor. I collapse, lying trembling on the floor, too shocked, too repulsed, to begin to process what has happened. The regurgitated figure gasps and sputters like a man saved from drowning. He is covered in a thick and pungent slime; he drags himself to his knees and turns to look at me. At first, he looks confused, but I see recognition dawn on him, and his demeanour shifts to anger. He hates me.

I heave and shudder as another body forces its way out of me, faster and even more painful this time, ripping through me like a fist being shoved through a rat. A woman slops out onto the ground, sputtering. She rolls over and looks at me. Like the first, she knows me, and she hates me.

"Tell me," Cain laughs, "how many did you kill?"

I don't answer, I can't, another body is being vomited from me, but I know the number: 57.

"I bet your mum and dad are in there too, they can't be proud of what you've become, surely."

Another body is jettisoned from me.

"That is the problem with swallowing so much guilt, Emily, you can't possibly keep it all down."

With increasing violence, I sick up body after body, until the apartment is crowded with them. There is hardly room to move. Cain was right, Mum and Dad are here too. As I watch, the figures of the men and women I have murdered begin to meld together, melting into each other, taking on a new, massive shape that fills the apartment with its terrible bulk. I can still see the faces of the individuals that comprise the legs and body and fangs of this new monstrosity. I start screaming.

"Afraid of spiders, are we?" Cain says, shaking his head in mock sympathy.

"If you don't deal with your guilt, properly, it will devour you, eventually. People do get what they deserve. Welcome to the building, Emily. Bon appétit, everyone," he shouts, raising his voice to be heard over my screams. Then he fades away and leaves me to the dark and the chittering hunger of my guilt.

The Boy on the 5th Floor

Alice Henley

"Hello? Is anyone there? Can you help me?"

Three solitary knocks against Sophie's front door. They echo around her dark flat. Having just plummeted into darkness with the television and lights all going out, she now finds herself surrounded by candles and the light from her phone. Looking at the time, ten minutes to midnight, she curses herself for not being in bed already and being free of any obligation to the tiny voice she can hear from the other side of her door.

"Hello?"

He sounds young, she thinks, voice not yet dropped, she can't ignore him again. Quietly stepping up to the door she looks through the peephole, creaking the floorboard as she does so.

"Hi."

Bugger, he heard.

"Please let me in. I live next door but my mum's not home and I'm afraid of the dark."

Slowly opening the door, the keychain still in place, she peeks down at the young boy on her doorstep. He must be ten - eleven tops. His hair matts across his face with a little bit of sweat. With sleepy eyes and dark circles, he looks like he's just woken. He seems small but it's hard for Sophie to make him out completely in the darkness of the hallway.

"Hi, Miss, sorry to disturb you, but I didn't know

what else to do."

"Where's your mum?"

"She's at work, she won't be home till the morning."

Trying to work out whether this is even legal, Sophie decides now is not the time to get involved in any legal domestic disputes. She looks out into the hallway, covered in graffiti, dark and cold, and lets the boy inside. He crosses the room and sits on the sofa, confidently looking around. He has a small backpack.

"What's your name?" he asks.

"Sophie, what's yours?"

"Alfie."

"Alfie? That's a nice name. I don't think I've seen you before Alfie, have you lived here long?"

"As long as I can remember, people don't tend to be too sociable here."

That's true, she thinks. She didn't actually know any of her neighbours and her and Paul had lived there for three, very long years now. Paul! He should be home by now. She relaxes slightly. She wasn't sure why she felt so unbearably uncomfortable but there was just something about this kid that gave her the shivers.

"What does your mum do?"

"She's a nurse. She always works late at weekends, it's their busiest time."

"Right, and usually... I mean do you always stay home alone?"

"No, my older brother is usually home too but he went out." Offering no more of an explanation, he continues to look around, taking in all the surroundings. Sophie can't decide whether he is looking around with judgement or just curiosity. Either way, he is beginning to grate. His eyes linger on her. She suddenly feels conscious of her small frame. She isn't actually that much taller than him.

"Why don't you give your mum a call? We can see what she wants you to do." She had no patience for children and this one seemed a little too sure of himself.

"Okay, pass me your phone and I'll call her."

"Please?"

"What?"

"Please pass me your phone."

"Okay."

She unlocks her phone and hands it over, crossing over to the kitchen to get herself a drink. "Are you getting a drink? Can I have orange juice... Pleeeaase."

She doesn't turn back to look at him, inwardly annoyed at the cocky attitude he is throwing her way.

Alfie starts to pretend to dial, keeping a close eye on where Sophie goes, where everything is in the kitchen. He clocks the slightly wonky door of the top right cupboard, the stain on the side top and the dripping tap. Lazy, he decides, or maybe she just doesn't have any help. Does she live alone? She is petite, easy to manage, he decides, and her hair is long and thick, which is useful. He starts to turn his attention back to the living room when she comes back. He talks into the dead phone.

"Hi, can I speak to my mum please? ... Yeah, it's Alfie... Okay thanks... our neighbour let me in... Hi Mum... yeah I'm okay, I'm with our neighbour... Sophie... no, just her, older than you, probably late 30s."

Now he was pissing her off. She mouths to him that she would like to talk to his mum and has her hand out for the phone.

"There was a power cut...Okay, bye then." He places the phone down on the table, slightly out of reach from Sophie.

"I would have liked to have spoken to her actually, Alfie." She puts down the glass of juice on the table next to him.

"She's really busy, she told me to wait here until she gets home."

"When is that?!"

"Don't know, around six."

"Well that's not convenient for me."

"Why? You're not planning on going anywhere, are you?"

"That's not the point, I only have one bedroom."

"I'll just sleep on the couch. No biggie."

"Excuse me but that's..." The key turns in the lock as Paul comes in.

"Alright babe, what a nightmare, the whole block is completely out, had to take the stairs. Trevor looks well stressed." Suddenly noticing the small figure sat on his couch, Paul turns his attention to Alfie. "Hello little man, you're not having an affair with my missus, are you?"

"No, no, sorry sir, sorry, I was just... I mean I..."

Sophie looks on in disbelief at this almost laughable display.

"Hey, hey, I'm just joking, don't worry, sorry, my lame humour."

"Can I speak to you in the kitchen please?" Sophie has been desperately trying to catch Paul's eye since he got in, ready to get this kid out of their flat. After witnessing that little performance, she is even more determined now.

"Oops, the boss sounds mad, excuse me little dude."

He gives Alfie a little wink who beams back up at him as Paul and Sophie head into the kitchen.

As they walk away, Alfie begins to size up this new player. He's tall but lanky, not much body strength, but still, it's an added complication. The pair in general are not too impressive. They can only be in their late twenties. He smirks as he thinks back to seeing Sophie bristle as he referred to her as late thirties. *Sophie is agitated, I shouldn't have wound her up,* he thinks. But he does enjoy seeing her lose her cool, and now with her boyfriend in his pocket this will be fun. He very slowly and quietly begins to pour orange juice over Sophie's phone, ensuring he soaks it, and then places the glass knocked over next to it. There isn't much light in here with only the candles so it's not too obvious. It surprises him just how many candles she actually has, both the kitchen and living room are full. He giggles, imagining Sophie's plans for romance ruined by his arrival.

"You need to walk him home." Sophie talks in a

hushed tone, aware of little ears in the next room. Paul goes over to the tap, turning it tighter to stop the drip.

"Huh?"

"Alfie, I want him to go home."

"Sure, who is he anyway? Why is he here?"

"He lives next door apparently, got scared when the electricity went out."

"Where are his parents?"

"At work."

"So he's on his own."

"He's fine, he's more than capable of going to sleep in his own bed."

"Soph, he's about ten, we can't leave him on his own."

"His mum did."

Paul turns to look at Alfie who has now curled up on the sofa looking tiny and far younger than the ten years Paul originally thought.

"Come on Soph, look at him, he'll be asleep in five minutes."

"He has been quite rude and pushy since he got in. I don't like him, I don't feel comfortable having him here."

"Are you joking? He's a kid, a tired and nervous one at that, you're being a little harsh. Come on, let me speak to him."

They go back into the room and Alfie immediately sits up, taking his feet off the sofa.

"Sorry, I was feeling tired. I can go, I didn't mean to be a pain... I just... Would you be able to maybe stay at my flat, at least until I fall asleep."

Paul turns to Sophie, who sighs and looks away.

Paul sits down next to him. "You don't need to go back to yours, you can stay here."

He takes his keys, wallet and phone out of his pocket. Alfie clocks the robotic way he does this. It's autopilot mode, subconscious working, conscious mind unaware. This is why people are forever asking where they put their keys, or if anyone has seen their phone. *Adults, always in a rush*, he thinks.

Sophie sits down and notices her phone.

"Oh, for fuck's sake, look at my phone!" She reaches across the table, grabs the phone and begins to shake off the juice, trying in vain to turn it on or get any kind of response from it. "You've broken my phone!" She storms out to the kitchen and Paul gets up to follow her. As he goes, Alfie quickly grabs the keys, wallet and phone. He turns the phone off and places it with the wallet down the side of the sofa, as far as his little hands will push them. He then gets up quickly, smoothly goes to the door and turns the key in the lock and then pockets the keys and sits back down. In his bag he draws out some chocolate brownies, he has at least fifteen in there. He considers pulling out two then, looking up at the pair in the kitchen, decides to break one in half. He can hear their tones are strained but can't quite make out what they are saying. This could be a challenge now but that makes it all the more rewarding when it pays off.

Paul comes back into the room.

"Ah she's just a bit tired little man, it's quite late.

I guess you must be too, huh?"

"I'm okay, I actually have something which might cheer her up, homemade chocolate brownies. My mum makes them, they're so good. Here, try it." Paul takes a bite.

"My God, they're great. Your mum is a talented lady. Soph, come in here."

Sophie comes in, leaving her phone in a bowl of rice in the kitchen.

"You got to try this brownie."

"I'm fine thanks, I'm going to bed."

Alfie speaks up, "I'm sorry, I know I've been a pain, honestly didn't mean it, I can go. Here, have this brownie, I promise you won't regret it."

She looks down at the big-eyed little boy sitting on her sofa, and across to Paul looking at her with a raised eyebrow. She sighs, she's not tired, she has been waiting for Paul to get home so she can unwind with him after a long day. She takes the brownie and sits back down. She bites into it.

"God, it *is* delicious. And you just brought these with you?"

"I like to keep a batch with me, they taste great with milk, let me get you a glass."

Sophie quickly stands, "No, no that's okay, I'll get it, one spilt drink is enough for tonight. Paul, do you want one?"

He nods, mouth full of chocolate. As Sophie sits back down, she and Paul finish their brownies and take a swig of milk.

"Well, looks like you ended up looking after us, now shall we get this sofa made up for you." Paul goes to get up, but Alfie puts a hand out.

"Would you mind staying up? Just for five more minutes." Paul settles back down.

"Sure."

"Can I use your bathroom?"

"Yeah, just down the hallway, first door on the left. I have a little torch here, take it." He takes the torch delighted, this will be super useful, he'll remember next time to bring one himself. Once inside the bathroom, Alfie looks at his watch. It's a quarter after twelve so he's keeping to schedule. There are only six flats on this floor, and with the regularity of these blackouts he knows he has a good few hours yet, probably the rest of the night. The plan was just to do one floor but two might be fun. He opens up his backpack and pulls out the pliers, the needles and thread, and bandages. Looking again at his watch, he decides enough time should have passed for them to be feeling a little spaced out. It had taken him some time to work out that the drug used for numbing the face for botox, botulinum, mixed with a little bit of ketamine can cause paralysis. The ketamine was easy enough to get hold of from his mum's latest loser boyfriend, and as far as the botulinum was concerned, the staff at the hospital were easy to charm, much like the idiot in the next room. Wasn't difficult to convince them that he wanted to be a doctor one day so would love to be shown around. Once he knew where everything was kept it wasn't difficult sneaking in and helping himself. Ensuring there was enough chocolate in the brownies to cover the taste was also a fun exercise. Flushing the chain and putting his instruments back into his bag, Alfie comes back into the living room. Paul seems semi-conscious, which was a little annoying, but Sophie on the other hand looks paralysed with fear which was just how he liked it.

"Woah, you guys look shattered, you should probably think about getting yourselves to bed, huh?"

Paul grunts and tries to get up but stumbles back down with a slight giggle. Sophie tries to let out a scream, but nothing works.

"Mmm, looks like you guys will be sleeping here tonight, eh?" Alfie moves around to face them and pulls out the coffee table. "You know Sophie, my mum always taught me never to take sweets from strangers." He places the torch facing up which creates a nice beam of light in the room. He zips open his bag and pulls out the pliers, needle and thread, and bandages. He threads the needle ready. Sophie looks on in panic and confusion, a single tear begins to fall down her face. Everything is so groggy, she can't move, the more she battles against it the more she seems to shut down. Alfie turns his attention to Paul.

"I have to say fella, you've taught me something, the state of mind of the patient really plays into the effects of the meds. I mean, clearly you are more laid back than your missus here, you even seem to be enjoying this, huh? That's good." Alfie pulls Paul's hand towards him and slowly opens the pliers, cutting around his thumb. In one motion he slices his thumb off, quickly placing a bandage over the gash. He pinches the wound and leans the hand against Paul's chest as he turns to pick up the needle. "Not the best light dude, but I'll try my best." He begins to stitch up the wound.

He turns to look at Sophie. "Don't worry, this isn't my first time, there won't be any bleeding out, this is going to be a really neat fix." Alfie removes both of Paul's thumbs and index fingers. "You're probably wondering why, huh? Well, it'll be difficult for you guys to write about me without the use of your hands. I can leave the other fingers, give you a chance at least." Sophie begins to pass in and out of consciousness, time having stopped. As Alfie starts talking about taking Paul's tongue it becomes too much and she feels herself losing her grip on consciousness. Alfie can't help but feel a little disappointed that she won't see it all, he must remember for next time to hold back on the ketamine, it's much more entertaining when they're awake. As he pulls on Paul's tongue, he begins to slice through it. There isn't as much blood as you might think, but a lot of tough muscle to get through. Once he has removed enough, he places a cold damp cloth into Paul's mouth. Looking into Paul's eyes he is amazed at how unaware he is of what's happening to him. He almost seems to be smiling at him. *Nice guy, shame you came home,* he thinks. Having finished up, he places the tongue, fingers and thumbs into a sandwich bag and moves over to Sophie. She has slumped forward and is unconscious. He pushes her head back and brushes her hair away from her face. Now becoming more of a clinical procedure, he gets to work. Fascinated with surgery the first time he heard his mum talking about a bad shift at the hospital with friends, Alfie knew this was the field for him. He thought about what he might do to Sophie, considering perhaps taking away her nose, perhaps an ear, but decided the crucial thing should be her communication skills. It was a risk performing so close to home. Although he wasn't actually in this block, he was in the one a couple of streets over, so it was important he was meticulous. He was quick with the hands but as he begins work on the tongue she starts to stir. She doesn't have control back yet, but she's able to move her head away and a couple of times she bites down on his fingers which hurts. But it wasn't long before she passed out again. She had annoyed him slightly and he knew how vain women were about their looks so decides the nose would be a lesson to her. However, he hasn't practiced this before so isn't sure what to expect, blood wise. He's relieved that it seems to be mostly cartilage, not so easy to sew up but not as messy. Once he has finished, he looks back to admire his work. It's always tempting to take a picture, but he'd watched too many crime dramas to know how easily people mess up when they become too proud and egotistical about what they've done. He walks into the kitchen to clean off the blood and tissue from his pliers and needle, he doesn't want to take any on to the next stop. It is nearly 1am now so he isn't entirely sure how many more he can get to. It's a Saturday night so he has that in his favour at least, most people will still be up. Just as he is finishing up, there's an almighty bang from outside the window. He runs into the living room and looks out to see fireworks. It was quite the display, the noise rousing both Paul and Sophie. Paul is now more aware of what is happening. Looking across at his mutilated girlfriend and down at his hands, he tries in vain to get up. He can't figure out what's happening. He can see but he can't feel or move. It was then he notices Alfie smiling back at him from the window.

"You're awake! We've missed having you to chat to, haven't we, Soph?"

At that moment, a very nervous and small dog comes rushing into the room, disturbed from his sleep by the fireworks and seeking comfort from his owners.

"You have a dog?! You didn't say. What's his name? Oh, sorry, ha, you can't talk right now. Hey boy, come here, it's okay." The frightened dog slowly and cautiously comes over, sniffing around Alfie. "It's okay, I'm not going to hurt you. Hey, are you hungry? Want some treats?" The dog's ears prick and Alfie grins. Sophie turns to Paul in horror as she guesses where this is going. Alfie opens up the sandwich bag, spilling its contents to the floor as the dog laps up the tongues and fingers in seconds.

"That's a boy, you saved me a job, huh. Good boy, good boy." The fireworks cease and Alfie stops looking down at the dog. He considers for a second whether to take the dog with him. This would certainly help with the clearing up and who doesn't like dogs? But after a pause he thinks better of it, doesn't want any excuse to be turned away. He takes in the scene one last time, sensing that Sophie and Paul probably only have a couple of hours before they feel more mobile, and he wants to hit at least one more flat before the night is out.

"Well guys, you've been great, really you have, but it's time for me to move on. So take care of yourselves. The wounds should heal nicely, they're clean, don't worry, but they might be sore. Your tongue is actually the strongest muscle in the body, and you've still got a bit left so that will heal really quickly." With that he picks up his stuff, unlocks the door and heads out, locking it behind him. The apartment is silent but for the sound of the dog licking his lips. Sophie and Paul look to one another in disbelief, unable to move. As they try to think about what they're going to do, they hear the sound of three knocks at the flat next door - and then a small voice calling out... "Hello? Is there anyone there? Can you help me?"

Riddled Inside Number 39

Philip Rogers

It had been a long day at work and an even longer journey home, but as he looked up at the flats, a sense of serenity overcame him. Knowing that he was finally home, he could forget about everything that had happened earlier in the day as he could now sit down for the evening and relax.

After the day he'd had, David didn't feel like taking the stairs, but as he could see the lift was currently located near the top of the building he decided it may even be quicker if he just walked. Compared with the possibility of entering the graffitied metal cage, which often carried the potent smell of urine from a late-night drinking session, the stairs didn't seem so bad after all.

By the time David reached the third floor he was already feeling fatigued and wondered where his youthful energy had gone. An unhealthy appetite for fast food, alcohol and twenty cigarettes a day, was probably the cause, and he wasn't sure any number of steps on his Fitbit would be the answer. Normally the accumulating number of steps and floors would be an added incentive but, with his phone running out of battery on the way home, it wouldn't be counted so what was the point.

Looking up at the seemingly endless staircase, David considered taking the lift for the remaining few floors, but the embarrassment of one of his neighbours seeing him unable to walk six flights of stairs spurred him on. Head down and moving on autopilot, a glass of red wine as a just reward kept his legs moving as they continued to lurch cumbersomely up each step.

As he was making his way up towards the fourth floor, he heard a voice coming down the stairs. It spoke angrily, with an aggressive incoherent babbling as he continued to have a conversation where he seemed to be addressing himself. From what David could make out, he was apologising for something he had done, but then interjecting on himself where he was trying to justify his actions. It was an angel and devil on each shoulder scenario, but he was playing it out in stereo sound so that everyone could hear. Unfortunately, unlike *Trainspotting*, real life doesn't come with subtitles.

Hearing the voice coming closer, David tried to look around the staircase and see if he could spot the figure coming down. David wasn't a violent man and always tried to avoid confrontation where he could, so at this moment he was considering going back down and taking the lift. Caught within two minds and misjudging the echoed voice coming towards him, he locked eyes with the stranger as he suddenly appeared from around the staircase.

Taking some of his weight with his arms to pull himself up, David put his head down and started walking up the stairs towards the stranger, keeping his eyes down to avoid another awkward contact of the eyes.

Looking at the oncoming steps he noticed that the stranger had stopped on the top step, the toes of his brown boots hanging over the edge as he swayed back and forth on his heels.

As David was almost aligned, the stranger addressed him. "What are you fookin' looking at?"

Great, thought David, *just what I needed today.* "Nothing," he mumbled as he tried to continue. "Just trying to get home." It looked as though the stranger was going to let him pass, but as he reached the top step a hand reached across him, latching onto the stair rail with a firm grasp. David tried to continue his tactic of avoiding eye contact, but he couldn't help noticing the man's arm. He was wearing a t-shirt which left the inked sleeve of his slim but muscular arms exposed. Whilst he was fascinated by his choice of old school sailor-inspired tattoos, it was the blood which got his attention. Whilst there didn't seem to be a wound, the blood was still wet.

With his options now limited and neither seeming favourable, David deviated from his normal rules of disengaged and turned to the man, instantly recognising that there was something very wrong. Like his arm, the man's face was covered in blood to the extent it was almost like he had bathed in it, and to make things more disturbing it looked as though it seeped into his eyes and stained them the same colour. They were like two snooker balls bulging out from his face with only the darkened pupils remaining in the centre as the distinguishing features. Whilst there was some bruising around the face, at a glance he couldn't see any actual abrasion to his skin or his head. At this point David wasn't sure if the blood was the man's or someone else's; either way, he really didn't want to know.

"Sorry," David said as he tried to politely lift the man's arm out of the way, but as he felt the muscles begin to tense, he knew they weren't going to move. It was like the ticket machine at the train station this morning when it didn't register his card, despite him trying to move forward to his destination he was denied the opportunity to proceed any further.

Knowing that he would be unable to make his way up the stairs, David decided to take his chances by retreating, but as he turned the stranger pulled him back by the shoulder and sunk his teeth into his neck. David squirmed and tensed his body as he felt the teeth piercing through his skin, but whilst the penetration was extremely painful, it was the burning pain that followed which caused David to scream. As the adrenaline kicked in, David heard the voice of his primary school gym teacher, who had once described the scenarios of fight or flight responses. David would have laughed had he not been in so much pain as he inadvertently shouted out 'Both,' turning to face his assailant and catching him off guard. Without thinking, David instinctively put his hands on the stranger's back and pushed him down the stairs.

David could do nothing but watch as the body fell awkwardly. Taken by surprise, the stranger tightened his body to try to stop the momentum, but his rigid posture only served to work against him. With gravity serving its purpose, the collision with the final few stairs seemed to be the most fatal.

With his body yearning to turn in one direction, the impact of his head on the steps made sure that his neck didn't follow. David winced as he heard the neck snap right before the now limber body dropped.

It was the fear that he may have just killed a man that initially made David's heart start to beat rampantly. But as the figure started to twist its body off the floor, it was fear of whatever *thing* he had nearly killed which made his heart feel like it was going to burst through his chest.

Despite the injuries sustained from the fall, his fractured neck clearly contorted at an angle and his leg dislocated and facing the wrong direction, the man didn't seem to acknowledge the pain. Initially he tried to walk on his injured leg, but inevitably fell as soon as his weight was applied. However, seeming focused on finishing what he started, he continued to use his working leg and arms to slowly manoeuvre himself up the steps.

"You gotta be fucking kidding," David mumbled to himself, as he started to run up the remaining stairs. The adrenaline had tapped into a reserve of energy he didn't know he had, even managing to bound up two stairs at a time. After nearly falling on the second stride, he thought better of it. Even though he felt out of breath and wondered if he had forgotten his natural ability to breathe, he didn't stop until he reached the 6th floor. In the panic he found himself fumbling with his keys and wondered why he had kept so many, especially as he didn't know what some of them even unlocked anymore.

After a missed attempt, with one eye still fixed on the staircase, he finally unlocked the front door and, in his haste, nearly fell through as he leaned his weight on it.

On stepping over the threshold David felt a sense of security but, unlike vampires, he didn't think that whatever was following him needed an invitation to get in, so he kicked the door shut with the heel of his boot.

Taking a moment to compose himself and gain some control over his breathing, David tried to comprehend what had just happened. He looked through the peephole of the door to the magnified hallway, half expecting a jump scare, but all he could see was the dreary white wall. Whilst he felt an element of safety in his flat, David's mind began to wander as he started to envision various ways in which the *thing,* for lack of a better word, might attack. He had watched too many horror movies and he knew the attack could come from anywhere, and with that thought he began to shuffle his body away from the letter box. Whilst he wrestled to try and convince his subconscious that the notion was ridiculous and it was all over, after what he saw on the stairs, he was wondering what else could happen tonight.

Unsure what to do next, David rested himself on the hallway console table and let out an overstated sign of relief, looking at himself in the mirror. Staring at his reflection, he suddenly noticed the blood seeping through his ripped shirt. With the sheer rush of adrenaline and chaos of the moment, he had almost forgotten the pain. Whilst he felt it subconsciously, he was more concerned about getting out alive and the burning sensation had been stored in the back of his mind to worry about later. Now with the adrenaline wearing off and having a moment to think, David became fully aware of the pain which had dramatically spread across his chest, neck and left arm. The wound looked painfully infected and the blood was seeping out with a white pus that was already beginning to congeal with his shirt. A rotting smell began to rise from the would as if it were days old, causing him to retch.

Painful as it was to remove, he eventually managed to peel away the fabric from the wound to reveal the extent of his injuries. The teeth marks had penetrated deep through his skin and the area looked infected, but what caused more concern was the inflamed bruising which had already spread. The area had swollen and had started to create a dark black bruising which looked plum in colour. Coupled with the swelling, it looked like it was ready to burst. Tentatively he touched his chest, expecting to feel a slightly tender sensation, but he could feel heat on his fingers. As he touched it, his chest began to burn as if hot coals had been placed underneath his skin. He screamed in pain and looked in the mirror to examine it further, when he noticed a small ripple as if something was there, moving beneath his skin. He moved closer to the mirror to look at his face for reassurance, but when he looked at his eyes even more questions were raised. His eyes were red like the stranger on the stairs. David addressed his reflection in the mirror, "What the fuck has that thing done to me?"

With the creature outside, David didn't want to leave the flat just yet and what could he say if he called the police? Would they even believe him? What if he was dead already? What would he do then? David needed time to refocus and decided the best thing he could do was take a shower to clear his head, clean the blood and hopefully clean out the wound. After that he could put on a change of clothes and then come up with a plan.

David stripped off and stepped into the hot shower, beginning to feel more at ease as he watched the red blood start to drip to the floor. It felt as if some of his stress was already starting to wash away with the stained water which flowed down into the plug hole. The burning sensation he had initially felt with the wound and surrounding areas actually seemed to ease under the heat; perhaps the hot water was helping to draw it out. David picked up shampoo and began to lather the soap through his thick black hair, but as he began to rinse it through, he noticed clumps of hair beginning to fall out into his hands. Looking down at the plug hole, he noticed that the water was starting to rise as the huge wads of hair were starting to block the flow. Touching his head again he could feel the smooth areas where his hair was now missing, the remaining falling into his hands.

David jumped out of the shower and grabbed a towel to dry himself, but whilst he wiped his face, he felt a painful lump above his left lip. As he pressed down on it gently, he suddenly got the taste of blood in his mouth and a shooting pain throughout his left jaw. After spitting out the blood, he used his tongue to explore the tender area of his mouth and noticed that a canine tooth was loose and starting to wobble. He moved his head upwards towards the mirror and could see that the tooth was really loose and starting to move on its own. David ran into the kitchen, grabbed a pair of pliers and brought them back into the bathroom. He had no idea what was going on, but he knew that tooth has to be removed, now, rather than later.

Using the mirror for guidance, he navigated the pliers into his mouth, took hold of the tooth and began to pull. He could taste the warm blood which was beginning to fill his mouth, with the overflow of the liquid now starting to run down the side of his jaw. He was finding it difficult to see what he was doing as his eyes began to tear up, so he took a moment's pause between pulls as the pain was becoming unbearable. He carried on until eventually the gum's clasp on the tooth gave way and the tooth came out clamped in the jaws of the pliers.

Whilst he could feel himself going faint, he had to check again as he presented his open jaw once again in front of the mirror. Looking inside, he could see what looked like a maggot wiggling inside of the vacant gum where the tooth was once embedded. David grabbed the wriggling maggot between his thumb and forefinger before trying to pull it out. But whilst he had a hold of it, it was almost like it was rooted in his gums and wouldn't move. Grabbing the pliers with his free hand, he used the instrument once again, this time to latch onto the maggot. Having got a hold of the creature, he once again started to pull. He was surprised that pulling out the maggot was as difficult as removing his tooth and the pain felt just as bad, if not worse. Eventually the worm conceded and David dropped it into the sink next to his tooth, before spitting out a mouthful of blood and turning on the hot tap to wash it away. Using a flannel, he covered the open gums in his mouth to stem the bleeding.

Feeling exhausted, David sat down on the toilet seat to compose himself once again, when the silence was interrupted by the vibration of his phone. Picking up his trousers from the floor, he began to search for his phone in the pocket and answered. Whilst there was no direct reply at the other end of the phone, what he could hear was the recognisable voice of his wife groaning in pleasure down the phone.

"Anna? Anna, is that you?" David began shouting down the phone, but still there was no reply, just the sound of Anna groaning in pleasure, followed by a man's voice in the background. David began shouting again down the phone, before throwing it in anger at the wall. Falling to his knees, David cradled his head in his hands as he began to cry.

Feeling faint, David put his hand on the floor to try and steady himself, but as he reached out the room started to spin. Losing control, he found himself falling helplessly to the floor. Paralysed, he lay there unable to move, unable to do anything but watch the ceiling continue to extend further away as the darkness gradually crept in.

Carrying several bags to the door, Anna was struggling to get the key lined up with the lock, as her next-door neighbour Nathan stepped out from his flat. "Do you want a hand, Anna? I can see you're struggling."

"No, no it's okay," she replied. "It's just like David always says when he's drunk - I'm almost in." Anna laughed as she crossed her eyes and stuck her tongue as if to mimic David's face. She liked to make gestured jokes with Nathan as it always made him blush and this was no exception. This time however, Nathan's usually awkward laugh was cut short with a smile as he responded with a question.

"I just wanted to check if everything was okay? I heard a lot of shouting earlier and I just wanted to make sure you and, err, well, see if David was okay" Nathan took a step forward as if to offer his help despite previously being declined.

"That's okay Nathan, I am sure it's fine. Probably just one of his silly horror films. I am sure he mentioned that some Nacho film was on tonight. I think it may be some low budget Mexican director. Mask of Bourne or something I think, maybe it's a crossover." Anna smiled as the key finally aligned with the lock, and just in time to make Nathan stop a few steps short of the welcome mat.

"It's a Mycho film. It's called Mask of Thorn,"

Nathan replied gleefully as if his Wikipedia knowledge of independent horror films would somehow be impressive.

"That's probably the one, you guys should watch these films together some time, I can't stand the sight of blood myself, I just don't get it." Anna pushed open the door, walked inside, and in a well-rehearsed action closed the door using her foot. "See you later Nathan," she shouted out as the door came to a close.

"You too Anna, be safe," Nathan replied softly in a withdrawn whisper. As it had been several times before, his response was more his own closure to the conversation for the things he wished he had said whilst Anna was still there. Withdrawing once again, this time more pensively in concern, he walked back into his flat.

Walking in and taking off her high heeled shoes which were beginning to make her feet ache, she called out, "Hi David, I'm home, can you help me with these bags? I've got some wine, but as it's late do you want to get a takeaway…' Anna barely finished her sentence when her attention was drawn to a blood-stained shirt on the floor. "David, are you here? What's happened? Is everything okay?" Wondering if she should have taken Nathan's advice, she took a step forward and tentatively pulled out a silver letter opener from the console table.

Anna called out again to David, this time with a more cautious whisper as if David would be the only one who could hear her. As she passed the entrance to the bathroom on her right, she suddenly noticed David lying on the floor with a chaotic mess surrounding him. Scanning the area for clues as to what happened, she found herself overwhelmed and didn't know where to start in putting the pieces together. The sink was covered in blood, as was the shower which had now overflowed onto the floor due to the plughole being blocked with mountains of hair. On the side were a bloodied pair of scissors and a razor.

Bending down to check on David, she put her hand in front of his mouth to see if he was still breathing and noticed a bite mark on his left shoulder. "Thank god," she said, feeling a faint breath. "David, are you ok? Can you hear me?"

As if he had been electrocuted, David reached out towards Anna's hand which was still near his face. Pulling it towards him, he clamped down on her hand with his teeth. In an instinctive reaction, Anna plunged the letter opener into the wound on his shoulder. As David's clasp loosened on her hand, she started to shift herself away towards the bathroom door.

David rolled himself onto his front and bridged his body up in an arch, balancing himself on his hands and feet as if he were getting ready to start a 100-meter sprint. Using the door frame for support, Anna scrambled to her feet, all the time keeping her eyes on David's movements. She tried to stay strong, but she could feel the tears building in her eyes.

"I'm sorry David, I didn't mean to stab you, but

what's going on? Why are you doing this?"

David looked up and glared at her with his red tainted eyes which showed nothing but anger. "You fucking bitch," he shouted as he projected himself forward like a cat, the ferocity of his launch and the element of surprise knocking Anna off her feet and sending her crashing to the floor. Winded and feeling pain in numerous places, Anna didn't have time to react as David straddled her, his full weight on her stomach. As she tried to push him off, she suddenly felt his ice-cold hands wrapped around her throat. She looked him in the eyes and tried to beg him to stop, but it looked as though the man she knew was no longer there. Whilst he shared the features, the cold hands were not the ones that held her and made her feel safe at night. Those eyes didn't belong to the man that said he would never hurt her. Whatever this man was, it wasn't her husband.

She could feel herself slipping away and in desperation reached up to pull the letter opener from his shoulder. "You're not my husband," she muttered as she thrust the knife through his cheek.

As he swiped her hand away from the knife, it gave her a moment of reprieve. With his grip disengaged, she gasped for air. But despite the injury, he seemed undeterred, looking down on her with those bloodied eyes she knew it wasn't over.

David removed the blade from his cheek without flinching, as if withdrawing it smoothly from a sheath. Holding it in the air, the blood dripped onto her face, the wound in his cheek opening as he smiled before forcing it through Anna's cheek.

"An eye for an eye, a cheek for a cheek," David mustered in a dark delirious tone.

Leaning forwards, David placed his hands on Anna's face and began to push his thumbs beneath her eyeballs. Anna tried to scream frantically as she pulled at his hands, but the thumbs kept sinking into the soft flesh underneath the eyelids. Within seconds the right eye had been popped out of the socket, but the pain continued for Anna as David pushed deeper. Desperately reaching up, she dug her long nails into the wound on David face, desperately digging as she tried to rip it open. It didn't have an effect and David continued to push down.

With his thumbs now deep into the eye sockets, he hooked them and pushed them into the side of her head with his fingers. His hands were now positioned on her head as if he was picking up a bowling ball with his thumbs in the holes. He lifted her head towards him and, once it was a few inches off the floor, he smashed it back down. Then he picked it up and did it again and again. David developed a constant rhythm as if he were performing CPR and he didn't lose any momentum as the head began to give way. Even when the skull had completely caved in, he continued to pulverise the remaining flesh, his fists punching into the floor.

Nathan had been sitting in his bedroom in silence, listening to the banging and shouting from his neighbours. After hearing Anna screaming again, he couldn't wait any longer and decided to knock on the door to check on her.

Nathan was surprised to see David open the door so quickly, and was even more surprised when he was invited in after being told that there had been an awful accident. Nathan couldn't believe his eyes when he saw the blood-spattered mess of what he could only assume was Anna, lying on the floor.

Nathan didn't have time to react as he felt a sharp pain to the back of the head which sent him falling to the floor. David stood above him and began to ask questions. "So, you thought that you could just come around now, even though I am here. What, don't you think I know what you have been up to?" Nathan adjusted his thick-rimmed glasses and held up his hands in front of him, confused as to what was going on.

"I honestly don't know what you're talking about David. I just wanted to see if you were okay, I heard the banging, the screaming."

David stepped forward so he was directly above Nathan and looked down on him. "I know what's going on, I've seen the pictures. Don't act like you didn't you know. Anna just sent them to me as you knocked." Nathan turned around again, eyes fixed on Anna lying on the floor. "Look," shouted David, holding up his phone with a blank screen. "Don't deny it, I have seen it all. I knew something was up, the way you looked at her. The way you were pretending to be all coy and shy. You were sleeping with her all along."

Nathan tried desperately to reply but began to trip over his words. "Honestly David, I don't know what you're… I mean, when did she… How? Just look at your face, we need to get you to a hospital." "No," David shouted as he kicked Nathan straight in his face, breaking his glasses in two. "I am going to give you something far worse." David lunged toward Nathan and bit into his arm. Stepping back, he pulled a knife from his back pocket. "Trust me, you are going to wish that I had killed you because this is worse than death," he shouted as he ran a blade across his own neck before falling to the floor.

Nathan sat there for a moment, stunned, not knowing what to do. He assumed that whatever was left of the body behind him was Anna and now David was there in front of him with his throat slit. *What the hell am I going to tell the police?*

He didn't know what he was thinking as he ran over to the flat opposite and knocked on the door. "Who is it?" a voice shouted from inside. Betty was eighty-nine and she always called out before making her way to the door. As it took her so long to get there, she would call to see if it was worth the effort of answering.

"It's me Betty, Nathan from across the hall. David's gone mad, he just killed his wife and then slit his throat. Can you help me? I just want to use your phone to call the police."

"Oh deary me," replied Betty as she slowly made her way to the door. Nathan became anxious as he waited for her to open the door and started knocking with more force. Finally, Betty arrived and opened the door. "It's all very surprising. He always seemed such a nice young man, they were a nice couple really. A bit strange, but…"

"Thank you," said Nathan as he walked through the door and promptly closed it behind him. "We can call the police in a minute, but first can you do something about this bite on my arm? It's really starting to burn."

The Noises Outside Room 50

MJ Dixon

"Who puts these out here?" Matthew wondered as he stepped from the elevator, its heavy metal door screaming as its ancient mechanics hauled themselves through the motions.

In his hands dangled the white plastic bagged spoils of a data entry supervisor, who made almost enough to afford rent on a shitty London apartment, in a shitty part of the city, eighty minutes away from the place he worked. The great British dream.

The corridor in front of him, the same usual five doors, dotted in odd numbers, two on one side and three on the other, forming an odd arrow toward Number 50, slap bang in the middle, looking right back at him. All of it looked the same as it did every evening, the murky, peeling, yellowed walls, calling out in desperation for a paint job, the dusty dented white door frames, surrounding the bland pale blue doors. Not pale of their own accord, but by years of aged fading.

Someone seemed to have spilled some kind of jam across the floor down the centre of the hallway, it was the chunky, fruit filled type. Dark and red and bloody everywhere.

Excellent, he thought. *I wonder how long it is before someone cleans that up?* He didn't hold out much hope. His neighbours didn't seem fussed about cleanliness. "Maybe I'll do it myself, that would show them," he muttered. He knew he was kidding himself as he stepped over it.

He was embarrassed for people to see that this was where he lived, but it was the building manager's job to fix this stuff and not his. In the four years that he had lived there, no one had ever made an attempted to spruce the place up.

That made the appearance of fresh new doormats outside of each apartment all the more bewildering.

Matthew wandered down the hallway, transfixed on them. Somewhat shaggy, like the ones you'd see on a farm for cleaning heavy mud from boots after a day mucking out the horses, but nicer, like they were made from soft animal hair.

They can't repair the handles to main doors, thought Mathew, *but they can throw fresh mats outside our doors?* It was typical behaviour for Castle Heights, slap a bandaid over a bigger problem and hope it distracts from the water damage, cracked ceilings and rusty pipes...

The elevator began to screech itself closed behind him and he turned and looked at it, his face displaying the kind of look that one would expect when hearing nails on a chalkboard.

"And heaven forbid they fix the sodding elevator," he grumbled.

Stopping outside Number 50, a shopping bag hanging from each hand, he stopped, placing his feet neatly before the shaggy rectangle.

COME ON IN, it announced.

"Quite presumptuous," he muttered as he looked down at it.

Looking back at the other mats, all of them

announcing the same slogan, he couldn't help but notice that they *did*, despite the spillage of fruit compote, tidy the place up a bit. Which was especially good news, what with him expecting guests this evening.

"They are quite nice I suppose," he smiled, and with that, he stepped over the doormat and hauled his bags of delights inside.

Matthew's apartment was never really a mess, he lived alone, picked up after himself, and it helped he was almost never home, the only thing slightly out of place was a small pile of takeaway menus that popped through the letter box every few days. He'd built quite a stack that had piled up on the radiator by the entrance to his abode.

He was usually up and out before dawn and rarely arrived home before 7.30pm. In these autumn months, he hardly saw the light of day. He often blamed that for his pale complexion, but if he was honest, he had never been particularly tanned, just another thing on the list of gripes about his physical appearance. From his dirty, bland, brown hair, to his skinny upper body that somehow only held weight around his waist, and his freckled, pockmarked face caused by years of severe acne as a teenager, the complaints were endless.

As Matthew dumped the shopping out on the kitchen counter, his eyes wandered over his Tesco treasures: crisps, posh spring water, a variety of chocolates (all weirdly caramel themed) and of course, some wine and beers. Popping his fridge open, he looked inside at the sparse shelves.

Nothing really but some cheap margarine and couple of microwave meals along with some low budget lager, the kind of stuff that was undrinkable, unless its sole purpose was to get you drunk and drowsy enough to fall asleep in front of the television, which just so happened to be Matthew's favourite past time.

He slammed the imported American beer bottles into the bottom the fridge and closed the drawer, but the wine, a red, he looked at.

Better at room temperature, right? It wasn't something he knew off the top of his head, but he'd heard that somewhere. Wine was definitely outside of his wheelhouse. All he knew was that if it was expensive, it was good and at £28 a bottle, he either had something very good or he had been 'very' screwed over by the Express Supermarket on the corner. Still, tonight was a night when he had to impress, even if it was against his will.

So, here Matthew was, unpacking cheesy Doritos and caramel chocolates into bowls, ready to 'impress' his workmates, placing them on the table and looking around at his dim apartment. The empty carton of a microwave meal sat on the small table next to his singular armchair. He looked around the room.

Where are people going to sit? he wondered. Being a bachelor, Matthew only had his trusty old armchair, his throne for watching TV, but that wasn't going to help him with his guests. *It's cool to stand, right? People stand at parties?* He wasn't convinced.

Opening the airing cupboard, he looked inside, finding some old fold-out chairs, the kind you'd have in your garden, but chairs Matthew had used for Buffy marathons with his fat mates during his University days. He pulled them out and arranged the pitiful mismatched seats in a line - it looked bad. He glanced at the table, its unappealing selection of snacks in equally unmatching bowls. This was not good. And he didn't have long before they'd arrive. His mind whirred as he tried to come up with a solution.

If only I hadn't had to work today, he thought, *I could have easily thrown something together*. He caved into his own thoughts. Who was he kidding? He never cooked; he didn't even know if he could if he tried. His idea of cooking was dialling a takeaway.

Wait, I could order something in. He glanced at the menus by the door. *Perfect*.

Cycling through the menus, he tried to pick something, something that would arrive before his guests, something that would look good.

Chinese, he settled on. *Everyone loves Chinese, right?*

He looked at the menu and hit the app on his phone. Smashing whatever he could think of into the the basket, he went to checkout. The total - £64.79.

Jeez, this little gathering is gonna bankrupt me! No matter, he just had to get through tonight, he could survive on bread and instant noodles for the rest of the month.

He clicked 'confirm', and looked down the app.

Your order will arrive at approximately 7.45pm. Just enough time to get it laid out before his guests arrive.

The guests, how many will there be? He hadn't given it much thought. It wasn't usually a large gathering, his team at work was pretty small. Plus, he had reference for how many people usually turned up to these things. He tried listing them in his mind.

Dave Morel, a man in his late 30s, he was pretty boring, didn't really speak to anyone, but he always showed up and sat and smiled and nodded, he was pleasant enough. Matthew actually really liked him, which was a good show, he'd been sat in the cubicle next to him for four years and Matthew has become accustomed to looking at the right side of his spectacles peering over the divider.

Tara Smith, the office bitch. She worked the same job as everyone else, entering numbers into computers, but for some reason, she thought she was God's gift, literally, being a 'Good Christian woman'. She was tanned (naturally so, she claimed), extremely attractive, a snappy dresser, but it was off-putting how much she knew it and even more so how she treated people at the office like shit, talking down to everyone and always having an eye on how she could climb the ladder a little quicker. For a woman who purported to be 'wholly Christian in her values' she sure acted like the other guy.

Sandra, the receptionist. She was probably in her

late 40s, not unattractive, but not eye-catching either. She also acted much older than she really was, doddering about the office, answering the phone at a snail's pace. However, she never turned away the chance of a free drink. He often noticed her sneaking a swig from a flask at the office; maybe it was just that she had a bit of a 'problem'. Although it was exactly the kind of job that would drive you to drink.

The main reason for that would be the Team Manager, Henry Handcock, a real piece of shit. He had been made Team Manager by his uncle, one of the 'upstairs bosses' that really ran the place, but he acted top dog, day in and day out. He was hands down the worst person Matthew had ever worked for - condescending, self-entitled and arrogant to top it all off, the kind of guy who wears one of those Bluetooth headsets and has 'important' conversations for everyone else's benefit. He liked to think these little meetings were him 'bringing the team closer together', but often it just highlighted how much Matthew really enjoyed his time alone.

The main draw for him was that he got to talk to Kelsey Little, his official office crush. She was small, blonde, bookish, beautiful, she was like a cross between a librarian and a surfer chick. Matthew often got to chat to her briefly whilst passing her desk on his way back from lunch, but in those few passing moments over the years he had gleamed several pieces of key information. The music she liked (Nu Wave Punk), the books she read (Trashy Young Adult fiction), the movies she watched (Low budget Indie Horror) and the fact she seemed to like cats, due to the copious amounts of little wooden cat models she had sat around her desk. Oh, and she was single.

But at these little gatherings, he would get a chance to catch her in much longer conversation. She was certainly the only appealing thing about it now that he really thought about it. Surely it would just have been simpler to ask her over for dinner?

No, that was too direct for Matthew, he was playing the long game. The long, long game in fact. Yes, gradually letting her know he was interested with a series of subtle hints until she finally accepts defeat and agrees to move in with him. It was the perfect plan.

Matthew quietly sat flicking through the TV guide on the Freeview box.

I wonder what I'm missing out on tonight. The usual nonsense. Some crappy horror on Channel 5 at 9pm. Some talk show, featuring some poncey 'filmmaker'. A game show with a funny name that he could never remember, but it had the guy on it, the one with the funny hat. And, oh wonderful, the boxing. That's why Henry had chosen tonight. He knew it.

Matthew rolled his eyes. He detested sports, he'd never been very good at them himself and watching other people performing any kind of sport, he found even more tedious. Yet he always found he had to watch the boxing, to be part of the cultural conversation at work. He hated it, and every time he did it he felt a little bit dirty, but if they were here, watching it together, then he would dodge that particular conversation bullet this time. Hopefully.

At least this night has another silver lining, he smiled to himself, *Kelsey and a Chinese, what a night it's shaping up to be.*

He looked at his watch. 7.46pm.

"Where's that food?" he muttered. "Should be here by now."

He looked toward the door. It was a big building, takes time to get up from the lobby.

A few moments later, the rusty sounds of the lift door echoed down the hall. "Ah, there he is."

Matthew sat flicking through the rest of the TV he was missing as he waited for the knock, but it didn't come so he got up and walked toward the door.

A horrific scream stopped him in his tracks, the doors were thick, and it was muffled, but he could hear it. Right outside his door. Then silence.

"What the hell was that?"

Matthew cautiously approached the door. He slowly stopped and moved his eye to the peephole. Out in the corridor, through the fishbowl view of the little glass, he could see, well... nothing.

It was completely quiet. But he had heard the lift door.

Maybe someone going down? Must have been. He turned and wandered back toward his trusty chair, looking at his odd arrangement of food and seats. He tapped his leg nervously. *Where was this food?*

It was 7.53 now. The guests were gonna be here

before any food arrived. Maybe he could brush it off.

"That'll be the food I ordered," he practiced out loud. "Hope you guys like Chinese." He imagined them all cheering. Kelsey giving him a smile, a knowing one, the smile a hero gets, and then he would take her in his arms and kiss her and his workmates would cheer and...

A knock at the door snapped him out of his fantasy. He whipped his head toward it with a jump.

Oh well, that must be the food. So much for his victorious moment. He looked at his watch, 8.01. It could be a guest, maybe this is the moment.

Another almighty scream, awful, blood-curdling, higher than before, like a woman's scream. He stopped and looked. It was definitely coming from outside. Then silence once more.

He moved on the peephole again. Still empty. Pulling open the door cautiously, Matthew peered out into the corridor. It was empty. He opened it fully. Nobody out there at all.

What on earth is going on? he thought as he slipped back inside. *Could be one of the neighbours playing a prank.* That didn't seem right. Maybe it wasn't his door. But it really sounded like it. Maybe some visiting 48 or 49.

But what about that screaming? he wondered. *Must have been one of the neighbours.*

He looked down and sat at the side of the mat was a pair of black rimmed glasses. He leaned down and picked them up. They looked familiar, maybe they belonged to one of the other tenants. Maybe they had been there all along. He had been focused on the new doormats when he came in, perhaps he missed them. He folded them up and stepped back inside.

Matthew wandered to the kitchen and opened the fridge, pulling out a beer. He would look cool, right? If he was sipping a cold one when his guests arrived. He opened the drawer, rooting for a bottle opener. The problem with drinking cans of discount, double strength, Danish lager is that they came with a ring pull. He looked through the drawer, had he not remembered a bottle opener? Or a corkscrew? He couldn't see one.

Oh no, he thought *How will we...* He paused, his panic subsiding slightly as he closed the fridge. A naked hula girl magnet was stuck to the door, it was a gift from his University flat mate who had gone to Hawaii for the summer a few years ago. Lucky for him it also doubled as a bottle opener and corkscrew. He held it in his hand. It was a little embarrassing, but he figured it would be more embarrassing should he spend the night opening bottles with his teeth. The thought made him wince.

Suddenly he jumped as a knock on the door grabbed his attention.

He turned, anger on his face. That time it was definitely his door.

Was someone messing with him? He shoved the corkscrew in his pocket, holding it between his fingers, ready for attack. He grabbed the door and tore it open, the face looking back at him hopped back in surprise as he came face to face with wide blue eyes.

Kelsey Little stood a couple of feet away, almost yelping as Matthew's face popped out the door. She looked at him, her face inquisitive. He realised he should probably say something.

"Oh Kelsey, sorry, it's kids, I think." He noticed he didn't make much sense. "Knocking on my door earlier, I thought it was..." He gave up. He noticed she clutched something in her hand.

"What's that?" he questioned.

"I found them on the floor." Her voice was soft and pleasant, its sound washed over him. "I assume Tara is already here?" She rolled her eyes. It was a thing they did whenever she was mentioned at the office, he liked that it has transferred over to 'out of office' conversation.

Then he frowned, why would she think Tara was there?

"No, you're the first one here." He looked at what she was holding more closely, really focusing this time. It was a small bracelet, a gold cross hanging from it.

"I thought this was hers." Kelsey held it up, it had a splash of red on it. "I think someone got that on it." She pointed down the corridor at the red mess his neighbours had left. "Someone has tracked it onto your doormat."

Matthew looked down. A fresh spattering of corridor jam was printed right across it. His face twisted. "Excellent, we just got these today." He looked at her. "Can't have anything nice in this place." He realised he was complaining already, so he smiled, trying to cover it.

"I didn't want to drag it in," she said.

"That's very thoughtful," he beamed, moving aside as she hopped over the jammy mat and into his apartment.

Kelsey looked around and Matthew noticed she was scanning, taking in his apartment.

Did she really think Tara was here? he wondered. *Oh no! Does she think we're having an affair?* He shook it off, he doubted she would have believed that. No, she knew him well enough to know he despised Tara. *But there is a thin line between love and hate*, he noted.

Kelsey put the the bracelet down on the desk by the door as Matthew wandered over behind the kitchen counter.

"Beer?"

She looked and smiled.

"I'd love one." He lifted up his embarrassing corkscrew, trying to conceal it and look cool at the same time. He thought maybe he managed it, as he handed her the beer and leaned back, trying to look casual.

Kelsey took a sip and let out a satisfied "Aahh" she moved her attention to his apartment. He hoped she'd notice his collection of DVDs and CDs, that would be a surprise for her.

"I've never been here before," she said, "but it looks just like I expected."

He looked at her, cocking his head, unsure how to take it.

"Er, thank you?" It was more of a question.

"Oh, not to cause offence," she said. "I just mean, that it's got a very 'London flat' kind of vibe. You know?"

He laughed, not really getting it.

"Not really, but if it's a compliment then I'll take it."

She smiled and took another swig. Not saying anything, she wandered across the room to the window and looked out.

"The view is kind of nice."

It wasn't, he knew that was a lie, it was grey and dull and boring, just building tops. But he liked how optimistic about even mundane stuff she always was, it was part of his attraction to her. "Thanks."

She looked at him and took another drink.

"I can't believe I'm the first here, I never am."

Matthew looked at his watch. 8.30. She had a point.

Where is everyone? he wondered. He looked at her and she looked back at him. Suddenly he realised that neither of them were saying anything, he tried to read her look, his mind raced. *Maybe she thinks I've killed them, maybe she thinks Tara is boiling in acid in my bathtub, oh god*! he panicked, internally. The silence was becoming unbearable. *Say something, ANYTHING!*

"I ordered Chinese," he said calmly, sipping from his beer.

"Cool," she replied and nodded.

He looked at his watch again. It was still 8.30.

"Although it seems to be running late."

She nodded, he looked at her, the silence began

to drift in again and, with it, Matthew's panic.

A knock at the door saved him, he darted his head toward it. He smiled politely, she smiled back.

"I should get that," he stated. "Might be the food." He stepped toward it when he heard it again. A wild screaming, muffled, but audible, like it was coming from right outside the door.

"Did you..." He turned to Kelsey, she was across the room, running her fingers across his CD collection, looking for Nu Wave Punk no doubt. He knew she'd be surprised, he had picked up CDs by some of the bands she'd mentioned, to try and build on their conversations, but of course he'd never really got round to listening to them and what he had heard was, well... awful. But she definitely hadn't heard the noise, or if she had, she had ignored it.

He turned back to the door and peered through the peephole. *No one there, again?* Surely someone must be playing a joke on him. Maybe this was Handcock's idea of a party game. If it was, Matthew wasn't impressed. He grasped the door and tore it open once again.

The corridor was quiet. He slowly glanced down, on the floor was a plastic bag, it had fallen in the floor jam and seemed to be full of...he looked closer... it was the bloody Chinese! Matthew leaned down over the doormat and picked it up. Holding the bag by both handles he peered inside. The food seemed okay, but it had been dropped on its side so some of the cartons had leaked a bit, although he was sure this wasn't enough from what he remembered ordering, some was definitely missing.

"They just dropped it on the floor and left?" he muttered out loud. "What kind of service is that?" "Everything alright?" Kelsey's voice echoed from the apartment.

Matthew pulled the bag in and closed the door.

"The delivery guy just left the food on the floor outside," he said. "Like, with no care in the world." "Maybe he was in a rush," she said. "I used to work at a restaurant, they expect those guys to deliver like 100 orders in an hour, it's crazy."

"Yeah, I suppose, it must be a lot of pressure," he said, half smiling. He didn't mean it. How hard could it have been to deliver food in a timely manner? With a bit of customer service? He was certainly paying enough to expect at least a smile and for someone to hand him a bag. The look on Kelsey's face told him that he would have to wait to complain once everyone had left, but he knew he *would* be complaining, and that someone would be fired for this. Or at least he wanted his £2.75 tip back - this was the problem with tipping with apps, no accountability.

Placing the jammy bag in the the the bin, Matthew looked to see what he could salvage. The prawn crackers had absorbed most of the oyster sauce that had leaked from one of the cartons, so they were for the bin. The noodles and special Chow Mein seemed contaminated with sweet and sour and vice versa. He threw those away. But there were cartons that seemed to remain sealed or hadn't leaked so badly. He enlisted Kelsey's help, watching as she cleverly transferred food into bowls and plate with no spillage. He used his app to list what each carton might be as they unveiled the contents, sliding them past him as they worked to gather the saveable food. It was like a montage in a movie, he was having fun and so was she, as far as he could tell. It had never happened before, a girl, in his apartment, making food just like a genuine couple. He could picture them cooking a meal together from scratch, maybe he wouldn't be such a bad chef after all.

Soon he had managed to create a miniature feast of beef and pork and chicken in various sauces and the surviving rice and wontons. Not bad. Probably about a quarter of what he ordered, but enough for two, maybe three people, if they didn't want too much.

But where were they? He looked toward the door, then at his watch - 9.05pm. *Very rude for everyone to be late*, he thought, *especially after I've made them this banquet. It's gonna get cold.*

"Everyone is late," he said to her.

"Shall I text Henry?" she said, pulling her phone out and starting to tap the screen.

"You have his mobile number?" Matthew seemed confused. "Is that not against policy or something?"

"Probably," she shrugged and tapped the phone as Matthew watched. *Why did she have Henry's number? I've never had Henry's number. Or hers. No one from office swapped numbers. Even these gatherings are organised by the electronic bulletin board at the office. I'm pretty sure that it was against company policy for the boss to have employees' personal numbers and the other way around. Why did she have it?*

Kelsey looked up at him. He realised he was staring at her, but she hadn't seemed to notice.

"You wanna eat?" Kelsey asked.

"What about everyone else?"

"Hey, if you snooze you lose." She smiled and playfully popped a wonton in her mouth whole, raising her eyebrows as she chewed on it.

"Fair enough," he laughed.

They started moving the food to the table. Matthew swept the crisps and chocolate aside and began setting the plates out. Kelsey, mouth full of food, another wonton probably, pointed to the chairs, gesturing to ask if she should move them to the table. He smiled and nodded.

Maybe this was fate, he thought. *Just me and Kelsey having dinner together, the start of something special*. Maybe this was his chance, they'd be living together before she even knew what was going on.

The night rolled on, Kelsey and Matthew listened to music that she chose, they laughed, they ate food, they drank beer and told jokes and funny stories. It was quickly becoming the greatest night of Matthew's life, all his trouble and anxieties began to drift away, he was in uncharted territory.

There was a moment when he thought he heard a knock at the door, but the music was loud and the laughter was flowing. Kelsey didn't seem to notice and as the scream echoed outside, it was almost completely drowned out by the 90s pop punk that she sporadically sang along with. He was almost sure he heard another scream, but now, in this moment, all he could do was focus on her. This was his moment, their moment, maybe one of these dreadful punk songs would be 'the song', the one for their wedding. He chose to be in the moment for the first time ever and it felt good. He was glad no one turned up, what a story to tell their children, a dinner party he threw, with no guests...

"Except your mother". He smiled at the thought, she looked at him.

"What?" she said, checking her face for any rogue sweet and sour. "Something on my face?"

"No," he said. "I'm just having a great time."

"Me too," she smiled. "It's nice, just you and me."

He glanced at the clock, it was 11.10pm. No one would be coming now. It was just the two of them, for the night.

Is this the moment? he thought. *Do we kiss? Do I kiss her?*

He looked at her, her face still a smile. He started to lean in, he was going to do it.

Suddenly her phone buzzed on the table, like a jolt of electricity. The whole thing shook, she whipped her head toward it, reached out and grabbed the handset. He'd missed his moment, but maybe it would be okay. She would just check the phone and it would be her sister or her friend and then they'd... "It's Henry," she said. "He's outside."

Henry? He thought. *Henry fucking Handcock,*

and at this time of night? That fucking bastard, he's ruined everything.

Kelsey went to stand. Matthew stopped her.

"No, I'll get it." He smiled at her and wandered toward the door. Maybe he would get lucky, maybe there would be a strange noise and an empty corridor, like every other time tonight. But as he approached, nothing. Just his luck.

He stood at the door and looked through the peephole.

"Please be empty," he begged in a whisper, but sure enough, there he was. Henry Handcock, in rounded fisheye vision, leaning against the wall a couple of feet away. "Fuck."

He opened the door and was greeted by the side eye of Henry Handcock, his greasy slicked back hair and pencil thin beard running down his jawline to his 'Zod from *Superman 2*' goatee. He was over dressed, in a blue shirt and tie, decorated with white collar and cuffs. His grey suit trousers and shiny, pointed dress shoes finished the look. He looked much too smart to be swinging by a colleague's house for drinks. He held his finger up, his phone in his hand and his other hand by his ear.

"Well you said that last time," Henry said, much to Matthew's confusion. "Will there at least be cocaine?" Matthew leaned out to see that he was talking into his Bluetooth headset. He kept his finger up at Matthew as he finished his conversation. "Right, well, I'll maybe see you in a bit." He tapped his phone and popped it in his pocket.

159

"Alright Matthew, how's the party popping? You know the lift is busted, right?" He took a long step over the doormat, pushing past Matthew. "Oh, and you need someone to have a bit of wipe down out here."

Matthew looked around, the jam seemed to have been tracked all over the floor, and more onto his mat. It was everywhere and, of course, just in time for his judgmental boss to arrive.

Nothing stays nice here, he thought, as something caught his eye.

Lying by the doormat was a Union Jack flask.

He recognised it. He leaned down and picked it up. It was definitely one he'd seen before, the one he'd seen Sandra drink from dozens of times. Sandra had been here. Tara had been here.

He turned and looked at Henry wandering into his apartment, taking it in. Henry turned and winked at him. Matthew stepped in, slowly closing the door.

He looked down at the wooden table, at Tara's bracelet, then the glasses he had found. He picked them up and studied them. There it was, the little silver square that he'd looked at over his cubicle every day, on *Dave's* glasses. Dave had been here too, they all had and then...

Matthew looked up at Henry as he greeted Kelsey with a smile and quick peck on the cheek. It made his blood boil as she smiled back, the sound draining from the room. All he could focus on was Henry as he moved in slow motion.

Henry killed them all! he thought. *They did come*

here and he was waiting and he killed them all... The terrifying thought dawned on him, *...and now he's come to kill us!*

Henry's voice suddenly cut through the silence.

"Oi! Matty!" Matthew looked up at him, his mouth agape. "You alright mate? You had too much beer?"

"Are you okay?" Kelsey stepped in. "You look like you've seen a ghost."

Matthew looked at her, trying to compose himself.

"Y... yeah," he stammered. "I... I'm fine." A perfectly reasonable response from someone looking at a serial killer.

"He been looking after you?" Henry said, looking at Kelsey. He turned to Matthew, "You been trying to get her drunk?" He laughed and then looked around. "Anyway, where is everyone? I know I'm fashionably late, but I thought they'd all be dancing the night away by now."

Matthew looked at him confused.

"I guess, they couldn't make it," he said calmly, trying to gauge Henry's reaction.

"Shame, that." Henry looked across the table of food and drink. "Looks like you two have been having quite the party." He grinned at Kelsey and she nudged him teasingly before looking at Matthew.

"We've been having a great time," she smiled. "Lots of good music."

Henry had stopped listening. He looked at his watch, 11.10pm.

"Oh, the boxing is still on." He walked to the TV and looked around. Glancing at the remote, he snatched it up and turned the TV on. "You don't mind, do you?" he said, looking at Matthew.

"N... No," Matthew said. "Be my guest." Henry was already looking at Kelsey.

"Pass me a beer, will you Kels?" he commanded,

Kels? Matthew thought. He's calling her Kels? He has a nickname for her? He has some nerve coming in here and murdering everyone and calling her Kels."

Kelsey handed him a beer as Henry pulled the armchair close to the TV and settled in for the match.

Matthew looked at him as Kelsey sat on the arm of the chair, watching it with him.

This has to stop, Matthew thought. *He's getting way too comfortable with her, and he's probably a murderer.*

He waited a few moments, his mind a racing. What to do? Should he call the police? Should he try and apprehend Henry Handcock himself? Maybe, he could hold him at bay with a kitchen knife until the police arrived... he'd be a hero, Kelsey would have to like him then, after all he'd have saved her life and...

"Matthew?" she said, slicing into his running daydream. "You okay?" She half mouthed it as to not draw attention to the fact she was asking, not that Henry would notice, he was now engrossed in the boxing.

Matthew beckoned her toward him quietly; she

162

frowned and got up, walking toward him with haste. "What is it?" she said,

Matthew put his fingers to his lips, his face red and veiny. Kelsey noticed, lowering her tone.

"What is it?" she whispered.

"I think..." He paused, Kelsey hanging on the silence. "...I think Henry is a serial killer."

Kelsey looked at him, she frowned and then looked at the man sat drinking a beer and jeering at the match on TV.

"Henry?" she whispered. "Are you serious?"

Matthew looked at her and then over her shoulder, he could see she didn't believe him. He needed proof, but wait, he had it.

"I know what it sounds like," he said, "but I can prove it." He grabbed her by the hand and pulled her toward the wooden table by the door.

She looked at the collection of stuff that had gathered.

"Tara's bracelet, right?" he said. She looked at it as he held it up. "You said it yourself, you'd seen her wearing it." She nodded. Matthew picked up the glasses. "These," he said, "are Dave's glasses, I've seen him wear them every day for four years. They were outside earlier."

Kelsey took them, studying them. She nodded, as if she seemed to be coming round to his thinking. Matthew grabbed the flask and lifted it up.

"And this belongs to Sandra," he exclaimed. "I've seen her use it at the office all the time. This exact one."

"Well, that seems like a HR issue..." she said,

"...but I get your point." She turned and looked at Henry. "And you think that Henry killed them?"

Matthew nodded.

"And why would he do that?" she asked.

"I don't know. He's a sociopath for sure, its not much of leap from there to the psycho kind of path, right?"

Kelsey looked at him. Her look was weird, like her feelings had been hurt. She became serious for a second.

"He's actually quite lovely," she said. "Once you get to know him."

Matthew looked at her, baffled as to why she was trying to defend him. The guy was a complete toad.

"Well," she continued, breaking the silence, "there's one way to find out." She turned and walked toward Henry, almost striding, with intent.

What the hell is she doing? Matthew's brain screamed as she stopped right next to him and blurted it out.

"Henry!?" Henry looked up from his beer, puzzled, his face painted with annoyance. "Matthew thinks you're a serial killer."

Henry frowned at her and let out a laugh that was joined by half a mouthful of beer. Matthew screamed in his head.

What the fuck is she doing?!

"You what?" he guffed. "What the bloody hell you been drinking tonight? Turps?"

"Are you, or are you not a serial killer?" Kelsey stopped and pointed to the table.

"Of course not, you nutty tart," he said.

"Well, how do you explain a bunch of stuff from the office being here?" She pointed to the table. Henry looked over at it. He stood up and stepped closer. "Matthew found this stuff outside in the hall and seeing as you're the only one who *did* arrive, I think we deserve an explanation."

"You're having me on, right?" Henry laughed and looked at them. Matthew's face was deadly serious. "Are you being serious?" he said, his neck pulling backward. "You think I murdered who? Tara? Dave?"

"A....and Sandra," Matthew added, shaking a little nervously. "I know you killed them Henry, I... I know you're some kind of sicko."

Matthew panicked as Henry approached him. What could he do? His phone was on the table by the food. The kitchen was too far away to grab a weapon. All he had was the corkscrew in his pocket. He whipped it at Henry's face as he stopped right in front of him. Henry looked at it.

"Well, I don't know what little game you're playing here Matthew, but it's all a bit fucking sick for my tastes." He turned to Kelsey and looked at her. "And you think he's onto something do you?" Kelsey looked at him, then she laughed.

"Of course not." She looked at Matthew. "Of course he's not a killer."

Matthew stood there stunned as the two of them stared back at him, he wasn't really sure what to do. Henry put his empty bottle down on the table with the corridor trinkets and turned right back to

Matthew's face.

"I'll talk to you on Monday," he said calmly. "Maybe we'll have a discussion about how you treat guests." Henry turned to Kelsey. "I'm meeting some people down The Swan if you wanna come."

"I'll be right out," she said. "Let me just have a word with Matthew."

"Suit yourself," he said. "I'll go have a fag in the corridor." With that he pushed past Matthew and walked to the door. Matthew caught him with one final sneer as the door closed.

He turned and looked at Kelsey.

"What the fuck was that?" he said.

"Come on Matthew, you can't just accuse innocent people of things like that."

"But I thought..." He looked at all the stuff on the table.

"Come on Matthew, the joke's over, it's gone too far," she said.

What was going on? Did she really believe that I had planted the stuff here? Why would I? Why would she think I would even do that?

A scream came from behind the door. Matthew turned and looked. The TV was loud, muffling the sound, and Kelsey didn't seem to notice. Matthew looked at her. "You didn't hear that?" he asked.

"Hear what?" she shrugged. "Enough is enough Matthew, I think maybe you need some rest." Matthew looked at her. Suddenly it all seemed to be coming together.

"Oh my god," he said. "Did you do this? Did you kill them?" He looked at the door. "Were you both in on this?"

Then, in a split second, the building fell into darkness.

The streetlights were too far away to make any impact on the interior lighting of the flat. Matthew scrabbled around in the dark. How did she cut the power? No, she was stood right there. It must have been Henry, she'd been the distraction and now he was alone with a serial killer in his apartment. He reached for his phone.

The table, he realised. Feeling his way across the room, he bumped into stuff as he went. "Matthew?" He could hear Kelsey's voice across the room. "Matthew, where are you?" she called in the dark.

He felt around, his hand landing in cartons of food. He knocked over some bottles, then he found his phone. A noise, the door of the flat opening. It was him, Henry, they were going to kill him. The council flat version of Mikey and Mallory, come to off him. He swiped on his phone and hit the torch icon, pointing it up to see his killers.

The spotlight from his phone landed on Kelsey, not ready to pounce, but stood by the open door to the corridor.

"I think I'm gonna go Matthew," she said sternly. He had never seen this expression on her face before, she looked mad and sad and angry all at the same time. "But if you wanted to get me alone, this was..." she looked around, "...this was a weird way of doing it."

She opened her torch on her phone and shone it down the corridor as she stepped out, shining it down to make sure she avoided the spillage on the floor.

Matthew, baffled, stood up, staggering after her. He stepped into the hallway, Kelsey's torchlight bouncing off the walls as she got to the elevator. The hall was empty. No sign of Henry, or anyone but her.

Kelsey was hammering the lift button as Matthew stepped into the corridor.

"Kelsey, wait," he shouted. "I'm not sure what is going on here, but I didn't have anything to do with it."

She looked at him down the hall.

"You can't just accuse people of being murderers Matthew," she said.

"I know," he mumbled. "Please come back, help me figure out what's going on? Henry might still be out here."

"No," she said. "He's gone to The Swan and that's exactly where I'm going." With that, she took for the stairs, disappearing into the dark. Matthew listened to her footsteps disappearing down the footwell as he stood, alone.

"What the fuck just happened?" he said, confused. Why did no one show up? Why was their stuff left outside his door? Was Henry behind it? What about the screams? None of it made sense.

Something wasn't right, he could feel it, right in his feet, like an intense pain. An actual, real pain. Matthew looked down, his feet were suddenly in agony, terrific pain bolted through his body. He pointed his phone torch down, to see his doormat. It was opening up, like a large hairy mouth, full of fangs, sucking him in, its teeth dragging him into its gullet. His phone landed on the floor as he tried to grab onto something, anything! He screamed.

As his neck and head were pulled inside, he saw, in the light of the phone's screen, Henry's earpiece, spattered with jam. But it wasn't jam, was it? It was blood. They'd all been eaten by doormats, vicious, man-eating doormats, and as he floated there in acid, and the bodies of his workmates bobbed around him, in various stages of skeletal digestion, Matthew realised that at least he

didn't have to face Kelsey again on Monday. Through the excruciating pain, he smiled as his face melted away.

Floor 8

Annie Knox

The eighth floor of Castle Heights is not technically supposed to be there. After construction in the 60s, workers walked away without looking back, none of them aware that at some point during planting beams, layering bricks, plastering walls and installing doors, an entire additional floor had appeared in the centre of the building.

If you get into one of the two service lifts in Castle Heights and reach for the button to take you to your floor, you will find your finger never hovers over number eight unless you put immense concentration into it. If you were to try and push on number eight, the lift would become inexplicably jammed, and you would have to sit in the bright red of the alarm light while awaiting the arrival of assistance.

Trevor - the assistance - would arrive in a timely manner and question what the hell you did to get the lift stuck. You would pause, scratch your brain, and wonder what the hell you *did* do. Because beyond getting into the lift, and being stuck in the lift, you would have a blank space in your memory. Nothing beyond a niggling sense in the back of your skull that you were very close to finding the answer to a question you couldn't remember asking.

The fire escape seems to hop from seven to nine with no plausible explanation - if you were to run the flights in a fiery panic, you would be able to swear truthfully, hand over heart, that you had covered two floors worth of stairs. And yet you would not have seen the eighth floor.

If you were to find yourself puzzling over who inhabits floor eight, no names or faces would spring to mind. If you were to ask Trevor, he would tell you that people lived in there, alright, people lived there. Who, you would pester. Who lives there, Trevor? And he would tell you again, infuriatingly vaguely, that make no mistake, *somebody* lives there. *People* live there.

And then he would abruptly lose interest in talking to you.

Sheri walked into Castle Heights feeling in the lining of her gut that something wasn't right. Gregory 'Greggers' Dixon walked ahead of her. When he had shaken her hand outside, the slick sweat on his palm had made her skin crawl. Catching sight of her reflection in the glass of the door as she approached, she wondered if she had overdone her make-up.

'Clarice: uninhibited, confident in her sexuality, empowered' had been the description of the casting she'd found online. She had read through the character profile and envisioned a sexier version of herself wearing a badass black latex bodysuit and towering heeled boots. She'd imagined herself kicking nutsacks, delivering those one-liners that make it to GIF status. Being hot, emotionally detached. Confident.

Being the complete opposite of herself.

The funny thing was the fact that Greggers had

sought her out.

A few weeks beforehand, she had been shocked and saddened when, upon posting a few selfies online and asking for advice on her casting type, she had been told 'girl next door', 'nerdy friend', 'funny geek'. 'That kid who does like half the work on the computer but then gets kidnapped despite being left behind for their own safety', and, the rotten cherry on the rubbish cake, 'your everyday girl'. Very much not Clarice. Which is why she had sighed, resigned to her fate to be boring, and clicked away from the page to hunt for more 'everyday girl' roles.

So, Greggers coming out of the blue had been flattering. His message had been professional, written in the plural - '*we* think you have a great look, *we* would love to invite you to an audition'. He had been friendly, polite, and very, very formal.

She hadn't questioned, even for a second, his legitimacy. Reading the script, Sheri had bitten her lip at the scarily sexy scenes and decided to ask about it once she had already blown the mysterious, multiple-personnel jury's socks off.

Now, catching sight of her reflection, she realised she might have gone a bit too wild with trying to fit Clarice's profile. It was getting on for quarter to nine, which apparently was the only available audition slot left. 'We really think you could bring a lot to the role,' the latest email had said. 'We're supposed to wrap up at half eight but we're willing to stay later to give you a chance.' *Lucky me*, Sheri had thought. *They must really like me.*

Red lipstick looked alien on her face - which was because she wasn't wearing it with the same confidence she had been when she'd left her house an hour and forty minutes ago. Her black, heavy eyeliner was thick on her lids, eyes panda-like. Her blusher looked like punches on her nervous-pale skin. Her hair - which she had washed, dried, straightened, re-curled, hair-sprayed and then jammed up into a complicated, plaited, half-up half-down style - looked stiff and stray hairs were starting to poke up left, right and centre.

'Please come ready to take on the character, however you may imagine her,' the email had said. 'We're looking for someone who we can immediately envision as our strong, confident lead female.' In the spirit of Clarice, Sheri had gone online and ordered herself a new top - nothing too sexy, just a black vest top with a cheeky bit of lace. She was wearing it with a pair of black tights, a cute skirt, and, of course, heeled boots.

The girl looking back from the glass in Castle Heights' front doors certainly didn't look like Clarice. No, she looked like a twelve-year-old who had accidentally put on an older girl's clothes and made a mess playing with her mum's make up. She looked like trash.

"You look...great." Greg gave her an awkward snort-grin-laugh, flashed a thumbs up while wildly avoiding prolonged eye contact. His irises hopped all over the place, scared to land for a second too long. "Really cool. Really...uh...in character. As you actors say. Ha!" The volume of the barked 'ha' made her flinch, and he cough-snort-grin-laughed again, wiping his nose with the back of his hand.

This, Sheri thought with clarity, *cannot be the person who was emailing me*. She followed him through the door, eager to get in front of the other casting directors and not be alone with this weird man longer than strictly necessary. She wished with her entire heart that she hadn't swallowed two whiskey miniatures for luck on the walk from the station. She was suddenly sure her entire body reeked of alcohol.

"Just taking her upstairs, Trevor," Greg told the old guy behind the counter. "If...uh...if that's cool? I cleared it all. With, uh, Tom. You know Tom."

"Aye." Trevor eyed Greg with displeasure, turned his gaze on Sheri. She felt an unexplainable mixture of defensiveness and pre-emptive anger. "I know Tom. He knows about this lass?"

Greg froze. "I'm just another actress," Sheri found her moron mouth opening and saying. "I'm just here to audition. Like the other girls." She tried to smile, convinced that the old guy thought she was a hooker.

He raised his eyebrow a little. "Aye? That right, is it?"

Sheri looked at Greg for help. Greg resembled a rabbit caught in headlights. There was an incredibly awkward pause.

"Well?" Trevor grunted. "Why're you standin' there?"

"R-Right. Right!" Greg grinned, cheeks bulging, and half-bowed at the concierge, whose nose wrinkled. Greg turned back to Sheri and did some awful, semi-curtsey sweeping action towards the lifts. "This way."

Sheri shot another smile in the concierge's direction. For some reason his hair made her think of her grandad, and she felt unhappy. Following Greg into the lift, she turned to see the doors shut slowly, like they were giving her a final chance to escape.

Greg let out an upsetting, high-pitched squeak of a laugh. "That man. What a weirdo!"

"Yeah... was he like that with all the girls?"

"Oh, yeah. Big time weird," Greg nodded seriously. "With all of them. Freaked some of them out, made them nervous. Touch of stage fright. You'll be alright, though. You look great."

Something in Sheri eased a little. "Are you sure? I feel like I've overdone it." Something caught her eye. "Oh - didn't the email say floor nine?"

Greg frowned. "Yeah. That's where we're going."

Sheri stared at the display. Buttons one to eighteen were available to press, and number eight was lit up. Very unmistakably, number eight.

"But..." she tried to ask, weakly. "But... you've pressed number eight."

Greg huffed. "Looks like someone's got stage fright after all. Are your eyes alright?" He snorted. "Did you have a few pints on the way here, huh?" Sheri cursed herself as she literally felt her entire face turn lobster-flame-volcano-hot red. Shame sweat broke out on her forehead, under her bra, down her back. Greg's laughter faded at the sight of her glowing cheeks.

"Oh." Greg bit his thumb. The lift stopped juddering, doors slid open. Sheri looked at the panel. One hundred percent, no doubt about it, they were on floor number eight.

Greg walked out.

"I'm sorry." Sheri tailed him. "I'm so, so - WOAH!"

She leapt right back into the lift, both feet leaving the floor with her body's knee-jerk reaction to the sight of three spiders waddling across the carpet. "Oh, god!"

Greg stared at her. "What are you doing?"

"Sorry, sorry." She was half-crouched into the corner like she was bracing for an earthquake. "God, sorry." *Stop apologising!* the part of her brain that wasn't paralysed with fear yelled. *You're acting like a crazy idiot!"*

The remainder of her brain was replaying just how close her feet had come to touching one of their gross little spindly legs and questioning if she should go ahead and jump out of the nearest window to get away from them.

"Sorry." *Damn it, Sheri!* "I just...I really, really don't like spiders."

"Oh." Greg looked at the floor like he was trying to spot a needle in a needlestack. "Well, looks like they're gone now."

They were sitting right there. Only bare inches from his left shoe. Three of them. Truly, unless one was blind, it would be impossible not to see them.

Had she wandered through a hallucinogenic cloud that day?

"Are you coming? Or…." Greg hovered. He was holding his hands close to his chest in a way that made him look a bit like a T-Rex. A confused, gawky, slightly creepy T-Rex.

"Uh, yeah. Of course." Sheri forced herself out into the hall, trying not to be overly obvious as she practically rubbed herself against the wall in order to tiptoe away from the spiders. "I just hate spiders so much. They really freak me out. Like, vomit freak out." She almost hurled as one of the spiders made a move towards her but managed to hold onto her stomach contents. "Sorry." *BLOODY HELL SHERI!*

"Anyway. About the - you know, the drink thing, I'm so sorry. It was only one of those miniature bottles. The tester bottles. Those like, five centilitre ones. Barely anything. I mean, I had two, so ten centilitres. I'm really sorry. I know it's unprofessional, but I was so nervous, and getting dressed up like this isn't my thing. I mean, for the character, I'd love it of course, on set, but to walk around London...I mean, if I was method, of course I would anyway, but…"

"Woah," Greg held out a hand, stopping them in the middle of the hall. Sheri absently wondered why it was so cold, and if she was safe standing in a hallway where the walls were coated in a layer of mould so thick she could spread it on her toast.

"Calm down." Greg gave her a flash of a smile, eyes flickering to meet hers and away, hers and away, like they were on springs. "Stop stressing."

"Okay."

"Deep breath," he told her, and he mimicked taking a big breath. Feeling a little like a child with a babysitter, she dutifully followed along, and did feel better.

"Look, I didn't want to say this and be...you know, unprofessional." He smiled, eyes going back and forth, back and forth. Did he get motion sickness? "But you really do look amazing. So in character. Like, the second I saw you, I could see it. Sheri, Clarice, what's the difference?"

He shrugged cartoonishly, and she laughed a little, even as the shame of being caught out stayed in the tips of her ears and nose.

"Really?" She tried for a cute shoulder shrug. "I thought it was too much."

"No!" He waved his hands. "It's perfect, you're perfect. Uh, for the film. Really cool and stylish. And... confident. Like the brief said….um...liberal. And… you know." He waved his arms around, drowning in his attempts to be supportive. Sheri felt some confidence starting to pump its way through her blood again.

"Do the…" he gestured with his hands wildly. "Do the line. The one she says when she kills the third guy. With the machete."

"What?" Sheri glanced around. "Here?" She knew she had a smile on her face. His flattery was working on her.

"Yeah!"

"Um...okay then. Okay." She set her feet apart.

No matter if she aced her audition, if this little practise was rubbish it would set a bad precedent. Consistency is key. Adaptability. Spontaneity. Authenticity. Always be ready.

Sheri rolled her shoulders back, flicked her hair - feeling better about it now, *of course*, if she was killing guys all over the place her hair would be a bit messy, *it was the character* - and cleared her throat. Cleared her mind.

"I told you. My bite is way, way worse than my bark."

She jumped back to standing normally, bit her lip, pulled a what-do-you-think-am-I-rubbish face at Greg. He let his mouth drop open, held his palms out in a wow-I-am-stunned way.

"Bam. I mean, that was it, wasn't it? That's the character!"

GOD, YES, THANK YOU, AND THANK YOU TOO SHERI, FOR BEING A LEGEND.

Outwardly, she beamed, held her hands together. "Are you sure?"

"Am I sure?" he laughed. "If it were up to me, you'd be cast already. Come on, let's go in." Greg led her to the room at the end of the hall – fifty-six, except the six was hanging upside down from the loose screw in its bottom, so it looked like fifty-nine at a jaunty angle.

"Um…" She wondered if she should just let Greggers realise his own mistake. "Didn't the email…didn't it say apartment fifty-seven?"

Greg gave her a look. "How much did you drink?" She felt herself flush in ice-burn shame again. "Aw, come on, I'm teasing. But seriously, what number are you seeing on the door?"

Sheri bit her tongue. Decided to just let him figure it out when the key didn't work.

From one of the nearby rooms a bunch of kids were laughing like hyenas, grating on her ears.

"Are you dyslexic? I had a mate at school who was dyslexic, and he used to mix stuff like that up. Ah - there you go."

To Sheri's amazement and confusion, the key worked.

She followed Greg in, and he shut the door behind her. The first thing to hit her was the smell - stale, musty, damp. It reeked, and she valiantly didn't react in the name of not upsetting any casting directors in the vicinity.

"So, is Tom one of the crew members? Should I take my shoes off?"

"Yeah, go on." The light flicked on and the hall was thrown into sharp relief. It was disgusting. Sheri wished fervently that she hadn't offered to remove her shoes. Gingerly, she tip-toed out of them and tried not to cringe at the uneven, bumpy, gritty dirty floor only a thin layer of sixty denier tights away. Greg grinned at her. They stood awkwardly.

"So...uh...what position is he? Tom." She tried to shake off the weird nervous feeling that was coming back. "Is he...a producer, or something?"

"Tom? Yeah, yeah. Tom's crew, alright." Greg led her through the apartment. It was absolutely vile. The light bulbs dangling from the ceilings didn't have lampshades and threw out a dim yellow glow.

There was only bare furniture there; a sofa in a small lounge, covered in a thick layer of dust, a dirty table with very upsetting stains on it. A few wooden chairs. A small kitchen sat behind the lounge area, and through an open door she caught a glimpse of a very nasty-looking bedroom.

"This is actually his place," Greg continued. "We're low budget, like the emails said. We didn't want to spend money on an audition space just for the sake of, you know, appearance." *Did he mean* professionalism, wondered Sheri, and then immediately felt like a cow. "So Tom, cause he's a producer, he offered to let us use his flat."

"Right. And, uh...where is...everyone?"

"Well, about that." Greg busied himself in the kitchen, not looking at her. "Remember we told you we were squeezing you in specially? Because we really thought you looked promising. Going to go places! Hollywood, one day, I'll put money on it."

The compliment successfully disarmed her.

"But, ah, they offered their time when they didn't really have any." A snort-giggle-laugh. "They all had to run to some networking event. There's this hotshot rich guy there. The guys want to talk him into funding the film. He might be able to give us proper money. You know, fifteen thousand."

"Pounds!?"

"Yeah!" He turned around, looking just as childishly enthusiastic at the prospect of a fifteen-grand film as she felt. In his hand was a glass of wine. When on Earth had he poured himself that?

He saw her gaze. "You don't mind, do you?" He took a sip. "It was a long day, you know, watching all these girls. And I figured you wouldn't mind since...you know."

"You won't tell the others, will you?"

"It's our little secret." He grinned over the glass. "You want? Ease the nerves before we do any of the scenes?"

"Um…"

"Oh, go on." He winked. "All the greats do it, you know. Hollywood secret. Keep me company."

Sheri, in all her naivety, honestly didn't think that it was the wrong thing to do. She thought it would help her have an edge on all the boring, plain, samey-samey girls who would have auditioned before her. Greg thought she was fun, she could tell. And, she reminded herself, people met in pubs and bars and offered each other jobs all the time, so it really wasn't that different. She'd seen it on the TV.

"Sure," she smiled. "Just a little."

As he poured she looked around the living room, went over to the old TV. It looked shattered. She could see the entire room in a bizarre, colourless reflection through the spider-web broken glass. There was her, all distorted, eyes like hollows in her head, and there was what must be Greg, just behind her.

Except Greg was still in the kitchen. Sheri spun around.

Empty room.

"You alright?" Greg came over, held out a very full glass. "Was I boring you?"

"What?"

He pointed behind her. Turning, she looked at the busted TV. What was he pointing to?

"Have you seen it?" he asked. She squinted at the screen. Was she going crazy?

"Seen what?" She took an absent sip of her wine, glanced at Greg. When she looked back at the TV, it was on, and it didn't look nearly as broken as it had a second ago. A movie's opening titles were playing.

"Oh!" She recognised it straight away. "Yeah, I have! Mask of Thorn is one of my favourite films. I'd love to play a lead in something like that."

"You will." He clinked his glass against hers in an uninvited and unagreed upon toast. "You'll be playing a lead role very soon, Clarice!"

"You really think so?" She took another sip. The smell of the wine, a deep fruity red, invaded her nostrils and she couldn't smell the damp anymore. "I haven't even done the scenes yet."

"Nah, I know. I knew when I - we - found you online. We knew straight away you were the one, but we have to go through this whole process. For appearances, you know."

Something popped up in her brain, a little warning sign. She forcefully pushed it back down.

"Shall we do the audition?" She took another sip, thoughts of red carpets on her mind. "How will the other casting people know if they like me?"

"I'm gonna film it for them." Greg went to the kitchen, started messing with a box on the side. He took out a camera. "So I can show it to them later."

"Right, makes sense." Sheri sipped her wine. It was what confident, sure-footed Clarice would do. "What were the other girls like?"

"Oh." He wrinkled up his nose. "Boring. Plain. Samey-samey, you know? No spark."

I've got a spark! Sheri thought. The room around her actually seemed a lot nicer the more she looked. She had been too judgy about the dust. The stains on the table just looked like patchy wood. Under her feet, the carpet felt plush, and when she glanced down, there was just a faint red stain near her feet - more wine? - but no dirt.

From somewhere nearby, she heard children laughing. *I heard that in the hall*, she realised, and let her eyes wander the apartment. *Did they follow us in here?* she wondered. *Should I point it out to Greg?*

The laughter stopped. *Never mind*, she thought.

Glancing back at the TV, she lowered herself down and tried to see past the scene playing out on the screen, past the steel mask and piercing eyes of Thorn. She could make out the shape of herself and forced her eyes to focus. Yup, there was Sheri, featureless and distorted, and there was Greg, putting a tripod up behind her, and there was an odd shape right at the bottom of the screen, a semicircle. Sheri peered at it, trying to work out what it was. The shape shifted and rose up until she could see two eyes staring back at her from the darkness. It was the top half of somebody's head.

Sheri gasped and jumped, wine sliding neatly over the rim of her glass down to where her fingers were clenched around the stem.

"You alright?"

"Sorry!" Embarrassed, she turned quickly, swapping the glass to the other hand and licking some of the wine away from her palm. Greg's eyes caught on the action briefly, before darting away.

"Well." He tried to scoff-laugh-snort. "That's what you get for getting so close to a horror movie."

"Right." She tried to laugh and took another sip of wine to calm her heart, which was thumping hard in her chest. There hadn't been anyone next to her, she knew that as surely as she knew that they were in flat number fifty-six with an upside down six that made it look like a jaunty fifty-nine, just as surely as she knew that they were on floor eight.

"Anyway, are you ready?" Greg grinned. The camera was pointed at her, ready to film. He pulled up a chair, sat facing her. "Any questions?"

"Um…" Sheri sipped her wine. Frowned at the doorway to the bedroom behind Greg. Was someone - no way was someone - there, in the shadows…

"Sheri?" She blinked back at Greg, who looked impatient. "Do you need to run the lines?"

"No!" She took another drink, put the wine down. "I know it. I can do it."

"Alright." He rubbed his hands together. "Let's start with the scene between Sheri and Robert, okay?"

"Oh. Um…"

He paused, about to press record on the camera. "Problem?"

"It's just…" Now Sheri was the rabbit in headlights. She had no idea what to do and was beating herself up for it. A professional actress would know! And now she had to ask, she was going to look like an idiot. Plus, she was absolutely sure now that she had just seen somebody move in the bedroom. In the dark. "It's just, that scene is quite…intimate? I've never had to do any…intimate scenes. At an audition. So, I don't know…" She bit her lip. "I feel stupid, but how do I do it? Cause most of it is…kissing and… you know. Not much dialogue. So how would I…um…"

"Sheri." Greg had a condescending smile on his face that made her hate him and herself equally. How dare he condescend her. How dare she be so unknowledgeable. "You just do it with me."

"What?"

"I'm the casting director." He laughed a bit. "Duh! Come on. You're talented, but you need a bit of know-how. I'm casting, so I need to see how you will perform. And the guys who will watch it later need to as well. This is an important scene for Clarice, for her liberal nature, for her uninhibited personality. It really is key. Okay?"

Sheri scratched her ear, starting to feel sick. Wine on an empty stomach. She hadn't eaten, just to avoid bloating before performing. "Um. But how will you watch it? If you're…doing it?"

Greg paused. "Maybe this is a mistake." He gave

Sheri a kind, disappointed smile. "You're lovely, and you're talented, but maybe this role is too much. You seem nervous. I was really rooting for you, but we need someone bold. Explorative. Perhaps you would be better sticking to milder roles. You know, girl next door."

The dreaded words. "No!" She tried to swallow back the shout, be more professional. "I mean, no, I can do it. I can. I was just surprised. I can do it."

Greg nodded, returned to the camera. "You'll have to learn to expect surprises in auditions if you want to get anywhere." He pressed record. "You need to be able to adapt."

She kicked herself mentally.

Greg settled into the chair. "Go on."

Sheri straightened her back, thought like Clarice, bold, brave, independent, uninhibited.

"You made a mistake coming here." She started towards Greg, who licked his lips and rubbed his thighs. It set off another warning sign in her head, which she again forcefully pushed back. She slid her jacket off her arms, carefully reciting the stage directions in her mind. One arm out, other arm, toss the jacket to the side, lean forwards. "You messed with the wrong girl. Because this girl... I'm sorry, but is there somebody else here?"

Greg, who had been leaning forwards, getting into it, frowned. "What?"

"In the bedroom." Sheri wrapped her arms around herself. The figure she'd spotted in the dark bedroom ducked out of sight. "There! I saw them again!"

Greg looked into the room. "No? No, there's no one there. Look, are you serious about this or not, Sheri? I've stayed late just to audition you."

"I really think there's someone in there. I heard a voice." Sheri shivered, cold. "Please could you just check? And then I'll finish the scene, I promise."

He gave her a look that downright scared her silly in her gut, that made her feel like she would be finishing the scene regardless of if she promised to or not.

Greg got up and moved towards the bedroom. Sheri's stomach churned. She really thought she was going to...

Be sick. Sheri spun around, hand over her mouth. There was no one behind her, and certainly no Spanish man, which was unquestionably the voice she had heard. Before she could call out to Greggers, several ballpoints of solid weight ran over her foot. Sheri slowly lowered her eyes to the carpet and was faced with the sight of a spider the size of a golf ball scuttling around between her legs. As she stared, momentarily paralysed, hundreds of spiders suddenly emerged from the thick fibres of the carpet, rising up like a wave. Little legs protruding from the ground, bodies molting up and out of the floor, scurrying over her toes. She felt them under the arches of her feet, spawning from the earth like demons bursting from hell. Ghost sensations ran over her calves and ankles as they poured up her legs towards her thighs.

"Don't they make you sick?" asked the little boy sat on the sofa, staring at Sheri with wide, bug-like

eyes. He looked perfectly innocent, considering he had appeared out of thin air. "*You said you hate them. You said they make you throw up.*"

"*THROW UP!*" screamed the woman standing behind Sheri, her icy breath a gust of cold against her neck.

Sheri found herself staring down at a puddle of vomit in the kitchen sink. She panted a little, removed her hands from where they were clenched knuckle-white around the counter, confused. Her fingers trembled violently. She lightly touched her forehead, where she felt wet sweat. The taste of puke in her mouth confirmed for her that yes, that was what had happened, she had thrown up.

In the middle of her goddamned audition.

"Sheri?"

"Greg." She wished she had just jumped in front of the train instead of getting on it on the way there. "I'm sorry. I thought I saw…"

"Is this some kind of joke?" He looked angry. "You saw spiders in the hallway, you're seeing people in the bedroom, you tried to convince me we were in the wrong hall, the wrong room…"

"I think I'm ill." Sheri blinked hard. Most of the wine was out of her stomach and in the sink, but she was still tipsy. Blinking hard again, she frowned as something became apparent to her - she had been right about the state of the apartment. It did look terrible. And god, yes, it smelt awful, damp and rotten. She stared at the sofa, sure that she was missing something. A second ago hadn't there been something sitting there?

"You know what, I think this is enough." Greg started to tuck the camera away. "I don't think you're right for the role, we aren't going to get anything here."

"But…" Sheri swallowed, struggled to focus her eyes. Every other time she blinked, it seemed like there were people watching her from the corners of the living room. "But you said… you said I was perfect. You said if it was up to you, you would cast me."

"I changed my mind. If you can't even do one little scene…"

"I can!" To her absolute horror, Sheri felt her eyes fill with hot tears. "I can do it!" They started trickling down her cheeks. Greg stopped packing up and sighed deeply. When he looked at the water sliding down her flushed cheeks, his tongue flicked out to touch his lips and then vanished back into his mouth again, a snake waiting to bite.

"Are you sure?" He reassembled the camera without really waiting for an answer. "Because I'm a professional, Sheri. I don't like wasting my time."

"No, I can, I promise, I'm not wasting your time. I promise. Honestly." She wiped quickly at the tears, blinked hard again. Each time she blinked, she was unsure of precisely what she was looking for, she just knew that she had spotted something that she wanted to get another look at.

"Alright." Greg sat back in his chair. "Let's go, then. The tears add to it, you know. The others will like it when they see it. Makes Clarice look more vulnerable."

"Okay." Sheri sniffled hard, walked past the little girl sitting on the kitchen counter clutching a torn-up, bloodied princess doll. The girl tried to grab at her arm as she went but missed. By the time Sheri glanced back, she had forgotten there was a little girl there in the first place. She felt more tears run down her cheeks, and jutted her jaw out defiantly, ready to start the scene.

"You didn't throw up enough," said the little boy on the sofa. *"You were meant to throw it all up. I'm going to show you more spiders."*

"No, I don't like spiders," Sheri found herself saying, and then wondered why the hell she had done so. Greg stared at her, starting to look a little worried. "I mean, you messed with the wrong girl."

"Did someone put you up to this?" Greg asked. "Did you get in touch with Tom?"

"The producer?" Sheri shook her head. A Spanish man somewhere behind her told her in a firm voice to *ask him why you have to do this scene.*

"Why do we have to do this scene?" Sheri found herself asking, and once again, wondered what had prompted her to. Something in her gut stirred her on though.

As did the sensation of a small child's hand slipping into her own, and a young girl's voice saying *"Ask him why he was the one who stayed behind!"*

"Why didn't you go to the networking event?"

"Ask him why you didn't see them leave!" called out the boy on the couch, who was picking his nose. Sheri blinked and wondered, absently, why she was

once again looking at the sofa.

"Why didn't I see them leave?" She squeezed her hand around the little girl's, feeling the Spanish man step up close behind her back, feeling the woman with the ice breath behind her other shoulder, seeing the twins in the bedroom appear at the doorway, the boy on the sofa giving her the thumbs up, the man with the axe in the kitchen, the dog with no eyes by the door, and dozens of others who were gone in the next blink. "I was early. I was forty minutes early. I was outside the front door waiting for a long time. Why didn't I see anyone leave?"

"You're crazy." Greg got up, looking furious - but also a little scared. He avoided her gaze, went to the kitchen and took an angry gulp of wine, totally unaware that there was a similarly angry looking man with a huge blond beard and an axe standing right behind him.

"Why did you ask if I had spoken to Tom?" Sheri found herself emboldened. "What would he have told me if I had?"

Greg drank more, didn't look at her. Tears started to build in her eyes again as the thought she had been denying for the past hour could no longer be pushed down. "Is this even a real audition?"

Nothing. The little boy was standing on the sofa now, bare feet crusted with mud pressing down the puffy cushions, watching her with sad eyes.

"Is it real?" She wiped her face with her sleeve, unashamed of the fact that new tears immediately replaced the old ones. "Is there even a film? Is

Clarice real?"

"She is," Greg nodded. "She is real. Completely real. For the actress that got cast in the role last week."

Sheri's stomach dropped out.

"A brilliant actress," Greg shrugged. "A brilliant actress who applied to the casting call with a great cover letter, and got auditioned in a real studio, like you do with real actors. She was brave, bold, vulnerable. Experienced, strong voice. Good posture, carried herself well. A real woman, not a stupid little girl. Not a stupid little girl who fell for some nicely written compliments from an obviously fake email address. Not a stupid little girl who turned up to her audition drunk and made a fool out of herself, dressing like some kind of cheap hooker."

Sheri sniffed a great load of snot back up inside her nose, scrubbed her face one more time, nodded, put her jacket back on, and walked out into the hall. She put her heeled boots into her bag, and removed the trainers she had packed, putting those on instead. Let her feet take her out into the corridor and down towards the lift, through the mould-ridden walls, beneath the ugly, dingy light bulbs, past all the different apartment doors. She was still dizzy and let her hand trail along the wall for support, leaving a long streak in the mould and making her fingertips filthy.

Arriving at the lift, she pressed the button to call it, still having to pathetically wipe at her running nose with her sleeve. The button didn't light up, so she pressed it again and again and again.

"Please," she told the lift, giving up on dignity. "Please. I just want to go home." To the ceiling she directed: "You cannot possibly be this cruel. Come on."

"You can't leave." She turned around and the little boy was right behind her, all innocent sad eyes. *"Only one of you can leave."*

"Right," Sheri nodded. "Well, Greg can stay then. Who are you, by the way?"

Sheri waited a few seconds. And then wondered why she was staring at the ugly carpet instead of still trying to call the lift. She turned back and started jamming her thumb against the button again.

"You're an idiot!" Greg's voice came from down the other end of the corridor. "Did you even think to check the film on IMDb? Her name is already credited! Did you even tell anyone that you came here? How stupid can you get?"

"If he's the one staying, someone has to make him stay." The boy was leaning against the lift doors. *"The lift won't come otherwise, and you'll both be stuck until you starve to death. It only stops here when it wants someone to stay."*

"How can you possibly know what a massive rusty crapbox wants?" Sheri jammed her thumb hard on the button. "Besides, I'm definitely not staying here." Tears continued to work their way down to her chin. "I'm going home."

"Who are you talking to?" Greg was leaning out of number fifty-six, drinking from his glass. His upper lip had a horrid red-wine moustache decorating it. "You really are crazy."

A dog with no eyes padded out the door, unnoticed by Greg, and peed on the floor before its hind legs fell off. Sheri stared at it in shock as it dragged itself down the hall until two spider legs grew from its hips and pushed its behind back up into the air, so that it could walk again.

She blinked. What had she been looking at? She was sure it had been something very disturbing but couldn't for the life of her remember.

"You have to make him stay." A little boy with peculiarly big eyes looked up at her from her elbow.

Greg was coming down the hallway towards her.

"Why am I here?" She blinked hard, vision spotting out. "If there's no… no… no audition. Why… am I here?"

Greggers swallowed down the rest of his wine, letting the cup fall to the floor.

"Are you really that naive?" He wiped away his blood-wine-red moustache with the back of his hand. Sheri's legs wobbled indecisively before decisively giving out and dropping her butt to the dirty carpet. "Why do you think you're here?"

He started to walk down the corridor towards her, eyes gleaming behind his big glasses.

"You needed to throw up more!" A little boy crouched down in front of her suddenly, scared and upset. *"I told you to throw up more."*

"I wanted you to do it willingly. A little extra-charged wine, the promise of a film role. But if you won't go along with it, then I guess I'll have to do it slightly differently."

Greg squatted down by her splayed feet. Her back against the elevator, she could feel vibrations running up and down her spine where the machinery of the lift was humming away.

Greg leaned down, staring into her eyes. She felt his cold and clammy hands through her tights as he wrapped his fingers around her ankles, lifted her legs up, and pulled.

Her back dropped to the carpet; head thudding down in a way that made her brain - scrambled by spiked alcohol - bounce around inside of her skull.

"Sorry about this." A boy poked his head out of apartment fifty-four, held his palms out over her body. Rough carpet dragged at her as she was slowly, steadily, hauled down the corridor by Greg, her arms limp over her head.

A crawling sensation tickled her sides, her ribs, climbed up to her stomach. Sensitive skin along her inner thighs prickled. She felt something clambering into her palms, down her wrists. Up her stupid lacy top, all around her bra, into the dip of her collarbones.

Using most of her little energy, Sheri lifted her head ever so slightly, and saw that her entire body was covered in spiders. Her stomach rolled, her mouth dropped open and she screamed as one took the opportunity to leap inside and try to wedge itself into her throat, eight legs scratching frantically at her vocal cords.

Greg yelled and dropped her legs, startled by the scream. He saw Sheri choking on the floor, thrashing like she had been electrocuted. Greg didn't see the spiders, nor the little boy who was watching. The little boy who Sheri, and only Sheri, heard scream *THROW UP NOW!"*

Vomit spewed from her mouth as her body buckled and curled sideways. The spider was propelled out of her mouth and flung away as red-wine-acid-puke fell from her gasping lips to the dirty filthy floor. The boy grinned and gave her the thumbs up as she huffed for air.

"Jesus!" Greg leapt backwards. "Gross!"

The boy pointed at Greg. *"Now you have to kill him!"*

"Yes." A little girl crouched by Sheri's other shoulder. *"Once he's dead you can leave, and we'll have some fun with him."* A dog with no eyes appeared by Greg's feet and licked his leg with a tongue that seemed to produce blood instead of saliva.

"How am I meant to kill him?" Sheri was, as she watched Greg's eyes widen in surprise, at least 98% sure she was dead and that this was purgatory. Or that she was about to wake up from some weird coma.

"You what?" Greg looked utterly lost.

Sheri forced herself up. "I have to kill you." He blinked. "The little boy says so. I want to go home."

Greg blinked again.

"Sorry," Sheri shrugged. "I guess you messed with the wrong girl."

His disbelief turned into amusement. "You idiot." A laugh hooted from his stomach. "You silly, stupid idiot! Do you think that there's still a chance of me casting you in anything? Is this all some bizarre act to get a role?! I tricked you into coming here to have sex with you, you fool!"

As he laughed, Sheri moved forwards, and stamped down hard on the glass he had let fall to the floor, which the little boy and girl were dancing around and pointing at eagerly. Ducking down, she picked up the stem of the glass and launched herself at Greg.

Yelping, Greg ducked out of the way and the glass skimmed his chest, a shard leaving a long scratch bleeding out of his shirt.

"You crazy bitch!" Sheri was too quick; not stopping to think she slashed and slashed and slashed until he fell on his back and she fell with him and slashed and slashed and there were dozens and dozens and dozens of people around cheering and jumping and dancing and laughing and the little boy and girl were both yelling at the tops of their little voices in excitement and blood was slashing up and over and around and in her face and hot in her mouth and slash, slash, slash, slash, the dog barked and barked and barked and...

Sheri blinked.

The elevator doors opened smoothly in front of her with a little *ding*. Legs slow and stilted, hobbling in, she wondered why she had so many pains and aches all over her body. Her stomach was churning for an unknown reason. The taste of bile sat on her tongue.

Right, Sheri, she thought to herself. *You were waiting for the lift. Why were you waiting for the lift?* She squinted at the buttons on the panel. *Why are you in the lift, you silly sausage?*

Taking a wild guess, she hit the button for the ground floor. Two kids, a boy and a girl, were playing with something that looked bizarrely like a human hand at the end of the corridor. As the doors started to close, they looked up and waved sweetly. Feeling a sense of familiarity with them, Sheri waved back. Maybe she had seen them on her way in?

The doors closed and the lift juddered into life. Her stomach rolled even more as it began its descent down, crawling back towards the Earth. Catching sight of herself in the blurry, dirty silver she was momentarily stunned - her face, her neck, her jacket, seemed to be covered in what looked like blood.

"Woah," she whispered into the lift. "Woah, what?? What is that?"

Peering closer, she poked at a cheekbone, watched her dirty fingers rub and smear the crimson into her skin.

"Oh god." She looked down at her clothes, damp and saturated with blood. "Oh my god! What the hell!?"

A second later the lift wobbled into place and the doors wracked their way open. Her mind went blank again. Tottering out into the ground floor, she blinked owlishly at the night sky outside, and then at the concierge, who was staring at her with his eyebrows almost up in his hairline.

"Excuse me." She tried for a smile, totally

unaware of how the whites of her teeth were shining through where red had stained her gums. "Could you tell me what the time is?"

He gestured at the clock behind him on the wall. 11.00pm exactly.

"Right, thanks."

Sheri turned to the door, ready to head out again.

"Wait!"

She turned back. He was standing, gathering up tools from the desk.

"How was yer audition?"

Right. RIGHT! She had come for an audition! "Uh, I honestly can't remember," Sheri shrugged. "Probably a no, I guess."

"And what floor were ya on?"

Sheri scratched her hair, which felt incredibly matted. She had definitely used too much hairspray.

"I think number….um…" *Think, think, why can't you remember?* "…it was supposed to be floor nine but...but… I don't think that was where we went." She stared at the carpet for a long second, lost in the void of the last few hours.

"Aye." Trevor looked at her, fully aware that she had somehow wound up on number eight. "Well. I got to go fix an elevator. We had a malfunction."

"Right, right." Sheri smiled again, her cheeks starting to hurt. "Okay. Well, have a nice night. Good luck."

Trevor watched the crusty blood-covered girl head out into the night, vanishing into the darkness once she was a few feet away. *Weird*, he thought, and then checked his watch. 11.02 on the dot. Better get the lift fixed before the drinkers roll in on their way to bed.

Outside, Sheri wandered towards the train station, the wind biting her skin. She continued to wrack her brains desperately, wondering if she had done well or not. There was just a huge, long emptiness where the audition should have been, with only a lingering sense of intense anxiety left behind.

Unknown to Sheri, good old Greggers was watching her walk away from the window of the not-meant-to-be-there eighth floor, surrounded by the other people who lived there. He wasn't about to have a good night, not at all, made especially obvious by the blond chap who kept leering at him menacingly while hefting an axe between his hands.

"You're one of us now." A little boy with wide bug eyes was grinning at him evilly, as Sheri turned a corner and finally vanished from sight. *"That means we can touch you."* The kid's face twisted into a grin that literally split his skin ear-to-ear, and a lolling great tongue fell between sharp twisted teeth.

The inhabitants of the eighth floor converged on the newbie.

***

Sat on the train, riding her way back to her life and back to more casting applications, Sheri caught the eye of some scared looking couple on the train and wondered why they were getting up and running away down the carriage.

Glancing out of the window, she just - only very slightly just - caught sight of Castle Heights as she was about to be whipped around a corner. And just before - just the second before - it vanished from her sight, as the time on her phone ticked to 11.40pm, she saw that all the lights in the building disappeared.

Then the train made its twisting, jerking turn, and it was put out of her mind.

The Unravelling in Apartment 58

Damon Rickard

On the 9th floor of Castle Heights, Lizzie and apartment 58 witness the clock turn 9pm. Well, actually, it is 9.04 because the clock was slow but neither knew and neither would have minded anyway. Accuracy of time keeping is not currently high on the agenda. The lights inside the apartment fill the rooms with a dull luminescence, the one in the lounge crackling with electricity like it was laughing at Lizzie. Pfffzzz, it said to her, over and over. She stares back at it, hating that it was the only sound in the room. Even her husband William remains silent, lit by the yellow hue of the incessant crackling light and the blue of the silent TV which he just sat staring at.

Lizzie, a slight black woman who had decided she was rather plain with no distinguishing features, had turned thirty earlier that day. There was no fanfare. No balloons or party poppers. Just an earlier trip to the store to get the weekly groceries. Thankfully, when she returned around 4pm, loaded with the fruits and vegetables of her labour, the concierge of the building, Trevor, was there to help her get the shopping up to the apartment. The lifts could take forever to turn up so, in his soft Scottish drawl, he offered to assist in carrying them up the stairs for her. Calling William would have been of no use to her.

"How is your fine man?" asked Trevor, as he

huffed his way up each stair, clearly trying to belie his unwanted age.

"He's as he should be," she replied. "No more, no less."

Her tone was stern when answering so Trevor felt it wise to change the subject. Perhaps they'd had a fight and the last thing he wanted tonight was to get in the middle of a domestic argument.

"Well, it's great to see you out," Trevor said as he continued his attempt to converse without bringing William into it. Lizzie turned and looked at him with a stare that ran his blood cold. "I don't know what you mean," she scolded.

Trevor's regret was instant, deciding not to say anything else unless asked a question. They ascended the rest of the climb in silence with the only sounds being their footsteps on the concrete steps and Trevor's heavy breathing, which was becoming noticeably heavier as they went. It almost started to sound like his breathing had an accent. The stairwells were cold and unwelcoming, a reminder of a forgotten building that was supposed to be a centrepiece of the area but never managed to become more than just another block of apartments, housing those in society that everyone else would rather not consider. A place where trouble could be considered normal, and the police don't rush to when called.

When they got to the 9th floor, they headed down the dingy corridor to number 58. Once there, Trevor put the bags down, pressed his hands to his hips and thrust his groin forwards.

"Need to stretch the old back out," he explained and Lizzie smiled.

"Well, thank you for helping, Trevor. That was very kind." She began fumbling for her key in her purse as Trevor watched on. "Thank you," she said again, only more forcefully this time.

"Oh. Of course. How silly of me. Enjoy your night, Mrs Creasey." Trevor turned to the lifts, clicking the call button and causing it to be illuminated. He looked back over his shoulder as Lizzie stood there, watching him, and he felt her eyes burning into him. He pressed the button again frantically in the hope that it would make the lift arrive sooner but could hear no whirring cogs of a lift moving.

"Looks like there may be an issue with the lifts," he said as he turned back around to Lizzie. She smiled back with a look that said she didn't care and just wanted him gone. So, he obliged, pretending to tip an invisible hat to her and marched off back down the corridor. When he arrived at the stairs, Lizzie could hear him take one large breath before hearing his footsteps patter back down to his greeting post.

Lizzie huffs as the annoying bulb snaps her back from her daydreaming, immediately thinking to herself she must remind Trevor about the light. He was supposed to have arranged for it to be fixed. She moves her attention to the TV and sees that William is in front of what looks like a low budget horror film on channel 5. She never understood why he liked such things. She huffs again and takes herself into the kitchen, the light crackling spitefully at her as she leaves. The kitchen was as clean as she could keep it, with markings on the walls that remained from the previous occupants. Often, she had stared at the stains wondering what took place to leave them there like a message from the past. All she knew about the previous occupancy was that one day they were there, the next they were not, so an apartment was suddenly available for her and William to move into.

A lot of the food from her shopping trip was still on the kitchen counters as Lizzie quickly lost motivation to find homes for most of it after her annoying stair climb with Trevor. Casting her eyes over it all, she was hoping to find a renewed sense of enthusiasm for stuffing cans in cupboards, but it never arrived, no matter how hard she stared at the cans, or the cupboards. She thought to herself that a few minutes laying down on the bed would sort her out and she could contact Trevor after that too. Pfffzzz. She was certain this place hated her almost as much as *she* hated *it*.

The bedroom was sparse, with just a small wardrobe, a small TV on a small table and small bedside tables either side of a small bed. Your usual bedroom staples such as a mirror, clothes strewn on the floor, and a hairdryer, completed the room's makeup. On her bedside table sat a photo in a frame and a phone charger. On his, an ash tray, even though he was forbidden from smoking inside. There was, however, one object in the bedroom, which was new to the space and looked wildly out of place. A box, or even what could be described as a trunk. It was large enough to be called such and appeared locked. Lizzie paid the unusual addition no mind as she lay down on the bed. The bed itself was just big enough for the two of them. Just. Once they had saved enough money, a new bed was top priority. She couldn't stand him rolling on top of her for much longer. It was always the same. They'd drift off facing in opposite directions and not long after she'd be woken up by a rogue arm flopping on her head, followed by him turning and ending up as much on her as he was on the mattress, snoring right in her ear. This was, of course, only on the nights he was home. Working late, he'd say. Had one too many at the pub so Doc is putting him up for the night, he'd say. But when he returned in the mornings, she didn't smell booze or the office on him, no, it was definitely something more unseemly.

The memories of the smell stuck with her as she drifted off to sleep, her mind replaying an unpleasant scene in her head.

"Who is she?" she'd yelled at William, the pffzzz of the light punctuating the end of her sentence.

"Have you taken your pills today? There is no 'she,' you crazy bitch," came his measured response.

"I can smell her all over you," Lizzie carried on, as she shot William a look that could make most men wither. He waved her away and started to walk off when she grabbed his arm. "Who is the whore you've been fucking when you leave me here on my own to look after everything?"

William remained silent and pulled her hand from his arm. "Look after everything? What 'everything' do you look after? Who has to look after who here? And touch me in anger like that again and I swear to God you'll regret it".

William had never been the gentlest of men but had never threatened her before. At least not like that. Normally it was threats of sending her away and getting her out of his life. She lost breath, shocked by his anger, and dropped to the floor. William calmly went over to his chair and sat down. Lizzie took her hands off the carpet where she'd used them to soften the blow as her backside hit the floor and covered her face, beginning to sob.

Lizzie's mind plays this over and over until she finally fades off and sleeps.

"Lizzie," comes the whisper, barely registering with her as she slowly comes around from her slumber. "Lizzie." This time she hears it more pronounced, and she shoots bolt upright in the bed, scouring the room. She sees nothing. The whisper sounds like it has come from right next to her, but the room is empty and felt lifeless, just as it was when she fell asleep. The only noise she could pick out was that fucking light in the lounge. Pfzzzz.

Realising she has no idea what time it is, she turns her attention to the clock on the wall and sees that it's just after 11pm, well, four minutes after for the purposes of accuracy. She thinks that Trevor would still be at his post so maybe he could come up and fix the light now before it finally drives her crazy, winning the battle of wills they had been fighting for some time now. Pulling herself off the bed, she moves with some effort as all her limbs feel heavy and she stands herself in front of the mirror to make sure she looks presentable before venturing downstairs. Studying herself, she notices stains on her clothes but is too weary to bother changing them. Then comes the whisper again. "Lizzie." The word sends shivers tumbling through her body, she spins round to try and spot where it's coming from. She begins slowly scanning the whole room carefully, the quietness now having become unsettling, but can make out nothing in there with her. She remains convinced she heard her name and that it came from very close by. Taking a deep breath, she turns back round to the mirror and in it she sees a dark, shadowy figure standing almost immediately behind her with burning blue eyes. Screaming, she swings round to once again see nothing but the emptiness of the bedroom. *Clearly my mind is playing tricks on me*, she tells herself. Even so, she quickly exits the room and heads for the front door.

She grasps the front door handle tightly, just about to turn, then realises she has forgotten her key. As she loosens her grip, she hears the whisper again. This time it sounds like the voice wasn't just close but mere millimetres from her ear. Terrified, she fastens her grip back on the door handle and hurriedly, almost violently, opens the door. Immediately she sees Tracey, her neighbour from apartment 60, standing there with her hand raised as though about to knock, causing her to scream again in shock. Tracey also jumps, startled by the sudden sight of Lizzie and the sound of her scream. Lizzie calms her nerves quickly and sees Tracey look her up and down and abruptly addresses her with, "What do you want?"

Tracey, taken aback by the curtness of the question, stumbles over her initial words. "Oh um, I, er heard, um, you scream or something. Ya know, a few minutes ago. I wanted to make sure you were okay. Especially after the noises earlier."

"What noises?" Lizzie queries. "And, yes, I'm fine. Took a nap and had a bad dream is all. Now if that's all then, if you don't mind, I need to go and speak with Trevor." Tracey tries to stop Lizzie from barging past and continues her questions.

"And William is okay with that? Is he there? Maybe I should speak with him. And isn't Toby visiting this weekend?"

Lizzie pushes Tracey against the wall. "I don't like the tone you're taking with me, Tracey. I'd advise you keep your nose firmly to your fucking self."

And with that Lizzie stomps off down the corridor, leaving a shaken Tracey trying to catch her breath. When she finally gets over the shock of what just happened, Tracey steps back up to the door and bangs on it.

"William?" she calls out, only to receive a deafening silence in response. "William, it's Tracey. Is everything okay? I just saw Lizzie heading off on her own." Still no response. Tracey bangs the door a few more times before giving up and heading back into her own apartment to call the police, knowing that it will be almost pointless to expect any help for some time.

The building is eerily quiet as Lizzie makes her way down the stairs. She isn't used to wandering the corridors or stairwells at this time, realising how lonely a place it feels at night. Every so often the distant sound of a TV set permeates the silence as she continues her descent. Nine floors seem so much further than she was expecting, even only just having come up them earlier in the day. She notices one thing that is incredibly pleasing, through the silence she could no longer hear the lightbulb. She starts slowing down to soak in the peacefulness, placing a finger against the wall and running it along the smooth surface to make sure she stays in the moment. Even the clack clack of her shoes on the steps is a delightful sound to her right now. Anything that isn't that electric crackle is heaven. Her finger hits the sign of the current floor she is passing, slightly pinching the skin and causing her to retract it, breaking its run. A faded 2, in what appeared to be a rusty red informing her that she was nearly at the bottom.

Lizzie rounds the corner at the bottom of the stairs after which the lobby of the block then comes into view. To her left sit the lifts, one of which has an out of order sign stuck to it, which she didn't remember seeing earlier. She then recalls the awkwardness of Trevor waiting for a lift that refused to arrive. In front of her stands an empty concierge desk which she just stares at. Why wasn't Trevor where he was supposed to be, especially as she'd just taken the effort to come and speak to him? The fact she just wanted out of the apartment was neither here nor there. As she stares, annoyed, at the space where Trevor should be, she notices a piece of paper on it and walks over.

'Gone to sort the lift. Be back shortly. Trevor,' was written in his scrawly handwriting. Lizzie decides rather than head back up, she will sit and wait so she heads back to the stairs to see if he turns up. She looks at her watch which reads 11:30pm. She decides to wait until 11.45 for him before admitting defeat and going back up.

The minutes tick by slowly. So slowly, in fact, that Lizzie feels like she had been sitting still for an eternity but, in reality, only five minutes have passed. The feeling of the passage of time once again going astray through nothing more than mind-numbing boredom. Five long and quiet minutes containing no sign of Trevor. She notices that the lifts had also been unusually quiet. One was seemingly not working but there is no whirring of the other one moving up and down between floors. Maybe that has packed it in for the night too. *Looks like it's the stairs back up as well then*, Lizzie thinks to herself. She begins focusing on the glass doors at the front of the lobby. The doors which once signified so much promise for the area but delivering little. The light inside meaning she could see little to nothing through the reflection of the lobby in the glass. She doesn't know what she was watching for, or indeed, hoping for. Just something that would mean this time would not just be spent in her head. To aid her distraction she once again focuses her finger on the wall and begins tracing a figure of eight on it, over and over. Repetition is good for keeping her mind calm. Around, up and across, around, back across and down. Around, up and across, around, back across and down. And just like that, as her watch turns 11.40pm, the lights disappear.

She looks back towards the glass doors which no longer reflect the lobby, yet she can still not see anything. There is no light outside either. Nothing from the windows of the other buildings in the area, no streetlights. Everything is black. And she is here alone. The panic begins welling up inside her and she is desperate to move but her fear keeps her welded to the step. She looks up the stairwell and sees nothing. She looks across the lobby and sees nothing. Then, breaking through the discomfort of the quiet, she hears footsteps on the lobby floor. Not footsteps as you would expect with the soft thud of a shoe sole or the clack of a stiletto heel, but the sound of skin slapping against the cold floor. They're moving slowly but with each step the sound grows louder. Louder means closer. "Trevor?" she whispers into the dark but fails to get a response.

Slap. Slap. Slap.

Her entire body is frozen still.

Slap. Slap. Slap.

The sound is getting closer and closer to her.

Then she hears it again. The voice. "Lizzie." It is no longer a whisper but a man's deep voice calling at her, a voice she recognises, one which is all too familiar to her but one it could not possibly be. The sound of William's voice should not be down here with her.

Slap. Slap. Slap.

The footsteps are right on top of her now and then out of the dark she feels a hand press against her shoulder. A hand which doesn't belong to anyone as she is on her own at the bottom of this dark, lonely stairwell. With that, her body brings itself into life and she jumps up, hurtling back up the stairs, taking as many as she can at a time. The noise of her running echoes up through the deserted stairwell. When she reaches floor five, she no longer has any breath and is unable to run any further. She stops, listening as well as she can over her own body trying to grasp oxygen. And, to her relief, that is all she could hear. The slapping sound of skin on floor has vanished. The only person with her, is her. She takes one extremely deep breath and lets it out as an extended and heavily relieved sigh. Still unable to reconcile what just happened, she carries on making her way back up the stairs.

Back on nine, she starts to walk down the corridor suddenly realising she didn't grab her key before she hurriedly left. Trevor would have a spare, but she has no idea where he is. As she stands there, staring down the corridor into nothing but darkness, she once again hears footsteps. This time from above, heading in her direction, and this time with shoes on. She peers around the wall up the stairs to see if she can see who or what is coming her way. Staring, waiting as her eyes slowly adjust to the dark. Then light appears around the corner, followed by a figure which then bounds down the stairs towards her. For one moment she loses all sense of fear and lunges at the figure, barging it over, the light falling to the floor and disappearing.

"What the fuck?" it says. "Lizzie? That you?"

She stares at it and slowly makes out that *it* is the boy, Darius, from up on floor 14.

"Why you jumping me like that?"

"You shouldn't sneak up on people," she replies.

"I ain't sneaking up on no one. What the fuck is wrong with you?"

Lizzie shrugs her shoulders which Darius can barely make out. He bends down to feel for his phone, brushing a hand across the floor until it bumps into what he is looking for. He picks it up and can feel the screen has cracked. He tries turning the torch on again, but to no avail.

"Fuck!" he says quietly to himself before turning his attention back to Lizzie. "You should be inside Lizzie. Especially with the power having gone out. Where's Bill? He not here with you?"

"No, he's back inside. You're right, I should be back in there. Where were you going anyway?"

"Heading down to see if I could get a signal and was gonna talk to our man Trev to see if he can get the power back on." He rubs his broken phone sadly, "Doesn't look like I need to worry about the signal now".

Lizzie glosses over the fact she caused Darius to drop and break his phone. "He's not there right now. I was just down there waiting for him when the lights went out."

"Let's get you back inside and then I can see if I can track down our missing Scotsman."

"Okay. But I've forgotten my key."

"Can't Bill let you in?"

Lizzie shrugs again.

"Well, let's see," Darius says and starts guiding her back to number 58.

Standing in front of Lizzie's door, Darius waits for Lizzie to knock but as far as he can make out, she's just standing there looking at him. So, he makes a fist with his hand and bangs on the door.

"Yo Bill. You in there? It's Darius. Got Lizzie out here with me. She seems a little confused."

Lizzie reacts to this assumption, "I am not confused, you little shit."

Darius ignores the insult and bangs some more. From next door, Tracey appears with a torch and shines it at them. Darius gets a good look at Lizzie in the torchlight and notices blood on her clothes.

"Yo Liz. What's up with the blood?" Lizzie looks at him confused.

Tracey then interrupts, "I saw that too! I wasn't sure what it was, and she pushed past me before I could get a proper look at it."

"Wait, you let her head off on her own?" Darius questions.

"Wasn't like I had a choice, but I've called the police to let them know they need to get here."

216

"Am sure they'll be here any fucking minute," Darius mutters.

Lizzie chimes into the conversation, "You called the police Tracey? Why would you do that?" and she starts to move towards Tracey. Darius quickly grabs her by the arm.

"Let's get you inside, Lizzie. Bill must be sleeping." He grabs his wallet from his back pocket and slips out a bank card. "Tracey, can you make sure you keep the light on the lock." Tracey keeps her hand steady so Darius can see what he is doing.

"You know how to do that?" she questions. Darius smiles back.

"It may not be my first time. But let's keep that between us, okay?" He slips the card between the door frame and lock, fiddles with it a little, it slips further in until he feels it slip into the right spot. Pushing the door at the same time, it slips open. "Go back inside, Tracey. I got this."

"We've got another one of these inside if you want it?' she says, referencing the torch. Tracey moves towards them and hands the torch to Lizzie.

"Thanks," says Lizzie.

Tracey immediately backs away. "Let me know if you need anything," she says to Darius. He nods and leads Lizzie into her apartment.

The beam from the torch cuts through the darkness, providing brief glimpses of bits of the apartment, Darius feels a disquiet steadily build inside him. Something is very wrong in here.

"Where's Bill?" he asks.

"He was sitting in front of the TV when I left,"

replies Lizzie. "But shhhh... can't you hear it?"

"Hear what?" Darius asks.

"Exactly. It's gone. Without the power, it can't torture me any longer."

"You're sounding pretty freaky, Liz."

Lizzie swings the torch around wildly, the light splashes up against the walls of the entry way and briefly catches the open doorway to the lounge, allowing the room a short illumination. Darius thinks he sees what looks like the back of a head as the room was lit up.

"It's the apartment, D." Lizzie is the only one he allows to call him 'D', it was something his mum used to call him, and he wanted it to remain special to her, but he has a soft spot for Lizzie, understanding her problems all too well from his own family history. As far as Lizzie goes, he didn't really know her when it happened, but his Aunt had told him that her kid got taken away after she had a breakdown and tried to harm it. And that she had to be locked up for a few years. Most people knew Bill and Lizzie and that Bill didn't like her to be out on her own as she could get confused easily, which led to her getting scared, which in turn led to her getting angry. That often led to her hurting herself rather than others. Lizzie knew she shouldn't be out alone so either something happened to Bill, or he's gone out and Lizzie's not had her pills that help her keep her mind right and also help her sleep.

"Is someone here with you, Liz?"

"Can't you feel it? It's asleep. The power cut made it sleep. For the first time since we moved in.

It's the first silence. It's laughed at me since it took my baby from me, D. Every day. All day." The light continues to dance around the walls as Lizzie continues to swing it.

"Stop swinging that and point it at the lounge," he says.

Lizzie senses he is getting upset so does as he asks. Darius can make out the shape of a head now, sitting in the chair just as Lizzie said.

"Bill?" he calls and heads towards the lounge.

As he gets close, the rancid smell hits him, a smell he knew from dead animals getting stuck in the small nooks and crannies of the crappy building he calls home. "Bill?" he says again, only this time his voice wavering, terrified of what he fears he is about to see. He inches closer to the man in the chair, very slowly, his mind's reluctance to know the truth seems to be winning the argument against his body's persistence in moving forward. However, that win is short-lived, and he reaches the chair and slowly turns to look, catching the shadowed face of a lifeless Bill. The torchlight manages to brighten the blood on his hands and he can just make out a gaping hole across his throat. Vomit suddenly fills his mouth and, as he throws up, the light disappears. He hears footsteps lightly dance across the floor, sounding like they're heading to the kitchen. The sound of a hand running itself against the wall, as though it were a guide rope. His heart rate increases, sweat starts to break on his brow and an overriding need to take a piss fills him. Next, he hears what sounds like drawers opening and closing and cutlery being clattered around. Then, suddenly, that noise stops. The hand is back against the wall and the light footsteps start again, coming back his way. All of a sudden, the torch is back on and shone directly into his face, blinding him. He moves to the side to see if he can get his eyes out of the direct light, but the torch follows his movement. And before he can catch another breath, the light darts towards him. It is upon him in a second and, just as quickly, he feels a blade enter his abdomen. The blade retracts, blood begins to rush out and Darius falls to his knees, the light still in his face renders him unable to see who is taking his life and he only hears Lizzie's voice. "Sorry D, but it's not my fault. If you told anyone about William, they'd come take me away again." He couldn't see Lizzie's face as she murdered him, just as he was unable to see the blade come for him again, puncturing his right eye and through into his skull, leaving him lifeless. His body collapses to the floor unceremoniously and Lizzie switches off the torch. She is much calmer now and quietly says to herself, "See, D, curiosity really does kill the cat."

Lizzie stands and stares as Darius's lifeless body oozes blood, the torchlight causing a shimmering effect on the ever-increasing crimson pool. She feels as though she should be sad, but all she feels is contempt. Contempt for these people saying she's not right and that she needs to be locked away. But she showed them. She drifts further and further into her thoughts. The torch is no longer aimed at anything, loosely hanging from her hand. Just as she feels like she could head back to sleep, a movement out of the corner of her eyes snaps her back into reality. She quickly swings the torch round to where Bill's body still sits, only she thinks his hand is in a different position. She moves closer to it, needing a better look. The image of him walking towards her as she sat on the steps fills her mind. How was he there and here?

"Bill?" she whispers into the dark. "Bill. Are you… awake?" No reply comes. "Bill, I think I'm getting confused again. I had to hurt little D as he found you and he'd have told someone that you were here like this. Because you've said I wasn't well, everyone thinks I'm not well? I'm fine. I'm absolutely fucking fine." She thinks back to earlier that day.

The key turned in the door lock. The familiar click of Bill returning from work. Lizzie had been waiting for this. She wasn't going to stand idly by as he lied to her and threatened her. She'd dealt with the whore girlfriend and now she'd deal with him. William walked through the doorway as he whistled to himself, entirely unsuspecting of the events that lay ahead. He slipped off his jacket, carefully hung it in the same place he did each day and ran his hands down it to prevent as much creasing as possible. He hated his coat getting creased. As he walked down the hallway to the kitchen he called for Lizzie.

"In here," came the reply.

"Where's here?" he asked.

"The lounge. Come join me."

He headed in and she was standing next to the TV, hands behind her back with a very strange look on her face. It was a smile, but it was oddly unsettling, as though she knew something he didn't.

"I took care of her," she said.

"Took care of who?"

"Your whore girlfriend."

"Lizzie, what have you done? How did you even get out to do whatever you think you've done? You really need to just settle down. Toby will be here shortly."

"I got out as I always do. Just by going through the front door, my love."

William walked over to her. He always locked the door when he left so she couldn't wander off and so was worried she hadn't been taking her medication.

"Have you had your pills recently?"

"Pills? My dear Bill, I don't need pills. I'm…. fine."

"You're not fine Lizzie. You're sick. You need to take the pills to stop yourself getting confused. Remember?" He walked a little nearer.

"I don't get confused, in fact, I don't think I've ever been clearer."

Bill went in to hug her and in one quick, unfaltering move she swiped a blade across his throat. Blood spurted out into her face as William reached up to wrap his hands around the wound in a vain attempt to stop the blood leaving his body. He dropped to his knees and stared up at Lizzie, his last thoughts being of confusion and fear as his limp, lifeless body collapsed to the floor. Lizzie, with a huge amount of effort, picked him up and placed him in his favourite chair, arranging his body to look like he always looks when he's watching the TV. She even took off his shoes and socks off as he liked to do. She turned on the TV and walked out of the lounge.

She undressed as she headed to the bathroom, leaving a trail of bloodied clothes behind her. The last stretch of the journey she completed naked, closing the door behind her and calmly running a warm bath. She ran her hand through the water as it filled the tub, creating small waves and the occasional splash. This focused her mind on where she was and once the bath was full, she slipped herself in, the clear water turning a murky red as she washed the death off her crimson-soaked skin.

The flickering of the torch brings her back to the here and now. She bangs it against her other hand, and the beam steadies but only for a short time before it flickers off. Lizzie is now in complete darkness. There is no light coming through the window from buildings around them. She searches for the wall so she can run her hand along it and get her bearings. Her hands flail all over the place, the wall nowhere to be found, and a panic begins to set inside her. She feels her breathing get heavier and faster, the sound of it exacerbated by the darkness which envelopes her. This is the only sound currently filling her ears. That is until she once again hears the terrifying sound of "Lizzie". William's voice sharply penetrates through the sound of her heavy breathing. What was once an all-consuming sound for her is now just a side note. The grip of fear has once again filled her. She can't look and see if he has stood up or if he's still sitting there as he calls her. Then she hears the now familiar slapping sound of his feet. Only not on carpet but it sounds more like it did downstairs on the floor of the lobby. She concludes it must be the linoleum of the kitchen, but how was he in there?

She is certain he didn't go past her.

Slap. Slap. Slap. Slap.

The feet are definitely moving in her direction.

Her flailing hands finally find a part of the wall. Any part will do and so she just hopes she's leading herself out into the hallway so she can head to the front door. She does so as quickly as possible to make sure she gets to the hall before he does.

Slap. Slap. Slap.

The rustling sound of skin against wallpaper disturbs the silence in-between his wretched, sickening footsteps. She feels she is heading in the right direction, her certainty only coming from the fact she is sure she would have been in the kitchen by now if she had gone wrong and would have therefore met this figure in the darkness on the way. However, her judgement of space and time is confused by the fear which she feels.

Slap. Slap. Slap.

All of sudden Lizzie finds herself flat on the floor. She has tripped over William's shoes which she lays there every day. Every day she would tidy them up after he slips them off in the lounge. Every day she would pick them up and bring them to the hallway. And now here they were, haunting her still. She is lucky that even in the dark she got her hands out in time to break the fall. But at least she now knows she is just a mere couple of feet from the door. From safety. A sense of relief starts to build within her, she even smiles, until she feels a cold hand wrap itself around her ankle. Screaming, she kicks out, not feeling her foot connect with anything and the grip grows slightly tighter. She kicks out again, still not managing to connect her foot to her assailant. The cold grip tightens further, and she begins to feel pain build as it becomes almost vice-like. Lizzie kicks out one more time. This time she feels something, and the grip loosens, just enough for her to get free and stand up. She practically leaps forward, hands out in front of her face, and they find themselves resting against the front door. Grabbing the latch, she rips it open and darts out. It is still pitch black.

She turns and heads toward the stairwell, banging on walls and doors as she goes, screaming for help. Once she realises she has run out of wall, she knows she has reached the stairs and, just as she starts to head down to safety, she hears footsteps heading up towards her. Terrified, she turns and goes up. Slowly, step by step and as quietly as possible. The echo of the footsteps coming up stings her ears. Up she goes, trying to guess which floor she is on. If she can tell the floor, she might be able to find help, but she doesn't know if she's made it up two, three or even four floors. She could even be up to floor fourteen for all she knows by now, where young Darius had come from. She wishes he hadn't come down. Not tonight. As then she wouldn't have had to do what she did. Stupid boy! As she drifts into her thoughts the terrifying sound of skin on floor emerges as if next to her.

Slap. Slap. Slap.

She screams once more and instinctively begins to run up the steps. Striding up a couple at a time. The darkness no longer a barrier to her movement. She huffs as she bounds up stair after stair, gripping the rail tightly as she goes. Her feet slapping down hard when there were no more stairs each time she needed to make a turn to go up the next flight. That feeling of expectation of the next stair to take your weight and then not being there, jarring her body each time it happens. Then, without even realising it, she is up against the roof door. The push of the silver bar the only thing between her being outside and stuck in here with William. She feels around the door for it and as soon as her wrists bang down against it, she pushes as hard as she can, praying the door had not been locked.

The door swings open and she almost falls out. She walks out a short way and stops, turning to face the door but unable to see anything. Almost breathless she whispers his name, "William?" Silence is the only return. She starts to slow her breathing down in an attempt to calm herself when from behind a bright flash occurs, followed by a loud bang. Startled, she jumps, looks behind and sees the bright explosion of a firework. It fades. She turns back towards the door when another one explodes in the sky. The light illuminating the scene in front of her temporarily, giving her sight of the doorway. She is alone and starts to feel safe and the light fades once again. Her mouth is dry from the fear and running and as she concentrates on trying to build some saliva a third firework bursts behind her. The illumination revealing something mere feet away. The figure of William silhouettes as the firework burns out.

"I'm right here with you Lizzie," he says.

Another bang, another flood of light, William having moved a foot further forward. Lizzie begins to back away.

"Why did you do it?" he asks.

Lizzie carries on backing up, slowly closing in on the edge of the building

"You know why! Because of you and your whore," she replies.

"Not me. Toby."

"I don't know what you mean."

"Why did you punish him?"

"I… I… didn't. I haven't seen him."

The next firework goes up and even though she has been backing away, William is closer than he was. She feels her legs touch the rim around the edge of the building and she almost loses her balance.

"But you have, Lizzie. You know you have. You saw him after you killed me."

"No. I wouldn't do anything to him."

"But you did before. And you did again."

"NO!" she screams at William.

Another bang, another flash of light. William is nose to nose with Lizzie. The scare this gives poor Lizzie is too much, she jerks backwards, her calves hitting the rim of the building, knocking her off balance. She starts to topple back and, unable to find anything to grab, gravity quickly takes over. She plummets towards the ground, her final moments prior to her death lit up in beautiful fashion with a background of colour and sound. Her screams pierce the night, eventually being cut out by each subsequent bang. She passes window after window before coming to the end of her journey on the cold, hard ground outside of Castle Heights. Her face forever etched with the fear of the last thing she saw, William staring over the edge of the building, watching her fall. Her bones now broken throughout her body and her skull caved in from the impact. Her life extinguished instantaneously as her blood slowly oozes out, providing a stain on the ground as a constant reminder of Lizzie Creasy's unravelling in apartment 58.

In Lizzie's bedroom remains a picture on her nightstand. A picture of her and a little boy, who is beaming and happy. She too looks genuinely happy, with her arm around the boy. He is wearing a brand-new blue cap that she'd just bought him for his 8th birthday. She wasn't able to afford much but Toby appreciated everything his mum gave him and so he wore it with pride.

Suddenly, the trunk in the bedroom moved, a muffled scream coming from within but, sadly, it was not loud enough for anyone outside the apartment to hear. The trunk was well sealed and would run out of air before too long. Once Lizzie's body is discovered, most likely in the morning, and upon being recognised, someone would go to the apartment to find no one answering the door. Eventually they would need to break the door down and would find William's lifeless body on his favourite chair and the body of Darius from apartment 89 on the floor next to William. No one would look in the trunk for a few days, upon which a third body would be discovered.

The Plumber on the 10th

Jack Joseph

He woke with a start and sat up wearily, his brain foggy and confused by the flashes of light outside accompanied by pops and bangs. He rubbed his eyes and walked cautiously to the window. Another flash, a streak of blue and red, soared up and exploded into a hail of stars about three floors above. He sighed with relief, just fireworks. They looked really close and he peered down and saw another rocket blaze up from the car park then crackle into flecks of light before him. He rubbed his eyes again and checked his watch for the time, just gone 1am. Still a while to prepare. He flicked the light switch on the wall, but the room remained dark. He tried again, knowing full well the result would be the same and it was. He scanned the room and realised everything was off, the digital radio display was dead, likewise the TV which had been on when he'd fallen asleep. Must be a power cut as all the bills had been paid.

"Christ's sake," he muttered to himself. He felt around for his leather holdall, picked it up and walked carefully to the bathroom as his eyes adjusted to the darkness. Once there, he locked the door, opened the old, weathered holdall and took out a blue plastic bag, which he draped over the empty toilet roll holder, a large, scented candle and a box of matches. He placed the candle on the shelf beside the sink, as he had done numerous times before, struck a match alight and turned it to the wick which smoked and burned into life, illuminating the small, immaculately clean white bathroom. He bent down to a cupboard and removed one of the dozen or so unlabelled bottles of toilet cleaner, carefully removed the top and poured all of the liquid contents into the toilet. He replaced the top onto the empty bottle and placed that into the blue plastic bag which in turn he placed into the holdall. He lit a fresh match from the candle and held it above the toilet bowl.

"Go dté tú sláne," he said, then dropped the lit match into the toilet, closed the lid, and pressed the flush. The water rushed through the system as he checked himself in the mirror. He was looking rough; he definitely needed a shave and possibly some surgery to get rid of the bags under his eyes.

"You look like shit warmed up, Danny," he groaned at his reflection. He was thirty-three going on sixty-three. His once bright blue eyes now seemed to be a faded grey, his tightly cropped brown hair now whitening at the temples. He stifled a yawn and threw the box of matches back into the bag. The scent from the candle was filling the air now and his nostrils twitched uncomfortably, he'd never taken to the smell of those things, they triggered his allergies. At least, he felt they did. The higher ups said otherwise, but then they didn't have his nostrils and they weren't the ones standing in their bathrooms having to breathe the fumes in. Still, the money was good and he was working from home so he shouldn't really complain.

Danny sat on the side of the bathtub and waited, listening to the little hands on his watch tick away the seconds. It was five minutes and fifty-two seconds when the sound of three knocks signalled the end of his wait. He stood up, walked to the toilet and opened the lid, a rush of air making the candle flicker. He reached into the bowl and pulled out a leather holdall, similar to his own, but without the wear and tear. He placed the holdall beside his and looked down into the bowl as a hand reached out, he took it and helped a wiry man in his late forties, up and out.

"Thank you," said the new arrival, brushing his tweed jacket, grey shirt and corduroy trousers down as he stood opposite Danny.

"Welcome," said Danny closing the toilet lid. "Card?"

"Right, yes." The man produced a small shiny, plastic card from an inside jacket pocket and handed it over. Danny checked it, ran his finger over a strip at the back and put it in his back pocket. The man gave a polite, if slightly nervous, smile.

"Name?" Danny reached into the bag and took out another, slimmer, candle.

"Arthur Mann."

"Where's the other half?" Danny grinned, lit the new candle then unlocked and opened the bathroom door.

"Sorry?" Arthur looked at him puzzled.

"Never mind," Danny shook his head, he thought that had been quite funny. "This way."

Arthur frowned, picked up his holdall and

followed his host out of the bathroom.

***

"How was the journey?" Danny asked, leading Arthur into the living room.

"It was rather nice, 'The Bump' was surprisingly pleasant," Arthur replied. He enunciated each of his words in a careful manner which bugged Danny.

"Good, good," Danny said. 'The Bump' had always split travellers, some had enjoyed it, some had barely noticed it and others had suffered travel sickness. One woman had claimed she had whip lash as a result of it and had rambled incessantly about compensation, like she was ever going to get it.

"Saving on electricity, are we?" Arthur flicked a finger around, though Danny didn't see it.

"Power cut," Danny stood by the window. The fireworks had stopped now.

"Cripes, how high are we?" Arthur asked in awe, transfixed by the view.

"Tenth floor," Danny said, then struck Arthur around the back of his head with the candle. The flame went out and the lights went out for Arthur as he crashed to the floor unconscious.

***

When Arthur painfully opened his eyes, he found himself tied to a chair in a room lit by yet another candle. There was nothing else in the room, apart from a large wooden chest, like one where a pirate would stash his treasure, over his left shoulder in the corner, a large, steel padlock holding it tightly shut, and another chair opposite him. On that chair sat his host.

"You broke my candle." Danny held out the candle, broken in two, and dropped it to the floor.

"You cracked me around my blasted skull with it!" Arthur's head pounded. "Why'd you do that? What is it with you and candles?" Arthur pulled at his binds, but they were tight and didn't budge.

"Who are you?" Danny said, his voice firm, but calm.

"Is everyone here obsessed with candles? Seriously, why the candles?"

"Who are you?" Danny repeated.

"I told you my name!" Arthur yelled back.

Danny sat in silence.

"I told you my name," Arthur said again, this time hauling back his temper. He wasn't in the best of positions to be provoking his host-turned-captor.

Danny sat in silence.

"Arthur Mann. You've seen my pass," Arthur muttered.

"I saw 'a pass'," Danny said blankly.

"My pass. I am Arthur Mann. Is this how you treat all your arrivals, is it some kind of test? I'm Arthur Mann. Now, will you please untie me?"

A distant knock interrupted them.

"Don't go anywhere," Danny stood and left the room.

***

In the bathroom, Danny lifted the toilet lid, a whoosh of air, the candle flickered, and a hand reached out from the bowl holding a folded piece of paper.

"Thank you," said Danny taking the paper.

The hand gave him a thumbs up then disappeared back into the bowl. Danny closed the lid and unfolded the paper. He read what was on it and sighed.

***

"Once more, who are you?"

"How many times are you going to ask me that? I'm Arthur Mann," the man tied to the chair replied. "This is ridiculous."

"Arthur Mann is a dead man," Danny held up the piece of paper. "You look good for a dead man."

"There must be some mistake," 'Arthur' pleaded.

"No mistake," Danny said. "It was the 'half a man' thing that bothered me."

The captive man didn't speak, he shook his head in confusion.

"With a name like that you would have heard that joke before, hundreds of times, probably"

"Oh, a joke, is that what that was?" 'Arthur' said sarcastically.

"Who are you?"

"Arthur..."

"If the next word out of your mouth is 'Mann'

then I am going to rip your fucking head off and flush it down the loo!" hissed Danny.

The man sat quietly, thinking over his options.

"Well?" Danny said quietly.

"I didn't kill him," the man said after a minute of silence. "I found him lying on the roadside, his bag beside him. He was already dead, I swear to you. I checked his pockets for identification and found the pass. I figured I could use it, he wasn't going to. What's the wrong in that?"

"It wasn't yours," said Danny.

"Nobody got hurt."

"Apart from Arthur Mann."

"Arthur Mann, I get that now. Arthur Mann, half a man," 'Arthur' sighed. "Stupid me."

"Indeed."

"Look, I know I did wrong, but I had to take the chance, surely you can understand? You know what things are like back there," the man pleaded.

"Not my business," said Danny flatly.

"Have you no heart?" The captive man was terrified at the thought of going back.

"Wrong is wrong."

"Let me go, what harm can it do to just let me go?" the man's voice cracked.

"I can't do that," said Danny.

"You can't send me back." Tears pierced through the man's eyes. "Please."

Danny didn't reply.

"Are you going to kill me?" 'Arthur' tried to read his captor's face.

"*I'm* not a killer," Danny glimpsed at the chest in

the corner.

The man tied to the chair felt his own chest tighten. "What's in there?"

"Hope that you never find out."

"What does that mean?" He pulled at his binds again, but to no avail.

"Who are you?" Danny asked and the two sat in the quietness for what felt like an eternity. Danny was used to waiting, he was a patient man.

"Stockley," the man finally said. "Richard Stockley."

"Thank you," said Danny. He took a pen from his shirt pocket and wrote the name down on the piece of paper he still held in his hand, then he stood and left the room.

Richard Stockley looked around the room in panic, hoping to spot something that would help free him from his predicament. Nothing, just that old chest which looked like it was growing in size, taking up more and more space.

The toilet flushed.

"Shit," gasped Richard. He hadn't foreseen this, it should have been straight forward. Get through, hand over the card, smile and move on, but he hadn't banked on that stupid joke over that stupid name and now he was here, stuck and facing lord knows what fate.

Danny returned and sat down.

"What happens now?" Richard tried to maintain a calm appearance.

"We wait for further instructions," replied Danny as if nothing rested on what those instructions were to be.

"You could let me go," Richard whispered.

"I can't do that," Danny said.

"Why not?" Richard implored. "Come on, I'm not a bad man. I did a wrong, yes, I admit it, but I did it for good reason."

"You did it for a selfish reason," Danny sat back in the chair.

"Everyone that comes here is here for selfish reasons then." Richard felt that was a reasonable argument. He was quite proud of himself for coming up with it so quickly.

"I don't care what their reasons are, I only care whether they're meant to be here or not."

"And what about justice? The system isn't fair," Richard said.

"The selection process is fair, the lottery, from what I…" Danny began.

"Lottery, is that what you believe? They are chosen by 'The Committee'," Richard corrected him.

"The Committee?" Danny had never heard of them, but then information was restricted here and he had never really sought any. The only information he ever truly came across was from the various arrivals.

"'The Diamond Dozen'," Richard noted the blank look on Danny's face with surprise, "you've never heard of them?"

"The Diamond Dozen - are you taking the piss?" Danny scoffed.

"I wish I was. The lottery is the story they peddle

to the people, but the reality is that there is no random selection process, there is no lottery. The selected are chosen by twelve people who sit at the very top of everything. Above government, above religion, above law. They decide who goes and who stays. They decide who lives and who dies. Luck doesn't come into it. Does that sound fair to you?" Richard took a breath and tried to read his captor's face.

Danny sat stony faced, giving nothing away, but, in his head, he was rummaging over what he had been told.

"I guess you were living deeper in the dark than you knew," Richard said.

"You want me to believe that none of the selections are random, they are all hand-picked by this 'Diamond Dozen'?" Danny kept a neutral tone.

"Yes," sighed Richard. "Want to know how they do it, how they decide?"

"That's not my business."

"Family, friends, business associates, the wealthy. They look after their own, that's how it works. There is no fairness in that. That's not just!" Richard was almost shouting as he finished.

"Where did you hear all this, some shadowy figure in a dimly lit alleyway?"

"My wife's former employer, he had contacts. But he's not the only one, I've heard whispers from others."

"Whispers?" smirked Danny.

"Yes, whispers. Does even the possibility of it not bother you?"

"That's not my business," Danny said blankly.

"What, the fucking hell, *is* your business?" roared Richard, his eyes spilling tears.

"I check the right people through and see them safely on to the next part of their journey."

"Why can't you check me through?" Richard pleaded.

"You're not the right person."

"According to twelve faceless people disconnected from the majority," Richard said with disdain.

"You don't even know if they're real."

"They're real." Richard was sure of it. "I'd imagine there's a similar set up over here."

"It doesn't matter anyway, you're not the right person."

"But I'm not a bad person."

"You're a liar and a thief, possibly a murderer."

"I'm not a murderer!" barked Richard.

"Hard to know if that's true seeing as you're a liar."

"Okay, that is fair, I lied. But what else was I to do? Should I have said, 'hey, I found this dead fellow and I took his pass and bag. I mean, it's a shame to let it go to waste, so I wondered if you'd mind ever so much to just let it go?' Should I have said that, would that have made any difference?" Richard slumped back.

Danny shrugged.

"I didn't kill anyone."

"That's not my…"

"Business, I know," Richard interrupted. "You

could untie me and look the other way."

"I can't do that," Danny said plainly.

"Not your business," Richard said mockingly.

"It's not," Danny was phased by this man. He had been doing this job a long time, met a lot of people, not all of them nice. But this was only the second time he'd had a 'Goose'. Things hadn't ended well for the first one, the chest had been opened and a heck of mess was the result. The bonus payment had been exceptional, but even so, he wasn't keen on a repeat. Still, if that was the decision, then so be it.

"Do you know what pedantic means?" Richard raised his nose.

Danny nodded.

"Well, that's what you are. Pedantic. A candle loving, pedantic twit, that's what you are," snorted Richard.

"I could happily do without the candles," smiled Danny.

"Why have so bloody many then?"

"They're part of the process, don't ask me to explain because I don't fully understand it myself. They serve their purpose, that's all that matters." Danny stood to stretch his legs and back.

"It's weird, if you ask me."

"Nobody asked you."

"No, but if they did."

That made Danny chuckle.

"Do you have a conscience?" Richard asked.

"I do."

"Why keep me here then?" Richard looked

241

imploringly at his captor.

"It's part of the job."

"You could be putting me to death, doesn't that bother you?"

"I don't know you," Danny said honestly. The man opposite him seemed to wither slightly, his shoulders dropped and his head followed. He could almost see the hope seeping out as if it were causing the man to deflate. Danny retook his seat and they sat there together for nearly three minutes before the man spoke again.

"I had a wife, Marie. She died, six months ago, as a result of the..."

"I don't want to know," Danny cut him off.

"Because you don't want to carry the guilt," Richard said.

"Because it's not my business."

"Sweet Mother of God, keep saying that and I'll kill myself!" cried Richard.

"That would save a lot of time," smiled Danny.

Richard half laughed, half cried.

"It's nothing personal," said Danny.

"Of course it's personal, it is very fucking personal. It couldn't be more personal!" Richard roared.

"I'm just doing my job," Danny raised his hands to indicate the decision was out of them.

"How many times have those words been spoken throughout history and how much blood was spilt because of them? How many lives lost?"

Danny didn't answer.

"A pitiful, pathetic excuse," Richard shook his

head. "You have a choice, there's always a choice."

"That choice isn't mine to make," Danny was genuinely apologetic.

"But it is," said Richard.

Two knocks came from the bathroom, Richard stared toward it, wide eyed, then turned his eyes to Danny.

"I'll be back in a moment," Danny stood.

"Don't answer it," begged Richard. "Untie me, let me go."

Danny looked down at him, then turned and headed to the bathroom.

"You stupid prick," Richard snarled through gritted teeth as he pulled once more at his binds.

"I heard that," Danny called back.

"Good, fucking good," Richard said in a hushed tone.

***

Danny entered the bathroom, locked the door, lit a new candle which he put beside the one still burning, lifted the toilet lid and a whoosh of air flickered both flames. A holdall popped up, he took it and put it on the floor as a man, dressed in a white boiler suit and a pair of bright white trainers, pulled himself up and out of the toilet bowl and into the bathroom.

"Derek," Danny grinned broadly as the pair shook hands.

"Danny." The boiler suited man called Derek grinned back as he smoothed down his mop of blond hair.

"They decided on *that* then," said Danny, feeling slightly guilty.

Derek nodded. "Where's 'The Goose'?"

"This way," Danny picked up the freshly lit candle, unlocked and opened the bathroom door.

"Cutting down on electricity, are we?" Derek said.

"Power cut," Danny replied.

***

"Aw, who's this now?" Richard rolled his eyes at the new man.

Derek didn't even look at him, he gently sat his holdall on the floor, knelt down, opened it and took out two bowler hats. He put one on his head and handed the other to Danny who did likewise. Derek took out a black umbrella, zipped his holdall closed and stood.

"Are you two for real, is this a bowler hat party? Where's mine?" Richard couldn't help laughing, this was insane. "Nice brolly."

Derek pulled at a chain around his neck and revealed a key.

"What's that for?" Richard stopped laughing and felt a quickly growing sense of fear.

Derek walked to the chest.

"Wait, wait, what's in there?" Richard looked imploringly at Danny. "Don't open it."

Derek put the key in the keyhole and turned it.

"Please, don't," Richard looked, in ever-increasing panic, from Danny to the chest.

The lock popped open.

"I'll go back, okay? I won't say a thing, I promise you."

Derek took the lock in his hand and a couple of paces back.

"Come on, please? Have mercy, man."

Derek reached out the umbrella and tapped the chest twice.

"Please, Brolly Man, please?"

Derek picked up his holdall as he walked back to the door, then he and Danny, taking the candle with them, stepped out.

"PLEASE DON'T LEAVE ME HERE!" Richard strained at the ropes and pulled forward.

The chest began to open.

The door closed and clicked as the lock was turned.

"Please, don't do this…please…" he looked back at the chest as it opened more. "Please."

***

"You're looking well," Danny said as the two men stood outside the locked room.

"You look like shit," replied Derek.

"Tell me about it," sighed Danny.

From inside the room, Richard yelled, "WHAT THE LIVING FUCK IS THAT?!"

"New suit?" Danny asked.

"Yeah," smiled Derek, "it's really comfortable. Looks cool, eh?"

"Not sure I'd use the word 'cool'," Danny laughed.

"GET AWAY FROM ME YOU FREAK!!"

"I think it looks cool," said Derek defensively.

"STOP THAT!"

"Listen, have you heard of something called 'The Committee' or 'The Diamond Dozen'?"

"Taking an interest in world affairs, Danny?"

"You've heard of them?"

"You know what they say, 'The Brolly Man comes, The Brolly Man goes, who knows what The Brolly Man knows?'" Derek enthused.

"I've never heard that before. Talking about yourself in the third person too, that's worrying," Danny grinned.

"AH FUCK, FUCKING SHIT!"

"I thought that sounded quite good," Derek laughed.

"You should get it printed on the back of your suit," Danny said. "It's true then, about this committee, that it's them making selections and not a lottery?"

"DON'T DO THAT, SHOO, SHOO!!"

"Nah, it's all a load of old bollocks. You really believe that twelve people run the whole world, presiding over governments and religions?"

"I don't know, you hear stories and some make sense."

"ARGH, BASTARD!"

"Stick to your job, Danny. We stick to our duties and we will be rewarded. You know how it works."

"Yeah, you're right."

"I know I'm right."

"FUUUUUCCCKKK!!!"

"How's Margaret?" Danny took his hat off and rubbed an itch from his head before placing it back.

"No idea, she left me," Derek said sadly.

"GET ME OUT OF HERE YOU MOTHER FUCKING BASTARD CU - !!" The cry was cut out and replaced by a loud, sickening gargle.

"Sorry to hear that. What happened?" Danny patted his friend's shoulder.

"An auditor."

A wrenching, cracking of bones came from the room followed by a munching, crunching and slurping.

"Margaret became an auditor?"

"Margaret wouldn't know her arse from an audit, no, she left me for an auditor."

"Ah. That's double shitty."

"I know."

"I hope her monobrow grows back, that'll serve that fucking auditor right," grinned Danny.

"I found her monobrow quite sexy," sulked Derek.

"Oh."

"Right," sighed Derek, pressing his ear to the door. "I think we're good to go. Hat on?"

Danny nodded and turned the lock as Derek opened the umbrella and held it in front of them like a shield.

***

The room was spattered red with blood, the walls, the floor, the ceiling. A bit of Richard Stockley squelched under Derek's left trainer.

"Damn it," Derek sighed loudly, "I've only just got these."

They watched a large, bloodied, furry hand slip back into the chest, the lid slammed shut and Derek reapplied the padlock, tugging at it to ensure it was secure. He returned to his holdall, closed the umbrella, returned that to the bag and took out a vacuum cleaner with '*Super Sucker 2000*' emblazoned across its side.

"Right, let's get this cleaned up," said Derek.

"One small problem," Danny pointed at the plug hanging from the orange device in Derek's hands.

It took Derek a few moments to register there was no power, "bollocks."

"We have two options, we wait for the power to come back on or..."

"Let's go with that option," Derek put the vacuum cleaner back in the holdall.

"I'll grab some beers," said Danny.

***

The two old friends sat on Danny's sofa, drinking beers and regaling each other with tales of times gone by. It was near six in the morning when the power returned. The tired and inebriated men quickly cleaned the room with the *Super Sucker 2000* doing all the hard work for them. With the work done, Derek bid farewell and went down the loo. Danny cleaned up, zipped his holdall and returned it to its place under the TV in the living room. He slumped down onto the sofa and fell asleep; it had been a long night. He hoped the next arrival would be less problematic.

Loathsome Reflections at 69

Grant Kempster

Bob stared at the man sitting across the room from him in the dying light, the final embers of the day fading away unnoticed in the grease-smeared window behind him. The man stared back at him through familiarly sad eyes. There was something else in there too, something Bob felt increasingly uncomfortable seeing. Was it shame?

"Ah, fuck ya," Bob spat before looking back awkwardly towards the TV in what would otherwise be the darkest corner of the dingy room. It was a cinderblock of a thing, as deep as it was wide with buttons lining one side and a series of dust-blocked speaker holes on the other. The fuzzy picture on it flickered as a middle-aged woman in a woollen hat interviewed a gardener about a murder for what felt like the hundredth time.

After a moment, Bob turned back to the man.

"Have we seen this before?"

The man shrugged.

"Probably."

"Fuck's sake," Bob snapped, picking up the paper on the coffee table next to him (so filled with opened envelopes, used tissues and assorted food wrappers, you'd have been hard pressed to fit a coffee mug on it). "The fuck's my glasses?"

Bob looked back at the man who pointed upwards to his head, with a playful smile that verged on sarcasm. Bob reached up and brought his glasses down over his eyes and began to read the TV Guide.

"Smartass," Bob quipped before sighing. "Jesus Christ. There's fuck all on again."

Bob turned back to the man.

"There's a film on."

"Fucking horror movie. We hate horror movies."

"Boxing."

"Bah! Not boxing like it was in our day," Bob almost snarled. "Not one of them has the talent of Ali or Clay. It's all gym muscles and cuddling these days."

The man was little more of a silhouette now, the window behind his head blooming as the last of the sun sank below the grotty concrete skyline. Bob looked at his watch and for the first time his spirits seemed to pick up.

"About time for a tipple, I reckon!" Bob grinned.

"Gets earlier every day."

"Ah fuck off," Bob chuckled as he huffed himself out of the worn tobacco-stained recliner and got unsteadily to his feet. He looked over and the man was no longer there. The smile left Bob's lips for a moment before he began to make his way to the back of the living room to his favourite cupboard. After a moment he stopped. "Shit, need a piss now. Back in a mo."

***

If you'd have asked Bob Trebor when he first started talking to his reflection, he probably wouldn't have been able to tell you. At a guess, maybe the year after Eve died.

Bob and Eve had been married almost thirty-five years and for the most part it was a happy one. Blissful? No, but happy nonetheless. They had their ups and downs and the last five years had been completely devoid of intimacy, which had been an issue for Bob, but not for Eve. On the last few occasions when he'd tried to tempt her into some form of sexual activity she'd laugh it off with her favourite phrase, 'I used to pause for men, but now it's the menapause for me!'

Maybe that was why, when Eve died suddenly following a stroke while doing the washing up, that Bob had deferred his grief in favour of becoming a man about town again. The world was his oyster, and he was determined to get into as many clams as possible. Only, Bob wasn't eighteen anymore, he was almost sixty-eight and the world had changed beyond all recognition. He'd stomached a few dates, but they all ended the same way, with him coming on too strong and them leaving him with his cock in his hand (figuratively speaking, thankfully) and the bill to pay.

Next on his list was hobbies. Eve had hated Bob's fascination with birdwatching, so he invested in a ridiculously expensive pair of binoculars just to prove a point and proceeded to make lists of all the birds he'd see throughout the day. It actually started really well, pushing him to walk in the local parks and woodland and filling his lungs with crisp fresh air that kept his spirits buoyant and the inevitable crash at bay.

But then the house became too much to run and Bob decided to sell up and move somewhere smaller, keeping a little in the bank for trips away for more bird spotting as and when he felt the need. No sooner had he moved into the 11th floor of Castle Heights than the depression hit. Within a week Bob felt the bottom fall out of everything. He stopped taking walks in the park, stopped watching birds all together (apart from the blonde in the building opposite, he'd sometimes watch her on a Thursday night) and now he just sat in his chair, watching TV and muttering to himself that nobody understood what he was going through.

He'd been in apartment 69 (so chosen because it matched his age, which he found funny at the time) for about two weeks when he'd been moving furniture around and placed the mirror on the chair across from him in the process. Exhausted by the shuffling of tables and chairs, Bob had plumped himself in his recliner and promptly fallen asleep. He eventually woke in the early evening, which had left him slightly disorientated, and when he moved forward to get up and caught sight of movement to his left, his heart nearly burst out of his chest. When he realised it was just the mirror he collapsed backwards again and laughed for the first time since Eve had left the Earth. When he was done he looked back at himself in the mirror, tears streaming down his face and smiled. There was someone who understood him and he could share his life with him every day. The mirror never moved from that spot from that day on.

***

Bob plopped himself down in his faithful recliner, full glass of whiskey in hand, and let out an audible sigh. These days he didn't need to move furniture to feel exhausted, just getting up and walking to the loo and back would do the trick. Bob flicked on the lamp next to him, looked over at his reflection and raised his glass. The reflection raised his in return.

"Cheers, big ears," Bob said with what was the closest thing he could muster to a cheerful smile before taking a big gulp. "What's it to be then? Edna Baggins solves Murders in Shropshire or that shit horror film Crown of Thorns?"

"Is it a Jesus film?"

"Now that would be interesting," Bob chuckled. "Bloke is wronged by one of his mates, is tortured to death and comes back a few days later to enact his revenge."

"I'd watch that."

"I'm amazed it's not been made already!" Bob laughed. "Nobody will hear your Christ for help!"

"That's awful."

"Edna Baggins it is then," Bob laughed.

"We could go out?"

Bob threw his head back as if he'd heard this a thousand times.

"And go where?" Bob sighed. "It's dark outside. Can't go out at dark round here, liable to get the shirt stolen off your back!"

"Nobody would want the shirt off your back. When was the last time you washed that?"

"Before the washing machine broke," Bob replied, knowing what was coming.

"That had to have been at least six months ago!"

"True," Bob admitted. "But I've got enough shirts to last."

"None of which have been washed in six months."

"So what? It's not like I'm going anywhere nice," Bob sighed.

"But the smell…"

"As if anyone will come close enough to smell," Bob said, taking a quick sniff of his pits. "Smells alright to me."

"Nose blind. Point is, you could go out. Pubs open 'til 11."

Bob looked out the window, contemplating it for a moment. But just a moment.

"Too cold out," Bob argued.

"It's always something, isn't it? Winter it's too cold to go out, summer it's too hot. Morning is too early, evening is too late and you're asleep all fucking afternoon."

"I've not slept today," Bob shot back indignantly. "So shove that in your pipe and smoke it."

"You'll be asleep before you've finished that glass, then you'll be awake in the middle of the night with nothing to watch but crap public service talk shows and reruns of 80s cop dramas."

"It's not that easy," Bob murmured. "You know it's not."

"Isn't it?"

"No!" Bob shouted, his blood starting to boil. "It's not! It's fucking not! So shut your stupid fucking face and stop going on about it! You think it's so fucking easy, why don't you come out of there and go for a walk yourself?!"

Bob watched his reflection for a response. Nothing.

"Exactly. Now shut up and watch TV."

Bob took another gulp of his whiskey and turned back to the TV. Edna Baggins seemed to suddenly have a revelation while in the middle of doing some knitting. He was asleep by 9.30.

***

There'd been a few times when Bob had thought maybe he had agoraphobia. He'd even looked it up at the local library to see if the 'symptoms' lined up with how he was feeling. At the beginning it didn't seem to make much sense to him. Bob had always been a very sociable person, in fact looking back he couldn't remember a weekend when he wasn't out down the pub with friends or round at another couple's house for dinner. It helped that Eve was that way too, almost to the point of being gregarious. Everyone would say how she was the life and soul of the party, and they were right. She lit up a room when she walked in, always with an infectious smile that seemed to fill most of her face.

People loved being around Eve and Bob had always assumed they loved being around him too. After she died though, that didn't seem to be the case any more.

There were invites up the pub at first of course, but they began to feel perfunctory after a while, always filled with questions about how he was feeling, was he eating and did he need any company. It was that which killed Bob's social life more than anything and, once it was gone, Bob found that actually he didn't miss it all that much. What was the saying? Misery loves company? Well in Bob's case Misery was pretty much happy on their own at home with a glass of whiskey or two. And the other Bob of course. They could both be miserable together. Anyway, when you have a bar four feet from your comfy recliner, why bother taking one of the rickety lifts down to the ground floor to go out into the bitter wind?

Bob had everything he needed right there in that small, dark flat. If he never had to step outside again he'd be happy. He had no doubt that the chair he sat (and often slept) in all day would be his deathbed whenever that time decided to come.

***

Bob gave a loud involuntary snort and woke himself up. It was pitch black outside now and the only light was coming from the TV in front of him, currently trying to sell him a luxury car he would never drive. He glanced up at the digital clock on the table next to him (he'd given up trying to read analogue ones six months ago – why bother?), it read 11:11.

"Heh," Bob feigned a laugh, "make a wish."

As one advert gave way to another, Bob considered going to bed but knew immediately it would be a pointless exercise. He'd just slept for almost two hours and the chances of him going back to sleep again any time soon would be next to none.

"Boxing then," Bob sighed. "Let's watch two pretty boys dance around each other shall we?"

He picked up the remote and flicked over to the Sports Channel. A rerun of the fight that had happened while he sat snoring in his chair greeted him. It looked as dull as Bob had imagined it would. Prod, swipe, hug and repeat. According to the announcers, the main event would promise to be much more entertaining.

"We'll see about that," Bob sniggered.

Taking the opportunity for a refill, Bob eased himself up and made for the drinks cabinet, making that predictable detour to the bathroom first. By the time he got back, the first fighter had stepped into the ring to thunderous applause. Plumping himself back into his chair, Bob settled in, ready for the night's entertainment.

As it turned out, the announcers weren't far wrong. These two actually had a little talent. Both fighters came out wanting to win and by round three, Bob actually found he was literally sat on the edge of his seat. One of the fighters, hilariously named Hammer, hit the canvas and the referee began the count.

"Come on! Get up you…"

Then everything went black.

"The fuck?!" Bob muttered. "Come on! First good thing on fucking telly in…"

Bob sat up a little straighter so he could see outside the window. Lights adorned many a window, as well as streetlights to a point. But everything else near Castle Heights was pitch black.

"Fuck's sake!" Bob shouted before looking around. "What are we supposed to do now?"

All Bob could see in the mirror was a faint silhouette.

"Candles," Bob stated. "Where's that smelly shit the Robinsons got me as a 'sorry your wife's dead' present?"

No reply from his reflection.

"A lot of fucking use you are," he mumbled as he got up and gingerly started moving towards the kitchen.

Actually Bob knew exactly where the candle was. He'd shoved it in a drawer with some of the paraphernalia from Eve's funeral, including her Order of Service and a Bible that the vicar had given him at the end. At the time, Bob had asked him what he expected him to do with it, to which the vicar had simply raised his eyebrows before deciding that the grief was talking. It wasn't. Bob had little time for religion, even before his Eve (and life) was taken away from him.

Grabbing a matchbox from above the cooker,

Bob made his way back to the safety of his recliner, placed the candle down on the table next to him and lit it.

"There," Bob said, happy that the adventure had worked out so well, "now I can see y…"

Bob stopped in his tracks, his mouth a wide 'O'. It must be the shadows flickering, caused by the candle, a trick of the light. Bob stared at his reflection, trying to make sense of what was staring back at him. He moved his hand in front of his face, testing it to see if it was real, but even that looked odd.

For some reason, the version of himself that was staring back at him looked dead. Totally and utterly dead. Sunken cheeks, hollow pits surrounding cloudy lifeless eyes, bared teeth extending from receded gums. Even his hand appeared bony and skeletal in the candlelight. Then it spoke, only this time Bob was pretty certain the words didn't come out of his mouth.

Bob shot upwards. No huffing and straining this time, bolt upright in a split-second. Once on his feet, he slowly allowed himself to peer sidewise at the mirror that should be devoid of Bob. It wasn't. The cadaverous spectre that kind of looked like him, a dead him, was still hunched over in the seat, its skeletal hands folded over the arm of the chair. Its lifeless eyes peering up at Bob as the thin remnants of its lips pulled back in what was meant to be a smile but looked anything but.

"What's the matter?" it asked in a raspy, gurgling voice. The sound of Bob's own voice twisted in such a way shot ice water through his veins.

Bob staggered backwards, knocking an assortment of paraphernalia off the sideboard behind him. Finally managing to pull his eyes away from the abhorrent visage in the mirror, he looked towards the door leading to the hallway. He was sure he could make it. His heart was thumping in his chest as if it was trying desperately to get out and he could hear his breathing, coarse and heavy. It was almost deafening. He might die trying, but he was sure he could make it.

Bob pushed off from the sideboard, as a swimmer would to begin a race, and attempted a run. He'd not tried anything above a brisk walk since he was in his 30s and his legs gave way after just three steps. As he hurtled towards the ground, Bob just had time to notice the coffee table corner thundering towards his temple.

***

Bob and Eve met on New Year's Eve in 1985. Bob had just crawled out from under a particularly torturous long-term relationship with a girl who had, quite frankly, made his life a misery. They'd been together almost ten years and he was beyond relieved when she decided to leave him on Boxing Day. Less than a week later, a group of his friends from work (who he'd barely seen outside of the office walls since he started working there) invited Bob to the local social club for New Year's. He nearly bit their hand off. Here was his chance to let loose, sow his seeds, finally be the man that he'd wanted to be for the last decade. No relationships from now on, just sex. Lots of it.

Then he met Eve. They'd struck it off immediately as Bob frankly refused to believe her when she told him her name. What are the chances?! That night they were inseparable. They danced, they drank, they held hands and then, just before the big countdown they found a quiet corner and kissed passionately as the crowds somewhere in another world counted down from 10 to 1. At that exact moment Bob felt like he could die happy. Fuck everyone else, here was someone he knew he could spend the rest of his life with.

As the cheers erupted, Eve pulled back, smiled sweetly, and wished him a Happy New Year. Bob had smiled right back and told her that the two of them will have a very happy one. Then the fireworks started whistling and exploding overhead and they went back to their kissing.

***

As Bob came to, the disorientation was overwhelming. The memory of Eve's face smiling at him the first night they'd met was still so fresh in his mind. He could almost see her face in front of his in startling high definition. Stranger still was that he could still hear the fireworks going off. They were even leaving intermittent multi-colour flashes across the walls.

After a few seconds, Bob's head began to throb and reality came flooding back. The fireworks stopped and the memory of Eve's beautiful face started fading away until he could barely remember what she looked like. What replaced them was the chilling realisation of what had just happened, or at least what had happened before he'd fallen and smashed his head on the table that was now lying around him in splintered pieces. Slowly Bob moved his hand up to his forehead to feel the place where the corner of the table had gouged into his skull. Sticky blood was still seeping from it, trickling slowly down his brow towards his nose.

Gingerly, Bob got himself into a sitting position, pushing the various pieces of broken table away with his feet. The room was still dark save for the candle on the other side of the recliner that was casting eerie swaying shadows all around him. As he tried to make sense of what was happening, a vision of the thing in the mirror flashed through his mind. Bob promptly vomited where he sat.

It had to be a dream. The longer Bob sat in a puddle of his own vomit and blood, the more he was convinced he'd just had a bad dream. One so bad he'd sleep walked and tripped. It wouldn't be the first time. Once he'd taken a piss in his mate's wardrobe.

Grabbing the edge of his trusty recliner, Bob slowly got to his feet.

"Come on Bob," he muttered to himself. "It was just a dream. Just a vivid, horrible fucking dream."

After a minute or two, he finally got up the nerve

to turn around and look at the mirror. When he did, he wished he hadn't bothered. In fact, he'd wished the corner of the table had finished the job. While the horrific visage of him was no longer staring back at him, the fact that it was no longer there at all was infinitely worse. Bob moved from side to side, desperate to see his own reflection but that wasn't there either. It was as if he just wasn't there at all.

Slowly Bob edged towards the mirror, hoping it was just a trick of the light. Yet no matter how close he got, he just couldn't see himself. He patted himself slowly around his body to make sure he still had some sort of corporeal form. Seemingly so… but yet… the reflection. Another mirror. He needed another mirror.

Bob staggered towards the bathroom, instinctively pulling the light cord when he got there. He cursed himself when the only outcome was a loud clicking sound. Swiftly, Bob stepped inside the room and looked towards where the mirror was. While it was incredibly dark, Bob's eyes had adjusted enough that he could at least see his dark silhouette looking back at himself. He breathed a heavy sigh of relief and as he got closer, the ambient light coming from the small window to his right just caught Bob's face enough for him to see more. He winced at the bloodied mess of his forehead, touching it as if to check that the mirror was telling the truth. But there was more. As Bob looked away from the gash, he saw his face and it almost took his breath away.

He by no means looked as awful as his deathly reflection had in the moments before Bob had panicked and tripped over his own feet, but the version of himself staring back at him was at least half way there. His eyes were sunken into bruised pits and his cheekbones seemed to be pushing through his almost opaque skin. Another trick of the light he convinced himself, although not really.

A noise from a room behind him startled Bob and he swung around, staring into the inky blackness beyond the bathroom door. As he started to walk he felt even more weak than he had done just moments before, reaching out for the towel rail to steady himself. A cursory look at his hand proved what Bob had feared was happening; he was rotting before his very eyes.

As Bob stepped into the living room, almost completely out of breath, he might have screamed had there been any breath left in his lungs. Instead he just stared at his faithful recliner and pissed himself where he stood. Somewhere in the back of his mind he cursed himself as he'd literally just been in the bathroom.

Sitting in his recliner was Bob. Not the hideous zombie Bob that he'd met earlier in the night, but the normal Bob. The Bob he'd been before the sunset, before the power had cut out, before… oh God.

"What was it Eve used to say?" The Bob that used to be a reflection but wasn't any more asked rhetorically. "You know, when we'd bitten off more than we could chew?"

Bob staggered into the room, his body buckled over partly with the pain of moving and partly because the muscles that used to hold him upright just weren't there any more. He got to the chair opposite the recliner – the one with the empty mirror still propped up on it – and slumped into it. He'd expected to feel the cold hard front of the mirror when he did so, but he must have lost the feeling in his back because he felt nothing.

"That was it. Be careful what you wish for," New Bob said with a chuckle in his voice as he picked up the candle, rose to his feet effortlessly and walked past Bob, whistling cheerily.

***

It didn't take long to pack. There weren't many clothes that Bob would want to wear that hung in his wardrobe, but that was okay, he'd grab a few bits at the airport and probably more once he'd got wherever he was going. They'd be cheaper there too. Bob zipped up the suitcase then got changed into the suit he'd set aside on the bed, wondering why people never wear suits anymore like they used to when he was a kid.

Bob set the suitcase down next to the front door. Just one more thing he needed to pack. He walked slowly into the dark living room and placed the still flickering candle down next to the chair with the mirror on before turning his attention to the window.

"There you are," Bob smiled. "Time to put you

to some good use again."

Bob picked up the binoculars and smiled.

"No peeping at blondie across the way anymore, I'm afraid!" he laughed before looking at the mirror. A huge grin spread across his face and for a moment the lips stretched unnaturally wide, but just for a moment.

Then, Bob left the room, whistling again as he did. As the heap of rotting flesh and bone that used to be Bob sat watching through glazed, dead eyes from inside the mirror, it was still possible to see the terror in its face as the door slammed shut and the candle snuffed out.

Dr. Levin in Number 77

Donovan 'Monster' Smith

Lester Levin coughed into his elbow, switching the channel over from the slasher film he'd been watching. The Lightweight Title Fight was about to start and he hoped it would drown out the kids who were being a bit rambunctious and unruly tonight. He jammed the volume all the way up, doing his best to ignore the disrespectful, ungrateful little brats. They were going to shut up and do as they were told, he'd make sure of it.

Number 77 had been his home for the last few years, and he rather enjoyed the seclusion and privacy it provided. All the neighbors on the floor kept to themselves for the most part, and no one ever complained, no matter what took place. The music was usually abnormally loud and blaring, covering up the multitude of screams from behind the locked doors.

He cracked open a can and took a long swig, wiping the sweat off his forehead with the back of his hand. There was still a ton of work to do, and he was on a very tight schedule with no time to spare. The trials were nearly complete, and he only had a few more tests to run before he could conduct his final experiment.

Doris popped her head in the doorway, smiling as she dried her hands on the apron she was wearing around her waist. She glanced at the television for a moment, then back at Lester. "Fight's about to start, huh?" she said, grinding her teeth. "This is going to be a snooze fest."

They'd been together since they were young, married for thirty-plus years, and still going strong. She often assisted him with his work in the laboratory, mainly cleaning up after him and making sure he stayed hydrated and fed throughout the day. She wasn't exactly a fan of what he did, but she knew better than to object and was great at keeping her mouth shut.

Dr. Levin, as he was otherwise known, had a Ph.D. in astrophysics and enjoyed tenure as a professor at a posh university somewhere off the east coast. He spent over half his life working in his given field and was highly respected and admired by his colleagues. His courses were extremely popular with the students, and his classroom was generally standing room only.

He loved science with all his being and knew from a very young age that it would be his life's work. There was nothing in the world he wanted to do more, and he pursued it with an unbridled passion that ultimately thrust him to the head of the pack. But that's where things soured and took a turn for the worst.

As a leader in his field, Lester regularly tested the boundaries and pushed the limits. He was a bit of an eccentric and was keen on conducting experiments behind closed doors, all in the name of science. Finding new ways to expand the laws of physics had always been at the forefront, and he wanted to be a pioneer.

However, as time went on, it didn't take long before he started to shy away from his responsibilities at work, becoming a bit of a recluse, concerned only with succeeding in his sick and ungodly experiments. He was obsessed with time travel and teleportation, and he'd do anything in his power to make it happen. Opening a vortex was his first quest, which he proudly achieved a lot faster than he thought he would.

As of late, his work had become increasingly stressful and problematic, despite the numerous breakthroughs he'd made. It'd taken a lot longer than he'd hoped for, but he was finally able to perfect his serum and ship some of his test subjects on through to the other side. The problem wasn't getting them there, it was bringing them back.

He'd sent plenty of guinea pigs through the wormhole, just over seventy to be exact, but he had yet to bring anyone back in one piece. Many had returned, but they were nothing more than a pile of mush - flesh and bone, hair and teeth. Those that did manage to make it back were unrecognizable monstrosities with countless deformities that no longer appeared human.

There were lumps and contusions the size of basketballs covering their bodies, along with arms fused to spines, eyeballs on ribs, and even the occasional foot on a face. Some had tails made out of femurs and large sections of cartilage plastered to necks, shoulders, and legs. It was a disgusting sight to behold, but Dr. Levin carried on regardless.

"Get him," Levin yelled at the television, gulping

down the rest of his drink before he headed back to the lab.

"Doris, let me know when the Heavyweights come out," he said, washing his hands as he prepped for his biggest excursion yet.

Grant Edgar landed a left jab followed by a right uppercut, staggering Louis Sandro as he fell against the ropes. Just as his knee kissed the canvas, Edgar popped him one more time in the head for good measure, which was met with a series of boos and hisses from the crowd. The bell dinged, signaling the end of the round, and both men headed to their corners for a breather.

Kabrina squirmed and kicked her legs in defiance, trying her best to wiggle out of the restraints she'd been confined in. She couldn't remember how she had gotten here, and she was scared shitless. There was tape over her mouth and she was in a cage of some kind, with no way out.

The room was shrouded in darkness, but once her eyes had adjusted she was able to make out other enclosures, other people. There had to be a dozen or so in total, everyone tied and taped up just like she was. It was some kind of perverse flesh farm, for who knows what.

Dr. Levin turned the handle and entered the room, letting in a small strip of light which made the rats wince and turn their heads in fear. He wondered who was going to be the lucky candidate tonight, and he slowly walked the floor, searching for the perfect patient. Very soon he was going to make history, he could practically feel it in his bones.

He was patiently waiting for the main title bout, as he knew it was going to be a loud, wild, ruckus of a fight. As soon as it came on, he'd crank the volume up as loud as it could go, and then begin his quest to solidify his name as the greatest scientist to ever live. He'd dreamt of the day since he was a child, if only his parents were around to see it.

As she struggled to break free, Kabrina tried her best to recollect how she ended up in such a precarious situation, but for the life of her, she couldn't remember a thing. The last she knew, she was out barhopping with her best friend Priscilla, and they ran into some cute guys who asked if they wanted to get high outback, to which their answer was "Yes, of course."

After that, it was all a blur. She had had one too many and was acting sloppy and obnoxious, and she must have royally pissed someone off, but other than that she couldn't think of any reason someone would want to do this to her. Why would they treat her like this when she couldn't possibly have done anything more than making fun of what they were wearing or cracking a joke about where they were from.

She knew she had to get out, and quickly, or else she was toast. And that's when the ugly old man in the white lab coat snuck up behind her and zapped her with a cattle prod, leaving her twitching uncontrollably on the floor like a wounded animal. He'd finally found his beauty, now it was time to feed the beast.

He strapped her to his table to administer the concoction and pulled out a long, thick syringe that he stuck into a bottle of bright orange liquid, which he then extracted. She slowly started to come to, her eyelids fluttering as she stirred. It was almost time, and he was beyond anxious to get started.

Her eyes opened and she was able to turn her head from side to side and look around. She noticed there was a second table to her right, with someone secured to the cold stainless steel. All of a sudden it hit her, the person lying next to her was her best friend, Priscilla.

Kabrina tried to yell, but the tape over her mouth stifled the sound and nothing came out. She writhed and thrashed against the metal slab, trying to find a little wiggle room so she could free herself. However, despite her best efforts, all she managed to do was tighten the straps on her ankles, wrists, and torso.

The fight was just about over and the final bell signified the end of the bout. Edgar had edged out a controversial twelve-rounder with Santos, clearing the stage for the Heavyweight Championship between Tom Nicholls and Graham "Sledge" Hammer. It was bound to be one hell of a spectacle, and it would make for the perfect smokescreen.

Doris popped her head back inside once more, giving him the nod that the time had come.

"Snoozefest, like I told ya," she said, trying to keep her eyes from wandering. "Big guys are up next."

"Thank you, dear. I'll start the process now."

"I'll be in the living room as usual," she said, closing the door behind her.

Dr. Levin laughed as he stuck the needle in Kabrina's arm and emptied the fluid into her veins. It would take effect very quickly and there wasn't any time to waste. He filled another dose and jammed it into Priscilla, watching as she flailed in protest. He kicked the brake release on the tables and one by one he scooted his test subjects into the chamber room for what he hoped would be his first successful trial.

It had taken him nearly his entire life, but he never gave up on his dreams and tonight he would become a legend. What he would accomplish would go down as the single greatest moment in human history. People would one day tell the tales of the first successful interdimensional time travel ever recorded, and his name would live on forever.

As he waited for the fight to start, he snagged a piece of chicken from the fridge and another beer to wash it all down with. Doris had always made the best chicken breast, and he was a sucker for it. Normally he'd have gobbled it down in a matter of seconds, but tonight he took his sweet time savoring the exceptional flavor. He needed all the energy he could muster, as it was an extremely grueling process and he had to be ready for whatever may come.

Tom Nicholls made his way to the ring and Dr. Levin looked on as he scarfed down the rest of the chicken and chased it off with a bottle of lager. It was time to get suited up and provide the last injections, and he'd never felt more ready in his life than he did at this moment. He tossed the remains in the trash and headed to his locker for a change.

The problem with all his previous tests was that the serum didn't hold up well when he sent subjects through. That's why they'd always return as globs of goo and slush instead of in one piece. Going through the vortex would displace their atoms and low-level radioactivity would weaken their cell walls. When the double helix is in its helical form, it's inactive. When it's unfurled, that's when it becomes active, and then it can transform and mutate.

Now, with the second round of booster shots, he was able to keep them intact when they went through and reappeared. He'd pinpointed the issue and adapted, and there was absolutely no chance it wouldn't work this time. All the steps had been accounted for and there was only one way to find out. He washed his hands and secured his mask as he stepped into the hazmat suit.

Graham "Sledge" Hammer shuffled on down to the ring, eliciting a barrage of cheers from his fans. He raised his arms in the air and danced around as he entered the squared circle, playing to the sold-out crowd. The audience went wild and let out a deafening roar as they checked his gloves and gave the okay.

All of a sudden there was clamoring in the flat next door, as "Sledge" Hammer punched at the air, putting on a show for all the spectators in attendance. If there was one thing the man knew how to do, it was entertaining. He was fired up and ready to do battle, smacking himself upside the head in a frenzy.

The Dugans had lived on the 12th floor longer than any of the other residents. Butch and his beautiful wife Ruth lived in number 76 and had three snotty children - one boy and two girls. Jake was the oldest at fourteen, followed by Lexie who was ten, and Lexa who topped the ladder at seven and a half years old.

They were an extremely loud family who was usually up all hours of the night, and sometimes it sounded as if they banged on the walls for fun. There were always yelling and arguing and whenever there was a fight on, without fail, Mr. Dugan would invite his buddies over for a night of drunken debauchery. Tonight there was a packed house and the hive was buzzing with excitement.

"I hope you're ready," said Dr. Levin as he administered the booster shot to Kabrina and undid the straps on the table.

Making sure not to do anything that would compromise his life's work, he gently picked her up and placed her inside the giant circular capsule, locking the door behind him as he stepped out. He hurried over to the control panel to commandeer the ship and switched on the pylons. They vibrated at such a high frequency that whatever was caught within the triangle when it started up, would vanish and then reappear within a matter of minutes.

It never ended well for his rats, but that was the price of being on the cutting edge of scientific advancement. Everything came at a price and if that's what it took, then so be it. It was all worth it in the end.

Nicholls and Hammer stood toe to toe in the middle of the ring, receiving their instructions from the referee.

"Touch gloves, gentlemen, and take your corners," he said as he stepped between them, separating them.

Dr. Levin waited for the signal, eager to get going. When the fight was loud enough to muffle the sound of the vortex, Doris would hit the switch and the light would turn green, and then he'd begin. Any minute now and his name would become synonymous with interdimensional time travel and it gave him goosebumps. He was twitching with anticipation, waiting for the bulb to flash his favorite color in the world.

The corners were cleared and the fighters took their positions, warming up as they waited for the bell to ring. There was a loud *ding* and the crowd went wild, whistling and howling like a band of maniacs as the zebra yelled, "Fight!" It was on and soon there was screaming coming from every flat on the floor, except one.

Mrs. Styles and her son had lived in number 80 for a little over a year and a half, and they were the quiet ones who no one ever saw. A few times Doris had thought that the place was empty, only to find the boy coming home or going for the night. His mother worked three jobs and was never around, leaving him to fend for himself.

On the opposite hand, the Beckers in number 78 were a noisy, rotten bunch; Jim and Katherine with their bundles of joy, Braxston and Ophelia. There's nothing more irritating than children throwing tantrums, and if there was ever a prize for getting under your skin, they definitely took the cake. No one liked them and everyone stayed as far away from them as possible.

Tonight they were as loud as the rest of the block, and Jim was doing his best to give everyone a run for their money. He was a bit of a macho man and had watched his father go pro when he was little, making his chest swell with pride as tears filled his eyes. It was a feeling he'd chase for the rest of his life.

Both fighters felt each other out for a bit, before chasing a few swings to best their opponent.

When it came to the sport in general, Dr. Levin wasn't much of a fan. He did indulge the occasional bout every once in a while, however, he never truly understood the point of the contest. Two men try to out punch each other and whoever is left standing, wins. After all the hospital bills and manager fees, how much could your average joe possibly make that would be worth the beating they took? Not enough, if you asked him.

And don't get him started on the main contender and champion. He despised them as much as he disliked the smell of horse shit on a warm afternoon. They were nothing more than glorified gladiators, barbarians of stupidity and brute force. Intelligence wasn't their strong suit like it was his.

He was born for this and had been chasing it his entire life.

Round one was coming to a close and suddenly the champ landed a strong right to Nicholls' ear, sending him to the canvas in the dying seconds of a vicious fight. He struggled to get to his feet, receiving a standing eight count as the bell sang its tune and they went to neutral corners. Luckily he still had plenty of time to shake it off and stage a comeback, and he was up for the challenge.

Kabrina woke up and had no idea where she was, again. She was groggy and could barely open her eyes. It felt like she'd been hit by a truck, her body numb and aching all over. The drugs were so strong, she couldn't move a muscle.

She was in some sort of weird, round, cage-like contraption with no clue of what was happening, and although she couldn't see, she was terrified to the bone. Where was she and what had the evil doctor done to her? She needed to get help, but her whole body tingled like it was asleep, and she was stuck.

From the corner of the room, Priscilla, tied to the table, was unable to do anything but watch the events unfold directly in front of her. She was out of the splash zone, but still in the line of fire, unbeknownst to Dr. Levin. Her straps were on extra tight, but no matter how much she fought it, she wasn't going anywhere.

The second round began and the fans were louder than ever. It was getting closer and closer, and the doctor was itching to get started. He tossed a few switches and a low distinct whirring sound began to engulf the room like a jet engine.

Nicholls danced circles around Hammer, delivering the goods as promised. He landed a couple of solid punches and the crowd went wild, erupting as the champ wobbled against the ropes. Doris sat with her finger on the button, waiting for the decibel meter to spike.

Dr. Levin was growing impatient and agitated and he wanted to just say screw it, to ignore the rules they'd put in place to keep them safe. But that wasn't the best reaction and, once he thought it over, he realized it was best to submit and not give in, no matter how much it pained him to do so. He hadn't gotten this far on his looks and physique alone, although sometimes he wondered what it would have been like to be more athletic and attractive, compared to brainy and geeky.

They were trading blows now and the champ was in serious danger of losing his title. Nicholls continued his relentless assault and battery, taking the second round by storm. The bell ended the round and Doris relaxed for a minute as the channel paused for commercials and station identification.

At the same time, someone knocked on the door of number 78, and Jim Becker answered. He was in a bad mood after watching his favorite fighter get pummeled at the end of the second. A dopey-looking kid stood in front of him with a name tag that read Meryl and a red hat and shirt that said *Dingo's Pizza*.

The third round was just about to start and Jim

patted his pockets for his wallet, "Aw, shit, kid. Hold on, I'll be right back," he muttered and disappeared back inside leaving Meryl standing there thinking maybe he had the wrong address or something.

It was on and Nicholls came out firing on all cylinders, taking it straight to Hammer. He could smell blood in the water, and he locked in on his prey. There wasn't any time to waste as the decibel meter buzzed with joy and Doris pressed the button, turning the light green.

Dr. Levin almost tripped over his own feet on his way to the controls. As he saw the signal he'd been waiting for, he tuned a dial and hit a few switches, sending his subject on through. The pylons vibrated at such a high speed that a pocket of air started to swirl and open, ripping the entire room apart with a violent, vicious whirlwind.

Out of nowhere, the circular pod disappeared from the room, and just as it did, it pulled Priscilla right along with it, decapitating her on the spot as she went. It was a terrible thing to see and before he had a chance to do a victory dance, Dr. Levin got a bad feeling that something had gone wrong. Something had gone very wrong.

The addition of Priscillas body to the process would definitely throw things out of whack, and that meant something was going to come back, but he had no idea what. He'd never made a mistake like this before, and he prayed it wouldn't cost him his life. There was a quick bright flash and the pod reappeared, smoking and slightly glowing.

The doctor cautiously approached it, unsure of what he might find, and he grabbed the handle and heaved it open. He was greeted by a wild, ferocious roar unlike anything he'd ever heard, and he instantly turned to run. Something that used to resemble Kabrina smashed through the doorway, exiting the pod, and he scrambled behind a chair, trying not to be seen.

It thrashed and shredded the room, crushing the controls and crippling the pod. Dr. Levin had no idea what to do, so he closed his eyes and prayed. He'd finally brought something back in one piece and achieved the impossible. Yet at the same time, he'd created a monster and no one was safe.

Butch jumped in the air, enjoying the fight with his buddies, drinks in both hands. He was shit-faced and loving it. Nicholls landed a left hook then a right uppercut, staggering Hammer. He ducked and threw another sweeping left hook, sending Hammer into the ropes and onto the canvas. The referee sent Nicholls to his corner and started his count. 1 - 2 - 3...

Suddenly the lights went off in the entire building and Doris freaked. "Lester, are you okay in there?" she yelled, trying not to kick anything over as she searched for a flashlight in the darkness.

There was no reply and she became frightened that he might be hurt. She needed to find him, and she located the doorknob and crept through, unaware of what was waiting for her on the other side. The monster grabbed Doris's head with one giant human-like hand and her shoulders with its other, smaller twisted hand, splitting her right down the middle as it ripped her in two.

Blood splattered all over the walls and furniture and the monster plowed right on through into the hallway, taking pieces of drywall and wood with it as personal keepsakes. It turned to its right and saw Meryl from Dingo's Pizza standing there waiting for Jim to come back with the payment and went right for him.

Jim was unaware of what was happening and came back to the door with a candle in one hand and his wallet in the other, ready to pay. "Must have been a blackou…" was all he got out before it tore through his head like fresh cabbage. Meryl tried to run but it grabbed him from behind and bit the base of his neck, detaching his spine and separating the skin from his skull.

The monster charged into the flat and Katherine Becker screamed at the top of her lungs, her children cowering behind her as the thing continued its bloodshed. After clearing the flat, it headed to the next one over, until it had successfully wiped out the entire 12th floor, one innocent victim at a time. Ruth Dugan was forced to watch her husband being disemboweled, preceded by the death of her three children who had their limbs removed while being eaten alive like little kernels of popcorn chicken.

The carnage continued outside for a while as the monster wreaked havoc, tearing the floor apart. It eventually made its way back to the doctor's place where Levin was still crouched behind a recliner, stuck in between the chair and a window. He was yet to be found, and he didn't dare move for fear of becoming its lunch.

Out of nowhere a slew of colorful lights flashed and sparkled in the night sky, lighting it up just long enough for him to get a good look at the *thing*. It stood nearly six-foot-tall and had one long muscular arm with a giant human-shaped hand at the end of it. It had thick, black, pointy nails, a huge lump of a shoulder with no neck and its head in the center of its chest. It slushed a single mushy rope-like leg that was trailing glowing green goo as it walked, crying out in anger as it maintained its search.

He'd done it. He'd actually done it.

His experiment had survived and made it back through, even if it was a vile abomination of man. He'd become the first person to ever successfully achieve time travel. It was real, and all thanks to him. He'd made it happen and nothing else mattered anymore. *Mark this day in your calendar folks*, he thought, grinning.

As the fireworks died off, just before everything turned pitch black again, the monster saw the poor old doctor crouched behind the chair, and it howled with excitement. It flung the chair aside with authority, and Dr. Levin never saw it coming. His body was mangled so badly, it looked like it had been attacked by a pack of wolves.

A few hours later, as the monster pressed on with its destruction, a dozen men in military suits came stomping through the wreckage, the vortex expanding out of control until it was almost too big to stop. They had to get a handle on the situation quickly or suffer the consequences. The experts had been called in to rid the place of its evil, and now the rest was up to them.

"It's alive," screamed one of the men in the green fatigues. "It's alive!"

Something Foul on Floor Thirteen

P.J. Blakey-Novis

When Nancy moved into Castle Heights a little over a year ago, she thought it was a shithole. But she was well aware that on her nurse's salary and having found herself suddenly single, a shithole was all she could afford. If someone were to ask her now what she thought of the place, with its peeling wallpaper, worn and suspiciously stained carpets, and bizarre odour that nobody could quite identify, she'd still call it a dump - but it was *her* dump.

Castle Heights, as grandiose as the name may have sounded, was far from being a palace. But as they say, an Englishman's (or English*woman*'s) home is their castle. What Nancy found was a community of sorts, not a heap of concrete stuffed with junkies and layabouts as she had expected. Her parents had never been to visit and had gone so far as to advise Nancy not to take the place. However, as they weren't offering to contribute to anywhere more suitable, they had little influence over the decision. Nancy told them about the flat, mentioning that it was number 81, but omitting the fact it was on floor thirteen. Her superstitious mother would likely have a heart attack if she knew that.

Within a matter of weeks, Nancy had met the occupants of her floor. Well, most of them. Apartment 81 was at one end of the corridor, with 86 at the other end. She'd had conversations with the elderly couple at 82, shared wine with Jane, the single mother at 83, ogled the two men from number 84 who were undoubtedly uninterested in women, and exchanged pleasantries with Herbert, the overweight but kindly middle-aged man at number 85. Nancy had never seen anyone go in or out of the flat at the end of the corridor. None of her neighbours had mentioned the inhabitants so she had presumed it to be vacant. Until tonight.

***

As a nurse, Nancy worked shifts, of course. She would come and go at all hours, allowing her to pick up on the routines of her neighbours. Maureen and Edgar at 82 hardly ever left the building. They rarely were awake past 8pm either, as Nancy had discovered one evening when she had knocked on their door, looking to borrow some milk, just before 9. Edgar had eventually made it out of bed and to the door as Nancy was re-entering her own apartment. Nancy apologised, of course, but Edgar was in good spirits. "We get to bed early these days," he'd explained. "Best not to be about too late, especially on this floor." What Nancy had taken as a joke at the time should have been heeded as a warning.

Jane from 83 was back and forth, sometimes carting her screaming toddler along to the lift and down to the play park nearby. She had been quite forthcoming about her situation when they'd shared drinks, how she'd got herself knocked up by her married boss who then suggested she find new employment. Nancy would bump into the men at 84 if she was on an early shift, often riding the lift with them to the ground floor. She'd never got around to asking what they did, but they were always sharply dressed by 7am and seemed to be heading to work. Herbert, on the other hand, did not work. His large frame required him to walk with a cane and Nancy would hear him wheezing along the corridor if he had the urge to leave the building, usually for cigarettes and a newspaper.

That just left apartment 86...the source of something rather foul.

***

Nancy had worked what she called a middle shift. These were by far her favourite as they were close to what could be called 'normal' working hours, albeit a long day still. She'd left a little after ten, taken the short bus ride to the hospital, and began her duties by 11am. Things were always busy and she ate little, rushing between patients. She told herself that busy was good, it made the time go faster, and before she knew it, 9pm had arrived. A 9pm finish does not always mean that, however, and Nancy found herself attending to one last patient before she could make her getaway, just missing the bus she would normally catch.

She waited in the cold for the next twenty minutes, before slumping into a seat on the bus, now thinking about food. Aware there was little available in her apartment, Nancy decided to stop at the corner store for snacks and well-needed alcohol. Tomorrow was a day off, a rare treat in itself, and she planned to drink a bottle or two of wine and sleep for as long as possible.

Nancy made it off the bus, in and out of the shop, and almost to the entrance of Castle Heights before things took a turn.

"Cold night," said a man's voice, a few feet from the main door. Nancy glanced up, seeing a figure in a black suit smoking a cigarillo, his dark hat concealing most of his face.

"Sure is," she muttered, reaching out for the door.

"I need to come in…would you mind?" the man said, stepping towards Nancy.

"You live here?" she asked, certain she had never seen him before.

"No. Just visiting…" he explained.

"You'll need to buzz whoever you're visiting to let you in then." Nancy opened the door, her stomach turning, fearful the man may try to follow.

"Tried that - no reply."

"What flat number? I'll let the concierge know and he can check they're home."

"Very kind of you," he said, tipping his hat a little. "Apartment 86, Floor 13."

Nancy made it through the door, closing it before the man followed, but she could have sworn he said, 'thank you, Nancy'.

The ground floor was gloomy, the build-up of dust, dead flies, and grime on the lamp shades keeping the entire building in a state of dimly lit neglect. On a chair sat Trevor, the concierge, somehow managing to read a newspaper in the poor light.

"Trevor," Nancy called.

"Nancy!" he replied in his thick Scottish brogue. "How are you this evening?"

"I'm fine, thanks. There's a guy outside, said he's visiting someone in 86 but they aren't answering. I told him I'd let you know." Nancy detected a flash of something in Trevor's eyes, fear perhaps, but it vanished in an instant.

"Okay, dear. I'll go and have a chat with him." Trevor folded his paper slowly, seeming to be in no hurry to get out of his chair. Nancy headed towards one of the two lifts before pausing.

"I thought 86 was empty?" she asked. "I've never heard a sound from there."

"Well, nothing wrong with quiet neighbours, is there?" Trevor replied with a shrug. Nancy stepped into the lift and watched Trevor open the main entrance before she hit the button for floor thirteen.

As the lift doors parted, Nancy almost dropped her bag of wine and snacks. She'd taken the lift at her end of the building, so it opened outside of her apartment's door but, even in the gloom, there was no mistaking what she saw. A crack of light illuminated the carpet at the end of the corridor, spilling from the door to number 86. Not only did it light up the floor, but it shined off the black shoes, the black suit, and that damned black hat of the man standing there. Nancy's mind reeled, wondering how he had gotten there before her, and with genuine surprise that flat 86 was indeed inhabited.

The conversation the man was having was too faint to be heard from where Nancy stood, but as she took a step out of the lift, her wine bottles clinked together loudly. She may as well have shouted, the sound shattering the quiet and drawing the man's attention to her. Unable to take her eyes away from him, Nancy took the few steps to her front door and fumbled for her keys. If he had been in conversation, that had been cut short. Now, he just stared at Nancy. She matched his glare but felt her heart racing, as though she were in danger, as though the entire population of Castle Heights was now at risk. Nancy looked away from the stranger to find the keyhole. As she turned her key in the lock, she risked a final glance back and paused. She hadn't heard the door close, but the man was gone, the door to 86 was shut tight, and all was silent. Once inside, Nancy slid across the chain on her door and began running a hot shower, an anxious feeling gnawing at her.

***

Once she'd showered and slipped on a clean nightdress, Nancy made herself comfortable on the sofa with an open bottle of wine and an assortment of crisps and chocolate. Deciding she was too tired to read, she flicked on the television, scrolling through for some late-night horror movie to watch. Time had little meaning for Nancy, she would work, chill out for a couple of hours, and then sleep - whether that was midday, or the early hours of the morning, it made no difference. It was a little past 11pm by the time Nancy found something to watch, a low-budget TV movie with some kind of sea monsters, and she'd made a dent in the first bottle of wine half an hour later.

The first scream came at 11.34pm. Nancy knew the exact time as she glanced at the clock instinctively. For a moment, she assumed it had come from the movie and wondered if she should turn down the volume for the sake of her neighbours. A minute later, a second scream rang out. This time the television was on a commercial break.

What the fuck? Nancy wondered, muting the television. Frozen in place, she listened intently for any other sounds, for someone else to go into the corridor to investigate. Five minutes passed in silence, Nancy barely dared to breathe, when another sound came. It was more than a scream, it was the sound of true terror, as though every damned soul in Hell itself was calling to her for help. There was a fraction of a second of silence before everything went dark and Nancy let out a scream of her own.

The silence was oppressive. There had been power outages at Castle Heights in the past, more so than with most buildings due to its poor maintenance, but usually it would only last for minutes. Often, people would congregate in the hallways and check on one another. Nancy sat in silent darkness, listening for any sign of movement but hearing nothing. She reached for her phone, flicking on the flashlight app. If it hadn't been for the screaming, Nancy would have just resigned herself to bed but there was no denying something was going on. And she was well aware she'd be unable to sleep if she didn't at least check on her neighbours.

Certain that Maureen and Edgar would be asleep and oblivious to the situation, Nancy slowly opened her front door. She flicked it onto the catch, pocketed her keys just in case, and took a few cautious steps along the corridor. Still no sounds. She wondered if she should really be knocking on anyone's doors at this hour - for all she knew, they were all sound asleep. Nancy hovered outside Jane's flat, deciding to text instead.

Hey, power went out. U ok? Was gonna knock but didn't want 2 wake Charlie.

A moment passed without reply and Nancy took another step along the corridor. Her phone was on silent but still vibrated so, when a call from Jane came through, Nancy let out another scream of her own.

"Jesus!" she muttered, swiping the screen to answer. "Jane...I'm outside your..." Nancy dropped the phone as the haunting screams of tortured souls echoed through the receiver. "Oh shit!"

Fearing Jane may be in trouble, Nancy began pounding on the door. Nothing about the situation was all right, nothing felt safe or even made any sense, and Nancy couldn't stop the tears from falling. After what felt like an eternity, Jane's door opened a little, the security chain holding it back.

"Nancy? What's wrong? Oh my God, has something happened to you?"

"I...You...called me..." Nancy stuttered, confusion swelling. "The power went out. Did you hear all the screaming?"

"I didn't hear anything, I was asleep. Probably just teenagers messing about outside."

"It wasn't outside. I texted you to see if you were okay, and then you called me, but it wasn't you."

"You're not making any sense. I haven't touched my phone - like I said, I was asleep." Jane removed the chain from the door and opened it wider. "Look, I'm up now, want a coffee?"

"No power for coffee," Nancy said, looking nervously up and down the hallway before following Jane in anyway. Jane flicked a few switches and verified that the power was out, before using Nancy's phone to light the way to her bedroom and retrieving her own device.

"It's not even switched on," Jane stated, her concern for her neighbour evident. Nancy explained the events thus far; the strange man waiting outside, how he had been on their floor visiting 86, the power cut, the screams, the phone call. "That's not all that weird," Jane replied, her shrug just about visible in the darkness.

"Seems pretty odd to me," Nancy said.

"What? Someone lives at 86, they just happen to be quiet. They had a visitor. That lift moves quicker than the one you took. There was a power cut. All pretty explainable…"

"And the screaming?" Nancy pressed.

"I usually scream when the power goes out," Jane said. "It can be startling, especially if it's night and the lights go off."

"The screams were before the power went out, just before. And the phone call?" Nancy held up her call list. "That's definitely your number that called me!"

"Fine, *that's* a bit weird but it must just be a glitch somewhere. Have you called down to Trevor?"

"Not yet, I didn't know if we should check on anyone else?"

"Why?" Jane asked. "Seriously, I'm sure they're all asleep or are big enough to handle a little power cut."

"Number 86 are awake because they have a visitor; he didn't arrive long ago. Maybe that's where the screaming came from."

"Hmm, you don't know who lives there, you said the guy in black was creepy, and you think maybe someone was, what, hurt in there? Just let Trevor deal with it."

"Fine," Nancy said, dialling the concierge's number. "Voicemail," she huffed.

"Just text him, that's what I do if I need something. He's probably busy getting the power back on."

Hi Trevor, it's Nancy from 81. There was some screaming coming from 86, I think. I don't know them so would you mind checking? Thanks.

A moment passed before the phone rang again, the vibrations making both women jump. "It's Trevor," Nancy said, swiping to answer. Once again, the sound of agony-filled screaming came blaring from the tiny speakers and Nancy held the phone at arm's length. Jane could hear it just as well and mouthed a 'what the fuck?', eyes wide. Nancy ended the call and looked at Jane. "That's what happened when you called me too."

"Yeah, that's fucking creepy. Maybe stay here tonight and we'll have a look around when the power comes on." Jane paced about the small living room, glancing outside at the deserted streets. "It's weirdly quiet out there. What time is it?"

"Just gone twelve," Nancy said, checking her phone. "I left my door open. I'll lock up and grab some wine if you want?"

"Want me to come with you?" Jane replied, grinning.

If Nancy had been honest then she would have given a resounding 'yes', but she tried her best to cover her fear. "It's two doors along, I'm sure I'll be fine."

Jane opened the door to her flat, keeping it wedged in place with her foot, watching as Nancy returned to her own home. She saw Nancy take a step inside. She jumped as the scream rang out, this time coming straight from number 81. Flicking the catch on the door, Jane ran the few metres to Nancy's doorway, looking over her friend's shoulder into the living room. It wasn't dark in there. Shadows danced across the walls and ceiling from countless flickering candles. They were everywhere - on every surface, standing on the carpet, along the windowsill.

In the centre of the room, on top of Nancy's coffee table, sat a small boy all in black. Legs crossed, head in hands, yet frighteningly familiar. Even after Nancy's scream, the child had not moved. Heart thumping, she took a step forward.

"Hello?"

Nothing.

"Did you light these candles?" Jane whispered to Nancy, staying one step behind.

She shook her head. "Hello?" Nancy called out again.

The child's head turned, suddenly, almost bird-like, in their direction. Jane let out a startled gasp. "Charlie?" she whispered. Nancy was about to speak when the child slowly pulled its hands away from its face. Time seemed to slow as the image before them hit home. *The eyes!* They weren't missing, as Nancy had first thought, but were pure, obsidian black. And big. Bigger than any human eyes should be. The women took a step back simultaneously, then another, as the child's mouth widened, not in a sinister grin but in a scream. From its apparently young mouth came the tortured sound of a thousand voices, deafening, angry. Nancy grabbed Jane and ran.

Jane darted into her own flat, into the small room where Charlie still lay fast asleep. Nancy appeared behind her, breathing a sigh of relief that the boy was safe. "It looked just like him," Jane said, fighting back tears.

"I know, but it wasn't."

"So, what now?" Jane asked.

"Police, I guess, but I'm not keen on using my phone." Nancy tried to call Trevor again, and the police, and the hospital. No answer to any of the calls, but her phone would ring soon after and the screams would fill Jane's living room once more.

"Then we need to leave," Jane stated, standing from the sofa. "The lifts will be out of action, so it'll have to be the stairs." It was the only logical thing to do but something pulled at Nancy.

"You're right, but I want to know everyone else is okay. Let's give the others a knock before we make a run for it."

"It's almost one in the morning," Jane replied.

"I know, but this is kind of an emergency."

Reluctantly leaving Charlie to sleep, they banged on 82, not caring if they upset Maureen and Edgar, but got no reply. They hammered at 84 and 85, certain that all those blood-curdling screams must have woken somebody but, again, no response. Without any real thought, Jane thumped on the last door - apartment number 86. The pair heard movement inside, hushed voices, a weird, metallic scraping sound. Jane and Nancy exchanged nervous glances as they heard a lock turn and the chain slide along and jingle free. Breaths held, flashlight casting eerie shadows, the women waited. The door opened silently, and they found themselves facing a girl in her late teens, wearing a black dressing gown.

"Oh, hi," Jane said, taken aback by the apparent normality of the occupant.

"Have you lost a child?" Nancy interjected, struggling for the right words. "I mean, there's one in my flat. And there's been a lot of screaming. Something weird is going on."

"I haven't heard anything," the girl replied.

"Are your parents home?" Nancy asked, now even more suspicious of the man who had been visiting.

"My dad's here," the girl replied with a shrug. "Dad!"

Appearing from the darkness was the man Nancy had met at the entrance. Something was wrong with this situation just as much as the mess in her flat. "He's your dad?" Nancy asked. "And he's come to visit you?"

"Go back inside, Dorothy," the man ordered, and the girl disappeared into the darkness beyond.

"Good evening ladies, how can I help you? It's rather late to be banging on doors, don't you think?"

"Seriously?" Jane retorted, now finding herself becoming agitated. "There has been screaming going on for the last hour or more, the power is out, there's a weird fucking child in my friend's apartment with candles all over the place, and now we find out people live in number 86. I don't care what time it is; I want to know what's happening."

"And what makes you think I know any more than you do? I'm simply visiting my daughter. Her mother is…away at the moment."

"Look," Nancy began, more than a little afraid of the man. "We didn't want to disturb you, we just wanted to check on each of the neighbours, make sure everybody was okay. There's been no reply at the other flats."

Before the man could respond, a high-pitched whizz filled the air, followed by another, and another. Outside was illuminated by a shower of fireworks, the bright blasts filtering through the windows of apartment 86.

"Fucking kids," Jane muttered, her eyes drawn to the interior of Dorothy's flat which was now lit up by flashes of red, blue, and green. Nancy also looked in that direction but the man in the black hat stared only forward. For the second time that night, the seconds seemed to slow. The women realised what was before them at the same instant the man knew they had seen it. Each flash of a firework reflected off the blood which soaked the walls, the furniture, even the ceiling. Dorothy stood naked in the middle of the gruesome carnage.

"Well, this is a little awkward," the man said with a smirk. "You are going to need to come inside, I'm afraid." The women took a few steps back, mentally planning to grab Charlie and make a run for the stairs. "INSIDE! NOW!" As he shouted these words his voice grew deeper, otherworldly, almost. The blast of fireworks continued to boom from outside Castle Heights. Nancy moved her head at the sound of a lock being turned, followed by another, and another. A wave of relief washed over her as three doors opened simultaneously. Herbert,

Maureen, Edgar, and the two men from 84 all stepped into the corridor.

Nancy shone her phone along the hallway, about to scream for help, when she felt the bile rise to her mouth. Five of her neighbours were facing her, each with eyes as black as the child in her apartment, mumbling something distinctively Latin in origin. They began to shuffle towards her as though in a daze and her mind connected the sight with a familiar zombie series on the television. Turning quickly, she grabbed a hold of Jane's arm, yanking her towards the open door of her flat.

"Run!" Nancy yelled, not pausing to wonder why Jane had not said anything. She tried to move her friend but found that she couldn't. Within seconds Nancy felt hands on her neck, Jane's hands, and screamed as she looked into those black orbs. The others were on her in seconds, the narrow corridor giving little room for escape, and Nancy knew she was finished as her neighbours shoved her into apartment 86 and closed the door, darkness falling over her.

***

Nancy came around to find herself strapped to a chair in a living room very similar to her own. Streetlights provided enough illumination through the bare windows to allow her to make out the basics of her surroundings, to see the man, or monster, perhaps, standing in one corner and puffing on a cigarillo. Nancy could see Dorothy, sitting on the floor in front of the chair, still naked and drenched in blood. The amount of blood was concerning, but that was not the extent of the horror - various chunks of skin, internal organs, and unidentifiable body parts lay scattered about the room. Even as a medical professional, Nancy couldn't tell if these were the remains of one corpse or more.

"What's going on?" Nancy asked. It seemed the most logical question, after all. Maybe an explanation would help but she held onto no fantasies of surviving this nightmare.

"Well," began the man, "it's all got a bit messy, I'm afraid. I should have taken more care, I suppose. Dorothy here had said everyone would be asleep." With this last sentence he gave the girl a sharp look, causing her to hang her head.

"Whose blood is this?" Nancy asked, not really wanting to know.

"Nobody important," the man replied. "It was just an offering. That's right, isn't it, Dorothy?"

The girl nodded her head.

"An offering to what?" Nancy said, hardly believing what she was hearing.

"To *whom,* not *what,*" the man corrected. "And if you're that interested, it was an offering to *me.*"

Nancy looked around the room as well as her restraints would allow, trying to assess the situation. Then she laughed, uncontrollably and hard.

"Because you're what, exactly? A demon? The Devil himself?" Despite everything Nancy had seen over the past few hours, she still had confidence in there being a logical explanation.

"Dorothy summoned me. She had some…shall we say…parenting issues? And to answer your question, I'm clearly not the Devil. I just work for the guy."

"Here's what I think," Nancy said, summoning an unexpected amount of courage and looking directly at Dorothy. "I think you're a little goth kid who got a bit carried away, hated your parents even though they were probably just looking out for you, and, maybe online, you found this fucking joker. Then he tells you to kill them and he'll come to help you. And by help, I assume you've had to fuck him?"

"That's gross," Dorothy replied. "And that's not at all what happened. You wouldn't understand."

"Gross?" the man interjected, feigning his feelings being hurt. "Thank you so much! And no, Nancy, that isn't quite right. Yes, Dorothy here wanted away with her parents. They were scumbags - I won't go into details as it displeases even us denizens of Hell, but she was subjected to things not at all appropriate for children. Yes, she found out about the ritual online, but isn't that how we learn anything nowadays? I may be what you'd call a *bad boy,* but I have certainly not taken advantage of Dorothy. She killed her mother with a knife to the throat while she was passed out drunk, said the right words, and that's when I appeared. Where we first met, in fact, downstairs. It seems so long ago now," he said, wistfully.

"Right, you appeared *downstairs.* Not here, in

303

the flat? And as a demon, you still struggled to get into the building? Righto…" Nancy said.

"DON'T DOUBT MY POWER!" the man yelled, his eyes flickering red, silencing Nancy for a moment.

"What about her father?" Nancy asked.

"Oh, that was all me!" the man said proudly, his mood switching in a split-second. "I hacked that fucker from anus to mouth and threw his insides about the place. And just to clarify, I never told Dorothy to take her clothes off, that was all her."

"What about the others? That kid in my flat…my neighbours?"

"What about them? The other residents of this delightful building are back in bed - they won't remember a thing. And that child, well, he's with me. He's still in training, I just put him places to scare people. Seems to be effective. Any other questions before we begin?"

"Begin?" Nancy repeated.

"Well, how did you think this would move forward? I'd wipe your mind and put you back to bed?" he asked with a laugh.

"Can you do that?" Nancy said, suddenly hopeful.

"Of course I can! But I won't. I'm afraid your time has come."

Nancy heard a mumbling from Dorothy and tried to listen. More words came, but it was just a whisper. "What are you saying?"

Dorothy looked up, turning to face the creature in the black hat. "You don't have to hurt her. She was trying to help."

"You're right, of course. Thank you. I don't *have* to hurt her. However, I *want* to hurt her. It's in my nature, you see. You summoned me, and this is what you get." The demon's hands pointed at Nancy and she felt a pressure building in her ankles. She couldn't see her feet due to them being tied under the chair, but she certainly heard the crack as each ankle broke, the feet now pointing inwards. That same pressure built up in her wrists next, bones breaking, hands hanging limply. Nancy tried to scream but her voice gave out, black spots filling her vision, her mind close to shutting down with shock and pain. Dorothy screamed but it was too late for her to help. Nancy felt each one of her ribs crack, one after another, sharp bone slicing through internal organs. As her mouth filled with blood, Nancy passed out, never to wake.

***

Jane was awoken by a racket outside Castle Heights soon after 3.30am. The sound of a military helicopter pounded overhead and, dragging herself to her bedroom window, she was shocked to see dozens of uniformed men surrounding the building. She reached for her bedside lamp, finding that the power was off.

"Nancy," she muttered, trying to discern between what had been real and what was a dream. She thought she remembered Nancy coming round, having wine, maybe, and talking to new neighbours.

Were they new? She couldn't remember. Jane made her way to her son's room to find him sleeping, then went to use the bathroom. Deciding that the fuzzy memories in her head were just blurry remnants of a wild dream, she was about to get back into bed.

The silence of the hallway was obliterated by a door swinging open and heavy boots running along the worn carpet. She heard banging on doors, including her own, and grabbed a dressing gown. Opening her front door, she saw each of her neighbours standing in nightwear, looking panicked. All except Nancy. Jane's eyes darted from one end of the corridor to the other as the soldiers entered both flats 81 and 86. There was yelling, words which were hard to make out, before two uniformed men ran from number 86 and vomited on the carpet.

"Everyone back inside! Nobody leaves," someone shouted, prompting each of the residents to return to their flats. Jane waited on her sofa for news, for some explanation as to what was going on, but nothing was coming. The official story she'd read in the papers a few days later: Couple Die from Drug Overdose at Castle Heights, Leaving Only Daughter.

As for Nancy, she must have decided to move on. Some of her clothes were missing and there was a note, after all. Jane couldn't be sure what had happened, everything was still so hazy. But things were looking up and Jane had a reason to be happy - she had a date lined up with one of her neighbours, a handsome man in a black suit from number 86.

The 14th

Tony Sands

"What you doin'? It's about to start," said Frank, munching on a crisp. On the TV, the opening bell rang to signal the start of the big fight, Nichols Vs Hammer. Frank had been very excited about it for days. Graham 'Sledge' Hammer was the overwhelming favourite, but Frank was a Nichols fan and, although he wasn't the most optimistic of people, he had hope that Nichols would pull off an upset win. Finally, the night was here and he was nestled comfortably on a sofa in front of a 65 inch OLED TV.

"I thought I heard something," said Fred, stepping back from the wall and joining Frank on the sofa. He plucked a crisp from the bowl on the table in front of them.

"You did, the opening bell," smiled Frank.

"No, something else, like...I dunno, just something." Fred ate his crisp and reached for another as they watched the fight.

"You're always hearing things," replied Frank.

On the TV Nichols and Hammer exchanged a couple of jabs.

"I have very acute hearing," explained Fred.

"You have very bad nerves," said Frank.

"Unlike you?"

"I have nerves of steel."

"My arse," muttered Fred, he sipped his bottle of beer and looked down at the table. "What happened to the pizza?"

"Gone."

"Really? I had about two slices."

"Three. Each. What a rip off. Lucky we bought so many crisps," Frank said.

"Last time we get a pizza from a place named Dingo's. You know the guy who delivered it was called Meryl? Meryl! 'Don't take my baby,' I said to him. Nothing. Just looked at me blankly."

"*A Cry in the Dark.*"

"Exactly," said Fred.

"Great film," they stated in unison, then found themselves leaning forward as the round neared its nervy end. Suddenly, Nichols was on the canvas having been caught by a fierce right.

"Told you he wouldn't last long," Fred pointed at the screen.

Frank sighed at the thought of listening to 'I told you so' all week, but Nichols got to his feet, the count stopped at eight and the bell signalling the end of the round came soon after.

"He's finished," chimed Fred, digging once more into the crisps. "Do we have any cheese and onion?"

"I just tipped everything into the bowl," said Frank.

A dull thump resonated from the wall behind them, startling both.

"See, I told you I heard something!" Fred said as they looked at the wall.

"Noisy neighbours," said Frank returning his attention to the fight. "Maybe they're watching this too."

"Maybe," Fred wasn't as convinced.

The second round soon took their mind off any worries though as Hammer almost went down under a barrage of blows from Nichols. Frank punched the air as Hammer walked unsteadily back to his corner.

"I think Tommy might actually have a chance here," Frank said excitedly.

Fred stood up and walked to the wall. The bell for the next round rang and the fighters came out. Fred smiled to himself, "it's just noisy neighbours."

"Eh?"

"Oh, nothing," said Fred. Frank was right, his nerves were bad, but then, all things considered, it was no real surprise. As much as he tried to forget what happened in 'that house' four years ago, it wasn't easy. His mind drifted back to that awful night...

"Holy shit!" yelled Frank, leaping from his seat.

On the TV, Hammer dropped to the canvas.

"Oh my, I didn't see that coming!" the commentator trilled.

"Hammer certainly didn't," came the pithy reply from his cohort who Fred assumed was some former fighter.

The referee started the count, "one!"

"Holy shit!' Frank yelled again.

"Two!"

"Did ya see that?" called Frank.

"Three!"

And then everything went black.

Frank and Fred stood in silence for a couple of seconds before the accusation came.

"What did you do?" cried Frank.

"Nothin', I didn't do a thing. I was just stood here," Fred said, his Liverpudlian accent crackling.

"What the fuck happened then?" Frank squeaked. "Was he counted out? Did he get up? And I hate the dark."

"I thought you had nerves of steel."

"Shut up, Freddy!" snapped Frank. He took his mobile phone out of his pocket and activated the flashlight. Fred did likewise.

"Don't act like you're okay with the dark," Frank continued.

"I never said I was, but then I never claimed I had nerves of steel."

A thump on the front door silenced them.

"Who do you think that is?" Frank aimed his light at the apartment entrance.

"Hopefully, an electrician."

***

They opened the door to a tall, gangly man with wiry hair and dark rimmed spectacles. He was in his late forties, around the same age, perhaps a little younger than Frank and Fred and was clutching a small, windup torch. He was surprised to see them.

"Hello?" said Fred.

"I was looking for Brendan, or Marie," said the man.

"Oh, yeah, they're away for a few days, taken

Theo to see his grandparents. We're cat sitting," Fred explained.

"Maxwell," added Frank. "He's the cat. Their cat, that we're sitting."

"Right, okay. Well, I'm Alex from next door. Have you lost your electricity?" he asked, peeking over their shoulders to see they indeed had.

"We have," said Frank, noting that there were no lights on the landing.

"It looks like the whole floor has," Fred said, looking around.

"Yes, any ideas what happened?" Alex asked, eyes on Fred.

"No," Fred stepped past Alex onto the landing. Another door opened, number 88, and an elderly West Indian lady poked her head out.

"Hi, Alice," Alex nodded at her, though she didn't see it.

"I've no electricity, what did you do?" Alice peered at Fred who was closest to her.

"Me? Why is everybody asking me?"

"Aren't you a maintenance man? You maintenance men are always breaking more than you fix," said Alice, stepping out of her apartment, pulling her bright purple dressing gown tighter.

"I'm not a maintenance man," Fred said.

"He's a cat sitter," said Alex, "for Brendan and Marie."

"Ah, I've never been a cat person," Alice said. "So, you gonna fix this or what?"

"Fix it? Are you still talking to me?" Fred felt like he was being reprimanded in school.

311

"I'm talking to anyone who will get my lights back on, I don't want my Darius messing with electrics."

"You worry too much, Nan." A light appeared behind her, followed by her grandson Darius who was a slim, boyish eighteen-year-old. He was in a t-shirt and jeans, his mobile phone providing the illumination. He had moved in with his nan when he was nine, due to his dad's lack of interest and his mum's ill health; he had been there ever since. This suited Alice just fine as she adored Darius and he was such a good boy.

"I don't want the risk of you getting electrocuted," his nan said.

"But it's alright if I get electrocuted?" whined Fred.

"I don't know you," she replied curtly.

**

Doors 87 and 89 opened in perfect synchronisation, as if rehearsed. Mr. Hernandez, from number 87, a short, balding, Spanish man, rubbed his weary eyes, he looked like he'd slept in his suit, which he had done, on the sofa, having had a very long day at work. He held a rather clunky, but bright, flashlight. Gabi and Paul, number 89, had been enjoying a horror movie in front of the TV when everything went black and scared the shit out of them. They both had phones lighting their way.

"Before anyone asks," declared Fred, "I didn't do anything, and I am not an electrician."

"Right," said Gabi, blankly.

"He's a cat sitter," said Alex.

"What is going on?" Hernandez asked.

"Blackout. Looks like it's affecting the whole block, lights have gone outside too," Paul had looked out the window from his apartment and noticed the very dark streets.

"Wonderful," said Frank, sarcastically.

"Who are you?" Paul shone his light at Frank accusingly, as if catching a perpetrator in the act of a crime, causing him to shield his eyes.

"Cat sitter," replied Alex.

Paul relieved the light from Frank's face.

"How many people does it take to look after a cat?" sneered Gabi.

"Guess it depends on the size of the cat," grinned Darius.

"Does anyone have a signal?" Paul held his phone out to show he had none.

Everyone checked, nobody did.

"Wi-Fi is out too," said Darius, his game having been cut disappointingly short.

"Where's Martin?" Alice nodded toward apartment number 90.

"Probably sleeping, like I should be sleeping," said Hernandez, looking back at his apartment longingly.

***

Alex knocked on Martin's door and it opened slightly.

"Martin?" he called gently. Martin was an elderly gentleman, always friendly, chatty and polite.

There was no reply and Alex looked around at the others for ideas as to what to do next.

"Martin?" he called again, a little louder. Still no reply. His torch started to dull and he gave it a wind, restoring the brightness.

"Go in and check on him," urged Alice, "he might be hurt."

"Or he might be okay and you'll give him a heart attack when he finds you suddenly standing in his flat uninvited," said Fred.

"I don't think you should go in," Frank added.

"For fuck's sake," Paul huffed and brushed Alex aside. He nudged the door open fully and peered in. "Martin, you alright?"

The silence was becoming heavier. Paul stepped inside, moving the beam of light from his phone around slowly. Light reflected from the glass casing pictures on the walls, but nothing stirred.

The others edged closer, trying to see in.

"Martin, it's Paul from number 89. You there?" He stepped slowly further along the short corridor. He felt chills running up his spine, but he couldn't lose face so carried on.

He reached the living room, his heart thumping hard in his chest and then he saw Martin, sitting in an old, high-backed armchair, unmoving. "Martin?" Paul moved quickly to him. Martin was still, his eyes staring into space.

"Shit," Paul exhaled, "shit, shit, shit."

Paul reached forward cautiously, intending to check the old man's pulse, when Martin grabbed his hand and sprang toward him wide eyed. "It's in the walls!" rasped Martin.

Paul, startled, fell backwards dropping his phone. "Fuck!"

Alex raced in, followed by Frank, Fred, Gabi and Darius. They found Paul scrambling to grab his phone and Martin leaning forward in his chair. He turned his head slowly to them and repeated the same words, "It's in the walls."

"Ah, Christ," whimpered Frank. "Of course it is, of course it's in the walls."

"I told you I heard something," said Fred.

"It's in the walls," Martin barked, glaring at them.

"What's in the walls?" Alex asked calmly, stepping slowly to his neighbour, hands out, trying to ease him.

Martin met his eyes then slumped back into his chair, unconscious.

"Martin?" Alex checked for a pulse on his neck.

"Is he dead?' asked Gabi.

"No, he has a pulse, but I think we'll need an ambulance."

"I'll go down to the ground and call one, Trevor should be around." Paul picked up his phone and stood up feeling rather sheepish.

"Trevor?" Fred said.

"The concierge," Gabi informed him.

"Ooh, posh, a twenty-four-hour concierge," said Fred. He hadn't noticed a concierge, but Frank had been in such a tizz to not miss the start of the boxing they'd rushed through the lobby.

"You'll have to walk, the lifts aren't working," Mr. Hernandez joined them.

"Fuck's sake," moaned Paul.

"I'll go," said Darius.

"Thanks, Darius, if you could," Alex smiled, and Darius headed out.

"We should go," whispered Frank to Fred.

"We can't leave them like this," Fred whispered back.

"Why not? It's not like they're on their own."

"That's true."

"And I don't like this."

"I can't say it's filling me with joy, but what about the cat?"

"When did you last see that cat?"

Fred paused in thought, it was a good question, he hadn't seen the cat since they'd arrived earlier that evening. "Do you think it's Maxwell in the wall?"

"You think the cat is in the wall?"

"In the fuckin' walls? The man's demented." Paul started to follow Darius when a *thump-thump* came from the wall, stopping him in his tracks.

"That doesn't sound demented," Fred sniped.

"Cat sitting pay well, does it?" Paul mocked.

"Come on, Paul, let's get home and wait for the power to come back on." Gabi pulled her partner away and out of Martin's apartment.

"Is he okay?" Frank looked from the wall to Alex.

"I don't know. He's breathing, that's good, right?"

"Is he diabetic?" Fred asked.

"I don't know," Alex felt helpless. "Mr. Hernandez?"

"I can't help, sorry, I don't know him very well." Hernandez shrugged, "he's a nice man, though."

"He is," Alex said.

"We'll wait with you," Fred said, reassuringly.

"I guess we will," Frank planted himself on the small sofa.

"I'll go and check on Alice," Hernandez turned and left.

Fred peered at the wall. "That noise didn't sound right."

"It's probably the plumbing, it's an old building," said Alex dismissively.

Fred took a seat, still unconvinced.

***

Alice watched Gabi and Paul storm past her into their apartment and was standing by the door to number 90 when Mr. Hernandez came out.

"Is Martin okay?" she asked with concern. She was very fond of her neighbour and seeing Darius race away to the stairwell gave her cause for worry.

"I couldn't say. He's breathing, but not awake." Hernandez shook his head.

"Poor Martin," she sighed.

"I'm sure Darius will get help."

"He is a good boy. I just hope he doesn't fall

going down those stairs in the pitch black. 'Don't worry, Nan, I got this,' he said, but how can I not worry?"

"He's a smart and careful boy, not the usual teenager. He'll be good." Hernandez patted her arm reassuringly.

"Want to come into mine whilst we wait for either the lights to come back on or the sun to rise? Whichever comes first."

"Okay, Alice, some company would be nice," he said, though he wanted nothing more than sleep.

"Right then, come on in."

***

"I hate this bloody place," Paul paced the corridor in number 89.

Gabi nodded in agreement, "I know, I know, but what can we do? It's a means to an end."

Moving into Castle Heights was only ever intended as a short-term measure. Paul's career in sales had been moving forwards rapidly and the business, a nail and beauty bar called 'Oh G's', that he and Gabi had started up and which Gabi managed, was building a steady, if unspectacular, trade. Frustratingly for them, things weren't progressing fast enough and they still weren't in a position to buy the house both felt worthy of them.

"That fuckin' bloke scared the shit out of me, I don't mind telling ya," Paul huffed.

"You did look stupid on the floor back there," Gabi snorted a giggle.

"Thanks, I feel much better now," Paul stomped into the living room.

"Chill out, babe, it would have freaked anyone out," Gabi said soothingly.

"That's twice I've nearly soiled myself tonight, first with the lights going out during that bloody film…"

"That scared me too." Gabi rubbed goosebumps from her arms, it had been a pretty scary horror film without the added frights.

"Then that Martin bloke, I mean, for crying out loud. What was that all about?"

"He was acting strange."

"He was acting like a nutter," sneered Paul.

"If you ask me, this whole building is full of nutters," Gabi reclaimed the glass of wine she'd been drinking before the blackout from the pristine, expensive, rather garish silver coffee table and sat down on the sofa.

"Amen to that," said Paul.

Thump-thump came from the wall, dull and ominous.

"Are they fucking around with us?" Paul snarled.

"Why would they do that?" Gabi flopped back into the soft cushions.

"Because they're all nutters, it's what nutters do."

Thump-thump, louder.

"Come and sit down, or even better, why don't you find those nice candles your mum bought us?"

Paul studied the wall. "Did you not hear that?"

"It's probably the pipes."

"Pipes? They've never made that noise before." He put a hand on the wall.

"Electrics? I don't know, maybe we could ask those cat sitters," she giggled to herself.

Paul pressed an ear to the wall.

"Fucking cat sitters," she snorted.

Paul listened hard, he was sure he could hear something moving.

"This place gets weirder and weirder, sooner we get out of here the better."

Paul thought he heard a whisper coming from behind the plaster, the hairs on the back of his neck stood up, fear overwhelmed him and then the wall moved, as if it were alive, and sucked him into it. In a split second he was gone. The wall wobbled, like a ripple in water, then stilled.

"Do we have any more wine?" Gabi swilled the little wine that was left in her glass around the bottom of it.

She sat in the quietness of the night for a few moments before turning her torch light around the room to find she was alone.

"Babe?" She put her glass down and stood up.

Silence.

"Paul, you there?"

Silence.

"Paul, don't fuck around."

Thump-thump.

"Oh fuck off!" she snapped.

Silence.

She walked up to the wall along the corridor where the sound had come from, washing the torch light around the room, empty. She felt very alone.

Thump.

"Fuck!" She bashed the wall with the base of her clenched fist.

Thump!

"Right!" She bashed the wall again.

Thump!

"Off!" She bashed it once more, but this time the wall sucked her arm in and, as much as she tried to pull back, it started to drag her in, her feet sliding along the wooden floor as she tried to resist. The wall snaked out and spiralled around her arm, tightening and squeezing. It pulled her closer and closer until her face was brushing it. "HELP!" screamed Gabi and then she too disappeared, leaving a ripple behind her.

***

Fred jumped to his feet, "Did you guys hear that?"

"Not the wall again?" Frank sighed.

"I thought I heard a shout," Fred looked toward the open front door.

"I didn't hear anything, sorry," said Alex.

Fred stood for a while longer then sat down, rubbing the back of his neck. "Maybe all this craziness is messing with my head."

Alex's flashlight dulled and he started winding it.

"Doesn't that get frustrating?" Fred asked.

"Not if it helps save the planet," Alex stated earnestly. "Humankind has done immense damage to the planet and I believe we should all do our bit to help save it."

"Oh," said Fred.

Alex finished winding as full light was restored to his planet-saving flashlight.

With that, they returned to sitting quietly in the dark until Frank finally found the silence was unbearable.

"Were you watching the boxing?"

"Not really a boxing fan." Alex didn't like violence, he had to switch the television news over on occasion and those soap operas were very angry shows, though his wife loved them.

"Oh," Frank felt deflated, which was better than scared. "It was a cracking fight, wasn't it Fred?"

"Great fight, you really missed something there," agreed Fred.

Alex didn't waste his time on nonsense, "I was watching a fascinating documentary on the indigenous plant life inhabiting the subterranean basin in..."

"That is fascinating," interrupted Fred.

***

"Thank you for keeping me company, I don't think I could go to sleep without knowing Darius is back safely." Alice pushed her curtain back and looked out the window. "It's very dark out there."

"It's very dark in here," said Mr. Hernandez as he safely navigated his way to a chair.

"That it is," Alice laughed. "I can't offer you a

cup of tea, but I have some cold drinks in the fridge. That'll be defrosting before long."

"I'm fine, thank you," Mr. Hernandez stifled a yawn.

"Long day?"

"The shop has been very busy this last two or three weeks." He rubbed his eyes, tiring more just thinking about it all.

"You work yourself too hard, at your age you should be putting your feet up," said Alice.

"That would be very nice, but my nephew has been unwell and my brother is on holiday, so we are short staffed. No rest for the wicked, eh?"

"I guess not," smiled Alice.

Pepé Hernandez came to England with his younger brother, Raul, more years ago than he'd care to remember, and it wasn't long before they had work in a warehouse and it was only a matter of months before they found, and took, the opportunity to buy a small grocer's shop which they both worked day and night in. Two years passed and the small grocer's became a bigger grocer's and then by their third year it was a mini market, then a supermarket. In the following decades they fought off large chains, maintaining a loyal and happy customer base. They kept prices fair and reasonable, and the business remained a family one, which was great, but also a pain, as you couldn't fire family.

Alice took a bottle of lemonade from the fridge and poured some into a glass. "You sure you don't want some?"

"You know, it might help me wake up a little, so

yes, that would be nice, thank you." Hernandez sat up in the chair.

Alice filled up another glass and, helped by Mr. Hernandez's bright torch, worked her way over to him.

"Thank you," said Mr. Hernandez, taking the glass as Alice settled into her well-worn armchair.

"I wonder what caused all of this," Alice sipped some lemonade, it was cold and refreshing.

"Hopefully, it won't last for much longer."

"If it does, we might need to find something stronger," laughed Alice and they clinked glasses.

"I have some wine, really good. Saving it for a special occasion, I can go and get it," Mr. Hernandez said.

"Aw, no, you wait for that special occasion," smiled Alice.

"This is a special occasion," he smiled back, "and you are a special lady."

"Stop it, Pepé, you're making me blush," gushed Alice.

Thump-Thump! The wall-mounted TV shook.

"What's this now?" scowled Alice.

Mr. Hernandez focused his torch on the offending wall and they both peered intently at it. Hernandez stepped up to it, listening.

Thump-Thump!!

"Blasted thing, my old heart can't be taking frights like that," said Alice. "It'll be the end of me."

Hernandez took a couple of steps closer.

"Be careful, Pepé."

"It's alright. Maybe it's rats?"

"Rats? I've got a hammer, I'll go get it."

Thump-Thump!!! Thump-Thump!!!!

"Those are some big fuckin' rats," Alice gasped.

"Maybe not rats," said Hernandez, moving closer to the wall.

Suddenly, the TV disappeared, right before their astonished eyes. Ripples spread across the white wall.

"What in the name of God just happened there?" Alice clutched the crucifix she'd worn around her neck for nearly forty-seven years.

"I don't know…I've never…" Hernandez struggled for words, his English failing him in all the confusion.

"That TV ain't cheap, you know? We paid good money for that." She liked that telly.

Pepé Hernandez rubbed his tired eyes. He was sleep deprived, that was causing all of this. It was the only explanation. He touched the wall where the TV had been and his hand sank into it, like it was wet sand.

"Dios mío," exhaled Hernandez. He tried to pull his hand back, but the wall had a tight hold of it and it was dragging him in. "No!"

"Pepé?" Alice was alarmed and helpless.

"Alice?" cried Pepé before he was lifted off his feet and sucked into the wall, taking his torch and the light with him.

***

Alex wound his torch again, the light brightening with each revolution of the small lever.

"Good exercise, eh?" smiled Fred and Frank laughed quietly to himself.

"I'm sorry?" Alex finished winding.

"You know, the winding, good exercise, strong wrists?" said Fred.

"Are you trying to be funny?" snapped Alex.

"Trying," said Fred with a slightly apologetic tone.

"He can be very trying," grinned Frank. "You know, a windup torch isn't a bad idea, my phone battery is going down, it's at forty-seven percent."

Fred looked at his phone's screen, "Mine's not bad, seventy-six percent. Your battery drains far too quickly, you need a new phone."

"There's nothing wrong with the one I have," Frank said defensively.

"Could either of you tell me the time, please?" Alex was becoming greatly agitated.

"Time he got a new phone," Fred sniggered.

"It's twenty past midnight," said Frank.

"Thank you. And I don't think now is really the time for humour. It makes everything feel darker," grumbled Alex. He dealt with a lot of annoying people in his role at Veganistic, where he was now store manager.

"I disagree, it helps us cope with the darkness. It gives us light, and light gives us hope," countered Fred.

"And with hope comes pain," said Alex.

"Nah, that pain was already there. Hope doesn't

bring pain, it brings the promise of better things to come. Hope is dreams, hope is aspirations. Without those things, we wouldn't cure diseases, we wouldn't travel, we wouldn't have learning. Without hope, we have nothing." Fred left his argument there.

"You didn't strike me as a philosopher," Alex felt embarrassed.

"You didn't strike me as a pessimist," said Fred.

"I apologise for my manner," said Alex. "Barbara, my wife, is out tonight. I'm not expecting her home anytime soon, it's usually a very late one when she's out with the girls. Which is a good thing, hopefully she'll be spared all of this."

"Hopefully," Fred smiled. "Look, that lad has probably called an ambulance by now and the power will most likely click back on any second. We'll be laughing about this in the morning."

"How are you not freaking out?"

"I'm shitting bricks on the inside," said Fred. "But Frank and me, we've been through worse."

Frank nodded, thinking back…

"There was this house…" Fred started.

"Was it a haunted house? Don't tell me a haunted house story, not now, I'm on edge as it is," Alex wound his torch.

"If you keep playing with it, it'll fall off," said Frank.

"It's so quiet," observed Alex.

And it was, incredibly quiet. Now that they were aware of it, Frank and Fred felt chills.

"Do you think the others are alright?" Alex

wondered.

"I'll go and see," Fred stood up.

"I'll come with you, stretch my legs," said Frank.

"What about me?" Alex didn't like the idea of being alone with a catatonic Martin and the silence.

"We won't be long," Fred assured him. "Besides, someone needs to stay with that poor fella."

"Better that it's someone he knows," said Frank, getting to his feet and heading for the door.

"Exactly. We'll be back in no time," Fred followed Frank out.

Alex breathed in through his nose and out through his mouth, deep breaths. He read somewhere that helped nerves. Or was it nausea? Either way, it wasn't working. He slowed his breathing down, closed his eyes and sat back in the chair. "It's going to be okay, Al," he told himself. He didn't see Martin's eyes flick open.

***

Fred knocked gently on number 88, the door was slightly ajar. He poked his head in and called quietly, "coo-ee."

"Coo-ee?" Frank mocked.

"What should I use instead? Oi?"

"What about 'hello'?"

"What does it matter?"

"It doesn't."

"Why are you making a thing of it, then?"

"Alright, alright. I'd say keep your hair on, if you had any."

"You're one to talk," mocked Fred.

They both smiled, humour proving a solid distraction from the unease they were feeling.

"Hello?" Frank called. "It's very quiet. Maybe they're not here."

"Maybe she and Mr. Hernandez are…you know?" Fred winked.

"I don't think that's what they're doing."

"Older people do 'do it', you know? My nan was like a rabbit…"

"Hello, Alice? Mr. Hernandez?" Frank called loudly, cutting Fred off.

They waited for a reply, but none came.

"Hello?" Frank called again,

Fred pushed the door all the way open, it tapped gently on the wall. The silence was eerie and swelled around them.

"Alice? It's the cat sitters," Frank raised his voice a notch.

"This is silly, it's only a blackout." Fred illuminated number 88's corridor and entered. Frank followed, feeling stupid now for being scared.

***

They found Alice passed out on the floor, at first they thought she was dead – it had been that kind of night - but she roused when they went to her.

"Take it easy," said Fred as she tried to sit up.

"What happened?" Frank asked.

"Pepé," Alice pointed weakly at the wall that had absorbed her neighbour.

"Pepé?"

"Mr. Hernandez, I'm guessing," said Fred.

"It took him," her voice was low, devoid of energy and she was in shock which had caused her to faint in the first place.

"What took him?" Fred helped her into a chair.

She pointed at the wall, Frank and Fred looked from that to each other thinking 'not again'.

***

"It's in the wall," said a distant voice. Alex tried to wave it off, he was too busy floating...he snapped his eyes open, adjusted his spectacles, raised his dimming flashlight and found Martin's face up close to his, noses almost touching. Martin's eyes were wide and wild. Alex yelped like a dog whose paw had been stamped on. Then his torch went out and darkness engulfed him, "FUUUUUUUUCK!!"

He desperately wound his torch.

"Martin, sorry if I alarmed you," Alex stammered. "We found you in a bad way, thought you needed help."

The flashlight emitted a dull glow, then it strengthened and Alex could see the room again, but there was no sign of Martin.

"Martin?" He stood and swooped the beam of light around. "Martin?"

Something grabbed his shoulder and he yelped again.

"It's me," came a voice.

Alex turned the light on the voice, stepping backwards into a chair and almost losing his balance.

"Fred, the cat sitter…" Fred put a hand up, as if to show he was unarmed.

"You scared the life out of me," said Alex.

"From the screams of ya, that was already happening," smirked Fred. "You okay?"

"I think so, Martin woke up, gave me a fright."

"Right." Fred scanned the room. "Where is he?"

"I don't know, one second he was in my face - like, literally, in my face. The next, he was gone."

"Well, he can't have gone far." Fred shone his torch down a second corridor that led to the bathroom and bedroom. "Coo-ee, Martin?"

They, cautiously, checked the bathroom and bedroom and there was no sign of Martin.

"He's not much for decoration, is he?" Fred observed.

"What do you mean?"

"He doesn't have anything on the walls; no paintings, no photos, no anything."

"I hadn't noticed, but now that you mention it, it is rather sparse." Alex looked at the blank, empty walls.

"Maybe he's wandered out," offered Fred.

"Wouldn't you have seen him?"

"In all of this carry on, who knows?" smiled Fred.

***

Martin wasn't on the landing and he wasn't in with Alice and Frank, who were very relieved to see them. Alice was still weak but regaining her senses.

"She said the wall sucked Mr. Hernandez in, along with her TV," Frank explained.

"It can't have," said Fred.

"I know what I saw," Alice retorted, her voice hoarse.

"Martin kept saying, 'it's in the wall'," Alex said.

"Where is Martin?" asked Frank.

"Not a clue," said Fred, "maybe Brendan's? We left the door open, so there's a chance he went in there."

"This might sound weird, Alice," Alex was studying the apartment. "But do you have pictures up on your walls?"

"Full of them, just take a look. My kids, my grandkids. You know, I even have a great grand kid?"

Alex looked at Fred and shone the light over the bare walls. Frank was puzzled.

"I'm going to look in Brendan's, I'll be quick," said Fred.

"Stay away from the walls," warned Alice.

"Yeah, I'll do that," Fred said.

"Freddy," Frank stood and joined him, "you're not going on your own. Something's not right here, we need to stick together."

"I'm fine with Alice," said Alex.

"I'll protect you, son," she said.

"Let's go then," Fred nodded at Frank and they left.

***

Brendan and Marie's flat felt cold, perhaps it was the temperature or perhaps it was fear, whatever the reason, it wasn't inviting.

"What was all that stuff about pictures on the wall?" Frank entered the living room just ahead of Fred.

"There are none," said Fred.

"So?"

"There should be, you heard Alice, she said she had loads of photos up of her family, but there were none to be seen." Fred shone his light on the walls of apartment 91, they were plain, white, bare. "There are none here either."

"Not everyone has pictures on their walls, Freddy," Frank said, more in an attempt to reassure himself than Fred.

"No, that's true. But, where's the telly?"

Frank's heart dropped at the sight of the blank space where the TV once hung. "We've been robbed. Brendan'll go barmy!"

"When was it stolen and how? You telling someone came in, filched it off the wall and scarpered down Christ knows how many flights of stairs?" Fred led the way into the bathroom, no Martin. The kid's bedroom, Theo's, was empty too.

They opened the door to Brendan and Marie's bedroom and saw a suitcase and a rucksack, sat by the bed.

"That can't be right. Are they back?" Frank felt extremely unsettled.

"I'm not sure they ever left," Fred said.

***

Alex finished refilling Alice's glass and put the bottle of lemonade down on the table.

"I know what I saw," Alice snapped.

"I'm not saying you didn't see it, I can't understand how, that's all. It doesn't make sense." Alex scratched his head anxiously.

A dull *thump-thump* seemed to sound all around them.

"We need to go," whispered Alice. "Now!"

"Yeah," Alex took her arm and began to slowly edge them toward the front door, "I think we do."

They were halfway along the corridor, almost at the front door when Alex's flashlight began to fade, quickly losing light. He slowed to wind it, light bloomed, and he found himself standing alone. The wall to his right appeared to ripple, then still. His heart rammed hard in his chest, "What the Jesus?"

Instinctively he stepped away from it and into the parallel wall which latched onto him, wrapping itself around his body and pulling him into it.

"Oh, God, no!! Please, no!!" he yelled, tears spilling from his eyes.

The wall pulled harder, oozing around his arms,

334

legs and torso like liquid tentacles of some starved, devilish milk monster, which seemed unfair to Alex as he had been vegan for a number of years.

"Help, please, please, help!! Help me!! HELP ME!!" The tentacles wrapped around his face, knocking his glasses to the floor, smothering his cries. They were hard, cold and relentless yet Alex still fought, determined not to be taken. The wall opened up like the jaws of a great beast, Alex's torch dropped from his hand, holding its light, and he was pulled into the nothingness. The wall rippled for a few seconds, then it settled and stilled into its usual form.

"Alex?" Fred charged in, flashlight waving wildly.

Frank was close behind.

"Alex? Alice?" Fred couldn't see either of them.

Frank looked down at the windup flashlight and broken spectacles, "Freddy."

Fred picked them up and looked at his best friend.

***

Hours later, when they recounted their tale to an army officer, they unashamedly explained that if racing down flights of stairs had been an Olympic event, they'd have shared Gold and claimed a World Record.

Sergeant Drake looked over her notes. "The walls took everyone on the 14th floor, that's what you're saying?"

"We never actually saw it, but yes. Martin, he was going on about something being in the walls," Frank said.

"Now, we think he's in one. Though it's hard to say which one," Fred added. "Then Alice said the wall took Pepé…"

"Mr. Hernandez," said Frank, helpfully.

"…then it took Alice. And Alex," Fred continued.

"There were those two from 89, we never saw them again. We think it got Brendan, Marie and Theo," Frank said.

"Okay, I understand, the walls took all the residents," Sgt Drake was already feeling weary from these two.

"And a cat," Frank looked at the notepad, waiting for her to add that point.

"And at least two tellies and loads of pictures," Fred said.

"The ones you put on the walls," Frank said.

"And not everyone, Darius went for help, so he got out," said Fred.

"Darius?" The Sergeant raised an eyebrow.

"Alice's grandson, he's around eighteen or nineteen. He's the one that called for help."

"Isn't he?" said Frank when Sgt Drake failed to reply.

"I'll have to check," she said.

"You're here because of the walls, right?" said Fred.

"Nope, that's news to me. But it's not the weirdest thing I've heard tonight," Sgt Drake said, donning her cap and peering through the tent flap. "Or rather, this morning."

"You're not here about what happened on the 14th floor?" Fred asked.

"Why are you here, then?" Frank asked.

"If you'd just wait here, gentlemen." Drake nodded at Private Harris and stepped out.

***

She looked up at Castle Heights which loomed high above them.

Army personnel went about their duties, the building's car park was now a functioning mobile army base of operations, a number of tents lined one side of the area, on the other were several military vehicles. Barriers were set around the block, sealing it off whilst the army dealt with the situation at hand and a lone helicopter scoped out things from above, its searchlight beaming down. Back on the ground, Sgt Major Wilkes waved to Drake as he approached.

"Anything?" He nodded to the tent behind her.

"Walls," she said. "Apparently the walls swallowed up all the residents on the 14th floor, though they think a young man called Darius made it out, late teens. Do we know if he did?"

"I'll check," said Wilkes.

"Thank you, Sir."

"Did they mention 'The Items'?" the Sgt Major asked, furrowing his brow.

"No, Sir."

"We have people on nearly every floor and no sign of them, though there is something very wrong with this place."

"I think that's putting it mildly, Sir," said Drake.

***

Back in the tent, Frank and Fred sat tired and confused.

"You wouldn't have any idea what's going on, would you?" Fred looked at Harris.

The soldier shook his head, "Sorry, mate, haven't a scooby."

"Our phones died, you see," Fred said.

"Even though his phone is *newer*, battery was flat as a pancake," Frank couldn't resist having a dig.

"Never happened before," Fred said defensively.

"And our van, completely dead."

"That has happened before."

"Do you know who won the boxing last night?" Frank asked.

"Nichols knocked Hammer sparko in the third," said Harris, he'd put a tenner on Nichols to win by stoppage so was pretty pleased with the result.

"Great!" Frank exclaimed happily. "We were watching when everything blacked out."

"And it all went to shit," Fred sighed.

"Didn't it just?" agreed Frank.

"What a night," Fred said sadly.

"Don't worry, lads, it'll be okay," Harris said with an encouraging smile.

"Yeah," said Fred, "we've been through this kinda thing before. Without the army, though."

"And it wasn't a tower block," added Frank.

"What happened?" Harris loved a good story.

"Well," began Fred, "there was this house…"

Floor 15: Fear Thy Neighbour

Matthew Davies

Marie looked up at the looming bulk of Castle Heights as she crossed the car park. The building was never going to win any beauty awards, but it was home. It was *her* home. She had worked and fought hard to get to this point. Her own flat, her own money, her own freedom.

She adjusted her grip on the two bulging shopping bags she was carrying. Both had been cutting into her hands for the whole bus ride back from town. She'd had to stand for the whole journey, as the bus had been packed with a mix of dead-eyed shift workers making a late journey home and drunks who'd had to the leave the pubs early having overestimated their drinking abilities.

As she crossed the car park towards the entrance, Marie felt eyes on her. That inexplicable sudden feeling of being watched. She carefully scanned the car park and caught sight of a figure sat in a car. The car was parked directly beneath one of the streetlights, so the driver, and the whole car interior, was obscured in shadow.

Marie paused involuntarily and stood stock still. She stared straight at the car and driver. Panic welled up in Marie as her mind began to race with possibilities. Had they found her? Had they come to try and take her back?

The driver slowly leant forward, moving out of the shadow and allowing light to spill across his face. Clive Paxton. "Mr Paxton" from Flat 98. Marie breathed a sigh of relief. Whilst her neighbour was, to say the least, a bit odd and creepy, she had no reason to fear him. Marie smiled and nodded, Clive did not return the gesture and simply stared back at her.

Marie continued across the car park and through the front entrance. In the lobby she was presented with a sight that made her heart drop. A tatty piece of paper taped over the call button for the lifts read 'Out of Order'. Great, two heavy shopping bags and now she would have to climb the stairs all the way to the 15th floor! Marie took a deep breath and then headed for the stairwell.

Clive Paxton sat in his car bolt upright. Good posture was important. No slouching for him. Clive watched his neighbour, the black girl from number 97, walking across the car park. Mary? Was that her name? He didn't much care. He wanted nothing to do with the other residents at Castle Heights. In Clive's opinion, the marked decline in the quality of the residents over the years was the main contributor to the decline of the block.

DIRTY FOREIGNERS! SCUM! The voice raced to the front of his mind, cutting through his thoughts and sending a chill down his spine.

Clive pushed the voice down in his mind. He didn't have a problem with anyone, so long as they worked hard and contributed their fair share to the country.

Clive noticed that his neighbour had stopped and was staring at him. He leaned forward to peer at her more closely. She smiled, nodded, and carried on towards the block. What was all that about? Clive leant back in his seat and checked his watch. It was 23:03 now, his eyes darted to "Mary" (he was sure that was her name) as she disappeared through the front entrance. He started the 55-second timer on his watch.

Clive had carefully timed how long it took the lift to travel from the 18th floor to the lobby. Once his timer ran out, even if the lift had travelled all the way down from the top floor, his neighbour would be in the lift and on her way up. Therefore, he could avoid sharing the lift and any potential "contagion".

SHOULD TAKE THE STAIRS, YOU FAT LITTLE TWERP! DO YOU GOOD TO GET SOME EXERCISE, the voice taunted.

Clive swallowed hard and breathed deeply.

"The exposure risk in the stairwell is far higher and I would be in there for far longer. The lift is the logical choice," Clive replied firmly to the voice in his head.

The voice gave no reply, but Clive knew it would lurk silently until the time came to attack and belittle him again.

Clive looked at his watch. Twenty-seven seconds left. He reached across to the passenger seat and retrieved his packet of latex gloves from inside his bag. He removed a fresh pair and put the packet back in the bag. Snapping on the gloves, he then pulled on a disposable mask and got out of the car.

Walking at his usual brisk pace, Clive headed across the car park and shouldered open the main door. He stopped dead as he saw the sign. 'Out of Order'.

WHAT NOW, BRAIN BOX?

Clive ignored the voice, crossed the lobby, and tapped the lift call button with his gloved knuckle. Futile. It would have to be the stairs.

But how long would the black girl be in the stairwell? She was carrying shopping which would slow her down, but those people were stronger in many ways, Clive mused. He'd give her fifteen minutes to clear the stairwell then he'd start up. He made his way back to his car.

Opening the driver's side door with his gloved hand, Clive then began to work off the now contaminated glove. At the same time, he pulled at the glove on the other hand, eventually leaving him with the two gloves balled together. What to do with them? He didn't want them in the car, who knew what foul things they'd picked up? Clive looked about the car park. There was always litter out here, a little more wouldn't hurt. He dropped the balled-up gloves and toed them under the car.

As he got back into the car, Clive removed his book from his bag. Dumping the bag on the passenger seat, he removed the book from its zip lock plastic bag. 'Panzer Divisions of the SS', it had been a great read so far and he could read another chapter in the time it took his neighbour to climb the stairs.

Out of breath, sweating, and the bags feeling like they'd cut through her hands, Marie finally reached the 15th floor. She paused, took some deep breaths, and then started towards her flat - number 97. As she passed by 93, she noticed a black streak running down the door. It looked almost like oil. That was odd, for all its failings Castle Heights was fairly clean. She also knew that Mr Paxton raised hell with Trevor, the concierge, if there was ever any mess. Perhaps having a weird neighbour did have its benefits?

Marie opened her front door and hauled the two shopping bags over the threshold. Home at last. She ran her eyes around the small flat. Everything was as she'd left it that morning.

"Of course it is," Marie said to herself.

Out of habit she always stopped to check if anyone had been in without her knowing. That was a legacy of her past and a habit she needed to break. As if on cue, her eyes fell on the picture of her mother. Creased, slightly torn and a bit faded, the small picture in its frame was the only personal item in the flat. Before she could get emotional, Marie switched her mind to other more immediate concerns: dinner.

Out in his car, Clive snapped his book shut as his watch began to beep, signalling that the fifteen-minute timer was up. He slid the book back into the zip lock bag, put it back in his bag and took out his packet of gloves. Dropping the packet onto the passenger seat, he then pulled on a fresh pair of gloves, grabbed his bag, and set out across the car park.

How to handle the stairwell? Obvious risk of contamination in there. Don't touch any surfaces you don't have too, he reminded himself. *Make sure your mask is on tight and don't dawdle*. He repeated this like a mantra.

Through the front entrance and then across into the stairwell. Clive took the stairs two at a time. No dawdling for him!

In no time at all he'd reached the 15th floor entrance. Heavily out a breath, Clive made for the door and pushed it open. Only then did he realize his mistake.

His gloved hand stuck to the door push plate. Something sticky, he saw it now, was smeared down the door. It was a milky grey colour that blended with the off-white paint of the door. Clive gagged behind his mask. Disgusting. As he pulled his hand away and the door swung shut behind him, he tore at the now contaminated glove. He hurled it away from him, across the corridor. Gingerly he worked the other glove off and sent it after the first. That was close!

Clive began to walk towards his flat and as he did so be noticed the filth down the front of Flat 93's door. "How can people live like that?" he muttered to himself. He would find Trevor and take him to task over the disgusting state of the place, and not for the first time.

He stood in front of the pristine door to his flat. It might look clean, but Clive knew that was a dangerous assumption. Who knew what invisible contaminants lurked on the door handle? A fresh pair of gloves was required. He reached into his bag for the packet and found…nothing. His mind raced, he rifled through the bag. Then he remembered he'd dropped the packet on the passenger seat but not picked it up again.

IDIOT! the voice said in a tone shot through with mocking laughter.

Panic welled up in Clive, his face flushed with colour.

"It's not my fault!" he said through gritted teeth. "She distracted me!" He shot a look at his neighbour's door at Number 97. "That black girl did it!"

BLACK GIRL MADE YOU STUPID? NO. YOU WERE BORN THAT WAY! the voice taunted him.

Clive's mind raced. What to do?

Go back to the car to retrieve the packet of gloves? No. Far too many contaminated surfaces between here and the car park.

Open the door with bare hands? The thought filled Clive with dread. He pulled himself together. He breathed deeply and closed his eyes.

"Just run in and get to the sink as quickly as you can," he said to himself.

Clive reached into his bag and pulled out his keys. Each key had a letter neatly stamped into the metal. 'WG' for the works' gate, 'L' for his locker, 'P' for his post box, and 'F' for his flat.

Clive unlocked the door, grabbed the door handle and then bolted into his flat. Holding his hand out in front of him as if it were on fire, he raced to the sink and began feverishly washing his hands. On the verge of tears, he desperately scrubbed at them. The water was almost scalding, but Clive paid no attention and continued to scrub.

PATHETIC! the voice sneered.

"Yes," Clive replied.

YES WHAT? the voice asked

"Yes. I am...I am pathetic," Clive lightly sobbed.

The voice had haunted Clive for a long time. It had started as the voice of his father; belittling and taunting him from beyond the grave. Then it changed. The voice of his father mingled with others until it was a choir of disapproval, criticism, and mockery.

WHAT NOW, YOU LITTLE WEASEL? the voice teased.

Clive tried to clear his head. His hands were raw, and he began to dry them on a paper towel. Gloves. Find more gloves! That was what he had to do.

He pulled open the kitchen drawer; nothing. As Clive started towards the cupboards a piece of paper on his noticeboard caught his eye. A neat piece of note paper with capital letters on it: 'BUY GLOVES'. Clive froze.

IMBECILE! YOU BACKWARD, WASTE OF SPACE! NOW WHAT? the voice cackled.

Clive stood still, his gaze fixed on the note.

'Shut up. Shut up! SHUT UP! SHUT UP!' Clive raged at the voice.

Marie sat in her flat with a bowl of noodles balanced on her lap. As she was lifting the spoon to her lips, she jumped at the noise from next door.

'What the...' Marie trailed off as the noise got

louder.

Mr Paxton was shouting something next door. Who was he shouting at? Why? Marie set the bowl aside and walked over to the shared wall. Tentatively she pressed her ear to it. It sounded like he was telling someone to shut up. Marie could only hear his voice, maybe he was on the phone?

Marie turned away from the wall as the noise from next door died down. She looked at the bowl of noodles, but the sudden noise had killed her appetite. She tided away the bowl and began to busy herself around the flat. She stopped to look at the patch of black mould in the corner of the room. It was getting worse, in fact it looked like it had grown since this morning. She took out her phone to take a picture. She'd send it to the Housing Association tomorrow.

That was odd. Marie had no signal on her phone. No mobile signal, data, or Wi-Fi. She looked at her router, the red light winked to show no internet. Bloody thing. She turned off the power, waited, and turned the router back on again. She waited. Still nothing. The red light winked.

"Great," Marie signed.

Clive stood in the middle of his flat, frantically looking around. How could he have been so stupid? No gloves. None anywhere. He'd torn the flat apart and could find nothing.

GO TO THE CAR! The voice took on a commanding tone.

"But...but...the surfaces." Clive started to hyperventilate at the thought of leaving the flat without gloves.

PULL YOURSELF TOGETHER WORM! The voice filled his mind.

Clive stood swaying, as if he were in a trance.

GO... TO... THE... CAR! the voice commanded again.

Clive lurched toward the door, as if propelled by an unseen force. He checked his pocket for his keys and left the flat.

Clive stood in the corridor as his front door closed behind him. Only now did he see it. Clive let out a whimper. The black oily filth from the door of Number 93 was also smeared across the handle of the stairwell door and he had no gloves. Clive snapped.

He strode over to Flat 93 and began to hammer on the clean part of the door with his fist. The sleeve of his jacket pulled over his hand as best he could.

"COME OUT HERE AND CLEAN UP THIS FILTH!" Clive raged, banging on the door. There was no reply.

Marie heard Clive shouting in the corridor from inside her flat. Before she knew it, she was stood in the kitchen and had taken a knife from the block on the work surface. She looked at her reflection in the blade.

"Breathe. It's not them," Marie said to herself. "It's just that weirdo from next door."

Marie kept hold of the knife.

Out in the corridor Clive stepped back from the front door of Flat 93 breathless. There was no one in.

SHE DID IT! the voice hissed.

"Who?" Clive asked in an almost child-like voice.

THAT BLACK GIRL AT 97, the voice purred. SHE MUST HAVE BROUGHT IT IN.

"Yes…yes. She came in before me! She did this," Clive chattered manically.

MAKE HER CLEAN IT! the voice commanded.

Now fully under the sway of the voice, Clive wandered back towards the door of Flat 97.

Marie jumped at the knock on the door. It was a firm knock, not like the hammering she'd heard from the corridor. Marie peered through the spyhole and saw Mr Paxton, from Flat 98, standing in the corridor. She stepped back from the door and thought about what to do next? Mr Paxton had never been friendly and was clearly a bit odd with his latex gloves on all the time. However, he'd never seemed dangerous. Marie knew what a dangerous man was like.

But Marie had seen enough to know that you should never assume a man was "safe". She slipped the kitchen knife up her sleeve and opened the door.

"Black! Filth!" announced Clive upon seeing Marie.

Marie stood in the doorway dumbfounded. Who the hell did this guy think he was?

"I beg your pardon?" Marie retorted.

"There is black filth all over the stairwell door and handle," Clive replied and pointed with a flourish back down the corridor.

Marie peered out along the corridor. The black streak from Flat 93 seemed to have spread somehow across to the door of the stairwell.

"Oh yes. Oh dear," Marie replied awkwardly. "I saw that on Flat 93's front door."

"Are you going to clean it up?" asked Clive.

"Why should I clean it up?" Marie replied indignantly. Again, who the hell did this guy think he was?

"How did it get there?" Clive retorted.

"What are you talking about?" Marie had given up being polite.

"The door was clean when I left for work. You came up here ahead of me and now there's filth all over the door," Clive replied.

"Why would I do that?" Marie stared at Clive in disbelief.

Clive searched for the words, but none came.

Marie had had enough. "I think it's something to do with Flat 93. Why don't you check in there?" She moved to close the door.

Clive's hand shot out to stop the door closing. "There's no one in," Clive said coldly.

Marie looked at Clive's hand and then towards his face. This was starting to head in a direction she didn't like. What was wrong with him? Marie decided to change tact.

"No one lives there, Mr Paxton," she explained slowly and politely. "It's only our flats on this floor that are occupied."

Clive looked at her with confusion. An awkward silence hung in the air between them.

"But you have keys...right?" Marie ventured. "You look after the flats? For Trevor?"

What was she talking about? Clive had no idea. Look after the flats? This was nonsense.

"What on earth are you talking about?" Clive said, rummaging in his pocket. "I only have four keys, my flat, my post box downstairs, the gates of the site where I work and my work locker." He pulled his keys form his pocket and held them up...all eight of them.

Clive stared at the keys. This didn't make sense. He only had four keys; they were all clearly stamped 'WG' for the works' gate, 'L' for his locker, 'P' for his post box, and 'F' for his flat. But as he turned the keys through his fingers there were clearly four more, each stamped with a number; 93, 94, 95 and 96. That corresponded to the other flats on this floor.

Clive turned to face the front door of Flat 94. Marie stood still, ready to slam her door shut but not wanting to move too soon and spook Clive.

Clive put the key stamped '94' into the lock and turned it. The door unlocked. None of this made sense, where had these extra keys come from? Clive felt like he was losing his mind.

LET'S HAVE A LOOK INSIDE, the voice suggested right on cue.

Clive pushed the door and it swung inward. A dank and putrid smell wafted from the interior of the flat. Clive reached in and flipped the light switch just inside the door.

The scene inside the flat explained the smell.

Piles of rubbish were stacked everywhere. Household waste, food containers, and empty latex glove boxes were crammed into every available space inside the flat. Here and there jars of fetid liquid could be seen as well.

DIRTY BOY! the voice jeered.

Clive wandered along the corridor to Flat 95 and unlocked the front door. A similar chaotic scene greeted him.

DIRTY, FILTHY, BOY! ALL THIS MESS, the voice jeered again.

"It...it's not mine," Clive replied. He walked back past Marie, who stood in her doorway with a look of concern and curiosity, to Flat 96.

Flat 96 was worse, the contents looked like they had begun to rot and congeal into a black mass.

Clive turned to the last door; Flat 93. He looked back down the corridor, Marie was peering into Flat 95, a look of disgust on her face. Marie turned to look at Clive.

"Is this...yours?" Marie asked in disbelief. "Have you been putting this in here?"

"No. I..." Clive trailed off, his mind in disarray.

"You told me you were looking after the other flats. Going in to check everything was okay. Not...not this." Marie was now level with Flat 94 and she pointed in through the open doorway.

OPEN THE DOOR! OPEN 93! the voice interjected.

Clive opened the door to Flat 93. A thick black slurry spilled out around the door and into the corridor. Clive backed away.

"Oh my God! What is that? Close the door! Mr Paxton? Clive? Close that door!" Marie implored.

Clive backed away from the black ooze as it pooled across the corridor. It spilled across from Flat 93 and reached the door of Flat 96 opposite, blocking the corridor.

THERE WE ARE, the voice said with a delighted tone.

"What *is* that? Where's it coming from?" Marie asked, pointing at the black pool steadily spreading across the corridor, but Clive paid her no attention. He just continued to back away.

Movement inside Flat 94 caught Marie's eye and she turned to look; she watched in disbelief as the detritus inside began to dissolve. First into a greyish brown mass and then, as it became more liquid, the colour darkened to the same jet black as the ooze spilling out of Flat 93. As Marie backed away toward her flat, she saw the same black ooze was now spilling out of Flat 95, already halfway across the corridor to Clive's front door at Flat 98.

Clive, still backing away from the pool steadily creeping forward from the stairwell end of the corridor, collided with Marie. He spun to look at her, a glazed expression on his face.

'Look!' Marie cried, pointing to the lake of black ooze now flooding in from the opposite end of the corridor. Clive seemed to snap out of whatever trance he'd been in and looked around. The door to his flat was now swamped by the black ooze and he & Marie were hemmed in, in front of the door to her flat.

"Quick, inside," said Clive.

Without thinking, Marie stepped back into her flat and Clive followed. The ooze seemed to react to this and began to, somehow, move quicker. To race toward the open doorway. As Clive stepped inside, a small amount of the black ooze had just begun to cross the threshold. Clive slammed the door shut.

As the door closed, another duller noise could be heard - a wet splat. Clive looked at the black ooze across the back of the door. As he'd slammed the door it had caught the end of the pool in the corridor and splattered up the door. Clive looked at the sleeve of his jacket. Black ooze had landed on the left sleeve and the material was being eaten away! He held up his left arm and watched as thin wisps of smoke rose from the melting material.

"TAKE IT OFF!" yelled Marie.

Clive sprang into action and wrestled the jacket off, throwing it into a heap on the floor.

"What is this stuff?" Marie asked.

Clive stared at the jacket on the floor, then looked at Marie. She was taken aback by the dead-eyed stare her neighbour fixed on her. As if he'd never seen her before in his life.

"Gloves," said Clive.

"What?" replied Marie.

"Do you have any gloves? Latex gloves?" Clive asked in a monotone.

Not fully understanding, but now very wary of Clive, Marie thought for a second. Then she strode into her bathroom and rummaged around in the cabinet. She found two pairs of gloves that she'd saved from hair dyeing kits. Marie realised she still had the kitchen knife up her sleeve, as the handle slid out slightly. She shot a look back out into the main flat where Clive stood motionless. She tucked the knife back up her sleeve.

Returning from the bathroom, Marie handed a pair of gloves to Clive.

"Thank you," Clive said, in the same monotone voice, and pulled on the gloves. Marie put on her pair as well.

They stood in silence, both looking at the front door.

"What is it? What is that stuff? Chemicals? Acid?" Marie asked again.

SHE THINKS YOU DID THIS, the voice whispered.

Clive turned to look at Marie.

SHE'LL BLAME YOU! WHO DO YOU THINK THEY'LL BELIEVE? YOU OR SOME POOR "ETHNIC GIRL"? THEY'LL TAKE HER SIDE! the voice continued.

YOU'LL TAKE THE BLAME, NOT HER. YOU'LL BE RUINED! YOU'LL BE NOTHING! JUST LIKE I ALWAYS SAID! NOTHING! The voice hissed the last few words.

"What should I do?" mumbled Clive.

Marie said something but Clive didn't hear her.

GET RID OF HER. FEED HER TO IT. The voice seemed to fill his whole consciousness.

Clive stepped towards Marie who was still talking.

"Did you hear me? I said we need to try and

356

contact someone. My phone isn't working." Marie held up the phone. Clive saw that the time was 23:40. "Do you have a phone…"

Marie's words were cut short as the flat plunged into darkness. It took a moment for her eyes to adjust. Moonlight spilled in through a gap in the curtains. She crossed to the window and looked out. The streets and buildings were in darkness, save for the flash of car headlights and the pale glow of the moon.

"Must be a power cut," Marie said and turned back into the room.

In the gloom she saw Clive lunge towards her, his movements obscured by the long shadows in the room. She grabbed at the knife from her sleeve, but he was on her before she could retrieve it.

Marie struggle, kicked, and screamed as she wrestled with Clive. Half trying to fight him off and half trying to draw the knife. She was surprised by how strong he was and how he seemed to shrug off her blows. Clive wrapped his arms around Marie and began to drag her towards the front door. She continued to fight as best she could, but her arms were pinned so she couldn't get to the knife.

"GET OFF ME! LET GO OF ME!" Marie screamed at the top of her lungs.

Clive made it to the front door and reached out for the handle. This was the opening Marie needed. She twisted her arms and was able to grab the handle of the knife with the ends of her fingers. As Clive dragged the door open, Marie got the knife free of her sleeve and grasped it firmly. The door swung open.

Marie kicked Clive in the shin with all her might. Clive finally cried out and stumbled back. Marie stood in the doorway, the knife raised above her head.

Clive hit Marie in the chest. Not hard enough to wind her, but hard enough to throw her off balance. She stepped back into the corridor, slipping in the black ooze and time seemed to slow down. She twisted in the air, spinning into the corridor, seeing it now covered in the black ooze, the floor looking like a black mirror in the moonlight. She dropped the knife and put out her hands. She splashed down into the inky black liquid.

Marie let out a scream as she landed. Clive leant against the door frame, unable to look away. Waiting for her to start burning like his jacket. Waiting for the black filth to dissolve her, to eat her alive.

Silence and stillness, only punctuated by Marie's deep panicked breaths. The black ooze was not burning her. It was unpleasant, yes. But not caustic like it had seemed when she saw it land on Clive's jacket. She pushed herself up on her hands and turned to look at Clive over her shoulder. The think black ooze dripped from her clothes and skin back onto the floor.

Clive looked on dumbfounded. Why wasn't she burning? What was happening?

GET HER, QUICK! the voice commanded.

Clive lunged after Marie, but she was too quick. Scrambling, she got to her feet and careened towards the stairwell door, slipping and falling as she went. The ooze had no effect.

Clive stepped after her. His foot slapped down, wet, into the black ooze.

GOT YOU! The voice sounded triumphant.

Clive took another step and faltered. He looked down. As he picked up his right foot to take another step, he saw the sole of his shoe had been eaten away. Unable to react quickly enough, he planted his foot back down into the wet black lake. Pain shot through his foot; the skin seared and burned. Clive cried out, just as the material of his left shoe gave out and the skin on that foot was exposed. He screamed louder and toppled forward, splashing down into the caustic black mass. He writhed and screamed as his clothes dissolved and his skin began to melt.

Marie pulled herself up using the handle of the stairwell door. She turned to look at Clive. He continued to drag himself through the ooze towards her. Skin hanging off in places, like wet paper. Why was she not affected? She didn't have time to ponder. She hauled open the door and threw herself into the stairwell.

The stairwell door silently closed behind Marie. Clive no longer screamed; all he could muster was a strained whine. He slogged on, trying to get to the door. The muscles in his legs became useless. The skin tore like tissue paper and the black ooze burnt at the muscle beneath.

GOT YOU NOW. SOON YOU'LL BE NOTHING! the voice said.

Clive struggled on, finally nearing the door. He stretched out his gloved hand towards the door handle. As he looked at it, just out of reach, he saw the glove on his hand begin to collapse. The ooze had worked its way into the glove. Slowly he watched as his hand withered to nothing, leaving the glove limp on the end of his arm, like a badly made scarecrow.

Clive gave up, he let himself fall and rolled onto his back. Unchecked, the ooze worked at what was left of his body, consuming it until the surface of the black lake was like a mirror again.

NOTHING. JUST LIKE I ALWAYS SAID, was the last thing Clive heard as a hysterical Marie plunged headlong down the stairwell, into the night.

Blue Daze on 16

Freddy Beans

Emily Whitmer didn't consider herself a violent person. She'd never even been in a physical fight before. Right now, though? Emily wanted to fight.

She knew better. She fucking knew better.

Emily had grown up with everything in life. Her parents had money. She graduated top of her class in high school and a few years later had a degree in finance. Short and curvy with eyes that captured men's souls. Emily knew she was the total package.

She had a favorite saying, when with friends.

"I may be short in height but I'm packed up nice and tight!"

It was juvenile and she loved that.

Bobby was juvenile too. She had thought she loved that about him but juvenile boys always end up doing dumb boy things. Usually, that left a hurt girl behind.

Emily was now in that girl's shoes, for once.

Her parents had raised her to be so much stronger. To use her mind and not be too boy crazy. To never let anyone hold her back. To always stand up for herself. Then, douchebag Bobby came around with his muscles and light blue oceanic eyes and she'd become a submissive mess.

She hated herself for that.

Bobby had arrived yesterday, after moving out just last week. Moved out, left Emily alone in shock, and wondering what exactly was wrong with her. Like most that are unceremoniously dumped, she was now stuck looking at herself with critical eyes. All of her mistakes now the elephant in the room that she couldn't take her eyes off of. She hated him for that.

Bobby had walked in then, like he did every room, with utter confidence. Opening up into a comfortable banter with Emily, when all she wanted to do was scream at him. Ask him why he'd left her and what the hell he saw in that tall Asian chick he was now with. Instead, she sat on the couch and bantered right back. Only coming up with clever sarcasm-filled retorts long after he'd left.

She hated herself for that, too.

He had a full load in his van but wanted to take Blue. Blue was the hyacinth macaw he'd received from his best friend Marcus back in the States. She'd offered to let the enormous bird stay a couple of nights if Bobby agreed to come grab it within two days. Bobby had hesitated, then smiled that toothy grin and agreed. "Not sure I can fit him in the truck, anyway," he conceded.

Emily hadn't cared if he could or couldn't. Deep down, she just wanted to see Bobby again. Truth was, she didn't want 'them' to end.

Yet, here they were. Separated, with Bobby already moving on.

She didn't like Blue. He creeped her out. She could handle a couple nights with the stupid bird but he still gave her the heebie-jeebies. His dead black eyes sitting in a sharp yellow ring. The hard, wrinkly, old man skin, fingered talons. Then there was that sharp beak the size of her fist. He could snap through most cages with a nibble. The steel cage in which he now sat had so far held strong but showed the damage from Blue's constant search for escape, nonetheless.

She felt some sympathy for the bird. Blue had only come under their ownership a couple of months back. He was really Marcus' pride and joy.

Marcus had researched the macaw for months before driving from Riverside, CA to South America. He'd purchased the thing down there, smuggled it back and treated it like the kid he and Barbara couldn't have naturally. Marcus doted on Blue. Teaching it as many words as he could. The two had become inseparable.

About a year later, all the good feelings ended.

Barbara had been brutally murdered in their home. Marcus had told them there were more than fifty some stab wounds.

Marcus hadn't been home during the attack and he was eliminated quickly from the suspects list. There were still holes left in him after that, as if he too had been stabbed. Blue became his emotional support animal and followed him everywhere. Marcus bought a leash so the large bird could hop behind him, though most of the time it insisted on steadily perching on Marcus' leather handler's glove. That's why it was surprising to Emily that Marcus just gave them Blue. A couple of weeks before they moved to London he offered up the bird as his parting gift.

Bobby had tried explaining it to her for his lost

friend. That the parrot reminded Marcus too much of Barbara. She understood that. Their relationship had ended so violently, she almost thought it might be absolutely necessary to purge.

Weeks later she figured out why he'd really gotten rid of Blue. Blue had taken up the unfortunate habit of mimicking Marcus' sad empty wails of "Barbara." When someone started to cry, the bird would inevitably howl the woman's name. He had Marcus' voice down pat. It had been off putting to hear her old friend's name cried out of this absurdly large macaw.

Emily shuddered but kept her tears back. Unfortunately, she'd heard Barbara's name a lot over the last few tear-filled days.

She walked to the window and looked out. Everything was so far down from up here. Sixteen floors seemed too many to her. She'd never lived in a high rise and she didn't like it very much. She preferred to walk out of her front door and jog down some local natural landscape. Emily didn't mind London; she just didn't prefer it over the States.

Here, it took several minutes just to get down to the first floor and she hated walking by Trevor in her workout gear. He was so awkward. It was clear he was into her, but he always said stupid shit like, "Nice day out, eh?" The only thing she liked about the old man was his Scottish accent. She had put up with all the leering just to get a taste of his accent. She'd always been a sucker for one.

Emily stood at the window and felt lonely and stupid. Too easily, she'd followed Bobby and his lying eyes here.

She had always wanted to vacation to the United Kingdom.

But live?

That was all Bobby. He'd convinced her way too easily. The tears fell again. She didn't wipe at the liquid, letting them fall from her eyes to the edges of her cheek and chin freely. The tears delicately dancing under her chin, before releasing their hold and dropping to the tiles underneath her feet.

Emily followed the cars below as they drove out of view. She picked another one and followed it until it eventually left her sight too. A minute went by and she scoured for more than moving vehicles. Two kids on skateboards, an older woman dressed to the nines, she could also make out a couple walking their smaller dog through the light fog.

There's a novel thought. Why couldn't I have a dog?

She looked at Blue.

No offense.

She grabbed the Maker's Mark out of the kitchen cupboard and poured herself a glass. The refrigerator ice cube dispenser groaned to life with her touch. Nothing came out but that dull grinding grating sound. No cubes. She hit the front of the fridge and one cube fell into her glass. The thing was freaking worthless. That was all she needed, for now. After this glass was emptied, Emily was certain she would need another cube…or three.

She thought about calling down to Trevor. He'd probably jump at the opportunity to bring her anything, even a single ice cube. She thought briefly about fucking Trevor, too. Just taking that old man and riding the life out of him, then sending him on his way. Making sure Bobby knew all about it on his next visit. Unfortunately, that path had a predictable ending. She'd only end up with an old stalking Scot. To boot, Bobby wouldn't be jealous. He never was. He'd probably laugh and tell her something carefree like, whatever floats her boat. This imaginary response pissed her off. Emily needed to find a way to cool down and thoughts of Bobby weren't helping.

The large gulp of cool whiskey warmed her deep inside. The tears had finally eased a bit and were now slow streams under her eyes.

"Barbara!"

Marcus screamed his dead wife's name, using Blue's ebony hued bill.

"Stop it!" Emily screamed at the bird. Her voice was gone. A weak squeak spilled out of her lips instead. She'd spent her voice screaming at Bobby last week. And again last night. She was sweet while he was collecting his shit but she screamed and called him every name she knew once he'd left. Part of her wanted to stay out here and show Bobby what he was missing out on. Another part of her wanted to run home and live with her parents for a bit while she picked up the pieces. She had no idea what she was going to do but Bobby had paid the rent for the next few months so she had some time. She hated being dependent on her ex but sometimes reality spoke forcefully.

Awk!

"Just shut the fuck up, please!" she scream-whispered it with the last of her voice. Her vocal apologies after came out in mere whispers. She looked at the bird who seemed oblivious to being cursed out or the following regrets. Blue flushed his feathers, bobbed his head up and down a few times, then relaxed and nibbled at the front of his plumage.

Why am I so pissed off? It's just a dumb bird, she thought before arguing with herself. *Because I didn't ask for any of this. That's why.*

It wasn't Emily who'd asked to be stuck in an apartment in bum-fuck London with this overstuffed parakeet. That was all Bobby. She had wanted the good life though. Shit, she'd had it too. Bobby had taken her everywhere. The highlight being California, or more exact, Los Angeles. Every night seemed important. It was all a blur. Dressing to the nines all the time. Lavished upon by a loving Bobby. She'd met important politicians and movie stars too. She was now angry the good life, like Bobby, had left her behind.

The bird squawked and shit on the newspaper below.

For some reason the defecation stuck in her mind like a shitty omen. A sign that her life would now be nothing more than squatted waste, squeezed out of her orifices.

Either that or it was a sign that Bobby was a shit stain. She opted for that choice.

The man was amazing though. He sure had a way about him. Or he had at first. Shit, he was still amazing. That was the problem. Bobby was a free spirit who meant no harm as he typhooned through god knows how many beautiful women's lives. He didn't care enough about the relationship and had no need to settle. Emily was the perfect fit. Then she wasn't any longer. It was nothing personal. Now this Asian chick fit and that's just how it was. It all made Emily feel so replaceable. It cut her to her core. She really wanted to tell Bobby how deep he'd cut her but she couldn't. Every time he walked in, she smiled and pretended she was okay. Waiting until he was gone before releasing her hurt. It wasn't healthy. She knew it wasn't. She had never had the ability to confront Bobby on serious shit. Always choosing the path of least resistance. Which should have been an early eye opener, but wasn't.

She kicked out in anger and hit the steel cage on accident. Blue squawked and flew to a higher perch. Away from the next leg attack, if and when it came. Emily almost told the stupid thing she was sorry but didn't. Swallowing unspoken apologies, Emily walked to the bookcase and looked through the assortment of mostly Stephen King, Clive Barker, Jack Ketchum and other dark writers. They were her favorite authors. Emily stared at the novel titles without seeing them for a while. When they slowly came into vision, she grabbed her favorite of the bunch Robert R. McCammon's *Swan Song*. She loved the book and it bore her adoration in long wrinkled creases and sun-aged pages.

She glanced at the clock, which read 7:30PM. Emily contemplated the television. They liked to call it the 'telly' here. That always made her giggle.

She seemed to remember a boxing match tonight? She could care less about the sport of boxing. Right now though, she thought watching a pair of half-naked men beat the living shit out of one another sounded on point. Her hands grazed over the remote a second before giving up and opting again for the novel.

She quickly set it back down unread and grabbed another healthy gulp of the whiskey. Finally picking up the novel with the intent to actually read it.

Emily practically knew the story by heart. She always saw herself as a humanitarian like Sue Wanda (Swan) and her faithful wrestler friend Josh Hutchings. To do good in the world.

Okay, and maybe have some good sent her way in return. Lord knew she could use it. She'd been looking for her protector for years. She hadn't found her Josh Hutchings. He was a make-believe character in a book of fantasy. She wanted that man in real life too. Someone that would understand her and her mission on Earth. Someone that would back her. At all costs. Not someone that runs off with the first well-stacked Asian he runs into.

Emily set the book down once more, without reading a page. Her mind was all over the place and she knew she wouldn't be able to concentrate. She was so pathetic, she didn't even have the energy to read. She felt close to the lowest she'd felt in her life. The tears weren't far behind.

Emily looked back fearfully at Blue. He was anxious and flitting around his cage, ending on a perch at her eye level. Jesus, he was a big ass bird. She guessed he was damn close to two feet tall. Probably stood at knee height to her. He cocked his head and stared back at her with his pitch black eyes. He looked sad. Which made his words somehow worse.

"Barbara!"

It felt like he was mocking her. She knew he wasn't. He was just a stupid bird after all, even if it had picked up some English.

Emily didn't like the way Blue continued staring at her and kicked his cage, purposely this time. She didn't care about the tears. She wanted this fucking parrot to shut up. She kicked the cage again and Blue flew in and grabbed the tip of her Chucks in his bill. She tried pulling her leg down but the bird held strong. She was balanced there, one foot holding her weight and the other stuck in an endless Rockette's kick. She could still feel her toes and wanted to keep it that way. Emily pulled her leg down hard, and the bird let go. The only evidence of attack was a thin slit at the top of her Chucks. She wiggled her little piggies and was happy to verify they were all still intact.

"Fucker!" she said as she slapped the cage. Blue flew in her direction and slipped his beak through the slit in the cage with his mouth open. It snapped shut hard, not far from her flesh. She had jerked back in just the right moment or he'd have had some bits of Emily in that bill of his. She couldn't fucking believe it. Was this fucking bird really attacking her?

She kicked the cage hard and it wobbled a few times before settling down in almost the same spot. Blue sat on the perch and just looked at her as his cage wobbled. Never taking his eyes off hers.

"Barbara!"

Blue bent his head after the Marcus impression and squawked loudly. It felt like Blue was taunting her. Emily couldn't help herself. She turned beet red and threw her tumbler at the bird. The glass exploded into a shard filled firework. Each individual piece slightly beautiful as they reflected off the fading sun peeking through her windows. Then the slits of glass falling unceremoniously on the tile below in the pitter patter of a hard rain.

It didn't shut Blue up. He was squawking endlessly and jumping from perch to perch. She became angrier temporarily, then noticed the red drops on the newspaper in his cage. She looked up and saw that he was dripping blood from a shard of glass embedded in his belly. Blue bent down and gripped the shard with his bill, removing it.

Emily felt stupid. She was arguing with a fucking bird. There was no doubt she was losing it. What the fuck was wrong with her? Was one boy really worth all this ridiculousness?

"I'm sorry, Blue." She meant it too.

She walked to the kitchen closet and grabbed the broom and dustpan. The chunks of glass were everywhere. She took her time cleaning them up and dumping the remnants into the kitchen trash can. There was a bunch still glistening on the bottom of the cage. She needed to clean those up and check on Blue too.

This gave her pause. She was scared of the damn thing. She had also hurt it. If memory served her well, he had even attacked her. Or at least tried to?

After a slight internal debate, she looked for the thick leather bird glove. As she slid it on her fingers, she began coaxing Blue.

"Relax, big guy. It's okay. I'm not mad anymore." It wasn't her voice any longer. Emily's voice was gone. What remained, reminded her of Kathleen Turner's voice. Deep and cracking. Emily found that oddly poignant. A lot of her was deep and cracking at the moment.

The glove on, she flipped the lock on the cage. Blue cocked his head at her and watched. The cage opened and he flew to the perch furthest away. It made her feel guiltier than she already did. She reached the glove in and Blue dropped to the perch below it.

"Damnit. I'm trying to help you. Okay?" Emily tried pleading with it.

She reached in deep to grab at the bird. Her right hand gripping the outside of the cage for balance. She extended quickly and the bird flew up safely to another perch. She opened up the glove to confuse the bird. Then took another stab. Reaching out slowly with the fingers expanded to block any exits he might think of. Blue expertly flew around her slow-moving fingers and landed next to her right hand, clutching the cage. His talons gripping the steel cage next to her digits as he closed his beak about halfway down her pointer and middle finger.

First, Emily screamed. A weak whisper, the only thing escaping her windpipes. She felt the beak rip right through her flesh like a spoon dives into mayonnaise. The next thing she felt was the beak hit her bones. Emily felt those bones weaken and give way. She heard what sounded like twigs snapping. Her eyes watched as her fingers were detached under new ownership. Both finger stumps started bleeding heavily. The pain was somewhere else. As if someone was holding it for her while she bled. Her first thoughts were about the stains her leaking may create.

She wondered if she was in shock. Emily came to the determination that if she was in shock she wouldn't have the cognizance to question if she was.

Blue took the pause in action to fly right at her face with his talons extended. She removed what remained of her right hand from the cage on instinct and slapped Blue hard.

The pain was immense. Shooting up her arm to her elbow, dying somewhere near her bicep. It would seem that missing fingers still caused quite a bit of pain.

She screamed at the top of her lungs. Roughly a library whisper.

Blue fell to the bottom of the cage.

"Watch out for the glass, fuck face!" Emily was quick to close and lock the cage. The enormous macaw was quicker squeezing through just as she closed the door. He was on her immediately.

Talons ripping at any unclothed flesh. Beak

reaching back, flying forward and embedding itself in her flesh over and over in a stabbing motion. Emily's open hands proved a pointless defense. The bird flew right between her open palms, talons gripping the bridge of her nose. She jerked back and felt her skin give. She couldn't breathe through her nose anymore and knew this was really bad. The stream flowing from her nose directly to her lips below reminded Emily to move.

Her eyes shut, she reached out blindly. Nothing. Her hands were sporadic in their search but the left found purchase on Blue's right wing. Blue looked at her hand, his beak reaching back to usurp more fingers away from Emily. She did the only thing she could think to do and slammed her arm down. A satisfying snap emitted from somewhere within the plumage of Blue's wing. Emily didn't let go, snapping her wrist up and down like she was cracking a whip. A sound, similar to white noise, came from the grinding and snapped bones. She let go in disgust with herself and her actions.

Blue flopped to the floor, one wing stuck open at an odd, upward angle, landing on his feet near hers. The macaw didn't say a word when he opened his beak, instead snapping it shut on Emily's right Achille's heel. Her tendon snapped with ease. The pain shot up the back of her calf and she fell. The cool tiles felt good on first contact. Then the bird was on her back, relentlessly attacking her everywhere. She froze. Maybe she really was in shock this time.

Everything stopped. Then she heard Barbara wail

the saddest, most alone "Marcus," she'd ever heard. Barbara was nowhere around. The fucking bird was mimicking Barbara now? Except that sounded like a dying gasp. Like Barbara was hurt and begging for Marcus' help.

A crazy thought entered Emily's mind. *Did Blue kill Barbara? Why would he do that? Was he jealous for all of Marcus' attention?* She couldn't be bothered with it more than that and started crawling aimlessly.

The bird was back to attacking her and she wasn't sure where she was going. She stopped and grabbed the nearest thing she could. The lamp worked perfectly. She swung it behind her and heard it connect. She saw the bird slide across the room and hit the wall near the front door in her peripherals. She didn't wait to see how he was. She hurt all over. Her entire body was aching but she crawled faster than she ever had need to before.

She started thinking of means to escape, while already on the move. Blue was blocking the front door and was getting up, heading her way now. She panicked and went for the only open door she could focus on. One she could close behind her. The bathroom door beckoned and she crawled as fast as she could for its safety, sliding across the cool tiles with Blue in hot pursuit.

She didn't need to look back. The soft click of his talons hitting the tiles, coming closer and closer, was all the motivation she needed. She reached out and grabbed the open door just as Blue landed on her calf. He dunked his beak into her flesh twice before she kicked out, sending him flying. The bathroom door closed. She was finally safe.

First Emily checked her pockets for her phone, but they were empty. She had a sneaking suspicion her phone sat waiting right next to *Swan Song*.

Fitting reading, she supposed. Swan Song *for her last turn around the sun. Swans were big and strong, weren't they? Surely, a swan could kill an overgrown parrot.*

Emily felt like she did at the end of her runs. Spent. Every muscle ached and she wasn't breathing properly. She was gasping for breath. She started paying attention to her breathing. Controlling it, like she'd learned in yoga class. Inhaling a long steady stream of air. It shuddered out of her roughly on exhale. After a minute, she felt much better and lifted herself up. Her hands splayed at the top of the sink for a bit. She looked at the missing digits of her right hand and momentarily was glad it wasn't her left hand. She could still fill a wedding ring!

Finally, she dared to look in the mirror. The sight scared her. She didn't recognize the face before her, only the curly dark hair surrounding it. There were little black suns all over her skin. Oozing blood seeped from all of them. Blue's beak had done her serious damage. Hard to look at but it wasn't what truly shocked her. Emily's nose did that.

It was cut deeply at the bridge near her eyes. Blood funneled out of the top of the bridge like a leaky faucet. The bottom half of her nose bent forward, only held on her face by the nostrils it hung by. She felt sick and weak all at once.

Emily closed her eyes and gathered her strength. She felt ridiculously tired and turned on the faucet to splash some water on her face.

She realized her mistake as it touched her skin. The pain was instant. Like someone had splashed acid into her open wounds. Emily yelled in her raspy whisper until her breath was gone. Her hands gripping the sink white knuckled so she didn't pass out. She waited until the pain passed, before finally turning the water off.

What was she going to do? She was bleeding too much and she was sure she needed help. She didn't want to bleed out in this bathroom, that was for sure.

Emily searched the cupboards for towels, wrapping every one she could find around her wounded body. Her right hand became a club. The missing digits and extending arm covered in the towels. She spent the next moments wrapping her neck and made sure to wrap her face up carefully, leaving only slits for her eyes. Finally, she wrapped her legs up as well as she could. Emily glanced in the mirror and laughed at the mummy looking back at her.

She felt safer. She was weak and her strength was ebbing but she felt she'd stemmed the worst of the damage. Bought herself some time, as she'd heard said in movies. She didn't have long and needed to make her move. The only way out was the front door. Emily Whitmer was going to fucking make it, too.

After getting a hold of her breathing, she cracked the door and couldn't see the bird. She knew it had to be near midnight by now. Then the lights turned off.

Emily closed the door and flipped the bathroom light switch.

On/off…on/off. Nothing.

For a moment she wondered if Blue had figured out how to cut the electricity. The idea felt stupid. Nope, Blue wasn't a MacGyver macaw. Emily was just experiencing some absolutely fucked up timing. Her breathing had normalized though, so Emily decided it was time.

The door cracked open slowly.

An inch.

Then half a foot.

Once it was large enough, she tried to hop towards the front door. Two hops in, she was amazed how great everything was going. The third jump stepped on a falling towel. Her right leg, which was flamingoed up to protect itself, came down for balance and she fell hard instead. Her elbows cracked as they took the brunt of the impact. It was a dull pain though and didn't debilitate her.

Emily crawled for the front door, not ten feet away now.

Then, the pecking started. He was all over her thighs. She could feel his beak slam into her ass and upper thigh area over and over again. She flopped over to protect herself, using her right-hand club for protection. The bird was knocked off, finally. She skootched herself back until she hit something - the

378

couch.

Fuck! She was now somehow further away from the front door. A couch pillow was grabbed and thrown at Blue, landing, harmlessly, far behind the bird.

Blue landed on her leg with one jump and started ripping at the towels protecting her there. She hit him with her club and his immediate reaction was to fly back right at her face. His talons grazed her before implanting themselves deep in the nape of her neck. Blue slammed his head into her skull. His beak embedded itself into the back of her head and must have gotten stuck because she could feel her head pulling back but the beak not being removed.

An opportunity.

Blue's left wing was up and she filled her eager palm. Emily found it easy to grasp and this time didn't crack it like a whip. She raised her right arm up with Blue clutched between thumb and ring finger, slamming her hand down on the tile below. A sharp pain cracked up her arm. She was pretty sure two of the remaining three fingers were broken from the impact.

Her neck felt wet all of a sudden. She chased the thoughts of what the talons did to her neck away.

"Marcus." The bird weakly mimicked Barbara one last time and fell lifeless a few feet away.

Emily let herself feel horrible for Barbara. She couldn't imagine how long it took her to die under this murderous bird's attack. Fifty stab wounds? Was Emily that far behind?

It sent chills up her spine. The tile was slick with

both of their blood. A crimson Jackson Pollock painting at her feet.

The crawl to the door was painfully slow. All of her remaining strength was needed to keep moving. She really just wanted to close her eyes and take a long nap. Fear of it being a permanent one offered new motivation.

Stopping six feet away to catch her breath, she heard a soft tick on the tile. If she hadn't stopped, she wouldn't have heard it. Tremors shot up her shoulders when she looked back and saw the bird wasn't where he had been unceremoniously slammed. He was up and wobbling in her direction. Blue was red with blood and looked like a living, breathing, old-school 3D effect.

His lifeless eyes. Those eyes pierced her deep as they unblinkingly stared in her direction. His broken wings stretching, still offering him balance.

She'd had enough. Emily wasn't going to back down to this overstuffed turkey. She growled. It surprised her. She slid her bloody legs on the tiles until she was sitting cross legged.

"Come on Blue!" Emily whisper-yelled at her attacker, her lips in a sneer. Emily growled deep in her chest. She felt feral inside. She wasn't thinking clearly. Only about ripping this bird to shreds. Rending him into a bloody, unrecognizable stew.

Blue wobbled her way. His beak opening and closing as he got closer. When he was a couple of feet from her, his wings flopped out, almost like he thought he could fly towards her. His broken wings stopped that from occurring.

Emily slammed both of her fists down hard on Blue, ending all thoughts of flight.

A sickeningly wet *skwick* came from the dead bird. She raised her hands again and slammed them down together, even harder than the last time.

Blue's dead eyes finally showed signs of life, his innards squeezing out of the orbits. There were a few holes in Blue now and all of them leaked bits of his insides.

The shaking started in her knees, crawled up her torso and didn't let up. Emily finally cried again, the fear of a squawked "Barbara" now gone. Tears fell and stung the open wounds below. Her long sobs the only sounds.

She lay down. Tired.

You don't want to die here next to this fucker, do you? she asked herself.

She inched herself on bruised elbows and aching thighs towards the front door. When she was under the handle, she sat upright, back against the door and tried normalizing her breath. Once it had settled down and she was ready to try moving again, she threw her hands up and unlocked the door. It wouldn't budge. Slowly she realized she had to move to the side of the doorjamb in order to open it.

The door finally opened to a dark hallway. There was commotion everywhere.

Emily felt faint. Everything was dark. She didn't think she would make it much longer.

A man ran her way. She couldn't make out anything he was saying, though she was sure it was in English.

Emily only saw Bobby. She knew she was going to give that asshole a piece of her mind. Whether he cared or not, he was going to listen to her and her feelings. She didn't give two shits if she looked like the Bride of Frankenstein when she saw him again. He was going to listen and understand he let a great woman go.

Right now though, all Emily wanted to do was sleep. She succumbed. Lids closing slowly.

She felt hands carry her to the stairs and then slowly, carefully down them. She wondered, wearily, why they weren't taking the elevator. It was filthy and reeked of piss, but surely that would have been quicker. Didn't matter, she was going to fucking make it!

Emily knew she had earned the hell out of the next chapter of her life.

She was excited.

The Connection on Level Seventeen

Richard Rowntree

Annie and Geoff, the couple at 101, had immediately exuded a vibe of *Rosemary's Baby* to Loretta. Not that they were old, Satanic, or indeed naked; more that they had welcomed her into Castle Heights with open arms and baskets of warm bread. There's something that feels unnerving and alien in a big city when neighbours want to introduce themselves and become a part of *your* life – however small.

It had been almost a year to the day since she moved into the apartment, full of enthusiasm for her new life. She was, she presumed, going to be elevated into the upper echelons of a society that she craved to be an intrinsic member of. A new city, a new outlook, a new *home*. A place, and a way, to erase the bad memories and carnage she was leaving behind. For good. At least, that's how she sold it to herself. But things never quite work out the way the protagonist expects. At least not in interesting stories.

Since leaving the hospice, Loretta had an unquenchable thirst for life. There was less than a one percent chance of getting out of there, unless you were a visitor, or a member of staff. She wanted to try new things, meet new people, explore new desires. But there was a crippling handicap that held her back. Her body had previously been ravaged by something she couldn't see – and now, something she *could* see had riddled her blood stream with a cure, one which came with its own price. She struggled to go outside. Not exactly an agoraphobic response, but more a comforting safety blanket of being in her own surroundings.

The dating app she'd been using had been working out in her favour – several times a week she entertained guests of both sexes in the privacy of her darkened bedroom. All on the basis of a no-strings-attached meeting of minds and bodies – though not necessarily souls. A lot of the gentlemen visitors were married – desperate for the excitement and anonymity of a casual rendezvous with an attractive, career-orientated girl, with no ulterior motives or expectations of companionship that lasted beyond their brief encounters. Some of the women were married too – though less frequently or, indeed, aggressively. Most were just lonely – seeking the tender touch of a like-minded partner.

So how had it got to this stage? Loretta's modus operandi in agreeing to meet with a couple had been twofold – she would challenge herself physically, that was first and foremost in her mind, but she would also stave off any impulses, presumably for double the length of time. But it's like a kid with a bag of sweets; eating twice as much doesn't fill you up for longer – it just makes you sick, leaves you empty, and, subsequently, hungrier than before.

When Doctor Atkins had offered up the experimental treatment, he had described it as "an old remedy for an ancient disease". People had been contracting cancer for time immemorial – its prevalence, however, was down to a lack of advanced medical scientific breakthroughs. Loretta's response had been that, at this stage, anything was worth a shot. The administration of the drug was straightforward – two small puncture wounds to the inside of the thigh. The scarring was unobtrusive until it wasn't – but by the time anyone would notice it, she hoped that the throes of passion would distract enough to render them as nothing more substantial than a footnote on a coroner's report.

The meeting had been arranged for almost a week by the time the door knocked. It was shortly after 10pm, and Loretta had, as usual, begun drinking around an hour prior – just to calm her nerves. She didn't bother dressing up for them anymore; if they had their kinks, she was well prepared in advance - an old wooden chest, filled with surprises sat at the foot of her bed. Tonight though, was a little different. The couple had declined to send pictures in advance - they were worried about it being some kind of scam – and they had respectable jobs, family and friends to think of before posting such things online, with strangers. It seemed a reasonable enough excuse, though Loretta had felt obliged to send them a selfie in advance of the engagement being confirmed. It had met with their approval, and the minutiae of the meeting had been clinical enough. She plumped the cushions on the sofa, re-arranged the vase of lilies on the coffee table and took one last, long swig from her thick recycled wine glass. She straightened her top and glided into the hallway.

The immediate after-effects of the treatment had been difficult for Loretta to categorise – not least because she had slept for almost a week with only occasional lapses in her slumber. There was an intense period of dehydration and tiredness, her appetite had waned and her teeth and sinus' ached; but beyond that, her recovery had been somewhat miraculous. The intense pain she had previously suffered, deep down in her soul, had eased to such an extent by the time she left the hospice, that both the nurses and oncologist were confounded. Her hair began to sprout, her vision sharpened, her senses returned. She never saw Atkins again post-treatment. Probably just as well. Her conflicted opinions on phytotherapy, and the questions she had about it, were best left tethered. She had signed the consent form without properly reading it – that had come much later – shortly before she decided to relocate, which was probably for the best. Its revelations had confused her at first, then enraged, and finally assuaged her.

If you'd have asked Loretta to guess what this couple was going to look like, she'd have offered up an incredibly detailed suggestion. They were going to be in their early to mid-forties. He would be wearing a suit, blue, without a tie. His hair was thinning. He had a strong jawline, cleanly shaven. She was slightly overweight, but attractive. Blonde, no… brunette hair, with a slight curl. She would wear more makeup than usual and dress in an outdated and frightfully too-clingy black dress. Tall heels. Both nervous. Both excited. She wasn't far off the mark with either – a kind of déjà vu swept over Loretta when she opened the door to her visitors. But it wasn't because she'd fantasised over these people – it was because she knew them. Annie. Geoff. Wow. So many conflicting thoughts filled her mind. So much *Rosemary's Baby*.

There was an uncomfortable hour or two to begin with, but once the anaesthetic had kicked in, Loretta was ready for the treatment. The doctor was assisted by a handsome male nurse by the name of Ivan. Ivan had been quite the soother of souls at the hospice. He attended every patient with the compassion of a saint and a phlegmatic temperament. Loretta's consciousness drifted between planes whilst they carried out the procedure. She was barely aware of what they were doing in the vale between her legs. She remembered seeing heads bobbing up and down, smears of blood, and smiling faces. Then darkness. The kind of all-encompassing blackness you only experience when you're in the countryside, alone, at midnight. It consumes you. Penetrates you. Envelopes you. Then it was done. The next thing she remembered was her mother floating around her in a haze, praying, clutching at her crucifix.

Aside from the awkwardness, there was a distressing unease to the whole situation. Annie and Geoff had obviously known in advance who Loretta was. The selfie had unequivocally proven that. And yet they had still proceeded with the charade. She must have passed them in the hallway at least once since it had been organized. And they hadn't said anything. Hadn't intimated it might be them. And Loretta was so taken aback by their presence that she had gone into fight or flight mode. And she had settled on the former. The smiles were uncomfortable, and the greetings disingenuous. But here they were, three of them, sitting next to the large glass wall on the east side of the building – breathtaking panoramic views of the city around them – sipping red wine, and contemplating their next steps. A knock at the door, and a further visitor was something none of them had expected. It was shortly before eleven by now and Trevor was apologetic about the hour. There had been some reports of the elevator not stopping on certain floors so he just wanted to make them aware that he was going into the service cupboard, situated on their communal lobby, to check the mechanism. It would only take a couple of minutes, but if they heard any banging they should not be alarmed. Loretta tried to engage him in conversation which might have helped her current predicament, but he needed to get on before it was too late. She smiled and bid him good luck before reluctantly returning to her unwanted guests.

However this was going to play out, Loretta knew that there was an imminent threat to her very existence. She ran through the possibilities in her mind and played them out in the great level of detail to which her mind had become accustomed. None of them ended well for her, but the outcomes were significantly more terrifying for Annie and Geoff, had they known the situation they had brought upon themselves. Best case scenario, it was a leave in the morning and start again in a new city situation.

Geoff had tried to break the ice, to get the conversation going in his own dissonant fashion. Annie had smiled tenderly at Loretta on more than one occasion. But the distractions were just too much to be able to comprehend. Every thought that fleeted through her racing mind had been about how this would go. The second, and, more likely the third glass of wine had settled her nerves to an extent – her fight response had dulled and her decision was made. She would feign some sort of illness, apologise, and see them on their way back across the communal hall. Yes, it would be uncomfortable seeing them in public spaces going forward, but it was definitely preferable to the level of upheaval she'd face if things went any other way. It was at that point her lightheadedness had gotten the better of her. She made an excuse and headed to the bathroom. Annie had looked moderately concerned, but Geoff had given her a reassuring glance.

The stark fluorescent tube above the mirror seemed to pulsate and the audible whirr of the extractor fan was like a whirlpool in Loretta's brain, growing louder with every revolution. She held tight to the towel rail to maintain her balance and turned, without thinking, to the mirror above the sink. Whatever it was that she expected to see there, it wasn't a reflection of herself. That had been gone now for some time. Her self-image projected something, but nothing her eyes could actually interpret as real. She was pale, drawn, and her eyes had become glassy. She didn't understand why, when she ran her tongue over her teeth, trying to regain a sense of feeling in her face, her incisors – usually so prominent – had felt flat and "normal". Her eyes didn't understand why they could see her, now, as she was, reflected back at them.

With an explosive speed and sound, the bathroom door was kicked open. By now, Loretta was laying prostrate on the cold, tiled floor. Aware of everything but suffering from a paralysis which weighed on every cell of her physical body like the Titanic's anchor.

Through a hazy, kaleidoscopic lens, she saw Geoff towering over her. It felt as though he were eight, no, ten feet tall. The distortion of her perspective was unfathomable to her poisoned brain. As he squatted athletically and took her wrists in his clammy hands, she tried to cry out, but only a saliva gargling moan of no real volume escaped her lips. He dragged her into the hallway and onward to the living room. Loretta didn't know how long she'd been in the bathroom, but it must have been time enough for Annie to have prepared what awaited. A large, phallic golden candle burned atop the coffee table, which had been moved to one side. Plastic sheeting had been laid out on the floor. It wrinkled as she was dragged into the middle of it, annoying Geoff to the extent that he and Annie had partaken in a minor disagreement about her methods, and about how she should have learned from her previous mistakes in this regard. Nevertheless, they worked as a team to straighten it again, and all was well.

The darkness in the apartment was paralysing in itself. In the movies, even when the protagonist is paralysed, they seem to be able to move their heads, to look around them, maybe even muster the energy or summon the inner strength to move a hand to grab a knife and fight off their attackers. The reality, though, was quite different for Loretta. Her head had naturally rolled to one side, facing the illuminations of the city through the glass wall, and she couldn't do more than blink every so often when her eyes became dry. The sounds she could hear behind her in the apartment were, therefore, all the more terrifying. Trying to place sounds when they're unnatural isn't always easy. Foley artists, for example, will use snapping celery to create the audible breaking of bones in a horror movie. Or hitting a watermelon with a baseball bat for thuds to the head. Loretta's mind was working overtime – the tinny clanging of china cups, the sharpening of a knife, the crinkling of a canvas sheet being unfolded. For all she knew, they could be anything. It was only via the vague reflections in the window glass she could even make out where in the apartment they were. But she knew something pretty horrific was about to happen to her. What she hadn't yet figured out was why.

When Annie knelt next to Loretta to gently roll her head one hundred and eighty degrees to face the apartment, our protagonist had begun to feel the painful tingle in her arms that you get when you awake in the night having slept too heavily on your shoulder. It was a positive sign, and she had surreptitiously hidden it from her attackers. How differently this evening had originally panned out in her mind! She had gone from being predator to prey. And Geoff was about to explain it to her in the kind of laborious fashion of Ernst Stavro Blofeld at his most incompetent. They had lost a child. Fourteen years old. Emilia. Before they moved to the city. Nearly six years ago now. Disappeared from a local park just after sunset in the middle of winter. Found ten days later in a ditch. Drained of all her bodily fluids. Six puncture wounds – three areas of her body, each with two teeth marks. Only the facts. There was no emotion from Loretta as she was informed of their tragedy because there couldn't be. The story went on for what seemed like ten minutes or more. But that was likely because it was punctuated by dramatic pauses, the storyteller running his finger over the sharp point of an English Oak stake that had been lovingly crafted and him having to reassure his wife that what they were doing was for Emilia.

Loretta had a psychopathy which rendered her entirely indifferent to their reasonings; she felt nothing for the dead girl, nor the vengeful parents. Her only thoughts were about escape. Maybe reconciliation, but, more likely, the requirement to rid these fucking monsters of their souls. What she was conflicted about, however, was whether she would give them the satisfaction of feeding from them. They didn't deserve that. Shit under her shoe – that's all they were. Her decision was made. The details of her plan would be difficult to execute, but not impossible. So long as her physical attributes performed as she needed them to. But it was at this point that Annie shuffled over and lifted Loretta's arms above her head. She held them down with a tenderness, and Geoff took out a silver-plated needle around six inches in length, and with the girth of the vein it was about to be inserted into on Loretta's left wrist. It slid in with ease – her skin offered no resistance – and the sting was tremendous. Silver will do that to you if you're a vampire. Although Loretta felt, she gave an Academy Award-winning performance in hiding it. Akin to lifeless. Geoff seemed not to be taking pleasure in the act itself, so much as to what was to come. Annie audibly winced in sympathy. Loretta's breathing was slow, her heartbeat steady. It seemed to anger Geoff – perhaps, he thought, the cocktail of drugs and garlic in the wine that he'd concocted had been slightly off this time. He wanted to make her panic, the way Emilia would have. In spite of this, he continued. Next came the crucifix.

Loretta's mother had never taken her crucifix off, so far as she could remember. It was a simple one, a tubular golden cross, a small and undetailed figure of Christ nailed to it. The assailant's one was similar, though more detailed, and wooden. English Oak no doubt – vampires didn't react particularly well to that, something similar to hay fever, not particularly painful, more uncomfortable than anything else. And as it bore down toward her forehead, all Loretta could think of was her mother standing over her in the Hospice bed shortly after her treatment, waving the damned thing around and it wafting the smell of sage flavoured joss stick into her nostrils. This one, though, was sent with malice. It burned as it touched her forehead, the skin shrivelled and smoked. It would leave an indelible mark, no matter what the final act of this evening presented. The skin of the forehead is very thin – perhaps it would disappear in time – and that was something Loretta would either have a plethora of, or very little. As she flinched, albeit subtly, it was the first indication that Geoff was getting excited, and that Annie was becoming uncomfortable. He held it with relish against Loretta's smouldering face, a broad smile breaking out as her voice whispered, "Please... stop..."

There were garlic solutions dribbled into her eyes, Rowan tree twigs forced under her fingernails, UV torches shined up and down the thin skin of her shins. It was a horrendous torture but, for Geoff and Annie's climax, there was the double whammy of that stake followed by a decapitation. It was approaching, Loretta could feel it. She had been feeling now for enough time to confidently speak out against them for one last time.

"Please, Geoff... please..." It gave him a thrill; he pictured poor, fourteen-year-old Emilia begging for her life at the hands of savages like this. He equated her level of pain with that which he was administering to one of "their" kind. A single tear drop ran down Annie's cheek as she did the same. He purposefully raised the stake above his head as he knelt over Loretta's midriff – his aim would take it directly into her heart, or what was left of it. A gleam in his eye. He took one more look at his wife, her sadness causing him to halt for a moment, and when he looked back at his victim he noticed, for a hundredth of a second, something which made his laboured finishing move redundant. The stake was two feet over his head as Loretta bucked her hips with such massive force that it sent Geoff flying forward, lowering his arms instinctively without releasing the sharpened stake. A foley artist might throw a bowl of pudding on the floor with great force to replicate the sound it made as it entered Annie's left eye socket and penetrated the back of her skull. But the sound was masked by the tremendous explosion of gunpowder and metal filings outside the apartment from below. A firework. A second. A third, fourth, fifth. Eardrum bursting – right outside the window. These moments of detail we revel in are those which Loretta had been planning so intricately for the last few hours. But they were over in the blink of an eye. A left eye, socket filled with wood and blood.

Geoff's face had hit the large glass window as he fell, and he was bleeding from the nose and lips. His appearance was one of a small boy who had fallen from a tree, but his determination to finish the job was stoic. He got to his feet and with a sense of panic he strained to look through the dim candlelight of the room for Loretta. The darkness was penetrated again and again with flashes of orange, green, white – the fireworks had been relentless for almost a minute by now. Wisps of blackness, with incredible speed, shot around him, disorientating him, giving him the fear. She was moving through the shadows, mesmerizing him. He turned, again, spun his torso left to right trying to slash at her with the large knife he had previously intended as a guillotine. The cracks of noise deafened him, dulled his senses, sending him into a state of confusion he couldn't escape from as she evaded him. With a solid blow to the face she knocked him clean off his feet. Then she disappeared. He regained his composure, stood. Once again, he was knocked onto his back against the floor by this demon. A third time he tried; he whisked like a tornado with the knife, spinning, holding it aloft in an attempt to wound and slow his opponent further than he had already done. But she was gone. And so were the fireworks. The darkness now enveloped Geoff physically as well as mentally.

He paused for a few moments, his breathing heavy, perspiration dripping from every facial pore. He glanced down at Annie – dear, sweet Annie – she hadn't really wanted any of this. He'd cajoled her into it and now she'd paid the price for his revenge. He swallowed hard and began shuffling toward the dark hallway. He'd have to leave, to regroup before returning. He inched into the darkness, wearily wielding the knife in front of his trembling body. An enormous crashing sound from the apartment below startled him to a whimper and made him instinctively look around him. Nothing. He continued toward the door, wary he was about to walk past both the bathroom and bedroom doorways. He backed against the opposite wall and crab walked past the bedroom. Safe. And then the bathroom. Safe. As he turned back to face the apartment and recoil from the evening's incidents, the front door to the apartment only now a few feet away, a misplaced calm fell over Geoff. For just a moment he lowered his knife and took a deep breath. He fumbled behind his back in the darkness for the door lever and pulled it down. Without taking his eyes from the apartment, he pulled it toward him, an ominous creak emitting from the unoiled hinges.

The lobby behind him was as black as the apartment in front of him, and the feeling of cold breath on his neck sent a shiver down his spine. "Hello Daddy…"

Also from Red Cape Publishing

Anthologies:

Elements of Horror Book One: Earth
Elements of Horror Book Two: Air
Elements of Horror Book Three: Fire
Elements of Horror Book Four: Water
A is for Aliens: A to Z of Horror Book One
B is for Beasts: A to Z of Horror Book Two
C is for Cannibals: A to Z of Horror Book Three
D is for Demons: A to Z of Horror Book Four
E is for Exorcism: A to Z of Horror Book Five
F is for Fear: A to Z of Horror Book Six
G is for Genies: A to Z of Horror Book Seven
H is for Hell: A to Z of Horror Book Eight
I is for Internet: A to Z of Horror Book Nine
It Came From The Darkness: A Charity Anthology
Castle Heights: 18 Storeys, 18 Stories

Short Story Collections:

Embrace the Darkness by P.J. Blakey-Novis
Tunnels by P.J. Blakey-Novis
The Artist by P.J. Blakey-Novis
Karma by P.J. Blakey-Novis
The Place Between Worlds by P.J. Blakey-Novis
Home by P.J. Blakey-Novis
Short Horror Stories by P.J. Blakey-Novis
Short Horror Stories Vol. 2 by P.J. Blakey-Novis
Keep It Inside & Other Weird Tales by Mark Anthony Smith
Something Said by Mark Anthony Smith
Everything's Annoying by J.C. Michael
Six! by Mark Cassell

Novelettes:

The Ivory Tower by Antoinette Corvo

Novellas:

Four by P.J. Blakey-Novis
Dirges in the Dark by Antoinette Corvo
The Cat That Caught The Canary by Antoinette Corvo
Bow-Legged Buccaneers from Outer Space by David Owain Hughes

Novels:

Madman Across the Water by Caroline Angel
The Curse Awakens by Caroline Angel
Less by Caroline Angel
Where Shadows Move by Caroline Angel
Origin of Evil by Caroline Angel
The Broken Doll by P.J. Blakey-Novis
The Broken Doll: Shattered Pieces by P.J. Blakey-Novis
The Vegas Rift by David F. Gray

Children's Books:

Grace & Bobo: The Trip to the Future by Peter Blakey-Novis
My Sister's from the Moon by Peter Blakey-Novis
Elvis the Elephant by Peter Blakey-Novis
The Little Bat That Could by Gemma Paul
The Mummy Walks At Midnight by Gemma Paul
A Very Zombie Christmas by Gemma Paul

Follow Red Cape Publishing

www.redcapepublishing.com
www.facebook.com/redcapepublishing
www.twitter.com/redcapepublish
www.instagram.com/redcapepublishing
www.pinterest.co.uk/redcapepublishing
www.patreon.com/redcapepublishing

Printed in Great Britain
by Amazon

72775120R00231